COWBOYS, DOCTORS...
DADDIES!

*The Montgomery brothers—
from bachelors to dads!*

Trevor and Cole Montgomery
are the best-looking bachelors in
Cattleman Bluff—not to mention the doctors
everyone wants to see!

More than one woman has tried to persuade
these men to say 'I do', but no one's
succeeded... Until two women move to
Cattleman Bluff and turn the lives of
these hot docs upside down!

Because it's not just the women
Trevor and Cole are going to fall in love
with—it's their adorable children too...

Don't miss this delightful new duet
from Lynne Marshall:

Hot-Shot Doc, Secret Dad

and

Father for Her Newborn Baby

Available now!

HOT-SHOT DOC, SECRET DAD

BY
LYNNE MARSHALL

Published in Great Britain 2015
by Mills & Boon, an imprint of Harlequin (UK) Limited,
Eton House, 18-24 Paradise Road, Richmond, Surrey, TW9 1SR

© 2015 Janet Maarschalk

ISBN: 978-0-263-24736-7

Harlequin (UK) Limited's policy is to use papers that are natural,
renewable and recyclable products and made from wood grown in
sustainable forests. The logging and manufacturing processes conform
to the legal environmental regulations of the country of origin.

Printed and bound in Spain
by CPI, Barcelona

Dear Reader,

Welcome to Cattleman Bluff, Wyoming!

When I first mentioned to my editor that I'd like to write about cowboy doctors, to be honest I expected a giggle. Instead I found support and enthusiasm for Trevor and Cole, the Montgomery brothers of Wyoming.

In Book One, *Hot-Shot Doc, Secret Dad*, Trevor literally gets the surprise of his life. Little does he know that the emphasis will be on 'family' when he hires Julie Sterling, a nurse practitioner returning to her hometown after being away for thirteen years. Funny how life has a way of sometimes putting us exactly where we belong...

A freak accident introduced Cole to medicine. He's the hero in Book Two, *Father for Her Newborn Baby*. When Cole has to step down from his highly respected position as a cardiology specialist and return to do country medicine for a while he's paired with Lizzie Silva, a 'rough around the edges' doctor from the streets of Boston. She comes with extra baggage...in the way of a tiny baby! Can things get any more complicated?

I'm proud to mention that this story is my twentieth book for Harlequin Mills & Boon®. I was thrilled to write two stories set in the gorgeous state of Wyoming, a place I love and can't wait to visit again. Plus, I got to write about not one but two weddings! I hope you enjoy the *Cowboys, Doctors...Daddies* duet as much as I enjoyed writing Trevor, Julie, Cole and Lizzie's stories.

Happy trails!

Lynne

www.lynnemarshall.com

'Friend' Lynne Marshall on Facebook to keep up with her daily shenanigans.

This book is dedicated to the beautiful state of Wyoming.

With special thanks to Flo Nicoll
for letting me write the Montgomery brothers' stories.

Lynne Marshall used to worry that she had a serious problem with daydreaming—then she discovered she was supposed to write those stories! A late bloomer, Lynne came to fiction writing after her children were nearly grown. Now she battles the empty nest by writing stories which always include a romance, sometimes medicine, a dose of mirth, or both, but always stories from her heart. She is a Southern California native, a woman of faith, a dog-lover and a curious traveller.

CHAPTER ONE

JULIE WAITED TO FACE the guy who'd knocked her up thirteen years ago.

"Ms. Sterling?" The young and attractive medical clinic receptionist called her name as if it were a crowded waiting room.

Julie was the only one sitting there, being that it was almost lunchtime. "Yes?"

"Dr. Montgomery will be with you as soon as he finishes with his last patient. He apologizes for running late. The appointment turned out to be a little more involved than expected."

"Thanks for letting me know." Julie's nerves were twisted to the point of breaking anyway over the thought of facing the man who'd once changed the entire course of her life. Now she'd get to balance on this tightrope over the roiling anxiety a while longer. Oh, joy.

Her goal was to not let on how desperate she was for the job. But how would she control these butterflies over facing him again after all these years? Short answer, she had to. She'd do whatever was necessary to get this job. Anything for her son.

What was that old saying about how you could never go home again? Well, Cattleman Bluff, Wyoming, population twenty thousand, was the last place in the world

Julie had expected to wind up. Her parents had bought her a ticket on a one-way train out of town when she'd barely been eighteen.

Now here she was applying for a job with a man she never, ever wanted to see again for a dozen different reasons that all boiled down to one in particular. But as a single mother, she'd do whatever it took to make a better life for her son, James. Twelve years old, with thirteen breathing down his neck come May, all hormones and bad choices, and already getting into trouble back in Los Angeles. James needed strong men in his life to set him straight, and the military school in Laramie seemed the best place for now.

Guilt stabbed at her conscience as it had for years. She'd made a rash decision at a tender age and had stuck to her guns no matter how hard it had been. Problem was, with James going wild, and now with the death of her parents, her bull-headed strength had run out. It was crunch time. After thirteen years of running, fighting and insisting she could manage on her own, she'd finally realized she needed backup. From a man.

The school was willing to take James midsemester. Of course, with his being there, that meant she'd be living and working over a hundred miles away from her son, but that was another sacrifice she'd have to make.

The school cost a lot, and the small monetary windfall from her parents helped tremendously toward that. All she had to do was cover their personal living expenses. Thankfully, she had a solid profession to rely on…if she got this job, that was.

If she didn't, she'd try for something closer to the school, but her parents had left her their home in the will, and these days only a fool would turn down free housing, even if it required moving to a new state.

Julie fought off another ripple of guilt and regret for the messy relationship they'd had—how her careless actions had been at the heart of it, but, even before, her parents' expectations for her future had been overbearing—and the fact they'd never mended it before their horrible accident at Christmas. Deciding to get out of the extralong winter, her parents had set out driving to Florida and had hit a patch of black ice a mere twenty miles from home. A swell of emotion built deep in her chest and pushed against her throat. She swallowed hard around it. All the years they'd lost because of the stubborn Sterling spirit, which worked both ways, theirs and hers. James had never really gotten to know his grandparents either... Now her eyes were welling up. She couldn't let this happen here. Especially not now. She had to stay strong.

Julie glanced at her watch and blinked the blur away. It was twenty minutes past her appointment time. She'd cut the doctor some slack, and use the gift of time to pull herself together.

Being a nurse practitioner, she understood how one appointment could turn into something much more than routine—a patient might come in for a diabetes check and their blood pressure would be out of control, or they'd happen to mention that they'd been having dizzy spells on their way out the door, or that the cut on their foot they'd neglected to mention before that moment had red streaks running up the leg. While working for LA County medical clinics, she'd learned anything was possible when dealing with health and patients.

Or, it could be that she was the last person on earth Trevor Montgomery wanted to see...

Julie took a deep breath to steady her crawling-out-of-control jitters. Focusing away from the reality of facing her fears and the downright sadness of losing her parents, and on to the task at hand. Getting the job. No matter what. And that ushered in a second wave of riotous anticipation. Of all the people in the world to need a job from.

She shook her head. Would Trevor even remember her after thirteen years?

To distract herself, she glanced around. The cozy waiting room was typical of many she'd been in, with the exception of having a cowboy rustic charm. Several oil paintings of cattle drives filled the walls. What else could she expect from Cattleman Bluff? The couches and chairs were in earthy tones, browns and beige with pops of orange, and made with natural wood, sanded and varnished, smoothed to perfection for armrests. The choice of magazines was decidedly Wyoming slanted, too. *Out West Today. Wyoming Home. Western Living.* Not to mention the huge cowboy boot–shaped umbrella holder beside the front door.

It had to be thirty degrees outside in mid-February. Back home in California, it seemed to be an endless spring, no matter what month. Fortunately her mother had left behind her warm winter coat and rubber-soled, faux fur–lined boots. Though a size too big, they'd do for today, and wearing them helped Julie remember her mother's softer, warmer side, the one she'd rarely showed as Julie had gotten older. Snapping away from where those thoughts might lead, she pondered how quickly a person could get used to the mild weather out on the West Coast. Had she turned into a weather wuss?

"Ms. Sterling, Doctor will see you now." The perky and blonde twenty-something receptionist held the door open. Julie's heart pounded as if she'd be meeting the president of the United States and would have to deliver his speech to the nation at the last minute, or something.

Get a hold of yourself. Trevor's just a human being, not God. Though he does seem to hold your future in his hands today.

What was that old trick to help settle nerves—picture them naked? It didn't take long for her memory to click in with a bigger-than-life naked-jock image.

Oh, no, not a good idea. Now she could add flushed cheeks to the ever-growing list of mounting terrors. The spiteful image flashed again as she fumbled to pick up her purse. Funny how some moments stuck in the mind as if they'd happened yesterday.

"This way." Blonde Rita, the receptionist, walked with a distinct sway down a short hall. Out of the blue, Julie wondered if Trevor was now married with children.

They passed four patient-exam rooms toward a modest office at the end, *gulp*, where Trevor Montgomery, the once-gifted high school athlete, exceptional student, all-around dreamy guy—not to mention the man who'd taken her virginity—waited.

Julie did one last futile battle with the panic jetting along her nerve endings, then threw in a quick prayer to help her get through the interview.

Trevor stood behind a huge rustic weathered wood ranch-style desk, smiling and reaching for her hand when she finally had the guts to look up. Tall, as she'd remembered, dark hair, piercing brown, almost black, eyes thanks to distant Native American heritage on his mother's side. Handsome as ever. She stopped in her tracks and took him all in.

She couldn't very well stand there gawking, so she tore away her gaze, and glanced around the office.

Matching woven iron lamps with stretched cowhide shades said classic cowboy chic through and through.

The steer antlers that were thankfully missing in the waiting room were mounted on the wall behind his desk, like a crown, exactly where he stood. No white coat for him. No, he wore a blue pinstriped, long-sleeved, button-down, Western-style shirt, open at the neck, no tie. No wedding ring either. The black Wrangler jeans with a tasteful, not overly large, silver-and-bronze intricately patterned belt buckle were de rigueur for these parts, and she assumed he wore boots, but couldn't be sure since he stood behind the behemoth desk. But obviously he did, right?

"Julie? It's great to see you again." Those eyes seemed to look into her soul. Thirteen years had transformed the good-looking young jock into a mature and handsome thirty-four-year-old man, by her count, complete with winter tan and creases fanning out from his eyes—the mark of a guy who still worked outdoors on his family's Circle M Ranch.

"Nice to see you, too," she mumbled and lied, forced a step forward and jutted out her hand, performing some kind of royalty handshake, one she'd normally never do. But since his mere touch had set off sparklers all the way down to her fingertips, she didn't want to hold his hand unnecessarily—even if it made her seem prudish. It was just all so awkward, wasn't it?

No ring. No picture of a family on his desk that she could see either. Didn't mean he wasn't involved, though, did it?

He didn't belabor the wimpy handshake. "I had no idea you were a nurse practitioner, with great credentials, too." His relaxed cadence reminded her how much she'd forgotten about home since living in LA for thirteen years. Things slowed down here, not that mad rush called daily life out West.

She nodded, not anywhere ready to find her voice.

"So what are you doing back in Cattleman Bluff?" He gestured for her to sit. She obeyed but perched on the edge of the chair rather than getting comfortable—no way that would happen anyway.

She cleared her throat, goading herself to woman up. "The truth?"

He nodded, a hint of intrigue darkening those already deep brown irises.

"My parents died in a car accident."

"I'd heard. What a tragedy. I'm so sorry," he said with a perfect mix of empathy and sincerity. *Good job, Doc.*

She gave a quick nod, unwilling to get sidetracked. Not now—she had to stay focused. Win the job! "Yes, well. They left me the house, and it turns out there was a place for my son at the military academy in Laramie for the rest of this semester. He's in orientation now."

"I've heard good things about that school." Though the one quirked brow proved he knew the school was a haven for troubled boys, and Cattleman Bluff had a perfectly good middle school just around the corner.

Her jaw clamped tight. His brow remained quirked. They stared at each other.

"Ah." She was grateful he trudged ahead rather than allow an awkward silence—probably just to be polite. "You know my brother keeps an apartment in Laramie. He prefers it there over Cheyenne." They'd hit their first rocky patch. Trevor—or Dr. Montgomery as he deserved to be called for today's purposes—segued smoothly as that driven snow outside the window into easy banter. "When he isn't gallivanting around the country lecturing and training other cardiologists, that is."

Julie raised her brows in acknowledgement, but didn't add a comment, not wanting to open the door for a deeper discussion on why her son was going to military school.

She'd heard of the great Cole Montgomery, practicing cutting-edge mitral valve replacements in the same fashion as cardiac catheterization, at Johns Hopkins Hospital in Baltimore. The guy who'd been the pride of Cattleman Bluff and the one person Trevor couldn't seem to outshine. The thought made Julie wonder why Trevor had settled here, practicing family medicine, instead of pursuing a more lucrative medical specialty like his big brother.

"So," Trevor continued on, since Julie was proving to be less than chatty. "You're certainly the best-qualified candidate for this job. I need someone who can pull their weight and work independently. The fact that you're also a licensed midwife is a big plus. Hell, you're probably better at delivering babies than I am." He flashed his trademark charming smile—nice lips, white teeth. Yeah, she remembered that smile.

"I've delivered a hundred or so babies over the last five years. Handled my share of difficult births."

"That's great, Julie. We'll need those skills, too." He laced his fingers and rested his elbows on the desk. "You're probably wondering why I'm hiring."

"Business is booming?"

He gave an obligatory smile. "Not quite. The reason is my father has had some health issues lately, and I need to be more help on the ranch. Some days, if you get the job, you'll be running the clinic all by yourself. Would you be okay with that?"

"I would." And she meant it. She'd been expected to pull her load in the last two clinics where she'd worked in Los Angeles, even when she'd protested that they were treating her as if she were a doctor, but not paying her the same wages. Fact was, she knew how to handle hard work.

"Some days it's deader than the prairie around here, then all of a sudden everyone gets sick. You just never know. And with winter almost over, people come out in droves. But I need to know my patients are in good hands when I'm doing my ranch chores."

"If you hire me, I'll give this job one hundred percent effort. I promise."

"You need the job?"

This was no time to play coy. *Of course I do!* "I do. That military school is pricey, and, last I looked, you're the only game in town."

"Fair enough." He sat straighter, reached for a pad of paper and a pen. "Then I need to do an extensive interview to gauge your medical experience, if you don't mind."

Great, now they'd play twenty questions—medical tricks, and treatment of the day—and she'd better come through. At least her jitters had settled down, thinking about medicine. "Fire away, Dr. Montgomery."

Twenty minutes later, after the most thorough and difficult medical interview in her life, Julie realized her palms were clammy. What if, after all of this, she didn't get the job? What would she do now that James was already enrolled at the military academy?

"If I hire you, I won't throw you in the fire. I promise to give you a couple of weeks' orientation, where you can shadow me and my patients, and learn the system. Or as long as you need. I'm proud to say I'm the only doctor outside of Cheyenne that uses computerized charting. It takes a bit of getting used to, but in the long run—"

"I'm familiar with that, depending on the system

you're using." County Hospital had been late to implement the charting system, and the one they'd used had been clunky, but she'd figured it out well enough.

"Great. So do you have any questions for me?"

Are you married? Do you have children? "Is there a benefits package, and how soon will it kick in—that is, if you hire me." How desperate could she sound?

"As soon as the paperwork is processed, and you've completed your orientation, you'll be covered." Trevor pressed the intercom then pushed back from his desk.

"Yes, Doctor?" Rita's chirpy voice was loud and clear and maybe a little too fawning.

"Could you bring in the new-employee paperwork?"

Julie inhaled, realizing she'd held her breath since her last question. "I've got the job?"

"It's yours if you want it." Trevor offered a far more genuine smile this time.

"Thank you." Now Julie smiled, too, anxiety streaming out of her body.

Rita arrived with a packet of paperwork, and handed it to Julie, assessing her more closely as she did.

"You probably want to have your lunch before your afternoon patients, maybe call your wife, so I can fill this out in the waiting room, if you'd prefer."

"No need. The clinic is closed on Tuesday afternoons. Otherwise, I'd introduce you to Charlotte, my nurse. I've got to finish up on Mr. Waverly's chart anyway. Feel free to stay right there." He went back to work but said as an aside, "Oh, and there isn't a Mrs. Montgomery. Just my old man, and, to be honest, having dinner with him every night is enough." He gave that charming smile over his laptop, slyly forgiving her for her none-too-subtle probing into his personal life. She pretended to be completely focused on the paperwork.

Though he did seem easy and open about still being a bachelor. She wondered if it had to do with being stuck in this small town taking care of his father while his brother lived the good life traveling and keeping two homes.

For the next several minutes, Julie filled in all the blanks about her personal information, but sneaked surreptitious glances at Trevor as she did. His mahogany-colored hair was still thick and wavy, covering the tips of his ears. After all this time, she remembered how she'd run her fingers through it the one night they'd been together, probably because she'd dreamed about touching that hair all that summer long. His square jaw was set while he typed away at his keyboard. He knit his brows and seemed very concerned about whatever it was he entered about poor Mr. Waverly's condition.

Once, he glanced up at the exact moment Julie did and their eyes met then skipped away from each other quicker than water on a hot griddle. Even so, the visual contact slid through her center, further jangling her nerves.

The man deserved to know.

But she needed the job. No way would she tell him! Not now anyway. Oh, man, why had she even considered coming home?

Round and round her thoughts chased each other. She was at the end of her rope and James needed... well, a father.

With her mouth dry and her hands clammier than ever, she finished her employment paperwork and handed the packet to Trevor. His lips torqued in a rigid manner as he took them, as if they were something sacred, then he used the intercom and asked Rita to process everything before she left for the day.

"Want to start tomorrow?" he asked, without looking at one iota of Julie's personal information, while handing everything over to Rita—who must have been standing right outside in order to get there so fast.

"The sooner the better," Julie said, relieved she'd have a new job before her final paycheck from her prior job was due.

He smiled tensely, and once Rita had left with the paperwork, Trevor shot Julie an anxious glance. Was he changing his mind? He followed Rita to the door, closing it behind her, further raising Julie's curiosity. What did he have up his sleeve?

"Listen," he said, stretching his lower lip and biting on it, as if the words were stuck just behind his teeth. Instead of walking back around his desk, he sat next to her. She'd been right about his wearing boots—black gator belly–patterned boots, to be exact. She stared at them rather than look at Trevor. "I'd like to ask you to forgive me."

What? She was unable to hide her reaction; her chin pulled in, brows shot up and she was quite sure her eyes bugged out—at least that was how it felt. She had a dreaded hunch about what he referred to, and for the record he did look contrite, yet she still couldn't quite make her brain believe it. "Seriously?" Did she say that out loud?

He made the wise decision of not attempting to touch her or even get too close. Though he leaned in and sincerity flowed from his gaze. "Completely. I messed up that night. There was nothing honorable about what I did. I took advantage of—"

"Wait a second, I may have been tipsy—well, we both were—but I still knew what I was doing. I had a choice in the matter. Made a bad one, but nevertheless."

Now he was the one studying his boots. "That's not the way it should be, the first time, you know?" He looked back up and nailed her. "A lady deserves some romance and wooing that first time. And I never even had the decency to apologize."

Oh, my gosh, he was going all chivalrous on her. *Too late, buddy.* She'd waited and waited for his call, which had never come. He'd had his chance to be honorable, but had never bothered. Even so, she decided to take the practical route.

"Now that I'm thirty-one, I can say with certainty that life isn't always the way it should be. That's just how it is sometimes." Without thinking, she reached for his forearm and squeezed. "We were both slightly inebriated, as I recall, and I'll let you in on a little secret—I went to that party hoping to see you. I couldn't believe it when you were interested in me, too. So—"

How naive could she have been? Any male would be interested in a willing woman at that age. Yeah, she'd learned that lesson the hard way.

"That still doesn't make it right," he said. "It's not like losing your virginity can happen more than once."

True, but how often did a girl get bells and whistles and romance with her first time? At least that had seemed to be the consensus among her friends back then, and, crazy as it sounded, it had helped ease her broken heart.

"It's weighed on my mind and I just wanted to set things straight since you're going to be working for me." He glanced down at her hand, still grasping his forearm, and her ringless finger. "I messed up that night, didn't have a clue you weren't like the girls at college. I took advantage of you, plain and simple. Please forgive me."

The remorseful expression, coupled with those dark,

pleading eyes, painted a gentlemanly and heartfelt apology. It warmed Julie's cynical heart by a few degrees, and brought out the forgiver in her. She let up on the tight clutch on his arm.

Truth was she'd packed away that chapter of her life years ago. What were the odds of getting knocked up your first time? Lucky her, right? Once the thrill of being with the guy of her dreams had worn off, he'd never called again, and the couple of missed periods had finally clicked in—better late than never, right? Julie had forgotten about that party and Trevor, who had already been long gone—she didn't forget about him that quickly—and she'd faced the tough reality that she'd soon be a single mother at the ripe old age of eighteen.

But today was about a job, not about losing her virginity and getting pregnant. "Apology accepted."

To be honest, many things weighed on her mind, too, about that night and the aftermath.

She'd already been enrolled at the University of Denver, and had settled into her dorm, gone through orientation, started her classes. After a couple of months and her normally irregular periods had just upped and quit, she hadn't been able to deny her suspicions any longer and had taken a home test. Even though they'd used a condom, she'd gotten pregnant.

Julie had called her mother. The woman who'd had big plans for her education. Julie had been the model student her entire life—actually had had no choice, with her mother being a grade-school teacher and her father the principal of Cattleman Bluff High School.

Her mother's voice had dropped at the truth. She'd flipped out, told Julie to have an abortion, so focused on her future, forgetting about Julie's feelings and thoughts on the matter. "Your life will be over because of that baby." She'd spit out the word *baby*, making Julie wonder if she'd ruined her own mother's life.

"They'll think you're only after their money, those Montgomerys," her father had said spitefully when he'd gotten on the phone. "They'll publically humiliate you, and us."

She'd shamed her parents and that had seemed to be all that mattered. Amazingly, with them, she and her baby had been left out of the mix.

Logically, because she'd been trained to think that way, Julie had transferred those implanted thoughts and doubts onto Trevor, the guy just beginning med school. With every ounce of guilt she'd felt heaped on her by her parents—as Julie's mother had gotten her father involved in the call, with both pressuring her into ending the pregnancy—Julie had bundled up her feelings and kept her mouth shut.

Trevor hadn't ever called her again. He hadn't given a damn about her. It had hurt like hell and she'd been alone in a new city, with no friends and parents telling her to get rid of it. As if a baby could be called an "it".

Hurt, anger and a large dose of immaturity had rounded out her decision. The good part was, against her parents' advice, she'd kept her baby.

The tricky part was, she'd chosen never to tell Trevor about her being pregnant because she hadn't wanted to be told to give up her baby by anyone else. She wouldn't have regardless, no matter how much her parents had pressured her. But they'd gotten through to her on the rest—she hadn't wanted to interfere with Trevor's dream of becoming a doctor by telling him he was going to be a daddy. He'd already proved he didn't care about her, hadn't once tried to get in touch with her since they'd been together that night. She'd feared he'd deny he'd been with her, put all the blame on her, as her parents had. It would have ruined her one perfect night with the guy she'd dreamed about all summer.

Julie glanced at the man sitting next to her, smiling benevolently, and tried her best not to betray her thoughts.

Would he have accused her of only being after his family's money, as her father had suggested? Being so young, she'd believed her parent's predictions. And she'd been hurt, so hurt when she'd been forced to realize she didn't mean anything to Trevor.

She'd been too young, immature, emotionally wounded and way too mixed up to work out all the particulars. How could she be expected to act rationally? But she'd stubbornly chosen to keep Trevor in the dark. She'd show him. At least that was how it had started out. Then the reality of being a single mom and supporting herself had kicked in, and she'd been bound and determined to prove her parents wrong. She could do it all. She *would* do it all. Trevor had practically been forgotten by then. Now all these years later, she'd have to face her decision and somehow justify it.

Here she was accepting an apology from a man who'd taken her virginity but didn't have any idea he was a father. That huge, and quite possibly unforgivable, reality twisted and tied into a knot the entire size of her stomach, making it hard to breathe.

"So you have my word that I'll only behave respectfully and professionally toward you from here on out." Could the guy sound any stiffer? Could she feel any worse?

Remember to breathe. "I appreciate that." She figured she'd better ensure one thing before moving forward with what she suddenly needed—had no choice, in her mind—to do. "And I definitely have the job, right? And not just because of that?"

He gave a relieved smile. "I expect you to be here at eight tomorrow morning. Our first patient is scheduled for eight-thirty."

She nodded, the rapid beating of her heart pounding up her neck and into her ears. She couldn't keep the lie going, not if she'd have to face this man every day at work. It would eat away at her conscience. Might even interfere with her job performance. She couldn't allow that to happen. For a millisecond she wished she'd never come back home, but James needed a chance at a better life. And she was hell-bent on giving it to him.

When she realized she'd been staring at her folded hands far too long, her gaze flitted upward to find Trevor's perplexed expression. Oh, yeah, he was onto the fact something else was brewing.

She owed him the truth. Hadn't he just taken a huge risk, bringing up their past, setting the record straight that he'd regretted their one time together?

Didn't he deserve to know there were consequences? How on earth would he react?

Her pulse switched to a fluttery rhythm, vibrating all over her chest. This was the moment of truth, and she couldn't let it pass.

"Trevor. Uh, about that night." She looked straight ahead, unable to engage his eyes for now. Could he sense the dread in her voice?

James is the most wonderful gift in your life. There's no room for shame over your son. Just tell him already!

"I mentioned I have a son, James. He's twelve. Twelve years, nine months, to be exact." Would he do the math instantaneously? She twisted an imaginary ring on her left hand, knowing she had to look Trevor in the eyes when she told him. Dreading it.

With every last nerve she could gather, she forced her gaze to his, praying he'd understand and not accuse her of lying. If he did, she'd have to quit the job before she ever started. "Well, since we're laying everything out on the table today, I want you to know that…" She had to swallow first, because her throat seemed to have closed down.

His stare drilled into hers and her chest felt as if it would implode. She took a sip of air and just blurted it out.

"You're the father."

CHAPTER TWO

TREVOR'S BREATH WHOOSHED out of him as if he'd just been kicked in the solar plexus. Well, metaphorically, hadn't he been? Julie Sterling—a one-night stand from the last night of a particularly great summer vacation—had just gifted him with the news. He was a father of a twelve-year-old boy and had never known it.

"What are you telling me?" He blinked, fighting off disbelief and a surge of anger.

Julie sat there, chin high, staring at him, looking far too young to be thirty-one.

In fact, right now she looked more like that pretty little gal with the wild curly brown hair and huge hazel eyes he'd played fast and reckless with that one night, all those years ago. She still had freckles across the bridge of her nose, and the thickest eyelashes he'd ever seen, and two minutes ago he'd been thinking how great it might be to get to know her again, how beautiful she'd become, how she still set off a reaction he'd forgotten about these past few years. Then she'd lowered the boom and hit him with the craziest news of his life. He had a son?

"I'm telling you the truth. I owe it to you," she said. "I got pregnant that night."

He needed to stand. Needed to inhale. Needed to

pound his fist into the wall. Was she a whack job, setting him up? His legs seemed undependable at the moment, so he leaned against his desk and dug his hands into his jeans pockets, because he didn't know what else to do with them. He finally remembered to close his mouth. "You're sure that I'm the one who got you pregnant?"

Yeah, he was being ridiculously slow on the uptake, on purpose, and maybe a little insulting, too, might even qualify as a jerk, but he'd proved that long ago when he'd never called her after they'd been together. He needed time to process this flabbergasting and life-altering information.

He was a father? What if he didn't want to be? Damn it, why hadn't she given him a choice in the matter?

She nodded, unwavering in her speculative stare, her hands knotted in her lap. "As you mentioned earlier, I was a virgin. I didn't run off and start sleeping around after that either. The OB doc tracked the pregnancy to nearly that exact day."

Trevor's hand flew to the top of his head, needing to check for a nonexistent cowboy hat. All these years he'd been a father? "Look, I'm sorry for how that may have come off. I'm just really thrown right now." Getting kicked off a bucking bull couldn't have felt worse.

"Understandably."

"Why didn't you tell me?"

She slowly shook her head. "I didn't want to ruin your first year in med school. Didn't want you to feel obligated to me." She glanced at the floor. "Didn't want you to tell me to—"

"Look, I honestly don't know what I would have done then. It would've been nice to have some say in the matter, but I'm pretty sure I wouldn't have told you to get rid of it. Er…him." He grimaced. "James, is it?" His head spun with the knowledge of his son. A kid he'd never had an ounce of input in walked the earth not knowing he had a father. Did James know that he was his father?

"James Monty Sterling."

"Monty? You know that's my dad's nickname, right?"

Still staring at the floor, she nodded.

So that was the one connection she'd kept to his family, and it was only a nickname. He ground his teeth to keep from spitting out the words flying through his head. Anger circled around like a hawk zeroing in on its prey. That urge to bash something with his fist returned, so he shoved his hands deeper into his pockets.

"That wasn't right of you."

Her startled look hit him square in the jaw. "It might not have been right, but it's what I did. I can't apologize for it, but if you don't want to hire me, I get it."

Could he face her every day, forced to wonder how different the boy's life would have been if he'd been in it? Would the kid have needed to go to military school if he'd had a father in his life? Why had she held out on him, and could he forgive her? Right now, he wasn't sure what any of the answers were, but he knew he couldn't fire her. To spite her, he'd only harm the kid. Instinct told him that wasn't right.

She'd come back to her hometown to deal with her parents' estate, and to put her, uh, *their* son in military school. All these years, she'd never hit him up for money or support on any level, even knowing his family was well off. There had to be something noble in that, except it was a boneheaded thing to do in the first place. She said she hadn't wanted to ruin his first year in medical school, yet she'd changed the course of her entire life by taking sole responsibility for the act they'd done together.

Taking that into account, some of the rage swirling through his mind simmered down.

Nope, it didn't seem fair to never know he was a father, but she'd called the shots, and unbeknownst to him he'd stood by in ignorance.

He could only imagine the nerve it took to drop that bomb, and how she'd had to swallow some major pride to apply for a job in his clinic in the first place. Had he been set up?

Something about her pouring out her heart to him after all these years, while having borne the burden of being a single parent for a kid who was half as much his as hers, made him zip through what was left of the shocked, angry and accusatory part. Before he realized what he was doing, he dropped to one knee to take her white-knuckle hands in his.

Her guts at finally telling him overrode his stunned reaction.

He studied her face. What the hell was he supposed to say?

"As you can imagine, I need some time to let this news sink in. I've never married and don't have any kids, so the thought of being a father to a nearly thirteen-year-old son is mind-blowing."

"I understand."

She let him hold her hands, but still didn't look at him.

"Your job's safe." Hell, he couldn't very well kick the mother of his child out on the street, could he? Nor did he want to. He'd been anything but honorable way back then, turned out so had she, but that was all history and it couldn't be changed. Right now was a chance to make up for it, and there was a kid in need of military school at stake. "But honestly, I'm going to need time to figure out what to do about the fatherhood part."

"Of course." Finally she engaged his eyes, looking amazingly earnest and so damn appealing, the expression grabbed his heart and squeezed it. Why did he still feel connected to her? Well, criminy, he was totally bonded to her by a kid, just didn't know it until now! "I'm fine with keeping this strictly between us for now. I love my son and that will never change, and I don't expect you to suddenly change your life. I'm just going for full disclosure here. New job and all."

He patted her hand, thinking how soft and fragile it was, how right it felt cupped in his palm. "Give me some time to work this through, okay?"

"Okay, but first you've got to understand I'm not asking for anything but this job, Trevor."

He nodded. "I believe you."

"So let's just keep this under wraps and move forward with my employment for now—is that okay?"

"If only it were that easy, Julie, but okay." He stood, shaking his head like it might help put sense into the latest news. It didn't. "At some point I'm going to want to meet him. Tell him."

"If that time comes, we've got to do it together. Promise me that."

He nodded. "Okay."

She stood. "I won't force it. Just so you know."

He nodded again.

"So I'll see you tomorrow morning, then?" A definite tentative tone to her question.

"Sure." Still stunned, he didn't have a clue what to do next, and his mind, in its currently baffled state, wasn't exactly coming up with anything else to say either.

Julie headed for the door, her bulky winter coat over her arm, the conservative navy business suit she'd worn fitting her narrow waist and rounded hips perfectly. He glanced at her shapely calves, remembering how he'd liked her legs in short shorts that summer. Man, had that gotten him into trouble…and all these years he'd never even known just how much.

He scratched his head, curiosity causing him to ask. "Do you have a picture of James?"

She stopped and turned. "Of course. You want to see him?" A cautious yet agreeable glint in her eyes led to a flicker of that girl from all those summers ago.

"Please." All kinds of new feelings buzzed around inside his body; his mind jumped from possibility to implausibility and back. He was a father?

She dug into her purse and produced a red leather wallet, opened it and immediately found a standard school photo and proudly showed it to him. "He's tall for his age."

He took it. If he'd doubted for one second that he'd actually been the father, he couldn't very well do it now. And shame on him for even holding out a tiny hope it wasn't true. The kid staring at him from the picture was a gangly version of himself at twelve or thirteen, but with Julie's lighter brown, curly hair and freckles over the bridge of his nose. He suppressed his reaction, but was pretty sure she'd already picked up on it. That DNA couldn't be denied.

"Thanks."

"You want to keep it? I've got plenty more."

Did he want to take the first step…? Hell, he'd done that thirteen years ago. "Sure. Thanks." How could he refuse?

Julie gave a demure yet hopeful smile. "I'll see you tomorrow morning, then."

He tore his gaze from the photo and exhaled, then watched her walk down the hall to the exit. "I'll be here."

Then he put the boy's picture in his desk drawer and closed it.

What the hell was he supposed to do now?

Rather than head straight to the house and face his father, since the sun had poked out that afternoon, Trevor decided to take a ride on Zebulon to help work through the residual anger directed at his newest employee. He also needed to check the area that his smartphone mapping app said was down. Until grazing-management technology was able to produce virtual fences and cattle headgear, he'd continue to do things the old-fashioned way—by hand. And today he'd use this possible boundary breach as an excuse to avoid facing his father. Besides, he needed more time to run the latest news through his brain—for about the hundredth time since Julie had told him he was a father.

He'd come home after graduating from college to help out on the ranch before heading off to medical school. He'd learned to work hard and play hard back then—he'd even finished his undergraduate work in three years instead of the usual four—and every weekend that summer, after helping out on the ranch, he'd hit whichever party in town that had promised the most ladies. Because he'd deserved it. At least, that was what he used to tell himself.

Sitting atop Zebulon, his buckskin Appaloosa, Trevor felt the frigid air cut through his lungs. He inhaled deeper, hoping the burn might shock some sense into him. Yet so far, he couldn't get Julie and James Sterling, his ready-made family, out of his mind.

Back then, the year he'd met her, word had traveled fast in their tiny town, and it had always been easy to find out about the weekend hangouts. It hadn't taken much to make a party. An old abandoned barn or a camp-fire ring, some bales of hay to sit on, car radios for music. The gatherings, as they used to call the weekly events, had always been well attended.

At twenty-one, he hadn't been a teenager anymore, but he'd gotten used to partying on weekends at the university, so he'd gone. Got treated like near royalty as a college grad, too. And that was the first time he'd noticed Julie. He'd asked one of his buddies who she was and he'd told him she was seventeen and had just graduated from high school. They'd spent most of that summer checking out each other, but something had kept Trevor from approaching her. He hadn't had any plans that included getting involved with a girl, not back home anyway, and maybe he'd instinctively known she might be trouble. Trouble? With that sweet face and sinful body?

Oh, yeah, trouble—big trouble. And damned if he hadn't walked right into it.

"Will you dance with me?" she'd asked that night, looking all innocent and pretty as summer itself in a little flowery sundress. It had been the last weekend before he was set to leave for Boston University School of Medicine. He'd held out all summer, but something about the way the campfire had outlined her wild hair, making it look golden with shooting solar flares for curls, had made him accept the beer she'd handed him, and the offer to dance. He even remembered thinking, *This is probably the dumbest thing I've ever done*, and yet he hadn't been able to help himself and had done it anyway. And it had been a slow dance.

He'd had a couple of beers already; even so he'd known he shouldn't talk to or dance with this girl, but he hadn't been able to resist. Not when she'd been right there, smiling so pretty.

Zebulon stopped without reason, and Trevor snapped out of his memories, realizing they were already at the fence line, and sure enough a couple of posts were down. He texted Jack, the ranch foreman, giving him the location, and waited for his reply.

And he remembered Julie's bright, though guarded, eyes from earlier, how they'd still enticed him. How they'd brought back memories of that last summer home before med school, and his taking advantage of the young woman's willingness that night. How they'd reminded him of innocence, both his and hers. She was right—she could have ruined the life he'd planned if she'd told him about the pregnancy back then. But she hadn't. That had taken some guts.

In order to get through her orientation at the clinic, he'd have to turn into the Tin Man. Even now her playful hair and matured features grabbed him in a place he'd rather forget. Yeah, the Tin Man approach was the only ticket regarding her working for him. Good thing his nasty breakup with Kimberley—how she'd dropped him like a bad virus when he'd chosen family medicine over a more prestigious specialty the fourth year of med school—had already taught him how to turn his heart to metal.

His cell phone blipped, bringing him back to the range. Jack had got the message.

Normally, Trevor would have thought to bring his fence-repair kit with him, but today he'd been so distracted by Julie's news, it had taken all his brainpower just to saddle up and mount his horse. He glanced upward to a cloudless sky, then downrange, seeing hundreds of head of cattle roaming on snow-spotted land.

Getting a girl pregnant hadn't been his plan that year. Not by a long shot. Hell, he'd just found out the week before his mother had had an abnormal endometrial biopsy and needed more tests. Worrying about her, and about how his first semester in competitive medical school would go, with his big brother's exceptional brain to compete with, he'd decided to let off some steam that one last weekend, before he'd have to completely buckle down.

And he'd danced with the girl with wild hair and the biggest eyes he could remember.

Zebulon whinnied about something, and Trevor glanced up again. Jack was already heading to the fence and had nearly caught up to him. Who knew how long Trevor had been sitting on the range, staring and thinking?

The man waved as he approached, then stopped. "Thanks for the heads up. We can't afford to have any more steer wander off. Not with the grey wolves showing up more and more in these parts."

"Thanks."

"Until we can budget for putting chips in our cattle, we'll have to manage like we always have." Branding and fences seemed so far out of date. Jack was in his early forties and kept up with modern ranching trends. Truth was, Tiberius—Monty—Montgomery was old-school, and not the least bit interested in learning new techniques, or utilizing software and technology for running his ranch. The man still insisted on keeping hand-written bookkeeping ledgers, which Trevor would have to transfer to his own computer books when he got home.

"I'll talk to Dad again about the cost to chip the cattle, and mention the long-term savings."

"You do that. Maybe he'll listen to you."

Trevor seriously doubted it.

The men smiled at each other and went their separate

ways, leaving Trevor to his mind-boggling thoughts. He
remembered the exact instant he'd realized Julie was a
virgin, he'd stopped thrusting for a moment and looked
at her. "Are you sure?" he'd asked. Though she'd grimaced, she'd bucked under his hips, urging him not to
stop. He had been soon taken over by his desire; the
fact they were having sex while lying in a foot of hay
in a barn loft for her first time hadn't registered. Nope,
it was only after they'd snuggled up close afterwards,
and he had smelled summer in her hair and sex on her
skin, that he'd started to feel guilty. He'd been on the
verge of bringing up the subject when two of her friends
had called her name at the barn entrance, told her they
were leaving and she'd better come with them. Julie
had jumped up, thrown on her dress and underwear,
then kissed him one last time and disappeared with her
girlfriends. That was when their situation had started
to sink in.

No, she wouldn't see him again.

She hadn't had a clue he'd be gone by Monday, yet
he'd let her go, then lain there and stared through the
cracks in the roof of the barn at the black summer sky,
thinking he'd done something he shouldn't have. Something he'd really enjoyed, but would regret. And he
hadn't even had the decency to see her home.

Well, at least she hadn't lost her virginity in the back
of the old beat-up car he'd been driving that summer,
his brother's hand-me-down. A barn loft had to be more
romantic than that. Right?

He racked his brain and knew he'd used contracep-
tion, just as he had all through college. No girl had gotten pregnant…until Julie.

Zebulon galloped toward the barn, like a homing
pigeon, obviously eager to get brushed and fed. Trevor

dismounted his horse and pushed the nagging thought of Julie and that night out of his mind. He should have at least said goodbye to her. It was the decent thing to do. He should have called and told her he was sorry for taking her virginity, too. Yet he'd done neither. Instead he'd left town for med school and never looked back. Soon forgetting all about her and that night.

Until her name and credentials had come across his desk on a job application.

His long-overdue apology hadn't been the least bit honorable. It had been obligatory and smarmy. What a heel he'd turned out to be.

Trevor walked the path to his home, the only place he'd ever lived, outside college and medical school, and gritted his teeth thinking it would be extra hard to hide his feelings from his father over dinner tonight. But he sure as hell would because this was one topic he did *not* want to bring up over one of Gretchen's casseroles.

But at least by hiring Julie today, he had a chance to make up for taking advantage of her thirteen years ago. There might still be a chance to win back a thread of honor. To meet his son and become the father the kid deserved.

The thought scared the tar out of him.

The next morning Julie kept her word and arrived at the clinic fifteen minutes early, butterflies swarming through her insides and gathering in her stomach. Charlotte, the RN, was there to greet her. Late forties. Graying dull brown hair pulled back tight in a low ponytail. Stocky and average height, wearing a glaring white uniform. Julie surmised the woman loved being a nurse.

"So you're our new RNP?" Charlotte shoved out a

sturdy and rough hand for a shake. "Nice to meet you. Call me Lotte, like my friends. What do you say I give you a tour of the joint before you shadow Dr. Montgomery?"

Grateful for putting off facing Trevor for a second time, especially since she could barely sleep last night from thinking of him, Julie smiled. "I'd love to, thanks."

Fifteen minutes later, having been shown how each examination room was set up, as well as the procedure room, where the medical supplies and ever-important linens were kept, Julie was escorted back to Trevor's office.

"Good morning," he said, looking intriguing and appealing with a day's growth of beard. The vision nearly made her stop in her tracks. Then she noticed his wild-eyed glance and understood how deeply she'd rocked his world yesterday.

Yeah, they both had things to deal with, and working together wouldn't be easy.

Julie greeted him with a catch in her breath. Those flashing dark eyes were responsible. As well as the perfectly ironed classic Western shirt. Why did she have to notice?

She'd taken extra care to wear comfortable yet stylish clothes today. Black slacks with matching low-heeled leather boots, and an ice-blue thin sweater that her hazel eyes would surely pick up the color from. She'd pulled her hair back from her face, with a folded blue, patterned scarf tied at her neck under the hair that dusted her shoulders. It was either that or a dull old black headband, and she'd gone for color and California style. Not that she'd wanted to catch Trevor's attention or anything.

These days, in LA, doctors and RNPs no longer wore white coats. She was interested to see if she'd be given

one here since studies had shown lab coats *carried
germs* instead of protecting doctors and patients *from*
them.

Trevor motioned her over. "Let me show you the
charting system."

Julie didn't want to get too close, but he used a small
laptop computer to sign in on for their first patient. Sure
enough, she had to get close enough to catch the scent
of his soap and masculine aftershave and the effect was
far too heady for this time of the morning. Fortunately,
the young man's information popped up, distracting her,
and Trevor explained the various windows to use and
entries she'd be required to make.

"Don't worry, I won't make you do this until you feel
ready." He tossed her a friendly smile that put her on
edge instead of comforting her. How would she handle
the entire orientation at such close range? She needed
to adjust her attitude and quick. If he could act detached
and businesslike so could she.

Switching to all business, she armored herself with a
professional disposition. Besides, Trevor seemed to have
already forgotten yesterday's news, and, even though it
cut deep, Julie was grateful for the hiatus.

Trevor stood, laptop in hand, and headed for Exam
Room One, where Donald Richardson, a twenty-seven-
year-old type-1 diabetic ranch hand, waited. His chief
complaint being nasal congestion for ten days and a
headache for the past four to five.

After a friendly greeting and introduction of Julie
to the patient, Trevor performed a quick examination
of his nasal passages. Based on the examination, plus
seeing a chart notation from Lotte, it seemed Donald's
temperature was elevated. Trevor told him it looked like
he had a sinus infection.

"Take off your shirt so I can listen to your lungs," Dr. Montgomery said.

Off came the shirt, and Trevor did not look pleased. "What's this?" He pointed to a colorful shoulder tattoo.

Donald gave a sheepish glance. "My new tattoo."

Trevor still didn't look happy, and Julie assumed it was because of the possibility for complications that diabetics might face with body art.

"Did you bring your daily blood-sugar numbers?" Trevor wasn't going to give the man a break just yet. He pushed some buttons on the laptop and brought up the most recent lab results, then took the small booklet Donald handed him. After glancing at the last couple weeks' blood sugars, and sliding-scale insulin injections, he shared the info with Julie. She glanced at the computer screen and saw that Donald's last A1C test was under 7 percent, which was a good thing.

"You know your kidney function has been borderline for a while now, and if you don't keep your blood sugar under control, getting a tattoo can be dangerous."

Donald hung his head, as if he was sick of hearing the diabetes story whenever he wanted to do or try something new. "I've been keeping it clean and there isn't any sign of infection."

"And that's a good thing. But would you do me a favor, and next time you decide to get a tattoo, or body piercing or anything invasive, would you let me run some lab tests first? The last thing you need is to put your life in danger. If your blood sugar is high, a tattoo can be a playground for bacteria. That bacteria can invade your body and cause all kinds of trouble. Which is exactly what you don't need."

"I've been doing pretty good with the blood sugars."

"I can see that. I'm just playing the devil's advocate."

From Julie's assessment, Donald kept his weight under control and looked healthy. But the outside package didn't always reflect the microscopic goings-on inside the body.

"I understand. You're just looking out for me."

"As long as we understand each other."

"Okay. I promise. But, really, isn't she a beaut?" Donald nodded at the tropical-inspired tattoo. "Whenever it's colder than the North Pole up here, I'm going to look at this picture and dream about being in Hawaii."

Trevor smiled. "That's another place you'd have to work extra hard to keep your sugars balanced. Hot sticky weather is a playground—"

"—for bacteria. I get it, Doc."

They exchanged a strained smile, and Julie fought to keep hers to herself.

"Well, the prescription I'm writing for the sinus infection should help, in case this tattoo springs an infection." He wrote it out, tore it off, and handed it to the younger man. "If you notice any pain, swelling, redness, warmth, streaks or pus on or near that tattoo you let me know immediately."

"I will, Dr. Montgomery, I promise," Donald said as he buttoned up his shirt.

"And I gave you seven days of antibiotics for your sinuses. Take all of them. After that, if you aren't completely cleared up, give me a call."

"Will do."

"Oh, and this is Julie Sterling, our new nurse practitioner."

They gave a friendly greeting, and within seconds Julie nodded goodbye and followed Trevor out the door. Essentially, she agreed with his assessment and plan for Donald. But before she could say a word, Trevor was heading to the next patient's exam room. He'd been adding all the pertinent data about Donald Richardson into the computer as he went along in the appointment. She wondered how long it would take her to become as proficient with the program.

He entered the next room and immediately washed his hands, as he'd done with the first patient, and made a friendly greeting while doing so. Julie would give Trevor an A for bedside manner—oh, wait, she'd already learned about his bedside manner...a long, long time ago. Man, she needed to erase that picture from her mind. And quick.

By lunchtime they'd hardly spoken ten non-medical-related words to each other, concentrating solely on the patient load and treatments. Their bodies being cramped together in small patient-exam rooms kept an unwanted heat simmering beneath Julie's cool and calculated surface. Try as she might, she couldn't ignore her reaction to being near Trevor.

At noon sharp, Lotte came waltzing into Trevor's office, while he was explaining the required codes for specific ailments and treatments and labs. Julie's head was spinning with intellectual overload and she was grateful when he handed her a printout of the codes. Until their fingers touched and some crazy tingly reaction nearly made her already-spinning head take flight.

"Come with me, Ms. Sterling," Lotte said. "May I call you Julie?"

"Of course." Thank heavens the woman was oblivious to anything beyond the clinic, because Julie was quite sure her cheeks had gone pink. She mentally crossed her fingers that Trevor hadn't noticed.

"Let me show you the lunch room. Did you bring your lunch?"

"Oh." Julie had been so nervous about facing Trevor again after the bombshell she'd laid on him yesterday that preparing her lunch had been the last thing on her mind. "I didn't bring one."

"Then let me give you a rundown of the local cafés." Lotte pulled Julie by the arm out of Trevor's office, and he barely glanced up, until Julie looked back and caught him taking a quick glance. Yipes, there went the head-spinning tingles again the instant their eyes connected. But just as quickly his interest shut down and he went back to the computer task at hand.

This all-business routine was wearing thin. Did it also mean he wouldn't see her as a human being? "I'll see you at one, then?"

He nodded, not bothering to look up again from his computer. "See you then."

She detected he was angry with her, and couldn't blame him, but also wondered if he was at all curious about James.

Lotte must not have realized that Julie had grown up in town and knew the main stretch like the back of her hand, so Julie let Lotte recommend her favorite spots. One of the cafés Lotte had named was new and Julie decided to give that one a try.

For a town like Cattleman Bluff, whose main claim to fame was the longest antler arch in the state of Wyoming—which she made a point to walk beside and then under while crossing the street, admiring the sheer number of antlers and the thick woven arch they created—the main street did seem to have a few new spots. An appealing dress boutique caught her eye, and a bookstore, actually a second bookstore since the first only specialized in used and unique books, went on her list of places to check out in the future.

The old-style café had a counter and she slipped onto the last available red vinyl stool to make her order.

Halfway through her ham sandwich and cup of home-made vegetable soup she heard the young waitress tell a customer his lunch was ready and waiting with a much cheerier note than when she'd taken Julie's order.

"Thanks."

Surprised by the voice, Julie turned to see Trevor accept the sack of take-out food, along with the huge and hopeful smile from the young server.

"Just the way you like it, Dr. Montgomery."

"You never let me down, Karen. Thanks. Put it on my tab."

The shapely waitress followed him to the door, and Julie couldn't help watching them talk briefly together before he left. Dating? Who knew? That was entirely his business, but, since Julie's pulse had stepped up a beat or two just seeing Trevor relating to the attractive woman, she chided herself for caring.

When Julie finished her tea she asked for her bill.

"Oh. No worries. That's been taken care of by Dr. Montgomery."

Julie raised her brows and noticed the waitress's carefully observant eyes watching her every move. "Oh, well, then, I'll be sure to thank him."

As Julie left the lunch counter she could have sworn she heard the young woman mumble, "I'm sure you will…"

Did she think she had claims on Trevor Montgomery any more than Julie did?

There was no way Julie could know the answer

to that, but one thing was sure: she'd bring her lunch tomorrow and skip eating at this café in the future.

The afternoon appointments were all fairly routine, and, since Julie needed time to tackle the computer charting, Trevor suggested she spend the rest of the day with Lotte and Rita. A relief to Julie, since being forced to watch Trevor all morning had caused a list of unwanted reactions, none of which were proper, so she took the assignment and ran.

Except he showed up in her office looking torn. "I've got an I and D in Exam Room Three. You want to take care of it?"

She understood this was an opportunity for him to evaluate her on an incision-and-drainage procedure. "Sure. Is it a boil or an abscess?"

"A boil."

She dropped what she was doing with Lotte and Rita, and followed him down the hall. He introduced her to Molly Escobar, a fifty-six-year-old librarian who had formed a ping-pong-ball-sized boil in her right armpit. The area in question was red, angry-looking and weeping pus.

Following protocol from her prior clinical experience for this minor surgical procedure, Julie first cleansed the skin with antiseptic and injected topical anesthetic to numb the area before using a scalpel with a sterile blade to make a small incision to allow the pus to flow out. As she worked she kept in mind that a regular boil looked the same as MRSA and the only way to tell the difference was if the usual antibiotics didn't help clear the infection. She'd save time and start with a broad-spectrum antibiotic active against both staph and strep just in case.

Once she'd drained the boil, and thoroughly cleaned the area, it looked clear of infection and had healthy tissue at the base, so she placed four sutures. Then she put on a thin layer of sterile gauze followed by a sterile dressing, which would need to be changed daily.

"I'm going to have our nurse show you how to change the dressing, and I want to see you back on Monday for a follow-up visit, okay?"

Dr. Montgomery had been as quiet as an overgrown barn mouse watching her every move, connecting with her glances whenever she looked up during the procedure, blinking his approval, evidently never feeling compelled to make any suggestions.

After Charlotte came to take Ms. Escobar to the procedure room, and they were alone, Trevor looked at Julie and smiled. "You have a gentle touch, Julie," he said, their eyes lingering briefly longer than necessary, and causing an unwanted reaction behind her breastbone.

"Thank you." She needed to step away from him. Now. "I'll go input the notes in the computer," she said, and sailed out of the room.

By 5:00 p.m. the clinic closed, and Julie walked with Lotte and Rita to the parking lot. Trevor was on his way out, too, and, without knowing, Julie had parked next to his car. She glanced at him, disturbed to find his gaze already settled on her, as she opened her door.

"Dr. Montgomery?" a man's voice called from across the parking lot.

Trevor looked up, smiled, and waited for the middle-aged man to approach. Julie moved around the car to put in her trunk a ream of paperwork given to her by Lotte to study that night. She dallied out of pure nosiness.

"What's up, Connor?"

As the man got closer Julie realized the guy was dressed shabbily and looked down on his luck.

"I was wondering if you can give me some advice about—"

Lotte spoke up from two cars down; evidently Julie hadn't been the only one to linger out of nosiness. "Mr. Parker, you know you're supposed to make an appointment for those kinds of things."

"That's okay, Charlotte, go ahead and go home," Trevor said, dismissing her in a kind way.

Julie was thinking the same thing—the guy should make an appointment, not hit up the doctor for a parking-lot consultation—but decided to keep her mouth shut if she wanted to stick around to find out what was going on, and if she valued her new job.

"Thanks, Doctor. With the cold weather and all, feet in boots all day and half the night—I'm working a second job as a security guard at Turner's Hardware—I've developed athlete's foot and I was wondering if you have any samples of that cream you gave me last time?"

"I don't, but I'll share a little trick. What you can do is urinate on your feet in the shower. Plug the drain so you can soak your feet in it for a minute or so. Doesn't cost a penny. Let me know how it works."

The man looked perplexed, but grateful and willing to give the old wives' tale a try. "Thanks, Doc. I'll be sure to let you know how it works."

As the man walked off Julie folded her arms, no longer able to keep her thoughts to herself. "You don't expect that to cure his athlete's foot, do you?"

"My grandmother swore by using urine on her cracked feet, even kept a jar of it for her winter-cracked hands, and folks have been recommending urine for foot fungus for years."

"Topical antifungals have something like forty percent urea in them, and urine has…what? Two point five percent tops?"

"Your point?" One arm on the roof of his car, looking over the top, he nailed her with a perturbed stare.

"Your treatment won't be very helpful for him. He might need a strong topical fungicide, or possibly an oral-medicine prescription."

He took his time to inhale, as though patience was his biggest virtue. "Look, the guy's health insurance has such a high deductible he can't afford to make appointments. Let alone buy medicine on the chance it may or may not help, or, worse yet, try oral medicine that can cause liver and heart issues as a side effect. The man's got six kids and a wife with a lot of physical problems. You heard him—he works two jobs. I'm just trying to save him some money, that's all." His brows formed a V as he dared her to challenge his wisdom.

Well, in that case… "Okay, I get it." She started to get into her car as he watched, but couldn't quite let the provocative subject drop. "Do you keep medicine samples for people like that? Or do you only rely on old homeopathic methods?"

Trevor continued to stare at her as though she was a cattle poacher. "I help when I can, but I've also got a business to run and salaries to pay. And the people around Wyoming have used home remedies for years, especially during the long winters when it's nearly impossible to get to a doctor."

Her hand flew to her earlobe, her tell for when she backed down. "Point taken." She slipped inside her car and started the engine, thinking she'd buy some basic pharmacy items and bring them to the clinic for people like Connor whatever-his-last-name-was.

The first day on the job, working with the father of her child, had started out restrained and ended up downright rocky. The last thing she'd expected was ending the day with an argument over whether or not a grown man should urinate on his toes in the shower.

What would tomorrow bring?

Was Trevor ever planning to discuss their situation again, or, as she'd suggested they keep things under wraps, had he taken it completely to heart—meaning forget it ever happened? Well, that stunk if that was the case, and her respect for Trevor Montgomery slid down the honor scale.

Still wanting to end the trying day on a positive note, because that was her tried-and-true survival mechanism, Julie lightly tooted her horn as she drove off. In the rearview mirror she saw Trevor standing, watching her go and finally giving a wave.

It wasn't the friendliest gesture, or the meanest. Truth was, she'd set the guidelines—"let's keep things under wraps"—and he'd taken her direction and run with it. Yet the fact he hadn't asked one question about James today smarted.

With one last glance into her rearview mirror before hitting the street, she consoled herself—at least he'd quit scowling.

CHAPTER THREE

THURSDAY MORNING, Trevor looked like hell, as if he hadn't had a second of sleep. The delicate skin beneath his puffy eyes looked bruised, his hair unkempt. He'd obviously skipped shaving.

"Can I see you in my office?" It wasn't a question.

Julie followed him down the hall, walked past him as he held the door for her, where she could tell he'd at least showered because he smelled fresh, and his clothes weren't crumpled in any way. Guilt stabbed at her for doing this to him, but how many nights had she lost sleep over her son?

Once inside, he closed the door, stood there and drilled her with his stare. "I need to know about James. From day one."

Did he expect her to take time away from her patients to tell him her son's life story right now? "Uh, I'm still unpacking, but I have baby books, with his pictures and milestones, if that would help?"

He nodded. His thoughts so deep he seemed to sleep-walk. "I'll come by tonight and get them."

"Okay." She turned to leave, but remembered something that had seemed so unfair the day it had happened. "Ironically, just so you know, his first word was *da-da*."

Trevor seemed shocked out of his stupor, the first sign of life glinting in his eyes. "You're putting me on."

She shook her head. "He was six months old, woke up all content in his crib. When I came in he was playing with his toes. He lit up when he saw me and said 'Ah-da-da.' For the record, it made me cry." After studying her shoes for a few moments to recover, she looked up.

Trevor stood still as a statue, watching her. He seemed to be trying to read her entire history, or was he assessing what the hell he should do with his newest employee? "I'll come by tonight. Get those books."

"Okay." She left and got on with her day.

The amazing thing was, the minute the clinic opened Dr. Trevor Montgomery acted as if nothing life altering had happened between them. His easy doctor charm returned, and he performed like the perfect mentor for her on her continuing orientation. All business. The man definitely knew how to separate work from personal life.

That night, at 7:00 p.m. Trevor knocked on her door. She'd had a chance to find the storage boxes with James's memorabilia and had dug out the first two baby books. Hoping all he'd want was to grab the books and run, she snatched them from the table nearest to the door as she rushed by to answer it.

Of course he still looked tired—agonized? He'd put in a long day just as she had. "Hi," she said, pushing the books toward him. "Here you go."

Proving to be a man of few words, he took them, looked at them as if they were the Holy Grail. If she could only know what was going through his mind.

"You can keep them as long as you'd like, but I do want them back."

Watching her, like he couldn't figure out whether to hate or thank her, he nodded. "Thanks."

She'd pegged him right. He didn't stick around, and she was grateful because if he asked the plethora of questions registering in his eyes they'd be up all night.

The next morning, the instant she hit the hallway in the clinic heading for her office he trailed her. "I need to talk to you."

"Okay. Let me put my things away, and I'll be right there."

Instead of letting her go, he followed her into her office, as if what he needed to say couldn't wait. He still looked tired, had probably been up half the night memorizing her son's birth, baby and early toddler records. "I've got a lot of questions and I need a million answers. Have dinner with me tonight."

The man wanted details about her son. Their son. How could she refuse? "Okay."

"We'll leave right after work, unless you have plans?"

"Works for me."

The instant the clinic closed, Trevor was at her office door, waiting. "We'll take my car."

He escorted her outside and as soon as he started the engine, he opened up.

"I've got to tell you, you did a great job recording James's first months. It was obvious you put a lot of time into those books."

"Thanks. I enjoyed it. Every day was something new with him." Uh-oh, had she said too much, rubbed it in that he wasn't in the picture to experience any of it? If she had, he let it pass.

"You mentioned he had surgery at fourteen months."

"Yes, he had cryptorchidism."

Trevor's head spun toward her. "Are you kidding? One of my testicles was undescended at birth, too. I had the same surgery when I was one and a half."

What were the odds of that? She knew one in thirty healthy baby boys had the condition at birth, but most resolved on their own and didn't require surgery. Was this Trevor's DNA speaking through her son? "They asked me if there was any family history, but, of course, I didn't know."

"I've got to be honest, I'm blown away about being a father. I—I just don't know where to start."

"I'll answer anything you ask."

"What if I don't know enough to ask?"

"I'll fill in the blanks. I promise." That sick spot that had taken up residence in her gut since blurting out about James being Trevor's son seemed to grow exponentially as she realized how many lives the information touched. Hers. Trevor's. Her son's. How would James take the news he'd had a father in Wyoming his entire life? Hadn't that been the foremost question on her mind since she'd told Trevor, knowing the only person left in the dark was her son? Especially after the horrible incident with her ex-boyfriend, Mark?

How many lives had she managed to screw up by keeping her secret?

They drove to that café she'd sworn she'd never eat in again. If he was dating that waitress, he wouldn't take Julie there for dinner, would he?

What did it matter if he was dating the waitress or not? Julie didn't have any right to the man. She'd sent his life into a tailspin, and he was simply trying to make sense of it. That was the only reason they were here.

She picked at her food as Trevor pummeled her with question after question about the pregnancy, the birth, the first few months and the first two years of James's life. He'd practically memorized her entries in the baby books. He grinned—which was a welcome change from

his serious attitude the past two days since being told—
when he mentioned specific pictures, both home shots
and professionally taken ones. And he teased her about
dressing the boy in some silly outfits, insinuating that
never would that have flown if he'd been around.

The implications vibrated through her, making it impossible to eat. But she'd put herself through this torture
because Trevor deserved to know everything.

He wanted to know what James's first day at school
was like. She backed up to tell him a funny story about
his first day in preschool, then moved on to kindergar-
ten and grade school. She noticed he hardly touched
his meal either.

By ten o'clock, her voice was nearly hoarse from answering all of his questions, and he finally checked his
watch. "Looks like we're closing down the restaurant. I
guess we have to leave."

Though she was grateful for his interest, she was
relieved that tonight's hot seat was about to end.

He drove her back to her car at the clinic. "Can you
bring more photo albums for me?"

"Of course."

He reached for her arm. "Thanks."

She swore she didn't pick up on any resentment beyond his sincere thanks, which proved he was a far better person than her. If the tables had been turned, she
would have been furious and would have made the with-
holder's life miserable.

She prayed he didn't have revenge up his sleeve as
she got out and headed straight to her car, noticing he
waited until she was safely inside, started the engine and
backed out of her parking space, before driving off in
the other direction. Thank goodness she had the weekend to recover before facing him again.

* * *

The following Friday afternoon at the clinic, almost two weeks from her hire date, Julie put the finishing touch on her personal office with a spider plant in a thick blue ceramic holder practically guaranteed to take care of itself, happy she wouldn't have to share close quarters with Trevor another day. She'd taken quickly and easily to his clinical practice and was eager to begin working with her own patients, beginning Monday.

A strong knock at the door made her jump while straightening the frame with her RNP certificate she'd just hung, making it askew again. "Come in."

Trevor opened the door and stepped inside her small but functional office, and her pulse shimmied a couple of beats. Shouldn't she be getting used to him by now? He'd been mysteriously quiet this week, but each time he'd asked, she'd brought more baby books.

"Not a bad couple of weeks," he said, working up to a slow smile. "I have to give it to you, you're a fast study."

So this visit was all business, and that relieved her no end.

"Thank you. I kind of got thrown into the fire out in LA. The county had so many patients in need of care, there wasn't time for a proper orientation. I had to learn to think on my feet, as they say."

He stayed where he was, not making a point to sit or give the impression he wanted to chat, but subtle heat in his dark eyes informed her there was more going on than shop talk. "I hope you don't get bored here. It's not often we see gunshot or stab wounds or whatever they do out there in LA."

She smiled. "I'm glad for that. ER wasn't my cup of tea."

He studied her for an instant as if trying to figure out

what her cup of tea might be, before his brows pulled down. "Look. It's been really weird knowing I'm, you know, a father, and I'm really grateful you've shared those baby books with me."

"It's the least I can do." She was breathy from his chosen topic.

He scratched the back of his neck, a man obviously trying to deal with an unsettling situation. "I think we should have dinner tonight and talk about what we need to do."

What they needed to do? Did that mean he wanted to meet James? "Dinner? Tonight?" She'd hardly gotten used to working with him yet, and last Friday she hadn't been able to eat a bite with him grilling her about James. How could she sit across from him, staring at his handsome face, and tell him she wasn't ready for James to meet him?

She'd been thinking about it, and the kid had so much to adjust to as it was, it wouldn't be fair to drop this on him out of the blue. As she had with Trevor? Her breath sank to the bottom of her lungs.

"Do you have plans?" Why did he look surprised that she might? Of course she didn't, but if he only knew what was going through her head— "I mean, I know this is kind of last minute, but if you have a previous en—"

"No. No plans." She spoke before she thought, since the original question had thrown her so much. And since she'd been home she'd yet to contact any of her old high school friends, might have thought about it, but wasn't even sure she wanted to.

"Then what do you say? Let's grab some dinner and talk some more. I know a place where we can have some privacy."

What did he have in mind? He looked as uneasy as

she felt, but considering their circumstances she'd cut him some slack.

"Is it too early to eat? I could pick you up later, if you'd like." Now he seemed downright flustered, which, on the big, otherwise completely competent doctor, was endearing. Maybe it wouldn't all be about James tonight. Maybe they could get to know each other a little more. She warmed to the idea of sharing a meal with him.

If he wanted to take her to dinner, then she'd oblige, but only because she owed the guy a lot for hiring her, for taking the news about their son like a man, for being interested in her son...and her? Her hand flew to her ear, where she pressed her thumb and forefinger over the earlobe. "No. Now's fine. I just need a couple of minutes to finish up here."

The relieved look smoothed out his brows, making him all the more appealing. And cinching a tiny knot in her stomach. "Okay, I'll be in my office when you're ready."

She nodded, then went back to straightening that picture again, flustered and fighting off a sudden ripple of nerves. She could handle the questions about James, but what if this was different? What if he actually wanted to spend time with her? Alone?

She took her purse into the ladies' room to pick out her hair—combs and brushes were useless with her curls, just making them frizzy—and to apply some lipstick. She wasn't sure why she wanted to freshen up for Trevor, so she used the excuse that it had been a long day and she needed a touch-up—that was how she would have explained it for anyone, even Lotte and Rita. Right. She needed to face the fact she wanted to look nice for him. There, she'd admitted it.

A few minutes later, feeling somewhat refreshed and

having calmed down a shade, she peeked around his
office door. "Ready." But glimpsing the big man at his
desk, with his broad shoulders and excellent hair, no
longer looking tired and confused, she knew all of her
settling down had been for naught.

He glanced up from reading a medical journal, did a
quick double take with warm eyes, as if she'd changed
into lingerie or something, and hit her with that appealing slow smile of his. "Let's go, then."

Maybe she'd put too much lipstick on, and did she
really need to use mascara? What was she trying to accomplish anyway?

More importantly, why did Trevor Montgomery automatically make her slide right into second-guessing
everything? She needed to convince herself that theirs
was nothing but a professional relationship and deal with
it, pronto.

She waited by his door, feeling a bit fluttery when he
passed, and then followed him down the hall.

The office was closed and both Rita and Charlotte
had already left. Being there alone with him felt too intimate, so she stood back, keeping her distance. Trevor
shut down the lights and activated the alarm system,
then closed and locked the back door. A take-charge
guy with fine narrow hips and sexy boots. Oh, man,
her plan to remain detached fell apart before they'd even
left the building.

The night air was frigid and woke Julie out of the last
of her long, hard day sluggishness. Being with Trevor
had jump-started the task. She looked upward, while
Trevor finished up locking and securing the building, remembering how many more stars there seemed to be in
the sky back home. If she was lucky out in LA she'd see
the Big Dipper and Orion's belt. Most nights she could

locate Venus, but that was about the extent of stargazing out there. She shook her head, enjoying the infinite vision. Remembering a little more about the hometown she'd left behind thirteen years ago.

"You ready?" he asked, watching her with clear interest, then glancing upward toward the sky himself.

"Sure."

"Beautiful, isn't it?"

"Absolutely." She inhaled and let the sight and the breath ease the remainder of her misgivings about sharing a meal with the father of her son. His demeanor was different tonight from last Friday night. He seemed relaxed, as though he'd worked through some of his feelings about being a dad. He'd obviously changed tack. Tonight he seemed to want to focus on Julie.

"Would you prefer to take two cars or do you want to go in mine?"

She hadn't gotten that far in her thoughts, but he made a good point. Since he was offering to give her some space… "Oh, uh, why don't I follow you?"

"You know, I've got a better idea. The place I have in mind isn't far from your parents' house. How about I follow you over there so you can drop off your car first?"

The topic of conversation tonight would be anyone's guess. Maybe about James. Maybe not. She couldn't get a handle on anything with Trevor right now, and, since slow, steady breathing could only accomplish so much with the nerves, she might have a glass of wine to relax, so letting him drive sounded reasonable. "That works for me."

The easing of tension around his eyes let her know she liked her decision. She had to give it to him: the guy was trying, not running away from reality. "Let's go, then."

The fifteen-minute drive to Dusty Road Lane and the

sturdy log cabin–styled house Julie had grown up in, and now owned, gave her time to organize her thoughts. She'd decided to share anything and everything else the man asked about James, but he'd have to do the asking. Yeah, that clinched it: she'd definitely need a glass of wine with dinner.

She didn't bother to go inside the house or to turn on the porch lights, she just parked her car in the garage and hustled back to Trevor's waiting silver hybrid SUV. Like a gentleman, he saw her coming and hopped out of the car, then beat her to the passenger door and opened it.

"Thanks," she said, wondering if it was the clean evening air or his cologne that tickled her nose. He'd definitely freshened up, too. The complimentary thought made her disguise a smile and a small swell of pride.

The classy leather upholstery felt cold on the backs of her knees as she slid inside the car. He'd left the radio on and George Strait sang a twangy, sweet love song that took her right back to her youth, and growing up in Wyoming. Not many people listened to country music in LA, and she'd gotten out of the habit over the years, but it felt good, welcoming even, to hear those clear and simple words and music. And it helped settle her sudden building nerves over facing Trevor at dinner.

He drove off without wasting a moment.

"So where are we going? Will I know the place?"

"Don't think so. Was Rustler's Hideaway around when you lived here?" He drove single-handed, not afraid to look at her while on the road, like a man with all the confidence in the world behind the wheel.

She'd never heard of it, but for the sake of not letting the conversation die she answered. "I don't remember the name. Sounds like a grown-up place." She laughed lightly, feeling a bit absurd, but realizing all she remembered from her hometown was being a kid and a teen-ager. If it wasn't a burger joint, an ice-cream parlor, or the old bowling-alley café, she'd probably never been there.

"You've got that right. They serve the best steaks in this part of Wyoming." He angled his gaze at her. "I know because my father sells our corn-fed cattle directly to them."

She'd given up steak when she'd moved to California thirteen years ago, not out of any kind of vegetarian decision, but because she hadn't been able to afford decent meat on a college student's scholarship stipend and part-time bookstore clerk's income. After so many years, she wondered if her body would remember how to digest meat, especially coupled with James most likely being the topic of dinner conversation.

She thought about asking how business was going for the Montgomerys, but worried how Trevor would interpret the question. She wasn't looking for a handout, but if the man was interested in helping with the costs of military school, she sure wouldn't turn him down. Knotting the fingers on her lap, she decided to drop the insecurity about how she might come off and be up-front with him for James's sake.

On second thought, no. That didn't sit well. It wasn't her style. Trevor had given her a job, and that was all she'd hoped for. Oh, man, she'd been all wrapped up in her thoughts, the car had gone quiet except for the radio, and all because she couldn't quit overthinking every little detail.

"Nice car," she said lamely.

"Thanks."

True to his word, the restaurant was within ten minutes of her house, and had to be new, or built since she'd left home, because she definitely would have remembered this place. Nestled in and blending into the side of a hill, with a view from the parking lot of the town of Cattleman Bluff in the valley below, the restaurant looked chic. She didn't remember her hometown doing chic when she was growing up. The entire front was glass, and the lights inside revealed a first-class restaurant with white tablecloths, candles, flowers and customers, already filled to capacity.

"Looks like we might have a wait," she said.

Trevor helped her out of the SUV and shook his head. "They always reserve a booth for my father."

Ah, so that was how the other half lived. As tense as Julie felt about having dinner with Trevor, the aroma of grilled meat made her stomach juices kick in. Red wine, baked potato, garden salad and a petite cut, not to mention some sort of freshly baked bread, seemed like the best meal in the world at the moment.

Then she looked into the dark and determined eyes of Trevor Montgomery just before he guided her toward the restaurant entrance with a large and warm hand at the small of her back, and her tingly reaction forced her to wonder if she'd be able to eat at all.

Trevor poured a second glass of wine for Julie, since she seemed to enjoy the first so much. Hell, from the looks of her, she was enjoying everything on her plate, too. His father's booth was in a cozy corner toward the back, on the opposite end to the kitchen. Candlelight and quiet music ruled the evenings at Rustler's Hideaway, which was owned by a chef and his wife from New York City looking for a quiet life in a big and mostly empty state like Wyoming. Last census, their population was just over half a million.

He'd about finished his rib eye and had yet to bring up the main topic of conversation—James. Instead he'd been distracted enjoying Julie's large warm eyes with the candlelight dancing in them, and studying her amazingly unruly hair as she devoured her meal. But he cautioned himself about letting down any walls where she was concerned. Since Kimberley had done her number on his head, he'd kept his women close and his heart at a distance. Worked for him, if not the ladies. Life was just easier that way, and, what with his father's illness and the responsibility of the ranch and medical clinic, he had enough on his plate to keep him far too busy for romance.

Since Julie seemed to be letting him set the direction of their conversation, so far they'd only discussed her first two weeks on the job. He'd dropped in tidbits about the changes in their hometown in the past few years, but mostly praised her for being an excellent clinician. She'd remained curiously quiet.

The waiter, who seemed to sense their every need, appeared at the table. "Dessert or coffee, Dr. Montgomery?"

Trevor looked to Julie, who spoke for herself. "Just coffee, please. Decaf."

"I'll have the same."

The instant the waiter left the table, scolding himself for not doing so before now, Trevor brought up James. "Tell me more about James. Now that he's a preteen. What he likes. What he does." Hating not knowing anything about the kid who was his flesh and blood, he shook his head and raised his shoulders. "Everything."

Julie put down her fork, leaving the bite of potato uneaten, her eyes dancing in the candlelight. It was so obvious how much she loved her son, and that drove the painful wedge in his gut a little deeper as he realized the boy was a total stranger to him.

"Why is he at the military academy?"

That flash of life in her eyes at the opportunity to talk about her son dimmed when he mentioned the new school. She briefly went inside herself as though forming the thoughts she'd share, then that bright flash reappeared.

"He's a great kid. Not that I'm biased or anything, but honestly he is." She smiled and it soothed the sudden cramp in Trevor's stomach. "He's smart and inquisitive. And funny, oh, gosh, he can be silly, a regular mimic." She ran the tip of her finger around the nearly empty wine glass. "He's good at math, too, and a voracious reader. Likes adventure stories. Let's see—" she glanced toward the vaulted wood ceiling with the antler chandeliers "—he loves to play video games, and hasn't seemed to find his favorite sport yet. Though he's coordinated and good at just about everything he plays." Her eyes came to rest on Trevor's, and a feeling he'd forgotten since his early dating days snaked through his body. Infatuation. It should have surprised him, but, glancing at Julie with her pert mouth and expressive eyes, he found that it didn't.

"Last summer my friend, Mark, sent him to camp at a small farm in Malibu. It lasted two weeks, and when he came home he was so excited, he couldn't stop talking about it. He loved taking care of the piglets, and how he got to see a foal born." She laughed like bubbling water, but something quickly troubled her as shadows closed in on her smile. She seemed to fight it off. "He said it was gross but really interesting at the same time. Oh, and you'll be glad to know he fell in love with the horses on that farm."

Trevor guessed she thought about saying "like father, like son" but thought better of it. He also wondered who this friend was who bankrolled the camp, but forced himself to let that pass…for now. "Then I'd love to bring him out to the ranch sometime, maybe take him for a ride. Does he ride?"

She hesitated. "He has, but not that often. Look, I'm not sure if that's a good idea."

"Bringing him to my ranch? Letting him meet his grandfather?" Hell, would he have the guts to tell Dad who the boy belonged to? But wouldn't it be good for the boy to get to know his father? Just what were they supposed to do? How should they handle this situation? More importantly, would Julie let him have any say in it? Until now, she sure as hell hadn't, and it still rankled.

"James is going through a rough time now. Last September when school started, he couldn't wait to tell his friends what he did over the summer, but they laughed at him and called him farmer after that, and he went all quiet about it. The next thing I know he's hanging out with a new bunch of boys who seemed like brats, and he started dressing different and acting different." She cast a mixed-up look Trevor's way, a confused and worried mother's expression. He remembered seeing it on his own mother's face during his teens, too. "It was like night and day and I never saw it coming. Then he got arrested for shoplifting and…well, that's when I found out a few more things and when I decided to get out of Dodge and bring him home."

Home. The word felt good to hear coming from Julie. Her admitting she still thought of Cattleman Bluff as home gave him hope, and he wasn't even sure why. By the distant thoughtful expression on her face, Trevor suspected there was more to the story than what Julie had told. He couldn't quite put his finger on it, but being called farmer by peers didn't seem like a terrible enough issue to send a boy in an entirely different direction. He wondered just what those other things that she had found out about James were. Maybe he'd get to the bottom of that once he met his son.

His son. Whew, every time he thought that he needed to sit back and let the shock roll over him for an instant. He was a dad. And he hadn't even met his kid. Man, oh, man, would the ache at having never known that until now ever stop?

The fact Julie seemed hesitant about bringing James into his life also twisted in his gut. He finally decided to ask the question sitting like a rock in the center of his chest.

"How come you never told me about the boy? Maybe not at first, but at any one point over all these past twelve years?"

Julie's chin shot up. The waiter brought the coffee, and for the next couple of moments she let herself be distracted by pouring cream and sugar into her cup. Then suddenly, as if a shot of determination had been served in the bone-china cups, she nailed him with those unbelievably sexy eyes.

"What would you have done if you knew you were going to become a father with a girl you hardly knew, when you were on your way to med school?"

Now it was Trevor's turn to stare at his coffee, to search the dark liquid for answers he didn't have, but still wished he'd had the chance to find out about. He lifted his cup and took a short drink. "I honestly don't know what I would have done back then. But you had twelve different years to tell me, yet you chose not to.

I'd like to think I might have done the right thing at any point in my son's life."

"The right thing? You mean, marry someone you don't know because you knocked me up?" She said it in a hushed voice, glancing around at the nearby booths for any sign of strained ears.

"Not a great way to put it." He also lowered his voice. "It's the truth. That's what it would have amounted to if you'd gone the honor route. It would have messed up your career and made you miserable. Even later, I didn't know if you were married and had your own family or not. I never would have been able to trust that you cared about me. I would have been miserable, might never have become a nurse. No, Trevor, that initial choice wouldn't have been the best one."

She recited her reasons as if someone else had handed them to her. As if she'd convinced herself they were sufficient and he should accept them without question. He took another sip and ground his molars, knowing what he was about to say wouldn't go over well, but needing to say it anyway. Especially since he'd been thinking about it all week. "It would have been nice to at least have had a choice in the matter." He said it levelly, without emotion, but how many times during the past two weeks had he yelled it at the sky when it was just him and Zebulon on the prairie, or when he was in the shower with the water running full blast? Damn it! "But you never gave me a shot."

Julie took a quick drink, sloshing coffee over the rim of her cup when she set it back in the saucer. Her chin, if it was possible, went even higher, and her lips tightened into a straight line. Yet she didn't utter another sound. He didn't have to yell it; he'd hit a raw nerve anyway.

After a moment's reprieve, they drank more of their coffee in silence.

"I'd like to go home now," she said, not sounding angry, just resigned, and putting her cloth napkin on the table as proof.

Trevor had a million more questions to ask, but figured he'd have to dole them out little by little as he gained more of Julie's trust. He raised his hand and the waiter was there with the check quicker than it took him to swallow the last of his coffee.

"I'm going to the ladies' room," Julie said as he dug in his pants pocket for his wallet.

"Okay, I'll meet you in the lobby." Whatever friendly moments they'd shared over dinner had vanished with his one honest remark.

The drive back to her house was even more awkward. Good thing it only took ten minutes, which seemed more like an hour. But when he pulled up to her house, it was completely dark as she'd left it, and there was no way he'd let her walk to her porch or go inside in the dark. He stopped the engine and got out of the SUV before she could protest, strode with determination around the front of the car and managed to get to the passenger door in time to help her out. Sure it annoyed her, he could tell by the way her shoulders straightened when he took her arm, but he didn't care. He was taught to be a gentleman, and he'd be one regardless of what she wanted. Even if he hadn't been thirteen years ago. Especially since he hadn't been back then.

When she stumbled on something while walking up the shadowed path to her porch, he helped her regain her balance, and he heard a faint "thank you" in response.

Trevor waited for Julie to open her door, fumbling in the dark for the keyhole, and then searching for the light switch just inside. The sudden burst of yellow illumination made him squint.

"So thank you for dinner, Trevor. And thank you for giving me a job." Her pride would be the death of her, and he was more determined than ever to tell her exactly what he had in mind. He'd had two weeks to think about it.

"Julie, just hear me out a minute, would you?"

She went still and gazed at him with suspicious eyes, her hand soundly on the doorknob for a quick exit.

"I want you to know a few things. First off, I totally respect you as a nurse practitioner. The way you've picked up everything these past two weeks has been remarkable. And until things went sour back there at the restaurant, I really enjoyed having dinner with you. It's great to see you after all these years, to find out a little about your life. From what I can tell, you're an amazing woman."

She raised a hand in protest. He was probably overdoing it now, but he didn't give a damn if he was going overboard or not, he'd made up his mind to tell it like it was and by the heavens he was going to. Besides, he'd made a snap decision beyond his plans for James—this one about her—while she was in the restroom back at the restaurant and there was no way he was leaving until he'd laid it out.

"Here's the deal. It's probably the dumbest thing in the world to socialize with one of my employees, but I'd like to do this again sometime. Not in the dating sense, but as colleague to colleague. I'd like to get to know you better, and to learn more about James." She started to say something, but he cut her off by lifting his hand, not wanting to stop until he'd gotten everything out he needed to say. "I'll leave it up to you when or if I get to meet him. I'll honor your decision even though it may be hard. Just keep in mind, I want to meet that boy, and I want him to know I'm his father. I want a relationship with him."

He put his hand on top of hers on the doorknob, forcing her to look into his eyes before he told her the snap decision he'd just made back at the restaurant. "I'd also like a chance to make up for the lousy start we had thirteen years ago. I was attracted to you back then, and, now that I know more about you, I'll be damned if I'm not still drawn to you. Not in a sexual way, but as a whole person. My colleague."

Maybe that wasn't entirely true, but that was all he could offer for now, and he wanted to make sure she understood he wasn't coming on to her in any way, shape or form. That he was, in all sincerity, wanting to know *her*, the woman she was now, at this exact point in her life, not that sexual fantasy he carried around from a long time ago. If he was coming on to her, it would be from a whole different angle, that was for sure. He wasn't in any place to want more these days anyway. Kimberley had messed him up more than he cared to let on. If Julie wanted professional, he'd stick by it, but couldn't they be friends, too? It seemed logical and safe for both of them. Yet, seeing her under the stars and...

"Trevor, I told you about our son because of my obligation to him. I'm happy to tell you about James. I put him in the military school because I believe he needs male role models, and I can't give him that. I'm not sure when the time will be right to introduce the two of you, but I agree you deserve a chance to meet him. I can't guarantee what will happen after that."

"Sounds reasonable." At least it was a first step. They

were both being so adult about their situation, it almost made him queasy.

"But I'm really not sure about the rest of your proposition."

He cocked his head and grimaced. "Not the best word."

"You know what I mean. I'm not sure about us seeing each other socially."

"Dating?"

"Is that really what you want to do?"

"To be honest I don't have a clue what it is I want."

"We're practically strangers."

"Exactly my point, so let's work on becoming unstrangers."

She glanced at the sky again. "That's way too uncomplicated for me." She gave a halfhearted grin.

"And that's how I like things." Especially where women were concerned. No entanglements seemed to rule the day. Yet regarding Julie, he was as confused as a lost bull. If he wasn't interested in getting involved with any women, why was he making an exception for her?

Well, duh, Montgomery—maybe because she's the mother of your son.

She nailed him with a worried glance. "I can't risk my job."

"And I'm not asking you to." He raised his hand as if taking an oath. "I promise not to let our seeing each other socially as colleagues and potential friends interfere with your employment. I'm just asking you to give me a chance, being that I'm your son's father and all."

Silence stretched over the next few moments as she worried her lips and fidgeted with the keys. He soon realized he held his breath.

"Oh, man, this is probably the dumbest thing I've ever

done, but," she said, "well, actually, the dumbest thing I ever did was to get knocked up at seventeen, but okay."

Something about the way she said it reminded him of the night she'd asked him to dance. *"Will you dance with me?"* He remembered thinking *This is probably the dumbest thing I've ever done, but...* On a rush of sweet memories from one night thirteen long years ago, that first summer he'd noticed Julie Sterling—the brand-spanking-new high school graduate, and virgin, as he'd later found out—Trevor let his logical idea slip through his brain cells and went straight for his gut reaction. To hell with being friends. He ducked his head, then moved in to kiss the woman on her doorstep.

A fleeting kiss.

He didn't go for sexy or overpowering or anything beyond a sweet meeting of their lips for old times' sake. Even so, the chaste kiss surprised him—how soft her lips were, how right they felt, how she hadn't resisted, how kissing her opened a flood of tender feelings he'd kept tucked away since Kimberley had dropped him just before graduating med school.

And that was the end of that kiss. No way could he set himself up with hopes and dreams only to get kicked to the curb again. These days when he kissed a woman it was only because they were about to engage in adult entertainment. And he liked it that way.

This kiss had been a throwback in time.

He pulled back to see Julie's eyes still closed, her features soft and dreamy under the dim porch light, and, again, it took him right back to that first moment when they'd kissed that summer night, while slow dancing to a heartfelt ballad.

"Goodnight," he said, his voice sounding husky.

She opened her eyes, as if lingering in their shared memory. "Goodnight."

"I'll see you Monday." He'd cleared his throat and sounded normal again.

"I'll be there."

He took a few steps down the path then stopped and turned, knowing he shouldn't but not wanting to censor himself. "For the record, I still remember kissing you that very first time." Kissing her just now had brought it all back. He used his index finger to point to his temple. "Got it stored right here."

She shook her head, bearing a disbelieving smile, but he could tell she liked what he'd said. Hell, he even wondered how much she remembered about their first kiss.

He forced a benevolent grin, rather than let on how much he'd enjoyed kissing her, and turned to walk the rest of the way to his car, thinking how he hadn't been completely honest just then. Yeah, he remembered that first kiss all right, but he couldn't let Julie Sterling mess with his head again. She was right, it was crazy for them to see each other socially, even under the guise of colleagues and friends, and he'd tell her as much on Monday.

Begrudgingly, he headed for his car, battling it out between his head and that soft off-limits spot he'd buried a few years back deep in his heart. Truth was, the real place he remembered their first kiss was right here. He patted his chest.

Trevor immediately groaned as he got back into the car. Julie's return with his surprise son, and what in God's name he should do about that, was about as complicated as anything could get.

CHAPTER FOUR

TREVOR'S KISS HAD SENT Julie reeling. It had taken all of her willpower to not let on how he'd shaken her to the soles of her boots as she'd stood on the porch, but she'd managed to make it into the house. There, she remained in the dark perfectly still for a few moments to work through her confusion. She flipped on the inside lights, and she heard him drive away.

The man wanted to see her socially, as colleagues, as friends. Sure. First off, what was that supposed to mean? And second, well, she wasn't falling for it. His decision was clearly based on guilt and some sort of honorable notion he'd had drilled into his Montgomery skull his entire life. Exactly what she'd always worried about. This socializing business wasn't because of her; it was for James's sake.

She wouldn't deny him the right to get to know his son when the time was right, but she'd leave herself out of the equation. If he thought they were a ready-made family, he'd better think again.

Julie walked across the living room, turned on another light, then went on into the kitchen and flipped the switch. She poured herself a glass of tap water and stood at the sink staring through the window at the pine trees out back.

It had been hard enough moving into her parents' house. She'd given most of their furniture to the local thrift store, keeping a few pieces she'd always loved. Like the solid-oak buffet in the dining room, and her father's cherrywood desk, oh, and that painting her mother had claimed would be worth something one day. That wasn't why she'd kept it, no—she kept the Western prairie scene because she'd always loved the colors and the way it made her feel, like complete solitude. And she swore she felt the warm summer breeze on her cheeks whenever she looked at the oil on canvas. In her mother's honor, she'd left it hanging, featured above the natural stone fireplace.

When she'd told her mother she was pregnant, you would have thought the world had ended. Her mother had broken into tears, sobbing even, muttering how Julie's future was over, how all their plans for her were ruined. As usual, Mom hadn't stayed defeated for long; no, she'd bounced back with fury. *End the pregnancy,* she'd said. *Stay at college like we planned. We can put all of this behind you and move on.* When Julie had fought back, refusing to do what had seemed convenient to her mother, but much, much worse to her, her mother had turned steely. *What are you going to do? Tell the Montgomerys you want to ruin their son's life, too? Don't think for one minute they won't accuse you of taking advantage of that boy for his family's fortune. They'll accuse you of horrible things. You'll regret you ever told them.*

Julie bit back the pain that never failed to overwhelm her when she let herself go down that particular memory lane. Thank goodness her aunt Janet out in California had taken a different view. She'd talked her sister off the ledge and convinced Andrew and Cynthia to send their daughter to her for the duration of the pregnancy. They'd agreed to see what happened after that, but it was obvious they'd hoped she'd give up the baby for adoption, then pick up and carry on with college in Colorado as if nothing had happened.

Wrong!

More disappointment had followed for her parents when Julie had given birth and fallen in love at first sight with her son. Who was she kidding? She'd been in love with the baby the entire pregnancy, and especially after that first sonogram. Aunt Janet had fallen in love with James, too. Her parents had sent money from time to time, but it had been her aunt who supported Julie while she got used to being a mother and all throughout the pregnancy. Even though theoretically she was an orphan now, as long as her aunt was alive she'd never feel that way.

She'd delivered James in May and gone back to school part time that September. It had broken her heart to leave him in daycare so young, but the program she'd enrolled in had offered free child care, and how could she refuse that? The next semester she'd doubled her units, and, being so impressed with the care she'd gotten during her pregnancy, and especially during labor, then following up in pediatrics, she'd decided to give up her prior major and go into nursing.

She'd found a part-time job in a bookstore and had gotten some scholarships for students with babies, but, hands down, her aunt had been the financial anchor in her personal storm. Knowing she had a place to live and food on the table had given Julie the freedom to explore being a first-time mother with all the joy and frustrations. She and her aunt had remained very close over the years; she'd even agreed to be James's godmother.

She had been the first person Julie had called the night she'd found out James had been arrested for shoplifting, and thankfully they'd had each other when word had come about her parents dying in the car crash. Julie didn't know how she would have managed with the estate otherwise. Or with the pain over the strain in their relationship that had remained ever since they'd suggested she end her pregnancy.

When the family trust had left a solid amount of retirement money to Julie, she'd insisted her aunt take half as repayment for all she'd done for her and her son.

Julie sat and slumped at the kitchen table, hanging her head over the glass of water. Life had seemed so simple when she'd lived here before. Now, it was anything but.

She let go and cried for the memory of her parents, forgiving them for their decisions that might have been brutal. *All we want is the best for you*, had been their mantra. Those words had wound up driving a wedge between them and Julie had never trusted them again. Now she found herself thinking the same thing about her son. What was best for James? Meeting his father? Possibly driving a wedge between her and her son in the process?

She forced herself to stand and went to the bathroom to get ready for bed. Once the house was locked tight for the night, she crawled between the sheets and stared at the ceiling. Her mind wouldn't let up.

Kissing Trevor, spending the evening with him, watching how he ate, the little quirks he had when he talked, how he glanced off to the right when he thought before he spoke, or how one brow always shot up when he questioned something, had brought that distant and faded summer crush back in living color. She could practically touch, taste and feel that late August night.

But she was a grown woman now. She'd suffered

through her tough times, and had prevailed over her challenging times. She'd succeeded when her parents had doubted her every decision. She'd become a registered nurse, a nurse practitioner and a midwife, but her biggest achievement was, hands down, her son.

Her son who needed a man in his life, and whose father lived only a hundred miles away from the military school.

Yeah, there was no way she'd get any sleep tonight.

Monday morning at the clinic, after slipping into her office and managing to avoid Trevor in the employee lounge, she'd jumped right into her appointments. After seeing two patients with the flu and one with a solid case of bronchitis, she stepped into the next examination room to tend to Alex Bronson.

He was a well-developed male, looking beyond his thirty-five years of age. From his history, she saw he was a cowhand and knew that his work was tough and demanding, the kind of all-weather work that aged a guy sooner than men in suits. Next she glanced at his chief complaint.

"Good morning. What brings you here today?" She already knew the answer, but wanted his take on the situation.

"I've had a canker sore and a sore throat for a couple of weeks," Alex said.

Julie did a head and neck assessment, finding a few enlarged nodes on the right side of his neck and beneath his jawline, and when she asked him to say "ah" to have a look at this throat, she noticed something that concerned her. Leukoplakia. "How long have you had that sore in your mouth?"

"Oh, that? That's just that canker sore I mentioned. Been there a little before I got my cold."

"You've had a cold? How long?"

"Well, not the usual kind, but I've been feeling poorly and, like I said, my throat's a little sore for about a month now."

"You smoke?"

"No, ma'am."

"Chew tobacco?" She already knew the answer from the state of his teeth.

"A little, yeah."

She also knew that many cowhands worked long hours doing backbreaking jobs and often chewed tobacco to keep going. Could she blame them? Unfortunately, the canker sore that Alex thought nothing about was concerning to Julie. Especially since he didn't show any signs of a true cold, but his lymph nodes were enlarged and the sore bulged in an unnatural way beneath the surface of his oral mucosa. But what concerned her the most was the velvety white plaque that spotted the back of his throat. She worried about oral cancer, yet didn't want to freak out the otherwise healthy-looking man.

"To be on the safe side, I'm going to give you some antibiotics, but I also want you to follow up with the ear, nose and throat doctor in Laramie."

Alex raised his brows. "Why? It's just a cold."

"A cold runs its course in seven to ten days. The sore-throat part should have been over by now, and to be honest I'm concerned about a couple of small spots in your mouth. Since you're a tobacco chewer, we can't be too cautious."

She opened the supply cabinet and found what she needed. "May I do an oral brush of the sore?"

"What's that do?"

"This will collect some surface cells and the lab can make a slide to check for any abnormal cells. Say 'ah,' please."

After Julie finished and processed her specimen, she washed her hands and her fingers flew over her laptop computer keyboard as she wrote her e-referral. She knew from experience that if you didn't hand a patient an appointment with a specialist before they left the office, the odds of them following through went down significantly. She pressed send, then looked up with a smile.

"While I'm waiting to hear back from ENT I'd like you to have some lab work drawn." She whizzed through the studies she wanted Alex to have, clicking them off on the computer screen, then buzzed for Charlotte.

While Alex put his shirt back on, Lotte knocked on the door before opening.

"Hi," Julie said. "Can you to take Mr. Bronson to the lab and draw some blood, then get a chest X-ray?"

"Sure thing," Charlotte said, with her usual can-do attitude, no questions asked.

"Oh, would you please deliver this to the pathology pick-up tray?" She handed off the slide she'd prepped from the oral brushing, which was safe inside a cardboard slide container with the patient's ID on it.

As the nurse led the patient down the hall, Julie got her first glimpse of Trevor for the day as he lingered just outside his office reading some mail. Oh, man, he wasn't playing fair. He'd obviously skipped shaving all weekend and had a serious start on a sexy beard, dark as his eyes. He wore a navy-colored vest over a micro-checked brown-and-blue soft cotton shirt, and had rolled the sleeves to his forearms, revealing the dusting of sepia-colored hair on his arms and a huge silver watch on his wrist. She loved that look on a guy, and when was the last time she'd seen a man in a vest that didn't involve a three-piece suit? His jeans fit perfectly, accentuating his long legs, and, for a change, today he wore brown suede and leather shoes.

Her thoughts flitted back to their kiss, and a tiny jitter bomb went off inside her stomach. She couldn't very well stand there gawking, feeding her vision with this gorgeous man. She scrambled back into her exam room and made a second slide with the discarded oral brush, then nearly jogged down to the lab to find the special stains she'd need to color the cells. For an early snapshot of what might be going on in Alex Bronson's mouth, she found toluidine blue stain and placed a few drops on the slide, swirling it around to cover the entire specimen, then shook off the excess. Next she delicately dropped a thin coverslip over the material to be viewed under the microscope and headed back down the hall to Trevor's office.

She tapped lightly on his door, even though it was open. He sat behind his desk, flipping through more mail, separating it into piles. He glanced up and smiled.

"Hey, good morning. You've been busy today," he said, obviously happy to see her.

"You weren't kidding about everyone coming in for appointments when the weather warmed up."

He smiled wide, his gaze pinned to her face. If she could only know what was going on in his mind. But that wasn't why she was there.

"Hey, I was wondering if you'd take a look at a slide with me. I just saw Alex Bronson and I'm worried about the state of his mouth."

Trevor scooted his chair toward the microscope he

kept set up at a small side desk and waved her over. "Let's take a look. You send a specimen for the big lab?"

"Sure did, and made an e-referral for an ENT appointment ASAP. I've got a bad feeling about this."

Trevor went quiet studying the slide in a consistent left-to-right manner, then stopped in one area, increasing the magnification, and focused in. "This doesn't look good." He pulled back, giving Julie room to step in and take a look for herself.

Several abnormally shaped nuclei had stained dark. It would be up to the pathologist to name the cells, but, to both Julie and Trevor, their fears for cancer just got worse.

"Damn," she muttered.

"I've been warning Alex about chewing tobacco for years. Done several community education lectures on it, too. The bad news just doesn't sink into their thick cowboy skulls."

Julie nodded in understanding. "I guess we'll just have to wait and see what turns out, but in the meantime I need to check my computer to make sure he's got an appointment lined up. Maybe I'll call to get him in before the end of the week. I want to make sure he has an appointment in his hand before he leaves the office today."

"It's worth a try. Good work, Julie."

She turned and noticed the sincere set to his eyes, the admiration and something else she was not prepared to name, and blinked her thanks. Then she walked off, wishing she hadn't gotten a nose full of his sexy-as-hell cologne while looking at that slide with him.

After a power-packed morning, Trevor got a call from his patient Francine Jardine. She'd gone into labor, and, it being her third baby, didn't stand a chance of getting to the hospital in Laramie in time. He hung up and dialed Rita. "Cancel my afternoon appointments. I've got a home delivery to take care of."

In seconds he was out the door with his doctor's delivery bag and headed for his car, and forty-five minutes later, after he'd arrived at Francine's home and had done an initial examination, he made a second call.

"Julie, I'm going to need your help at the Jardine residence. It's an urgent situation. Mom's fully dilated, and the baby's in a transverse position. Not a chance in hell she'd hold out until we got her to the hospital. We're going to need to turn this baby."

"I'll be right there. Oh, where does she live?"

"Charlotte will give you directions. I've got to go."

Trevor solemnly walked back to his patient, realizing he might be performing an in-home cesarean section before the end of the day if he and Julie couldn't turn the baby.

Fifteen minutes and six contractions later, Julie arrived with more supplies and some medicine to help Francine relax. She'd also brought the portable oxygen canister. Good move.

Julie gave Francine two liters of oxygen via nasal prongs if for nothing more than to help clear the worried mother's head.

Trevor sipped some water and spoke quietly to Julie. "Have you ever had to do this before?"

"I've had a couple of instances where the baby wouldn't turn and we slowed down the labor to get the patient to the hospital for a cesarean. But I've also been successful in internally turning the baby on occasion."

"Well, there's two of us, and I'm hoping we can manage to get that head in the vertex position, but I've got these big old rancher hands, which are fine for delivering calves, but… So, listen, even though she's fully dilated, I think your hands could get in there better and move the head downward."

Julie nodded, and, though tension set her eyes, Trevor knew Julie was the best backup he could hope for at a time like this.

"But if I have to, I'll perform the C-section here, because there's no way either of them would make it to the hospital in Laramie in time."

They both finished their water and went back to the mother-to-be, then, after explaining their plans to the distressed woman, Julie did an internal examination, then set about pulling and pushing the baby's head into the down position.

It seemed like forever, but, with near brute force and a very cooperative mother, Julie finally managed to engage the baby's head in the proper position, and forty minutes later Trevor did the honors of birthing the baby.

"It's a girl!" he said, handing the infant off to Julie.

Soaked in sweat and looking weak as a kitten, Mrs. Jardine smiled. "This one's going to be as stubborn as I am." Then she flopped back onto the bed as Julie placed her newborn on her chest and snipped the umbilical cord.

He glanced at the women, wondering if Julie had had that same look of unconditional love on her face when she'd first held James. Who'd been with her through labor? Had she had to go through everything alone? He fought off that familiar sad pang lassoing his chest every time he wondered about his son and Julie, and forced himself to concentrate on putting his soiled equipment into a thick plastic bag for the return trip to the clinic. If only he'd gotten in touch with her after their first night.

Trevor took one more look at Julie and the new mother, fighting off that unnamed yearning that had sprung up lately, then drew a long cleansing breath and gave a quick thanks for the healthy birth of this baby, and for Julie coming back into his life.

"Mrs. Jardine's kids are due home from school soon. I'll stay with her," Julie said. "But maybe Charlotte can arrange some child care for the tots before Dad gets home and while Mom and baby bond?"

"Sounds like a plan." Trevor flipped out his cell phone and made the call, and glanced peacefully at Julie and Francine as they fussed and cooed over the newest addition to the Jardine household. There went that yearning again.

As his respect and admiration for Julie grew, something else wagged its hand, insisting on being acknowledged—animal attraction. Pure, unadulterated, gut-level physical attraction to the woman.

This wasn't how it was supposed to go with his newest employee. Hell, he hadn't been the slightest bit ready to find out he was a father, but this, oh, no, this part of the equation—being attracted to the boy's mother—wasn't a good sign at all. He'd quit getting involved with women beyond physically for the past few years. So far, that approach had worked just fine. Not at all a possibility with a colleague, though, and especially a friend.

This tugging on his heart and body by Julie Sterling was definitely messing with his logically thought-out five-year plan. Women, beyond a purely peripheral position, had never been added into the mix. And he couldn't let that change now.

CHAPTER FIVE

Friday morning, Julie arrived at work smiling. She'd gotten to talk to James on the phone Thursday night and knew that Sunday she'd be able to see him for the first time in four weeks. She couldn't wait to sneak a hug in before he could protest. He'd sounded good, but complained about being homesick. If she wanted the best for him, she'd have to stand firm and make sure he finished out the semester.

As she booted up the computer in her office she took a deep breath, realizing she'd made it through the entire week without Trevor suggesting they have another "not a date" date. His solid voice carried down the hall as he talked to someone on the phone, sounding happy.

She looked at her schedule of appointments for Friday and prepared for another busy day. This was what she loved doing: helping people, figuring out what was wrong and finding the best way to treat it. She'd felt meant to be a nurse from the time she'd made up her mind to go into the health profession, and knew the skills would always provide her with a job. Even back home in Cattleman Bluff.

Thank you, Trevor Montgomery, for giving me this job.

And speaking of Trevor—he'd suddenly materialized at her office door.

"Hey," he said, smiling, standing tall and looking like he belonged in a *Western Living* advertisement instead of a medical clinic.

"Good morning." She smiled back, unable to prevent it.

"I just got off the phone with my brother. Do you remember Cole?"

All she remembered, being that he was probably eight years older than her, was that he'd been the kid everyone talked about, especially her parents. *"Look at this, Julie..."* Her father or mother would share an article from the local newspaper with her about Cole Montgomery winning the statewide geography bee or participating in the National Academic Decathlon competition and being the captain of the team the one and only time Cattleman Bluff High won. She'd seen the trophy in the display case in the high school foyer, where it probably sat to this day.

Wait a second, she also remembered something about an accident, a bad accident, and it had to do with the junior rodeo competition one summer.

"Who doesn't know Cole? Well, I've actually never met him."

"So this is your chance. He's home for a quick visit to see the old man. Thought it might be nice to have you over for dinner tonight."

"Tonight?" There it was: he'd swooped in for another surprise attack. What was it with Trevor, always waiting until the last minute to make his move? Not that she had big plans, but she had hoped to finish up unpacking the house this weekend before she made the trek to Laramie on Sunday to see James. And until this very minute, she'd hoped he'd forgotten about their conversation on the doorstep last Friday night. After all, he hadn't said a peep about it all week.

"I know it's last-minute, but Cole just dropped this on me, too."

She'd cut him some slack since the clinic had gotten off to a quick start on Monday and had never slowed down since, and evidently Cole had made last-minute plans, too. Must run in the family. But did this mean he wouldn't have invited her out if his brother hadn't decided to come for a visit? For some crazy reason, she felt miffed.

"Wouldn't you rather have family time together? Just the three of you?"

Trevor scratched the back of his neck. "Well, you might think so, but Cole and Dad have a knack for arguing and, to be honest, I thought you might be a buffer. You know, put them both on good behavior with a lady present."

She had to laugh about being used as protection by big ol' Trevor Montgomery. "Are you kidding me?"

He shook his head, looking chagrined. "You probably think I'm a jerk, but, honestly, I meant to invite you out to dinner all week, just never got the chance."

"So, we're still going to do that becoming unstrangers thing, then?" She'd unintentionally lowered her voice.

"I think we should." He'd lowered his, too, plus added an earnest-as-hell expression.

She sighed. How could she resist that kind of charm even if it was only out of obligation? "So what's for dinner?"

Now he grinned and the office seemed to brighten by a shade. "I don't have a clue, but you can rest assured that Gretchen will whip up something special for her favorite Montgomery boy."

Did Trevor inadvertently leave off the *s* in boys? "Who's Gretchen?" And how did it feel to always be the second-best kid? Being an only child carried stress and responsibilities, but it did have a few advantages, such as she never had to wonder who Mom loved best.

"She's been our cook since Mom took sick—that's years ago now. And she was old then, so she's got to be pushing seventy."

"Well, I hope she doesn't work herself to death on my and Cole's account." Half teasing, but a touch concerned, too.

"She'll love every minute of it, and you better clean your plate, too." Now that he'd sealed the deal, his thumbs slid easily into the belt loops on his Western-style slacks.

Julie was subtly taking it all in when Charlotte rushed down the hall as if competing in a speed-walking event. "Dr. Montgomery? Alan Lightfoot showed up with a nasty cut. I think he'll need stitches."

They made quick plans for that night, and Julie insisted on driving out to his house, then Trevor rushed off to see his add-on patient. Yep, looked like Friday would be the same as the rest of the week. Busy!

Julie had offered to drive to the ranch herself, mostly to be able to make a quick getaway in case the Montgomery clan started tearing into each other. Or, in case being around Trevor got to be too unnerving. Who knew what to expect? But, to be safe, she'd be prepared.

She grabbed the clinic laptop and walked toward the exam room with her first patient, wondering why her stomach suddenly felt a tiny nervous knot over an introduction and a meal that wouldn't happen for hours and hours, and a big question mark about why Trevor had insisted she meet the family.

* * *

Being early March, the days were still short, and Julie drove slowly once out of town and on the open and dark roads of Cattleman Bluff. There were very few street-lights in these parts, so she depended 100 percent on the GPS in the small car she'd purchased with some of her parents' estate money.

With plains that seemed to go on forever and that were rich with the native grasses in this southeast sec-tion of Wyoming, the area was perfect for grazing cattle. But the expanse of land left a girl wondering if she might get lost and never get found if she took one wrong turn.

Just when she'd decided she was definitely lost, she saw the lighted Circle M Ranch sign off in the distance at the beginning of a long and winding road. She sighed, relieved, then quickly took a deep breath to tame the jit-ters licking her insides over seeing Trevor on his home turf. Not to mention meeting his father and brother.

"Relax, Sterling, it's not like Trevor is going to drop the bomb about being a surprise dad to his own father tonight," she muttered, fingers mentally crossed that that wouldn't be the case. Nah, that wasn't exactly the kind of competition a younger brother wanted to win.

A minute later, still driving the entry road without a building in sight, she began to wonder if she'd made a wrong turn after all, and then around the last curve, in the distance, sat a sprawling single-story ranch-style home, a manmade front lawn complete with shade trees, and across the paved driveway, sitting farther back, a classic barn and stables. All spotlighted by perfectly placed lights along the yard.

As she got closer she took note of the interestingly stained wood that fronted the house. At first the house looked more red than brown, like an old barn, but on closer examination the wood looked naturally bleached with red, brown, blond and even some greenish sections. She wondered if the floodlights made that effect.

Smack in the center of the sprawling ranch house was a silo covered with the same antique wood, and the rest of the house seemed built around it, then down on the far end the roof rose up to a second story.

Wow. She'd definitely never been here, and couldn't wait to see how it looked on the inside.

Trevor must have been watching for her because before she could finish parking he was out on the huge front porch and taking the steps down to meet her.

"This is something else," Julie said, getting out of the car. "I never got to this side of town when I lived here." She joked, but, as with all jokes, it stabbed at the truth.

"Yeah, we are out of the way a titch. Have any trouble finding us?"

"No, but that Circle M sign about twenty acres back is a little misleading." She understood his family owned thousands of acres and heads of cattle. This was what the Montgomery name stood for in Wyoming, except for the fine-print disclaimer that both of Monty's sons had gone into medicine instead of cattle ranching.

"Well, come on in and warm up. Dad's eager to meet you."

Why? "Really?"

He took her by the arm and led her toward the porch. The pressure from his firm grasp, even though over her coat sleeve, set off a warning. *Don't get used to this attention. It'll never go anywhere. See to it.*

"Sure. He knew I was hiring. Plus I admit I've been bragging about you a little since you started working at the clinic."

He'd just paid her a huge professional compliment, which stunned her, causing a hesitation before she said, "Thanks."

Once inside, as he helped her shed the coat, she took note of his jeans and blue plaid shirt, and then the tooled dark brown leather belt and firmly broken-in boots. Totally in his element, he embodied a natural-born cowboy appeal, and Julie found it hard to look away.

"Come on, let me introduce you to my dad and Cole."

Those simmering jitters in her stomach started stroking her spine at the prospect of meeting his family. He guided her into the living room that had a two-story-high ceiling. Huge and grand and very Western with a floor-to-ceiling rock fireplace taking up a good portion of one wall. There was a small staircase that led to a furnished loft and library toward the back of the room.

"Dad, Cole, this is Julie Sterling, my new RNP."

"What'd I tell you about using all those medical abbreviations with me?" Tiberius Montgomery said, standing with the aid of a quad cane. "Nice to meet you, young lady. Thanks to you I'll be able to see my son a little more often."

She wondered, considering Monty's condition, if he ever got up to the library to read anymore.

"You mean ride him hard and hang him up wet, more likely, Dad," Cole jumped in. A slightly taller, darker version of his brother, he painted an imposing picture. Flashing dark eyes, his face all sharp angles and curves, oozing with character. Thick dark hair cut shorter than Trevor's, and styled for a sophisticated big-city look.

Then Julie zeroed in on the scars, one on either side of his temples, and a couple smack in the middle of his forehead above each eyebrow. They were the marks of wearing a halo brace for cervical fractures. So there had been an accident. Had it happened at the junior rodeo? The long-ago story was vaguely familiar.

Mr. Montgomery had walked to meet her, no easy feat with the one weakened side and the heavy quad cane in tow. She reached for his extended hand.

"It's so nice to meet you, Mr. Montgomery."

"Oh, hell, just call me Monty like everyone else."

She smiled, took his hand and glanced into the old man's eyes, the exact same shape as the ones she saw in both of his sons, but his were green. Though his face was craggy and worn, and his hair thinning and silver, the intensity in those eyes was still alive and strong.

Next she officially greeted Cole, the bigger-than-life version of Trevor. No wonder Trevor had spent his life overachieving!

"So nice to meet you."

"The pleasure is mine. And thanks for helping out my brother. He's got a lot on his plate helping at home and running that clinic."

"It is a busy clinic, that's for sure."

A short, plump woman with dyed red hair appeared in the arched doorway in front of the silo section of the house, drawing Julie's attention away from Cole's scars. "Dinner is ready."

The family cook, Gretchen, looked as if she knew how to handle a house full of men with her stern expression and sturdy schoolmarm shoes, and Monty dutifully responded. "Well, let's eat, then."

To get to the dining room, they walked through the round silo section of the house where hardwood floors and Western antiques filled the space. With the amount of oil paintings hanging on the walls, it was apparent this section of the house was their museum. Imagine, a house big enough to have its own art gallery inside.

It made her wonder if Trevor's mother might have been an artist.

Incredibly inviting aromas from the kitchen changed the course of Julie's thoughts.

If the little comments she'd picked up here and there at work from Trevor about Gretchen's fantastic cooking were true, Julie was in for a treat. Too bad her tummy was tied in a knot.

The dining room was long and rectangular with the entire outside wall made of floor-to-ceiling windows. A rustic dining table long enough to easily seat a dozen people looked like it weighed a ton. They all sat at one end.

As the plates of food got passed around, everyone starting by serving Julie first, the Montgomery men made easy banter about Cole's flight in, Trevor's ranching-accident patient that morning at the clinic, a man his father knew of and Monty's ongoing in-home physical-therapy rehab—which he hated.

Julie soon realized from the conversation that the man had been having a series of small strokes, TIAs, over the past few years. No wonder Trevor felt compelled to stick around Cattleman Bluff.

Behind Monty on the wall was another oil-on-canvas painting of a lovely middle-aged woman, and Julie quickly understood where both Trevor and Cole got their dark, thick hair. It had to be their mother who had Native American blood somewhere in her family tree.

Trevor must have noticed Julie studying the painting.

"That's a self-portrait."

"Is it your mother? Was she an artist?"

"Yes."

"So, Julie." Monty refocused the conversation toward Julie when the topic of his health issues and now his deceased wife came up—a man still in command of his castle, or ranch in this case. "How does it feel to be home again? Trevor told me you're originally a Cattleman Bluff girl."

"I'm still getting used to it. I've been out in California for so long, my blood must have thinned. I can never get warm enough."

"Spring will be here soon enough," Monty said, dabbing a piece of biscuit into gravy and taking a huge bite. "You'll warm up then."

"How's business, Cole?" Trevor asked, accepting the roasted potatoes and carrots from Julie.

"Going well." All three men appeared to enjoy eating, as they spoke in short sentences in order to shovel more of Gretchen's man-style food into their mouths.

"What is it exactly that you do?" Julie asked innocently, as, beyond his being a cardiac doctor, she didn't have a clue about his business.

"I stumbled onto a new noninvasive method to replace mitral valves using the same technique as angioplasty."

"He's being humble. He created the method." Trevor spoke up.

Julie lifted her head. "You go through the groin artery?"

Cole nodded, too busy chewing a piece of pot roast to embellish.

"Yeah, he's made quite a name for himself," Trevor said, "and now he spends all his time on planes flying all over the country showing other docs how to do the procedure."

"That's amazing." Julie meant it, and she noticed a fleeting look in Trevor's eyes when she did, communicating it was the story of his, Trevor's, life.

"The traveling is a pain, but, if it helps more people avoid the more invasive open-heart surgery, I'm glad to do it. And so far the success rate has been great. I can't complain."

"I know the dinner table isn't any place to talk about surgery, but maybe later you'll explain to me how you switch out a bad mitral valve for a new one through a space the size of a femoral artery."

"I'll be glad to."

Julie glanced at Monty, with a smile on his face. He definitely had two sons to be proud of, but she worried Monty overlooked Trevor's steady, dependable nature for the brighter star in Cole.

Immediately after dinner, as they moved away from the table, Cole explained his technique to Julie, and she had to admit it was fascinating. Before dessert, they all agreed they needed time in between the courses, so Trevor handed Julie her full-length coat and invited her out onto the porch for some coffee. Just as they hit the door, a friendly disagreement between Monty and Cole began to heat up in the two-story living room, echoing off the cavernous walls.

"Come and sit with me outside. I'll turn on the heating lamps." Trevor smiled to himself over the shocked look on Julie's face—that pretty face he'd already gotten used to seeing every day Monday through Friday—as he hadn't really given her a choice. Sit outside? At night? In forty-degree temperatures? "Come on." He helped her put the coat on, liking the chance to inhale her light flowery perfume. "You'll enjoy the fresh air. It'll help wake you up after Gretchen's killer pot roast."

She gave a reluctant smile, but didn't fight him as he helped her with first one arm, then the other, into her coat.

He chose the most comfortable chairs, high-backed

rockers with thick cushions that molded to the back and bottom, then flipped on the heating lamps strategically placed around the porch for anyone's sitting pleasure.

"So what do you think about my big brother? Pretty awesome guy, huh?"

"Very. Did he break his neck at some point?"

The astute and direct question took Trevor aback; Julie's perceptive assumption about the scars on Cole's forehead and temples showed she really knew medicine. "Good observation. Yeah, he used to take part in junior rodeo and got thrown from a horse. Mom never wanted him to go into rodeo, but there was no talking Cole out of it. He was damn good at it, too. Then one day, his second year on the junior rodeo circuit, he got thrown for a loop. Just lay there, couldn't get up. Mom about flipped out. Turns out he'd fractured his cervical spine, needed surgery to put screws into his skull and had to wear the halo brace and plaster jacket for three months. He was fifteen, and Mom treated him like he was one of her fragile teacups the whole time." Trevor laughed, remembering some of the heated arguments between Cole and Mom back then. "Anyway, that accident is what made Cole decide to become a doctor. He was fascinated with everything that went on in a hospital. So, as bad as the accident was, I guess it was one of those meant-to-be moments that changes a person's focus in life."

Sort of like the day Julie told him he was a father.

He took a sip of his coffee, enjoying watching the vapors rise from the cup, but enjoying having Julie to himself again even more, which quickly bothered him. What were his intentions with this woman, the mother of a son he'd yet to meet? Damned if he knew, but, like that stupid moth circling the heating lamp, he couldn't seem to stay away.

She looked thoughtful as she drank her coffee, holding the cup with both hands, snuggling into her coat and scarf under the heat. The dim porch lighting cast lacy shadows over her face and hair, and the effect was sexy as hell. Ah, now there he went again, getting all tangled up in the wrong intentions.

"You know, we both have something in common," she said, matter-of-factly.

Something in common? Now that was a surprise to him. "Really? How?"

Beyond creating a kid together, he couldn't think of a single thing they might have in common. He'd come from privilege and she'd come from, well, he wasn't even sure, but he had a strong suspicion, by the thoughtful breath she took, she was about to tell him exactly what they had in common.

"We've both been in situations where our dreams were postponed by reality. My getting pregnant. Your father's failing health making you stay close by while your brother travels the globe and gets all the attention."

Her direct observation stunned him. He'd thought he'd finally dealt with the resentment toward his brother, who lived the glamorous life with all the freedom, but her comment released a quick rush of buried animosity. He couldn't deny it. "If I didn't know you were right, I might try to argue that wasn't the case at all. That I chose to come home and take over the town clinic when old Doc Stewart decided to retire before he dropped dead."

"That's the second thing we have in common. Our parents brought us home, whether we wanted to come or not." She took another sip of her coffee and stared off into the night where, in the distance she could hear the comforting lowing of the cattle settling in for the night.

Her parents had died in a car accident, his mother had gotten cancer while he was in medical school, changing the course of his plans. He'd wanted to become a surgeon, but had known he'd need to take a residency in a big city to follow that dream. It would have kept him away from home when his mother was in the last stages of the disease, so he'd opted to go into family medicine, a far less prestigious specialty, but a solid one that touched many more lives than a surgeon could ever hope to. And the three-year residency had been in his home state, close enough to get home on a regular basis, so naturally, when Dr. Stewart had planned his retirement the day Trevor had finished his residency, there hadn't even been a decision to make.

In the meantime, Cole had been well on his way to making a name for himself in the field of cardiology. But Trevor had gotten to be nearby the last three months of his mother's life. At the end, he'd taken over her hospice care in the home she'd loved. It might not have been the big dream he'd held on to for Kimberley's sake, but it had been the right thing to do, and he'd always treasure those last days and weeks with his mother. As he'd come to find out in life, every decision cost something. He'd paid the price of losing the woman he'd thought he'd wanted to spend the rest of his life with.

Now his father's failing health held him here.

"Right on both counts. Running this ranch takes a lot of work beyond what our foreman and crew can take care of. Dad is nowhere near ready to give up the reins, and, though he depends heavily on Jack, he needs my support, too." Trevor took one last sip of the coffee that had quickly turned tepid from the night air, and thought as he did. "But I think your son may have had more to do with your decision to come back to Cattleman Bluff, right?"

She nodded. "I'd already looked into military schools in California, but there was no way I could afford them. Then I got word about my parents. Crazy how that happened."

They sat in companionable silence for a few moments, but Trevor could tell there was a lot on Julie's mind. Maybe if he kept still and quiet, she'd open up. Truth was, he wanted to know her better, learn more about the woman who'd raised his son. Alone.

"Not to go all philosophical on you or anything, but having my baby so early, the baby who derailed my plans, well, the experience gave me a gift I couldn't ever imagine on my own. I had to live it, and you know what? I'd never trade that for anything. All the hard work to have a baby, go back to school, jump into the reality of adulthood and raising a son. Nope, I wouldn't trade in a moment of it for anything."

The positive expression she'd so proudly worn the second before melted into something far more somber, and soon dipped into a troubled frown. Without thinking, he reached for her hand and squeezed. Maybe it was his touch, or maybe it was going to happen anyway, but she broke down, as if the weight of the world were suddenly too hard to bear. Not knowing what else to do, he squeezed her hand firmer and kept his mouth shut. Being a doctor had taught him a skill or two in the listening department.

"I used to doubt my mothering skills, and I admit I was selfish. I didn't date much because I'd heard so many awful stories about men resenting their girlfriend's kids. It scared me, you know?"

He could totally understand her fear. All anyone had

to do was read a paper or watch the news to understand what she was talking about. Hell, he'd seen an example or a dozen of that kind of abuse in his own clinic.

"And James deserved a man who really cared about him. But he got into trouble, and maybe there was a guy out there who could have turned that around."

Him? If only he'd had a chance, but Trevor knew there was no way life could be orchestrated. It all worked out the way it did, and all anyone could do was deal with it. He let go of the ribbon of anger threading through his thoughts.

"I feel guilty, like my parenting skills weren't enough, that I shouldn't have robbed him of his father." For the first time, she looked directly at Trevor. "You. I shouldn't have kept him a secret. I'm sorry."

"Julie. We're in a crazy situation, but there's no beating yourself up over this." Something nagged at the back of his mind. Hadn't Julie said she'd been seeing someone before she moved back home? "Didn't you mention a guy who helped pay for that summer camp for James last year?"

She took a long inhale, and with her free hand put the coffee cup on the nearby table. "Yes. We were dating. That turned out to be a big mistake, too. I finally thought I'd found the right guy. He got along great with James. I thought, maybe, just maybe we'd finally become a family." She glanced at Trevor, then quickly away. "He even proposed. But I came to find out that Mark, that was his name, had sent James to that camp to get time alone with me, which was fine, but once James got home, he took him aside and told him how things were going to be from then on. Evidently, my son wasn't a very big part of the picture. James broke down and told me after he'd had to spend the night in juvenile hall—the poor kid was scared to death, and I needed to know what in the world he'd been thinking stealing something that didn't belong to him. That's when I realized that once Mark married me he planned to send James away to school so he'd have me all to himself. He'd told James as much. Told him I didn't want him anymore."

Her tears flowed without effort, and she shook her head. "My baby thought I didn't love him. I messed up by getting involved with a man and my boy got hurt, then he acted out, and now he's been sent away to school anyway." She cupped her hands to her forehead, holding her head, and quietly cried.

Trevor ached to soothe her. And he wanted to deck that Mark guy.

"Julie, from what I've seen and heard, James couldn't have been any luckier to have a mother like you. You made the right decision about dumping the jerk and moving home. That boy knows he's loved."

She smiled through her tears. "I hope so."

"I know so." Trevor wasn't used to consoling women; he was used to hanging out for kicks and having sex with them, but not really getting to know them. Not since Kimberley anyway, and sitting here with Julie was almost too reminiscent of that old feeling. He didn't know if he liked it or not, but he was here with her, and she deserved his full attention. Hell, it had been his idea to invite her out here for dinner to meet his father and brother; he must have had some kind of reason beyond just wanting to see her again.

Julie's raw honesty struck like an arrow in his chest. He had thoughts and plans about the son he'd never had a chance to know, and now was as good a time as any to bring them up.

"I'm just kind of sad, hearing all the tough things the

boy has gone through." He didn't want to sound angry or resentful about his true feelings, so he tempered his honest reaction. "I regret never having the chance to be a father to him. I wish things had been different. Maybe we can make that up to him. Will you let me do that?"

Julie lifted her head, wet eyes flashing terror one moment and hope the next. She swallowed hard. "Sunday is family visitation day. Will you come?"

CHAPTER SIX

TREVOR HAD INSISTED on driving Sunday morning, and picked up Julie bright and early at eight for the hour-and-a-half drive to Laramie. He looked freshly shaved and had combed his hair more into submission than usual, and the notion he'd done it to make a good impression when meeting James touched her heart.

After driving thirty minutes on smaller roads, they got onto Interstate 80 for the last seventy-five miles of the journey. Trying her best not to be so aware of Trevor's presence, his scent, and the way he filled up his side of the car, Julie looked over the day's schedule. Welcome event at 10:00 a.m., a tour of the dorms after that. She'd have to wait until nearly eleven o'clock to get time alone with her son. She figured she'd introduce James to Trevor after the luncheon, not telling him he was his father, of course, but introducing him as her boss. Then she'd give them some time together to talk horses and ranches and anything else they wanted. Hopefully, James wouldn't think it weird that his mother had brought a strange man on the first visit, especially after what had happened with Mark, and how he'd told James he wanted him out of the picture.

"You look worried about something." Trevor spoke

up, ever perceptive—another trait she both liked and loathed about him, because it kept her on her toes.

She might as well come clean, since the cowboy seemed to be able to see right through her. "I was wondering what James would think about me bringing you for the first visit, that's all."

"You think it's a mistake? 'Cause if you do, I can wait in Laramie while you—"

"No! I wouldn't hear of it. You're giving me a ride and practically holding my hand through all my angst about putting him there in the first place, not to mention you're his father—how could I ask you to wait outside?"

He gave an appreciative smile, and she thought she saw something deeper in those eyes. Oh, man, she couldn't let herself get wrapped up in Trevor Montgomery's natural-born charm. Things were complicated enough as it was.

"I'm not a proponent of lying to a kid, but you could tell him you needed a ride and I offered to drive, if that's okay?"

"No, I won't lie to my son."

"Didn't think so, but I was just trying to be helpful."

"Don't get me wrong, I do appreciate your support, though."

"Then that's the angle we'll take. You were nervous about the long drive and seeing him after four weeks, and I offered to bring you so you wouldn't have to navigate the highway. Which is true for the most part. We'll just leave the father business out of it."

She let that angle process for a few moments. If she were driving, her mind would probably be all over the place and she'd probably get lost faster than lightning on a chain-link fence. Funny how the local vernacular kept coming back, now that she was home. "I can deal with that. Okay. And thanks, because overall it's true. My mind is everywhere right now, not on the road." Home? Trevor? Would James ever come to think of Cattleman Bluff as home?

"Glad to be of service."

Honestly, sometimes the man seemed like a throwback in time, like a character from an old Western movie, he was so polite. She could practically see him touch the brim of his hat, if he were wearing it. But it made her smile and think highly of him. She really needed to think in the polite realm of things because the way he drove with one hand, the other's long fingers resting on his thick, masculine thigh, combined with that nearly noble profile, well...

"How about you?" It occurred to her that Trevor should be nervous for his own reasons.

"Is my mind on the road?"

She appreciated his attempt to lighten the mood by playing dumb. Another plus. He really needed to stop it. "Are you nervous?"

"To meet a son I never knew about until three weeks ago? Nah." He exaggerated the *nah*.

"You do look cool as a cucumber."

"Pure facade."

"Do I detect hair product this morning?"

He unconsciously patted his head and hair. "Too much? I want to make a good impression."

"Once you put your hat on, your hair doesn't stand a chance anyway." She referred to the dark brown wool felt cowboy hat that sat on the console between them in the car.

"Yep. Nothing like hat-hair ridge to look authentic. Say, has your boy ever met a cowboy before?"

"Aren't too many in the Los Angeles area."

Trevor laughed lightly. "Guess not. What if he doesn't like me?"

"How could he not?" She liked just about everything about Trevor, which could get her into trouble and ensure more heartache, but then her reasons for liking the man were completely different from her son's. But what if James didn't like Trevor because of Mark?

The tiny knot in her stomach kept growing the closer they got to Laramie.

They continued on in companionable silence, occasionally opening up with thoughts or questions, but mostly remaining quiet for the rest of the ride to the military school. It didn't go unnoticed that they had to drive by Wyoming Territorial Park, at the center of which was the prison, to reach the school. Hadn't the school taken the boys on a field trip there last weekend? Or was it only to Frontier Town? What if James felt as if he was in prison at the school? Oh, her doubts about placing him there just wouldn't let up, and once again she was glad Trevor drove. Bottom line, she had to stand firm by her decisions for her boy's sake.

Once at the military academy, they parked and walked to the front of the school, where a large group of families gathered at the auditorium entrance. Exactly at 10:00 a.m. the doors opened and they got ushered to their seats by upperclassmen.

Julie's pulse jumped around inside her chest as she was watching for her son, realizing today was a monumental day whether James knew it or not. He was about to meet his father.

Now her cheeks flushed, too, but having Trevor by her side gave her confidence that things might work out for the best. She prayed the two would like each other and form a bond. James needed that desperately.

Soon the various classes entered, their cadet uniforms reminding Julie of police officers with the long-sleeved pale blue shirts, epaulets on shoulders, patches on the sleeves and gray slacks with black stripes down the leg. Hardly thinking, with her heart thumping so hard she felt it in her ears, Julie reached for Trevor's hand and squeezed for support. Immediately, Trevor placed his free hand on top of hers. It felt so natural, yet unraveling to be touched by him.

James entered with his seventh-grade class, looking straight ahead, and walking with the best posture she'd seen on him ever. She still needed time to get used to his shorter military haircut, especially since he'd been wearing the scraggly longer style with his skateboarding friends back in California one short month ago, and she really did love his thick wavy hair.

"That's him," Julie whispered and pointed out her son to Trevor, second row, fourth in. He sat straighter to get a good look. Pride for their son welled in her chest.

"He's taller than I thought," Trevor whispered, his laser stare assessing James.

"I swear, he grows on a weekly basis these days."

Trevor smiled, and patted her hand, and Julie wondered if he was thinking back to when he was that age himself, or if he was as amazed by their son as she was. From this angle, with Trevor's strong, jutting-out chin and his bright eyes devoted solely to checking out James, she voted for the amazed option.

And why did the hand-holding feel so intense and wonderful?

No, she couldn't let herself dream of something that wasn't possible.

Within minutes, the introductions were completed and a few short welcoming speeches were given, and then a tour of the dorms, where the spotless rooms of two to three bunk beds each were almost unbelievable. The upperclassmen guided the tours and told how their days began at six and lights-out was at ten. How the boys were responsible for themselves and their schedules, and excuses weren't accepted.

Then finally it was time for the meet and greet. Julie could hardly wait to get a hold of her boy. He stood in the school foyer along with everyone else, in the at-ease stance and looking so young. Yet he seemed far more mature than the last time she'd seen him the day she'd brought him to the school. James's eyes lit up and a lopsided smile creased his serious face the instant he saw her.

Do not cry. Do not cry!

Wow, she'd never connected the dots before—that smile was a younger version of Trevor's knock-your-socks-off grin.

"May I hug you?" Julie didn't have a clue if that would be okay with James or not, and the last thing she wanted to do was break any written or unwritten rule.

"Hi, Mom," James said, letting Julie erase the distance between them, and accepting her hug and kiss without protest.

She fought to not overdo it, so after one kiss on the forehead and a quick tight squeeze she let up and stepped back. "Hi, James."

She wanted to say *Hi, baby* or *sweetie* or *honey*, just about every endearment she'd ever said to him, but for the sake of her son she reined it all in. "You look great. How are things going?"

"Not bad. Better than I thought."

Hopefully he was being honest. Trevor had stood back, and Julie glanced over her shoulder as James led

her away to the visitation garden. They'd made their plan
and Julie would stick with it. Trevor already understood.

"Would you like some lemonade?" James asked as
they passed a table with cookies and drinks.

Who was this polite kid? Not that he'd ever been rude
to her, but surely he'd never been this formal when it had
been the two of them? "Sounds good. Thanks."

Like a young man, James got their drinks and led his
mother to a secluded table to visit. Over the next hour
she got an earful about the school, how things worked
and what the academic classes were. She found out about
study hall, lights-out and mandatory sports classes. Her
mother's instinct wasn't detecting any red flags, and
again she hoped with all her heart she'd made the right
decision putting James here.

After a brief tour of the dorms earlier, her hunch was
he'd fit right in. Her son was a social animal, with a good
personality, when he wasn't being teased or tormented
by jerks. She prayed there weren't any jerks or bullies
in his dorm room.

Soon, it was lunch time, and after that Julie brought
up Trevor. "James, I've brought a guest today, my new
boss. I've been telling Dr. Montgomery all about you,
and he was kind enough to drive me here."

After a quick perplexed flicker in his eyes, James
relaxed. "That's cool. Where is he?"

Julie turned and found Trevor directly behind her,
talking to some other parents, but keeping her and James
in his peripheral vision. She waved, and her heart flut-
tered at the thought of introducing father to son. Trevor
stood holding his hat, chatting, but noticed her immediately, as if he'd been keeping tabs on her and James—
which Julie was positive he had—and smiled. The effect
of his handsome gaze on her senses never ceased to

surprise her. Damn, he was good-looking. And damn if her son wasn't his younger spitting image.

Trevor strolled over, a kind expression smoothing out his brows, and waited for Julie to introduce them.

"James, this is Dr. Montgomery. And this is James."

They smiled and shook hands, and Julie could only imagine what must be going through Trevor's mind.

Trevor reached for the boy's hand and shook, hoping the friendly mask he wore wouldn't give away the gamut of emotions stirring throughout his mind and body. It felt oddly like meeting himself when he was a preteen.

"How's it goin'?" he asked, feeling lame the instant it left his lips.

"Pretty good."

"Seems like a pretty good place to go to school."

"I guess."

Oh, man, it felt like his saddle was slipping, and he couldn't fix it. If only he could figure out how to get the boy to open up. "You know, your mom is out of earshot. If you want to be honest, I'm all ears."

The time-travel version of himself thought, quirking a corner of his mouth as he did. "Sometimes it feels kinda like I'm locked up."

"You can't do whatever you want when you want to?"

James shook his head.

"You don't get any free time?"

"If we get all our morning classes' homework done, after sports, we have an hour before dinner. Then we have to get the afternoon classes' homework done before lights out."

"Have you been getting all your homework done on time?"

"Sometimes."

"What would you do if you got that free time?"

"Back home, I'd ride my skateboard. I don't have one here, though."

"So if you had a skateboard, you think that would be incentive to get you to finish your homework on time?"

James flicked a hopeful glance at Trevor, then nodded. Trevor sure hoped the kid wasn't playing him, but his gut told him otherwise.

"You want me to talk to your mom about that? Not that I have any influence or anything, but she seems like a very reasonable person." He was careful to say person rather than woman, which was the only way Trevor thought about Julie lately, not as his RNP or that girl he used to know. Nope. She was a woman, and she was driving him crazy. Now that he'd met his son, he ached to come clean, tell him who he was, but they'd made a deal, he and Julie, and he'd stick to it. Today was just a meet-the-kid kind of day. The rest...well, they'd just have to wait and see how things worked out.

"That'd be good. Thanks."

"Okay, then. Oh, hey, your mother tells me that you like horses."

James nodded thoughtfully.

"Did I mention I happen to live on a ranch?"

"No, sir, you didn't."

He wanted to tell him to knock off the formal sir business, but what exactly should he tell the boy to call him? He wasn't about to let him call him by his first name, in case the time came when he might be called Dad. Dr. Montgomery sounded so dang formal, and *hey, you* was just too common.

"I notice they call you kids by your last names around here."

"Yes, sir."

"Why don't you call me Montgomery instead of sir?"

"Okay." James was looking more confused by the minute. Evidently he wasn't expecting to see Trevor beyond today.

"So back to my mentioning the ranch. It's a cattle ranch, but we have all kinds of horses."

"That's cool."

"Yeah, and I found out today that parents can sign their kids out for home visits on the weekends if the kids are keeping up with their schoolwork and chores."

Now he had James's full attention.

"What I'm saying is, how would you like to go riding with me next weekend, that is if it's okay with your mother, and provided you stay on top of your studies all week?"

"Would she do that, do you think?" James's hopeful gaze almost did in Trevor.

"I don't see why not. I'd really enjoy your company, and I've got some pretty awesome trails I could take you on. Oh, and I'm her boss, so I think we stand a good chance she'll say yes."

James smiled and something inside Trevor's chest popped wide open. He wanted to be the father his son had never had. He wanted to make up for lost time. He wanted to be the male influence on the rest of this boy's life. He wanted to love him as his own. Which he was!

But hold on.

All in due time. The kid had enough new things to get used to. Knowing he was talking to his birth father might set him back. A lot. "Let's shake on it."

Just as they shook hands an announcement came over the loud speaker. "Visitation day is about over. Take the next five minutes to say your goodbyes. All cadets, fall in with your company at fourteen hundred hours, sharp."

Trevor wanted to forgo the handshake and hug the daylights out of the boy, but practiced discipline and settled for the manly shake. Julie rushed over, not the least bit concerned about protocol, and hugged James. By the slight quiver to James's chin, Trevor understood the boy was fighting back his true feelings, too.

"Mom, I know I messed up, and I'm trying to make up for my mistakes."

"I know you are, honey. You know I love you no matter what, but I want the best for you, and right now I believe this place is it."

"I guess."

"Hopefully one day you'll understand."

They hugged again, and Trevor saw the truest kind of love that ever existed, the love of a mother for her child, the kind he'd felt from his own mother until her last day. The scene moved him deeper than he'd felt since his mother's dying day. It was his turn to fight back the emotions surging through his core and up the back of his throat, swallow, and take a deep breath.

One thing became apparent as he stood there watching Julie and James hugging and weeping: he wanted to experience the same thing, to let himself open up and feel love without limits for the son he'd never known he had. He had a lot of years to make up for, but he'd do his best, starting with bringing James to the ranch.

Trevor cleared his throat. "Uh, Julie?"

She turned, huge eyes glistening with moisture. "Yes."

"Not to put you on the spot or anything, but James and I were thinking it would be fun to go for a horse ride at the ranch sometime. Would that be okay with you?"

Now that hovering, hopeful cloud switched over to Julie's sparkling eyes. "I think that's a great idea."

"Cool!" James jumped in.

Not to become putty in the boy's hands, Trevor manned up. "You know the deal, right, James?"

"Yes, sir."

"Remember, you can call me Montgomery." For now.

"Okay, Montgomery, I'll keep my end of the bargain. I promise."

The final alarm sounded and Julie managed one last kiss before James rushed off to his Charley Company. Trevor stood there with a kind of pride he'd never experienced before, and he hardly even knew the boy.

Julie's hand slid around his elbow, and Trevor looked down, suddenly feeling like a family man.

"Great kid," he said.

"I think so, too. He just got off course, but now I know I made the right decision."

"I think so, too."

They smiled at each other, and a new understanding planted itself deep inside Trevor's chest. Meeting James was the beginning of a whole new part of his life, one he planned to stand by from here on out.

As they walked back to the car, Julie felt snug on the crook of his arm, and her light perfume teased his nose. It would have been so easy to stop and kiss her again, but he reminded himself he didn't do that kind of relationship anymore, and Julie didn't deserve the kind he'd become way too good at.

"I was thinking," he said as he opened the car door for Julie to get inside.

"I've heard that can get people into trouble." She smiled sassily up at him, just before slipping inside.

"So true. But let me run this by you. I was thinking about buying James a skateboard." He closed the passenger door and took his time strolling around to the driver's side, to give her time for that little gem to sink in.

"Seriously?" she said the instant he opened the door.

"As incentive for him to keep up on his schoolwork. He told me they get an hour of free time before dinner if they've finished all their morning classes' homework."

"They do pile the work on here, and he told me he feels locked up."

"Yeah, he told me that, too. It's hard not to feel for him, but it's for the best."

"I know, I have to stand my ground on that. Isn't the horseback riding enough incentive for now?"

"Well, yes, probably, but I'd kind of like to give him something he can keep and maybe think of me when he uses it."

"That's very sweet." There was that too-good-not-to-look expression Trevor found harder and harder to resist on Julie. "So what'd you think of him?"

Slipping back into stiff-upper-lip mode, Trevor tightened his jaw. He couldn't possibly let her know what he really thought, how everything had changed in one afternoon, and that he planned to be a part of the kid's life from here on out. "Nice kid."

Fortunately, she didn't buy his subtle response and socked him in the arm. "What'd you really think?"

"Like I just traveled back in time and met myself." *Like I want to be a father in the truest sense of the word.*

CHAPTER SEVEN

THAT EVENING, TREVOR INSISTED he and Julie have dinner together before he took her home, and they stopped at the Sweet Pea Diner on Main Street in Cattleman Bluff. Having lived in California for so long, seeing the main street in town often reminded Julie of a movie set. But she loved how her hometown worked to keep history alive instead of bulldozing everything down and starting over. She remembered coming to Sweat Pea Diner with her parents for fried chicken sometimes on Saturday nights when she was a child, and that made her smile as they walked inside.

"Wow, it smells great," she said as a rush of buttermilk biscuits and frying chicken hit her head-on. "Must have been hungrier than I thought. My mouth is watering."

"You hardly ate lunch, I noticed," Trevor said as they followed a waitress who seated them in a black vinyl booth with a speckled beige Formica table top. It was by the window, which was covered in lacy valances and half curtains. The lady in the pink apron with Sweet Pea Diner in bold black print across her chest handed them menus and left.

"I was too nervous to eat. I kept wondering what James would think about your being there."

"If anyone should have been nervous, it was me."

"Were you?"

"Very, but it didn't turn out so bad, did it?"

"No. The day was pretty darn good." She smiled and studied Trevor's face; his brows nearly met as he looked over the menu. The choices didn't seem that perplexing, and she wondered what he might really be thinking so hard about.

Once they ordered, they got their sodas right away along with a basket of those delicious-smelling biscuits. Julie dug right in and buttered one, spread some of the homemade Sweet Pea honey on top, and took a big bite, the crazy sweetness melting in her mouth. Wow, she'd forgotten how great the local orange-clover honey was while out in California.

"So I guess you'll have to ride out with me next weekend to sign out James for the day," Trevor said.

"I sure will. I'm going to be jealous to share him with you, but I want him to get to know you."

"Why don't you plan on having supper with us at the Circle M, then we can drive him back to school together?"

It sounded like a lot of togetherness to her, but since she wanted what was best for James, and she was pretty sure that meant bringing his father into his life, she'd go along with Trevor's plans. For now.

She took another bite of biscuit, this one not quite as sweet as the first, then looked at Trevor. He'd broken her heart so thoroughly when she'd been seventeen that she didn't think it was possible to ever pick up the pieces again. If it hadn't been for the pregnancy back then, she'd sworn she couldn't have gone on living. Ah, the overdramatic days of being a teenager. Thank goodness they were over! She'd never put herself in a position again to let a man make or break her life.

Yet in her heart, she still worried about how much pain Trevor could cause, and this time not only to her, and held back on every natural reaction she felt toward him. He couldn't be as good as he seemed. There had to be a catch—there always was with men. Maybe one day she'd meet a man she could trust, but so far...

"Do you recommend the fried chicken or the meat loaf?" he asked, still reading the menu as if it held the key to life itself.

"Hands down, the chicken. Of course, I don't remember ever eating anything else here." She glanced outside at the old bowling alley across the street, remembering her parents being in a bowling league with other teachers, and how she'd got to hang out and drink milkshakes on Friday nights. When she'd turned sixteen, she'd applied for her first job as a bowling-shoe clerk, helping people find the right size and making sure they checked them out and paid for renting them. She used to take her breaks outside no matter how cold it was, to get the stench of stinky feet and sweaty socks out of her nostrils.

Julie fought off the urge to grin over the fond memories.

Trevor took her recommendation and they enjoyed an old-style meal together—there was that word, *together*, again. The dinner came complete with mashed potatoes and gravy—the real kind, not instant whipped—along with overcooked green beans, and while they ate they recapped the day.

Julie had never seen another man's eyes light up while talking about her son before, and she believed Trevor when he told her she'd raised a great kid.

"But you've only just met him, and don't forget he

got caught shoplifting." She pointed with her fork before stabbing a sliced piece of fried chicken breast.

"I know good character when I spot it. He made a mistake, that's all." Trevor nailed her with his sincerest expression. "He was asking for help, and you got it for him. You did the right thing."

Why his opinion meant so much, she wasn't sure, but his kind words gave her confidence she hadn't really been feeling before now. "Thank you."

There seemed to be more on Trevor's mind, but he got busy eating his dinner, and before she knew it two fresh peach cobblers showed up with coffee.

"I can't ever resist cobbler when it's on a menu," he admitted.

She wasn't trying to impress him or anything, but she decided to let him know she'd learned a thing or two from her momma before she'd moved to LA. "I happen to make a pretty great apple crumble, in case you're interested."

His brows lifted and his eyes flashed a playful glance. "You mean you've been holding out on me?"

"I don't tell just anyone that I can cook."

"I understand. You don't want a man to like you for all the wrong reasons."

"Oh, yeah, if word got out in Cattleman Bluff, I'd have men beating down my door. Of course, they'd all be over fifty, but a single mother can't be too choosey."

He gave a good-hearted laugh. "If my dad didn't have Gretchen, he'd be first in line, too."

"You think there's a chance for me with your dad?" she teased.

Trevor's face got serious; his hand flew to hers. "Not on your life, because I'm going to be the first in line when you decide to date again."

Direct, straight down the line, his comment set off a reaction in her chest like a strike at that bowling alley across the street. She couldn't dare mess up the early relationship between Trevor and James by getting involved with him. Yet Trevor kept dropping hints. Was she misreading him? Maybe he was just playing along with her and she'd taken him too seriously. Maybe it was his way of being nice.

And what happened to not ever letting a man mess with her head again?

"The day I bake an apple crumble, you'll be the first to know, okay?" *Why did I just say that?*

"Sounds like a deal."

He insisted on paying for dinner, and they drove home in awkward silence. She'd played around too much back at the restaurant, and he'd misunderstood her, putting a whole new spin on baking. Now he was so deeply in thought, she expected him to drop her at the curb and head straight home.

But she was wrong. When they arrived at her house, he jumped out, as always, and opened the door for her. Proving good Wyoming manners went deeper than any misunderstanding between a man and a woman.

He walked her to the door, and before she could unlock it he cleared his throat. "I need to tell you some things," he said.

The porch was no place for a serious conversation, and that was definitely the impression she got from his earnest comment—a conversation was about to be had. "Why don't you come in, then?"

She opened the door and flipped on the lights and he followed her into the living room. The house wasn't nearly as settled as she'd like it to be, but things were getting there.

"Can I get you anything to drink?"

"I'm fine, thanks," he said, sitting on the cream-colored microfiber love seat in front of the modest fireplace, practically filling the seat up with his broad shoulders and long legs.

Would it be weird to sit beside him? So close? There was hardly any room left and they'd have to touch. She opted to sit in the brightly patterned accent club chair a few feet away. Julie folded in her lower lip and bit down as she waited for whatever Trevor wanted to tell her, a breeze of anxiety whispering through her.

He traced the brim of his hat with his fingertips, turning it round and round in the process, while he stared at the black granite tile on the fireplace. "I want to be a part of James's life. I don't know how I can just step in and begin, but I want to. I want him to trust me and know he can depend on me, and I know that takes time, but I want that. You know?"

His honesty touched her so deeply, she could barely breathe. She'd longed for a man to care like this for James since the day he was born. But she'd been fooled before.

"Seeing the two of you today," Trevor continued, "I can't explain how it touched me, it's too hard, but I've never felt anything like it. I want that, too." He looked up and nearly knocked her out of the chair with his heartfelt expression. "The thing is, I understand that people don't love each other just because you want them to. It has to be earned. But I want to earn that with James, no matter how long it takes. I want him to think of me as his father, not just because I'm the biological parent, but because I'm *being* a parent for him."

Julie's eyes welled up; the man was saying the magical words she'd always dreamed about for her son, and she believed him. He wasn't just spouting platitudes. Seeing her with James had moved him, and he truly wanted a slice of that parental pie for himself.

Overcome with hope and optimism, Julie got up and went to Trevor. She sat beside him on the love seat, saw the early signs of moisture in his eyes and threw her arms around his neck. She couldn't help herself. She'd come face to face with the father of her son, had taken the chance to tell him, risked jeopardizing a job over it, but discovered the true character of Trevor Montgomery in the process. Her gamble had paid off like nothing she could have dreamed up.

His arms circled her waist and back; they hugged and laughed, and cried a little, too, but good tears, like long-lost-family tears. She took his face in her hands and looked deeply into his eyes; she'd never noticed before now that they were lighter brown at the center with gold flecks. "I'm going to hold you to that, Trevor. It's all I've ever wanted for my son."

She kissed him lightly, and though she'd meant it to be a completely different kind of kiss—a tender kiss of thanksgiving and appreciation for the man—it didn't turn out that way. With the melding of their mouths, warmth spread over her shoulders and down her back; a surprising need to be close to him reached inside and wrung her out.

His arms roamed her spine as he pulled her closer, smashing her breasts to his chest, opening his mouth, kissing her deeper, meeting her tongue with tiny flicks of his, then slipping between her lips. She kissed him back, sliding her tongue over his, then heard a sound deep in his throat as his need to take over became apparent. She let him kiss her to near dizziness, let his eager mouth explore and take whatever he wanted. The warmth quickly turned to burning, and she was confused. She couldn't let their sexual desire for each other interfere with the fragile new relationship between Trevor and James.

His hands felt so good on her back, kneading and massaging her into stupidity. No, she couldn't let this happen, no matter how badly she wanted it. She couldn't let things go any further.

One moment her hands were on his shoulders, enjoying their width and power, the next they slid to his chest where his muscles tightened under her touch. Just one more kiss before she ended it, just one more taste of his velvety mouth. So selfish of her.

She had to stop. There was too much at stake. Her hands pushed against his chest, and she pulled back her chin, breaking their touch, hating the feel of cool air in place of his moist, inviting lips.

"This was a horrible idea." She croaked the words as she glanced into his fiery eyes. Raw sexual passion burned there for her. The tips of her breasts tightened even more at the sight of him, and his wanting her.

He didn't utter a sound, just stared at her, hungry-eyed, with promises of ecstasy, if only she'd keep kissing him. Knowing he saw the same desire in her, she let out a ragged breath, pleading for him to understand. The moment of danger stretched on as the burning gaze in his nearly black eyes slowly flickered out. He inhaled and regained his composure. They stared at each other until it was safe and their passion vanished.

It had been too close.

"I just wanted to thank you for caring for James. I didn't…"

He touched his forehead to hers. "You didn't mean to drive me crazy?"

They snickered together and it released more pent-up

tension. "We can't confuse things any more than they already are, Trevor."

"Might be true, but it sure would be fun trying."

For him it might be fun, but for her making love to Trevor Montgomery would mean something completely different. "Please understand."

He kissed her forehead. "I do. But I've got to tell ya, you kiss like a crazy lady, and I like it."

No sense in being embarrassed; she'd reacted exactly how she felt. Something about Trevor had always done that to her. Surprisingly, all these years later that feeling hadn't changed. But for the sake of her son, she'd bury the lost love she still carried for Trevor deep inside, just as she had for the past thirteen years.

She could never again allow her personal desire to interfere with her son's welfare.

Trevor drove home, thanking Julie for stopping him from making a huge mistake. Her kiss had set him off on a road he had no intention of turning back from. He wanted her. Like a madman. The way he wanted contact with his sometime girlfriends around town. But those consensual arrangements were meant to keep feelings out of the mix.

Julie deserved better from a man, but these days that was where he was at. Good thing she'd put on the brakes.

He chose to ignore the thought niggling way at the back of his brain... *Julie is different.*

Well, of course she was, she was the mother of his kid. Surprise! She wasn't exactly the kind of woman he could screw and forget, now could he? Not any more, anyway. Not her.

Yet, seeing her with James today, seeing how deep their mother-son love was, had reached inside him and changed something in that cold hole he called a heart. Hell, he'd told her how he wanted to act like a father, to *be* a father, now he damn well better live up to his braggadocio.

The kid deserved a dad.

Julie deserved a man of his word.

And he deserved a chance to prove himself to both of them.

Taking the woman to bed would ruin everything.

Monday morning, Trevor was back to all business at the clinic, though Julie made it challenging by wearing a skirt. He'd catch glimpses of her legs as she walked into her examination rooms, and on more than one occasion he had to take a moment to recover. Damn, she had great legs.

Tuesday morning, she tapped on his office door and asked for help with a difficult patient diagnosis. After evading her eyes, pretending to be engrossed in the lab results on his computer screen, he followed her into an exam room and gave his expert opinion on atopic dermatitis versus rosacea, while pretending he couldn't smell her shampoo in that wildly misbehaving hair of hers. Thank goodness the clinic closed down on Tuesday afternoons. He spent the entire afternoon on the ranch, working alongside Jack and his crew, vaccinating cattle.

Wednesday was easy since he'd set up a day of house calls, traveling as far as Medicine Bow National Forest in the morning, where a family of campers had all come down with a fever and a rash, and ending up at old Jake Jorgensen's place to make sure he'd been keeping up with his heart meds and that his blood pressure wasn't acting up.

Thursday was tough, though, as it was the monthly

staff meeting—Julie's first. Fortunately, Charlotte did all the talking, and Trevor was able to avoid eye contact with Julie by staring at the Italian cold-cut sandwiches Rita had ordered in for lunch. But as Julie slipped out of the meeting to take a call he watched the sway of her hips and noticed how her hair bounced around her shoulders when she walked.

After nothing more than civil work-related conversations all week, on Friday Trevor had to talk to Julie since they needed to make plans for the trip out to Laramie and the military academy the next morning.

Though hesitant to be up close and personal with Julie for the ride out—only because he knew it would wreak havoc with his good sense and make him want her all over again, and not because he didn't otherwise enjoy her company—he used the office intercom to contact her.

"Julie, can you come to my office?"

Within a minute or two, she stood at his door, that sweet, innocent smile of hers driving him nuts.

He really was excited about bringing James out to the ranch, though he wondered how long it would take for his father to catch on that the boy was his grandson, and that the story about helping out a troubled kid was a bunch of hooey. On that level, he was nervous, knowing he'd have to, sooner or later, tell his dad that he, Trevor, was a father.

And on that note, he needed to broach a touchy subject with the lovely woman standing before him in a dark gray pencil skirt and a periwinkle blouse with a bunch of inviting ruffles down her chest. Damn.

"Time to make plans for tomorrow?" she asked.

"Yeah," he said, his hand cupping the back of his neck as if she'd just put a crick there. "I know I said I'd pick you up at eight, but maybe we should get a much earlier start, say six?"

Her shapely brows lifted nearly imperceptibly, those huge hazel eyes attentively waiting for his reason.

"That way it will be nearly eight before we check him out and almost ten before we can get started on that ride. I was thinking of taking him out to Sheep Mountain."

"Wow, I don't know if that's a good idea. He's only been on horses a few times."

"You think we should stick closer to home, then?"

"This time, I would. See how he takes to riding, then maybe the next time you can cover more territory."

Trevor smiled. "I like the sound of next time."

She smiled back. "I do, too."

Next time made him remember her kiss and how he'd tried his damnedest all week to not want a *next time* but had failed miserably. But right now he took back control over that weakness for Julie's sake. "I bought James a skateboard, and I just wanted to let you know I plan on giving it to him tomorrow."

"That's okay." She didn't look happy.

"I'm not trying to bribe him to like me or anything, but we had that conversation about keeping his grades up and all. Any reports about that?"

"I figure we'll find out tomorrow when I sign him out for the day."

He couldn't waste another minute beating around the topic he really needed to bring up. He laced his fingers and planted them firmly on his desk. "So tomorrow, if at some point the time feels right, are you okay with me telling James I'm his father?" The thought made Trevor's mouth dry up and his pulse race. Had he just said that?

She inhaled and forced her shoulders to relax. Her delicate hand flew into a clump of light brown chaotic curls near her temple, and she gripped them. Slowly she let out her breath and removed her hand. "Trevor, that's something we need to do together, when the time is right."

"I wasn't lying when I told you I want to be his dad, Julie. But what I'm hearing is that you're not ready to tell him." He leaned forward on his desk. "If it helps at all, I'm as nervous as you must be about this. The thing is, will the time ever be perfectly right? Maybe we should just jump in."

She shook her head, comprehension flashing in her worried-looking eyes. "Like we did the night I got pregnant? Hell, no. We need to give this time, think about how best to go about it. Plan a day."

He tightened his chin, stretching his lower lip, and nodded, even though it went against everything he was feeling. "Okay. When do you think that will be?"

"Not just yet. I'm sorry, but I can't rush this. He's still traumatized over Mark."

"I'm not Mark. I'm his dad."

"It'll take time for him to understand that. Can't tomorrow just be about James getting some guy time? Some bonding time, like you said you wanted?"

"I guess it'll have to be."

"Thank you for understanding. See you tomorrow at six, then." With that, she nodded and left.

"I'll bring the coffee!" he called out after her, not caring who heard him.

Something told him he'd need a lot of caffeine tomorrow because he probably wouldn't sleep a single second tonight.

True to his word the next morning Trevor appeared on Julie's doorstep at one minute to six by her kitchen clock. She was putting the finishing touches on a couple of breakfast burritos filled with scrambled eggs, pinto beans, cheddar cheese and salsa. It wasn't exactly a cowboy meal, which would include meat and biscuits with whatever else got splashed onto the plate, but good old SoCal food and good enough for the drive out to school.

She'd taken him at his word about bringing the coffee.

Rushing to answer the door, she stopped quickly to smooth back her hair, which she'd foolishly attempted to put into a ponytail, but which looked more like a cascade of curls on the back of her head. Even as she patted she realized that half a dozen curls around her face had already escaped the elastic.

"Right on time," she said, swinging open the door to find his friendly face with an early-morning twinkle in his eyes.

He'd come dressed for riding in a pastel-blue long-sleeved shirt with thick navy vertical stripes, a larger-than-usual belt buckle and well-worn jeans highlighting his narrow waist and hips and extralong legs, and some really broken-in riding boots. And he stood like a man who knew how to ride the range.

Julie took a moment to catch her breath.

"Coffee's in the car. Something smells great."

"Oh, yeah, let me grab the burritos and my jacket and we can be on our way."

On the drive out to school, they sipped their coffee and ate their food and enjoyed watching the sprawling landscape lighten up in shades of purple and gold to finally greet the day for miles and miles. She could live to be a hundred but would never get tired of looking at the majesty of Wyoming.

She liked that she didn't feel pressured to always be on top form with Trevor. If she wanted to talk she could and if she wanted to keep her thoughts to herself, well, that seemed okay with him, too.

"The boy owns jeans, right? Not those shorts they wear for skateboarding." Trevor broke into her thoughts.

"Yes. And I took the liberty to buy him a shirt this week. It's in my purse."

"You call that a purse?"

True, her big handbag could pass as carry-on luggage, but she swore she needed everything inside, which today included a Western-style shirt for her son to wear when riding with his father.

She inhaled a shaky breath and stared out the car window, hoping and praying for the right thing to happen today, even though she wasn't sure what that might be.

Later, the signing-out process from school went like clockwork, and she promised to have him back by lights out, 10:00 p.m., that night. After the first six weeks in school, provided the boys kept their grades up, they'd be allowed to go home for the weekends. So far, James seemed to be on track. She'd been counting down the weeks since she'd first brought him to the school, for when she could have him at home again.

It was heartening to see how excited James seemed when he saw Trevor again.

"Hey, you ready for a long ride today?"

"Yeah. What's my horse's name?"

"I've been giving that some thought, and I think I might loan you Zebulon. He's my horse, so I know he'll treat you right."

"Cool!"

Before long, they'd arrived back at Cattleman Bluff, and Trevor dropped Julie off at her house.

"Be careful today," Julie said, grazing the top of her

son's head with a kiss. "I don't want to find out about any broken bones."

"I promise to set them straight, if that happens," Trevor said, trying to keep things light, not all angsty the way Julie obviously felt about the day.

"Take good care of my son."

"Ah, Mom!" James protested.

"I will. We'll see you around five for dinner, okay?"

With one last raggedy breath, Julie got out of the car and nodded her head, thinking this would be the longest day of her life, waiting, wondering if they hit it off. Would her boy realize Trevor was his father today, or just a really great guy who bought him a skateboard?

Only time would tell.

Julie showed up for dinner exactly on time, and with a fresh-out-of-the-oven apple crumble. Gretchen escorted her in, and she found Monty sitting comfortably in his favorite chair in front of the fireplace. Trevor and James were nowhere in sight.

"Hi," she said to Mr. Montgomery.

"Hello there, Julie. Come keep me company."

Though well into his sixties, the man still had a lot of life in those sparkly green eyes. She wondered how Trevor would look as he got older, but decided it was a silly thought and pushed it aside.

"The guys not back from riding yet?" She tried to sound casual, but failed.

"They are. Trevor's showing the boy how to remove the tack, brush the horse and pick out the hooves. All that good stuff."

"That's great. Did they have a good ride?"

"If I judge by the way the boy couldn't shut up about it when they got home, I'd say yes."

A smile stretched across Julie's mouth, and her chest dropped with a sigh.

Monty reached for Julie's hand, looked her straight in the eyes. "That boy looks an awful lot like Trevor. Is my hunch right?"

Just after she'd sighed with relief, her heart seemed to triple-flip and tumble down to her stomach. She broke eye contact and stared at her hands. What should she do now? Would Trevor be livid if she told the truth? Had Monty already questioned him? If so, had Trevor denied it and would her confession make him a liar? She pressed her lips together, trying to form the best and most diplomatic answer she could come up with.

Mr. Montgomery seemed to wait impatiently.

"Mom! You should've seen me on Zebulon. He's so cool."

Saved from answering Monty, who dropped his hand from hers, Julie quickly flicked her gaze over his knowing glance as she turned to greet her son. James grinned like an emu as he crossed the room. She stood and reached to hug him, grateful that he offered a half-second hug in return before backing off and hitching his thumbs in his jeans pockets. And looking so much like another cowboy standing in the room.

"Did you get any pictures?"

"Yeah, I took a selfie with Zebbie."

"I snapped a few," Trevor chimed in.

With Monty's strong suspicions, her hunch was that Trevor hadn't told his father yet. Now she was grateful her son had interrupted the conversation with him.

"Mr. Montgomery tells me you had a great day riding."

"It was so cool. You should see how big their property is, Mom."

She relaxed and started smiling again, getting lost in her son's enthusiasm.

"He's a natural. You'd think riding was in his blood," Trevor added, taunting her. She flashed him a look, and the corner of his mouth turned up.

"Montgomery said I can come and ride anytime I want."

"That's awfully nice of him."

"Dinner's ready." Gretchen appeared at the wide arch separating the living room from the dining room. "And Ms. Sterling brought dessert."

"Do you need to wash your hands?" she asked James.

"Nah, Montgomery made me before we came in the house."

She glanced at Trevor, who wore a silly grin. Over the hand-washing, or the fact she'd brought dessert?

Julie waited and helped Monty stand, then walked slowly with him to the table. Before they reached his chair at the head, Trevor rushed to pull it out for his father. While the man sat, using his quad cane for balance, Trevor's fingers brushed the back of Julie's waist.

"You brought dessert?"

She tossed him a quick glance. "Apple crumble."

A slow smile spread from one side of his mouth to the other, completely replacing that silly grin. "You hitting on my father?" he mumbled, close to her ear.

Julie gave him a "whatever" stare and let Trevor pull out the chair for her, closest to his dad.

Forty minutes later, after another wonderful Gretchen meal had been devoured along with way too many compliments about Julie's apple crumble, she glanced at her watch and decided to be the bearer of bad news.

"You know, we're going to have to hit the road pretty

soon to get you back to school in plenty of time for
curfew."

"I know." James sounded dejected, as if he thought
he was going back to jail or something.

"Mind if I tag along?" Trevor asked. "I'd be glad to
drive."

"I've got my car here."

"I'll follow you to your house and we can leave from
there."

It seemed like he wouldn't take no for an answer.

"Do we have time for me to see what my room looks
like, Mom?"

With all the activity and hectic visits, she hadn't once
thought about showing James the room he could call his
own whenever he came on the weekends. "Sure. I guess
that settles that, then."

Once they arrived at her house, James rushed down
the hall. "Which one is it?" he called.

"The last one on the left."

The boy disappeared inside. "I'm going to change before I go back to school," he said. "Real quick, I promise."

Trevor shook his head and smiled. "I guess he doesn't
want to be caught dead in cowboy riding gear."

"He was born and raised in California, you know."
She got serious, quickly, not knowing how long she'd
have to ask what had been heaviest on her mind all day
and evening. "So things really went well?"

Trevor made a decisive nod. "He really took to riding.
I had him loping and he even galloped like a natural."

"That's wonderful. Listen, I have to tell you, your
father hinted that he knew James was—"

"I was what, Mom?"

Her heart nearly stopped beating as her mind worked

like a madwoman to find something to say. "He said he knew you'd be a good rider. He could tell just from looking at you." Fingers crossed he'd buy her lame answer, and she'd try to forgive herself for not being completely honest with her son.

"Really? Cool."

"You do have a knack," Trevor said. "Maybe because you have good balance from all the skateboarding you do."

"You think?"

"I know. Had proof today." Trevor gave him one pat on the shoulder, and they headed toward the door. The shock of seeing the two of them standing in her parents' house—her house now—nearly did her in. James truly was the younger version of Trevor, and if anyone would know that, Monty would.

She wondered how Monty and Trevor's conversation would go later tonight. Maybe, the older man would already be in bed to spare Trevor the cross-examination, but she knew in her bones that a father-son talk about the boy would be inevitable.

And in that case it was time to tell James who his father was.

An hour and a half later, they pulled into the military academy's parking lot with a half hour to spare. As James jumped out of the car, resigned to spending the rest of the semester at the school, Trevor stopped him.

"Hey, wait a sec. I have something for you." He walked around the car to the trunk and popped it, then removed his gift. "I know you're going to keep up on your schoolwork, so I wanted you to have a new skateboard for that hour of free time every day."

James's eyes grew as wide as they could go. "Seriously? Wow." He took the skateboard and looked it over. "It's a Landshark!"

"I'm told that's one of the best."

"I've wanted one of these for years," James said, joy bubbling out of him. "Thanks so much." It seemed he wanted to hug Trevor, but didn't know how to start it.

The thing that surprised Julie was that Trevor seemed just as awkward about hugging or not hugging James. They settled on a knuckle knock and skipped any expression of affection, which disappointed Julie. But at least James had thanked him.

"We better get you checked in." Always the bearer of practicality, Julie led the way inside the school.

The drive home zipped by, what with Trevor telling her everything about his day with James. He laughed and smiled, and she believed with all her heart that he liked James.

"So who did you bring that apple crumble for, me or my dad?" His rakish smile made her laugh.

"Your father, of course." She couldn't resist teasing, and the playful look she got in return was totally worth it.

He pulled into her driveway and parked, then reached across the car and took her hand. "One thing I want you to know for sure. I like our kid. In time, I know I'll love him."

His words wrapped around her like hope and promises, and they warmed her right down to her toes. "I hope that day comes soon."

"I know it will."

"I had a lot of time to think today." Why bandy about the main topic in their lives? She took a breath and went for it. "What do you think about us telling him next weekend? We can take him for a horseback ride, the three of us."

"I've got the perfect spot to take him. It's by a waterfall. We can bring some snacks, then sit him down and tell him who I am."

His sincerity did her in. She almost gushed, *I love you, Trevor Montgomery,* but thankfully got a hold of herself before she did. "You really want this, don't you?"

"More than I've ever wanted anything." He shifted toward her and his lips covered hers in a hot and greedy way. This time, instead of letting practicality step in, she sunk into and savored his hungry kisses, which quickly put a stop to any thinking at all.

Somehow they made it into her house with one thought shared between them—how quickly they could get each other out of their clothes.

Maybe it was the secret they shared or the fact that Trevor hadn't once tried to shirk his responsibility as the boy's father since he'd found out. Not that she'd asked him for anything, but that he'd willingly offered to become a part of her and James's lives. Or maybe it was because he was still the sexiest man she'd ever laid eyes on, and she couldn't believe her good fortune that he seemed to see something in her he liked, too.

But most of all, as they grappled with buttons and zippers, kicking off her shoes and pulling off his boots, the real draw between them was because of a long history going all the way back to one night in a barn on a warm summer night.

He pulled her onto the bed, her mattress feeling so much softer than the itchy straw in the loft of that barn thirteen years ago, and peeled off the one remaining item separating them, her lacy underpants.

Once they were naked, everything seemed to slide

into slow motion. Trevor clearly knew how to please a woman, and right this moment all his attention was on Julie.

His hand slipped underneath her hair, cupping her nape, drawing her close for tender kisses, and in between, his gaze worshiping every corner of her body.

"You're so beautiful," he whispered, kissing her cheek, then her neck, releasing a rush of tingles and chill bumps across her chest. He dipped his head and kissed her breast, lifting it, running his tongue over the tip. When he gently sucked, her head dug into the pillow and she lost her breath.

How long had it been since a man had made love to her like this? Making her feel she was the center of the universe, his only wish to please her? She reached for his head and kissed the crown, the other hand tracing the breadth of his shoulder. His back was strong, his torso long and muscular, his hips narrow, leading to powerful thighs. She ran her hands over the rock-hard mounds of his glutes when he got up on his knees, then down the backs of his legs.

Longing burned bright in his midnight eyes as he laid her back and skimmed her sides with his fingertips, tracing along her hips and legs and inner thighs, releasing chills from his touch and giving her that look of wonder. Before long her knees were over his shoulders, his head at her center, and he kissed the tender folds between her thighs, igniting a shock of sensations. She had to work to settle down, to get used to being kissed there, to being stroked by his tongue. First flicks and swirls, then probes, forcing tension and longing and crazy thrills spiraling throughout her body. He wouldn't let up, and she could hardly take his unstoppable touch as she clutched the sheets to anchor herself. The room shimmered as his tongue caused an explosion deep inside, undoing her, sending her mind flying, her body blissfully tingling and vibrating.

She was lost to him.

He'd been frantic and intent the first time they'd made love when she'd been a virgin. Now they were both experienced at lovemaking and he'd matured, knowing how to treat a woman, how to please and how to drive her wild. She was the lucky recipient of his attention tonight. She wouldn't waste it.

Once she'd recovered from her orgasm, she gently moved his shoulders away, got up on her knees and pushed him back to the mattress. She crawled over him, straddling his hips, pretending to be unaware of his full and throbbing arousal, choosing to kiss him deeply, mouth to mouth. He shared her taste as their tongues tangled in messy, sexy kisses. She sat up and her hands skimmed the muscles on his chest. Working on the ranch kept him in tip-top condition. Lucky her.

Scooting down his legs, while still tingling between her thighs, she focused on him, and his long, strong erection. She wrapped her fingers around him, enjoying how hard he was; her thumb ran from tip to base and back. He moaned his pleasure. Still holding him, she leaned forward and kissed his chest, teasing his small tight buds, then running her tongue the length of his torso, enjoying his slightly salty taste. She inhaled his musky male scent and reached between his legs to cup all of him, then shimmied down further to taste him, to kiss his ridge, to run her tongue over the length of him.

He liked it.

She glanced up at him, loving the view from down there, his chin jutting ceilingward, every muscle on his chest and shoulders taut. "If you keep that up," he said in a rough whisper, "this party will be over before it starts."

She'd sworn years ago she'd never let this happen again, yet here she was wanting nothing else.

"I hope you brought a condom because I don't have anything here," she said, afraid the answer would be no.

His head shot up. "Well, I hope you don't get the wrong impression, but I sure as hell did."

His candid answer made her laugh as she eased up on her hold and let him find his wallet. He was a grown eligible man—of course he'd be prepared. She loved seeing him stand, proudly naked, his muscled thighs looking powerful, his stomach showing the results of crunches at the gym beyond working the ranch. She couldn't wait to be wrapped in those strong arms again, to be devoured by his mouth.

The mattress dipped when his knees hit, and he crawled toward her, having already sheathed himself. She rolled into him, soon covered by his hot, smooth skin. He pulled her closer, stomach to stomach, breath for breath; they kissed and eased their way back into their rhythm.

Several minutes later, with her worked to near frenzy from his attention, he finally thrust into her welcoming heat, his strength filling her, stretching her to capacity.

He rode her gently until they adjusted to each other, then moved faster, went deeper, and she met him each step of the way. Heat licked through her center, up her back and out to her breasts. Everything tightened with expectation.

He rocked her faster; she shifted her hips for the best sensation, bearing down on his force and friction. *There, right there.* Throbbing and tingling, she kept up with his pace, nearing her tipping point. She squeezed tight around him, then let him ride and push her to the limit, indescribable sensations whipping up inside. She begged and whimpered for more, right at the edge of the magic.

His power and speed drummed into her until she gave way with the sensation of flailing into the night, spasms and tingles and…euphoria.

He growled and followed her into the stratosphere, their bodies interlaced closer than imaginable, spinning out of control together in pure bliss.

CHAPTER EIGHT

SUNDAY MORNING, JULIE WOKE with her head on the hard pillow of Trevor's chest. He was asleep, his fingers buried in her hair, their bodies entwined like a braided rug. Her eyes popped open. How should she handle this? They'd spent most of the night making up for thirteen years, and having sex again with Trevor Montgomery was something she'd sworn she'd never do. Had she jeopardized the whole point of telling him he was James's father?

Relationships were always messy, and she couldn't very well date the dad and break up when things went sour like normal dating—not when her son was just getting to know Trevor.

Oh, hell, what have I done?

"You okay?" Trevor asked with a deep, inviting morning voice. She must have squirmed while buried in her thoughts for him to wonder.

She rose up and almost coldcocked him with her head to his chin. "Oh! Sorry! Uh, just thinking." She sat up the rest of the way.

His squinting-from-morning-light gaze drifted to her breasts, and immediately, with lids fully open, cast a total look of appreciation. Just like last night. Not the way to have a serious conversation. She grabbed the sheets and covered herself. His sweet expression changed to a scrunched-up morning face. "What's up?"

"I think you know."

"What if I guess wrong? Do I lose points?"

Okay, maybe she was expecting him to read her mind, maybe she should come right out and say what she thought. "Where do we go from here?"

"Right this minute? Because I'd kind of like to carry you into the shower with me."

She lightly cuffed his chest. He smiled and pulled her near. "I propose—"

Her head shot up again. No collision this time.

"As I was saying, I propose that we explore the possibility of being a couple."

That was a crazy idea. "That could ruin everything with James."

"How so?"

"What if we don't like each other? Then what?"

His warm hand skimmed her arm, raising a path of goose bumps. "I think we've already established we like each other. The bigger question is, will our dating get in the way with my spending more time with James?"

"We can't let that happen."

"I don't want to, but I've got to tell you—" he nibbled her neck, then traced the line of her jaw with kisses "—I like James's mom a lot."

Was it okay? Had she ruined any potential bonding between Trevor and James? Or, worse yet, would he feel obligated to be with her son in order to be with her? Or vice versa. "It's just so complicated now."

"And it wasn't before?"

"Good point." Truth was there was no *un*complicated version for their story. "I don't think we should let James know about us, though."

"If that's what you want."

"But it would be fun to do things together, the three of us." She wanted a chance to watch the interactions between Trevor and James, couldn't deny that. "After we tell him."

"You know I'm all for that, too."

It suddenly occurred to her that she was a woman in a modern world and going to bed with someone didn't mean the same thing as it did in her parents' time. Or when she was a teenaged virgin. But in her heart, making love with a man was still a *big deal*. A very big deal. She'd never been able to be casual with love affairs. Didn't want to. Trevor, however, gave the impression that casual was his preferred method of dating. "I don't usually jump into bed with my dates."

"We were on a date?"

She cuffed him again.

"It's not like we haven't done it before, Julie bean."

"Thirteen years ago!" Did he just call her *Julie bean*?

"I liked how we picked right back up." He grinned while he spoke, and she knew he was teasing her, but she wanted to slug him out of frustration, mostly with herself, but just the same...

She held his jaw so his eyes could only look at hers. "Promise me that nothing between us will be more important than you getting to know James. Than your stepping in as his father."

"I promise." He looked sincere, too. When she let go of his jaw, he sat and got up, then headed for the bathroom. "But you're the one who made the apple crumble. I'm just saying."

She plopped back onto the pillow and stared at the ceiling. Had she thrown down the gauntlet with that damned crumble? She had definitely given him mixed messages. They'd jumped into bed together and now she'd have to pay the price of muddying the water where James was concerned. *Good going, Julie, always a mess up.*

"Are you coming, J.B.?" he called from the bathroom, shower water running full blast. And the nickname had morphed into initials?

Truth was, she'd be crazy not to enjoy a shower with her boss and the father of her kid this morning. The damage had already been done, and they'd agreed to work on being a couple.

As long as he didn't feel obligated to take the mother if all he really wanted was the son.

"I'm waiting."

As if mesmerized, she got out of bed and followed the sexy voice into the bathroom.

All the next week, Julie spent way too much energy making sure no one at the clinic could suspect anything was going on between Trevor and her. Even when he'd slip up and call her JB. Three out of the five days after work, they'd spent the night together. She'd discovered things about making love with Trevor she'd never dreamed before, and each and every day she learned something new to like about him.

When James got to come home on the weekend, she and Trevor agreed she should drive out to pick him up herself.

After getting James set up in his room, which she'd completely finished painting and cleaning, she made him lunch and they caught up on how his classes were going.

"I'm doing okay, Mom. I got to ride my new skateboard three days this week."

"That's great. Keep up the good work."

"In my opinion, it should've been four. Their rules are too strict."

"Why do you think that?"

"I only had two more math problems to finish and they wouldn't budge. Homework not done, no free time."

"Rules are rules. If I'm supposed to be at work by eight, I can't show up at ten minutes after eight every day."

"They shoulda let me skate."

They ate roast beef and cheddar cheese sandwiches in silence, but she decided not to go for overkill on explaining the importance of following rules. Sure, life was full of grays, but for now James needed to learn the black and white parts. Was he ready to find out who his father was?

She took another bite and noticed James had a strange look on his face as he chewed. "When I go to Dr. Montgomery's today, will his dad be there?"

"Sure. Why do you ask?"

"He kept giving me weird looks last Sunday."

Oh, no, the man had been obvious and James had noticed. How could she respond? "Really?"

"Good thing he didn't meet me when my hair was long. I don't think he's used to being around teenagers."

"That's probably true, though you're not technically a teenager yet."

"Maybe I look like an alien to him."

She laughed, thankful he'd given her a way out. "Maybe."

"I can't wait to ride Zebulon again today."

Her prayers were answered for a change in topic. "I'm so glad you enjoy horseback riding."

"Montgomery—he told me I could call him that—

said he'd let me watch how they feed the cattle today, and I could maybe help out if I wanted to."

"Fantastic!"

"Why's he being so nice to me?"

And there went that quick elevator ride from her chest to her lap. "He's a good man."

"You thought Mark was a good man, too, then we found out he only wanted you."

The kid had figured that one out the hard way, and she worried it might color his outlook on life. "It's different this time." She patted his hand, knowing that couldn't change the hurt he remembered, wishing she could erase the moment Mark broke his heart.

The boy twisted his lips in thought, perhaps weighing whether he could believe his mother after the horrible experience with her last boyfriend.

"I know Trevor is different. Please trust me." From what she'd learned about Trevor being a man of his word, she believed it. He'd stayed in Cattleman Bluff as a family-medicine doctor to be there for his family rather than pursuing a bigger medical career. He also had a strong sense of loyalty to his town. He'd let his brother live in the spotlight and never complained, though she suspected he sometimes resented the hell out of that. From what she'd seen at the clinic, he was a fair and benevolent boss with his employees, even when they pushed him too far, and a damn fine doctor, and people around town liked him. He had a sincere desire to be a father to a boy he'd never known about, when he could have thrown a fit and demanded DNA testing before he'd accept the news.

And he'd been a considerate and generous lover, too. Damn, now her cheeks started to burn.

A hard triple knock on the front door saved the day. "Coming!"

James's eyes lit up. "That's probably Montgomery!" He jumped up and ran to answer the door.

There was no faking it with James; he genuinely liked the man. The tricky part was, so did she, but she'd sacrifice anything for what was best for her son. And today was the day.

They'd changed their earlier plans and decided to tell James over dinner at her house that night after they'd taken another horseback ride together. But, it being early spring, as soon as they returned to the ranch one of the Circle M cows got ready to drop a calf, and James wanted to watch the delivery. Then another calf got born, and before the guys knew it Julie showed up with dinner in a wicker basket and James's travel bag ready for the ride back to school.

Trevor caught her eyes, his expression worried. *It's okay*, she mouthed. She wasn't in a rush to tell James, even though Trevor seemed to be. Mild guilt tinged her relief.

As James cleaned up in the barn for the ride home, Julie approached Trevor. They shared a clandestine kiss. "Next weekend, for sure, we'll tell him first thing," she said.

"Sounds like the best plan. We can't exactly tell him on the ride home then drop him off."

The following Wednesday, Charlotte rushed past Julie's office door, heading for Trevor's office. Within a minute, he called her on the intercom.

"We've got two women in full labor. At least that's what they both say. Meet me in my office."

She went directly to his office, where Lotte stood.

"I spoke to both women. Mrs. Lewiston has four other kids, and she sounds ready to go right now. Mrs. Rivers says her contractions are about every four to five minutes, but she doesn't have transportation to Laramie General. Her husband works the oil rigs and is gone for long stretches."

"I'll cancel my morning schedule and head out to Mrs. Lewiston's since her delivery sounds imminent," Trevor said. "Julie, I think you can keep your schedule this morning but, soon as you're done, head out to Mrs. Rivers, in case I can't get there. I'll tell her to call the clinic if there's any change. Lotte, put a call into our local midwife, see if she's available to help out with either of these women in case we need backup. Oh, and cancel all this afternoon's appointments."

All having received their marching orders, they fanned out in three directions. Julie had just finished with her last morning appointment, a preop physical for George Mathers, who was scheduled for a knee replacement in Cheyenne the next week.

Back in her office, while she was restocking her delivery bag the phone rang, and she assumed it would be her mother-to-be, Mrs. Rivers. She answered smiling and thinking reassuring thoughts. Until she heard it was the military academy.

"We wanted to let you know as soon as possible. James has gone missing. We haven't checked every possibility, he may still be on campus, and trust that we won't leave any stone unturned, but we thought you should know right away."

Breath caught on the spasm in her throat. He'd gone missing? "How long?"

"We don't know for sure, but he wasn't present for roll call at breakfast today."

"Have the police been notified?"

"We are following protocol, ma'am. The police have been called. We will find your son."

She could barely think, let alone calm the jitters inside. What should she do about the woman in labor? If James had run away from school, would it make any sense to drive out there? Panic drove her to speed-dial the number she'd used the most lately.

"Please leave a message." It went directly to Trevor's voice mail on the first ring. He must be delivering the baby.

"Trevor, it's Julie. James has run away from school. I'm freaking out, but I'm on my way to the Rivers delivery. Please relieve me the instant you can. I've got to find James!"

A half hour later, Julie was at Anita Rivers's home distracting herself from full-out panic by focusing on the mother. She performed the first examination. Mother's vital signs were within normal limits. The fetal heart rate was normal and the baby appeared to be in the anterior position. The mother insisted on a home delivery, and nothing seemed to suggest it wouldn't be a smooth one.

Using sterile gloves, Julie did a pelvic examination and assessed the cervix was eight centimeters dilated; the cervix was softening and over fifty percent effaced. First stage of labor. It could be a long afternoon or not, depending on how the next hour or so went. She hoped Trevor would get there soon.

"If you feel up to it, Mrs. Rivers, you can walk around or lie on your left side. Would you like some ice chips?"

The anxious woman nodded.

"Would you like me to help you up first?"

"I'm okay here, right now." She was on her bed, which was now covered in absorbent barriers in case her water broke during the contractions. "I'm so glad you're here," she said, before Julie could leave the room.

Maybe soothing Mrs. Rivers's nerves would help soothe her own.

"Oh, oh, oh!"

With Julie on her way back from the kitchen, Anita had obviously started another contraction. It had only been two minutes since the last one. Julie rushed to the bedside to hold her hand, right when her cell phone rang. She couldn't very well abandon the laboring mother to answer her phone. After several rings the signal indicated it went to message and, soon after that, another signal indicated a message had been left.

Once the contraction was over, and Anita's white-knuckle grip let up enough to free her hands, Julie rushed to the phone.

Trevor had left the message: "I'm on my way to the Rivers house. It was an uncomplicated delivery here, and the local midwife is with Mrs. Lewiston for follow-up. I've been in touch with the local police chief—he's my dad's best friend. He assures me they'll be on the lookout and they'll find James. Everything will be okay. Do you hear me? I told Larry everything and he assures me they'll find our son. See you soon."

"Our son." It was the first time Trevor had gone public with his being a father, and the thought made Julie a little swimmy headed. She glanced at her watch. It had been almost fifteen minutes since she'd listened to the fetal heart rate, and right now, no matter how many concerns, fears and worries she had, she still had a job to do.

"Okay, you're fully dilated, and baby—what's the name going to be?"

"Chloe. It's a girl."

"Well, Chloe's heart sounds good and strong and she's

nearly fully engaged. By the time your husband gets here, he may already be a daddy. If you don't mind, I'm going to unlock the front door so Dr. Montgomery can get in, in case we're busy delivering a baby when he arrives."

Anita couldn't answer, and by the painful look on her face she was already in the throes of another contraction.

"Try to breathe through it," Julie said, rushing to unlock the front door then speed walking right back to her patient. Thankfully it was a small house.

"I feel like I need to push."

Slipping on a new pair of gloves, Julie noticed fluid leaking onto the padding. "Let's bring your knees up. When I tell you, push!"

More fluid gushed out, but the contraction ended before anything major had happened. She was auscultating the fetal heart rate, since she didn't have access to an internal monitor, as Trevor appeared in the room.

He might as well have been a cowboy in a white hat riding a horse to save the day with the swell of gladness she had over seeing him.

"Hey, how's it going?" he asked, low-key, steady as a rock.

Knowing he was here for a professional reason, and his question was about Anita's labor, she tried to sound cheery, though her heart ached and her head was on fire with panic over the situation with her son. "I think the new kid on the block—Chloe—will be showing up within the hour," Julie said, trying her best to look happy for her patient, above all being professional.

Anita smiled with expectation, but soon that smile changed to impending pain. Another contraction.

"I'm taking over now, Anita. Julie needs to go find our son. He's run away from school," he said while washing his hands in the bathroom sink. Julie handed him a sterile towel and pair of gloves, amazed by what he'd just said.

"Why didn't you say anything?" Anita bore the look of a woman who understood how frightening it would be to have a child missing.

"We had a baby to deliver." She patted Anita's shoulder, and the woman looked up with a grateful expression just before biting her lips.

"Take off now. Head over to the police station for an update. Let me know what you find out," he said, stepping in on this contraction.

"I'll call the instant I find out anything," Julie said, already rushing for the front door.

"Good luck!" Anita called out, but the second word turned into a yell as she'd obviously gone into another massive transitional contraction.

Once in the car, Julie decided to go straight home first, hoping beyond hope her boy might be there. But how in the world would he have gotten there? In her desperateness, she felt compelled to check.

Panic and fear swirled through her mind like thorny vines. She couldn't let anything keep her from focusing on finding her son. Worry wouldn't help a bit.

As she drove she thought about Trevor back at the Rivers's house nobly taking over so she could get to the police station, and she realized, again, that he'd told the police chief and their patient that the missing child was his son. Their son. She wondered how soon Monty would have his hunch verified, and even though it was the craziest time in her life—her son had gone missing—she smiled as a calming feeling took hold. Things would work out. They'd find her son. They had to. This part of Wyoming wasn't anything like LA; her kid would be safe. She told herself that story over and over, praying it was true.

Again, Trevor popped into her head—he'd be with her as soon as he could for the search.

And after today, everyone in town would know that Trevor Montgomery was a father.

But that feeling didn't last long as horrible thoughts about everything that could happen to James barged back into her mind.

She pulled into her driveway, parked at a weird angle, because she didn't care, then rushed into the house. "James!" she called over and over as she checked each and every room, including the basement, hope and anxiety mounting in equal measure. But he wasn't there.

She called the school for an update and was heartbrokenly disappointed with no news as she clutched one of James's T-shirts to her chest. She went back to his room, the one he'd yet to sleep overnight in, and cried. *Where are you, James? Please come home.*

It wouldn't do any good to melt down, so she wiped her eyes with shaky hands, drank a glass of water and drove to the police station in the center of town.

"Is Chief Jorgensen here?" she asked at the front desk. The tiny office felt cluttered and closed in on her, or was that panic taking hold again?

An older silver-haired man appeared at an office door. He still looked good in his uniform, without the usual paunch of middle age, though his face was mapped with lines and fissures. "Julie Sterling?" he said. "I remember your parents."

Oh, yes, of course, he was the person who'd called her after her parents' fatal accident.

With a caring smile, he gestured for her to come. "Let's go into my office."

She followed him inside, but, unable to sit down, paced. "Any word? Anything?"

He solemnly shook his head. "Nothing yet. But I've pulled three units and put them exclusively on this task, and asked another handful of officers to work overtime so we can comb our county from one end to the other. Trevor provided me with a picture. He texted it to me—"

Wait, Trevor had a picture of James on his cell phone?

"May I see it? Uh, to make sure it's recent?"

The chief riffled through the piles of papers on his desk. "Here it is." He showed her the picture, which must have been taken just last weekend. It was a great picture of James smiling in the full-on Wyoming sun, an expansive range scattered with cows as a backdrop. "I've sent out a BOLO to our neighboring precincts, since we can't be sure that this should be an AMBER alert or not. Yet."

The thought of an AMBER alert—a child abduction alert—made Julie need to sit on the nearest chair. "What's a BOLO?" She hardly had enough breath to ask.

"Sorry. Be-on-lookout. It's usually used for suspects, but I justified it in this case, being your missing boy and all. And his most likely wanting to get to Cattleman Bluff." He stopped shuffling papers and looked directly at her. "We are covering every main road, as well as back roads and trails in this area. And we are working in coordination with the Laramie PD, which is doing the same, and the Wyoming highway patrol."

"In other words, you're doing everything you can to find my son."

"Yes, ma'am, we are."

She believed him, but until she had her son in her arms there was no way she'd rest. "What can I do?"

"If he has a cell phone, call him. Let him know how

worried you are. We've been calling, but it goes directly to voice mail."

Hoping they hadn't inundated James with calls that would fill up his voice-message storage, she dug into her purse and found her phone, immediately speed-dialing. Her brain had blanked out when the school had notified her. Since then her thoughts had been skipping everywhere, riding the waves of panic and full-out fear. Not thinking straight. Otherwise she would have thought of this earlier. Her call went straight to voice mail, so she texted.

Where are you? Please call me. I need to know you're okay. Please call. Love, Mom.

After several moments without response she texted again.

I'm worried sick, please reply.

She couldn't give in to the dark feelings flitting through her mind; she had to remain hopeful that her son was okay. If he ran away from school, once they found him and she hugged him, she'd throttle him for putting everyone through this horrible mess. She bit her lip to keep from crying. Someone entered the room behind her.

Soon large, strong hands rested on her shoulders, lightly massaging. It was Trevor, and his presence brought welcome support.

"Chief Jorgensen, any news about our son?"

"I was just filling Julie in on everything we're doing. Rest assured we're doing all we can. We'll find your boy. My suggestion is that you both go home and get some rest, because there's nothing for you to do here.

We've got your cell-phone numbers and I'll personally call the instant I hear anything. Keep trying to make contact on his phone."

Julie checked her phone screen hoping James had replied, and somehow she hadn't heard it come in. No luck.

"We understand, and appreciate your help. Julie, let's go home." Trevor took her hand and led her out of the office. How could he look so calm? Why wasn't he freaking out like her?

"Thank you," she remembered to say on her way out. Then halfway to the parked cars another question came to mind. "Who's with Anita and Chloe?"

"Once I did the initial pediatric assessment and the baby was fine, I asked Charlotte to come be with her until Anita's husband got home. I've made arrangements for the county visiting nurses to follow up with both mothers and babies tomorrow."

"I'll be fine, Trevor," Julie said, sticking out her chin with faux bravery. "I want to stay here in case James shows up."

Worry had etched into her brow so deep, Trevor thought she might never be able to smile again. If they didn't find the boy, he wouldn't either. He'd been fighting back his worries since the instant he'd heard the news; he could only imagine how Julie felt. "I don't think you should be alone. Let me stay with you."

"Please. Go home." She clutched her cell phone in her hand. "It's been a long day. You delivered two babies. Let Gretchen feed you some dinner."

"What about you?"

"I couldn't eat if I tried."

Not until James showed up. Trevor got it. He was beginning to understand exactly how she felt. It wasn't because her panic had worn off on him; no, this fear belonged to him and him alone. He loved his son. Barely knew the kid, but he knew love when he felt it. If this was what parenting felt like, how had Julie made it through nearly thirteen years alone?

Against his better judgment about leaving her by herself, and only because she was adamant about it, he'd do as she wished. "Okay, but you call me if you need me, and I'll check in every hour." Trevor took Julie into his arms and squeezed her close, loving the feel of her, thinking how precious she was as he kissed the top of her head. No words could describe how heartsick he was that something bad could have happened to their son. *Their son.* He cursed himself for not telling James who he was when he'd had the opportunity, and vowed to fix that as soon as he had the chance.

"I'll be fine, go," she whispered, just before she bussed his lips. He didn't believe her for one instant. She'd be a wreck until they found James.

"You need to know something first." He waited until he had her undivided attention. Would it be fair to tell her he loved her in the middle of chaos? Would she hear him? Nope, now wasn't ideal even though he'd mean it with every single fiber. He'd realized it last week when all he could think about was Julie, and how he couldn't wait to be with her every night. How easily they'd slipped into being comfortable together, how great they were in the sack. She'd reminded him why people needed to be open to love, because missing out was such a waste. It had been way too long since Kimberley. All the stand-ins since then had never measured up. Not until Julie. No, she wasn't ready to hear that, but there was something she needed to know right now that might, just might, give her hope. "I love our son."

Tears welled in her eyes as she stared at him with a grateful smile. "I believe you."

There was no way he wanted to leave, hell, they'd just had a major breakthrough, yet she pushed him toward the door, obviously wanting to be alone. The least a guy could do for the woman he loved was follow her wishes.

He glanced at his watch as he walked to his car; it was almost four-thirty. Soon it would be dark and the odds of finding James would be that much less. They'd first noticed him missing before seven this morning, but there was no telling when he'd taken off, or where on earth he could be by now. Could James be desperate enough to try to get back to California? What if Trevor never saw him again? A sick feeling balled up inside as he got into his car and headed for the ranch.

Halfway home, a text came in from Jack.

Your old man says to get home quick.

He pressed on the gas, worrying that his father might be having another stroke—what more could happen today?—and nearly fishtailed around the first curve, driving like a madman to get to his dad.

CHAPTER NINE

ONCE OFF THE HIGHWAY, heading for the Circle M Ranch, Trevor grabbed his cell and speed-dialed Jack, who answered on the first ring. "What's up with Dad? Is he okay?"

Instead of replying, Trevor heard the phone being shoved toward something. "I'm fine," the gravelly and irritated-sounding voice of his father said after fumbling with the device for a second or two. "When were you going to tell me you had a son?"

Thankful his father's health wasn't the issue, Trevor still needed to take a deep breath to tackle the topic of his son. So Chief Jorgensen had been in touch, had he? "Not before I told James. I figured he deserved to be the first to know when I had my coming-out party." He gritted his teeth. "Not sure I'll get the chance now. Any word?" He made a quick, one-handed maneuver to avoid a large rock in the road, and swerved.

"Hell, there's been all kinds of sightings reported. Old man McGilvary evidently picked up a kid outside of Thistle Gardens, gave him a ride on his flatbed for twenty-five miles or so. Someone else saw a kid riding a skateboard on the road, downhill, going at a pretty damn good pace, too."

"And no one thought something was wrong about that?"

"Plenty of folks thought something was wrong, just assumed it was some kid playing hooky from school, but no one thought enough about it to report it until later when word got out. And to my mind, the bigger question is how the hell did a kid get all the way to Thistle Gardens on a skateboard?"

The wonder of that feat had just occurred to Trevor, too.

"Look," his father said, "I think we've got a problem with a trespasser right now, and I think you need to check the stable when you get here. Zebulon just might have company."

Trevor's pulse jumped at the hint. "You saw him?"

"Let's say, I didn't investigate. I figure that's your job."

"Thanks, but *do not* let him take off again."

"You think I was born yesterday? We've got the stables under surveillance, but that kid has proved pretty damn nimble footed to make it all this way."

Trevor ended the call and tossed his cell phone onto the empty seat next to him. His immediate instinct was to call Julie, but he figured he should make contact with the boy first. He couldn't bear the thought of giving her false hope, in case nimble toes had moved on. She'd get that call the instant he had James locked in his arms.

It occurred to him how amazingly well his father had handled the situation. He hadn't made any accusations or flung any curse words. Hell, he'd even sounded amused by the possibility his grandson had managed to travel a hundred miles in a day with nothing but a skateboard and his wit, and was currently hiding out in the Circle M stables.

And they said old dogs like his dad couldn't learn new tricks.

Amazingly relieved, but still cautious and a tad edgy, Trevor arrived home and parked in his usual spot in the driveway. He took a long stealthy gaze in the direction of the stables, while pretending to adjust his hat, then casually started toward them. The clinch that'd had a hold of his stomach since finding out that James had run away tightened. Trevor could have lost his son before he ever really had him. But the kid had come here. Home.

He might have missed out on his son's being born and his first twelve years, but he sure as hell could be there for him from here on out.

As he entered the stables the scent of hay and horse dung hit him straight on. He thought he saw a shadow near the back of the building, down near Zebulon's stall. "James?" he said quietly. No answer.

The horse whinnied quietly, his usual greeting, ears twitching with lips pulled up exposing big old yellow teeth in greeting. His tail switched back and forth because of a couple of pesky flies. Trevor put his hand on Zebulon's neck, feeling his heat, then moved down to the muscular shoulder. The horse's nostrils flared and he made a quick exhalation. Yeah, he was trying to tell Trevor something. Evidence of carrot bits were by his front hooves. Trevor had shown James where they kept their fifty-pound-bag carrot stash just last Sunday.

"James, I know you're here, so please quit hiding. Your mother and I have been worried sick about you all day."

Still no answer.

"You're going to give your mom gray hairs, and she's way too young and pretty for that." He saw movement in his peripheral vision, and slowly turned to the left.

James stepped out from O'Reilly's stall, looking wrung out, filthy and probably wondering how much deep horse manure he'd be in for today's adventure.

And he was the most beautiful sight Trevor had seen since Julie first came back to town.

Trevor didn't want to overwhelm the boy with emotion, though that was the only thing pumping in his veins right then. He decided to go the old cowboy route, and make light of the God-awful situation—what could make a kid run away a hundred miles?

"Boy, you look as weary as a tomcat walkin' in mud."

For his effort Trevor received a head shake that said, *That was totally lame.* But Trevor smiled anyway, finally able to breathe again, and approached James. It was obvious the kid was using everything he had left to hold it together. Trevor recalled several misadventures of his own at that age. That was the problem with half-baked plans—they never turned out the way a kid imagined them.

He got to James and pulled him into his arms, finally holding his son, his only desire to comfort the boy. He smelled like day-long sweat, even though it had probably never hit seventy degrees today. James didn't resist, even kind of melted into Trevor's hold, resting his head on his chest. With Trevor finally having his son in his arms, relief washed over him like spring waterfalls at Medicine Bow Peak. A thought occurred to him—when had the child last been hugged by a man?

"You realize your momma's going to kill you after she kisses you to death, right?"

A muffled, quick laugh emitted from the area of Trevor's chest. Man, the kid was bony, and he even felt a little shaky right now. "You hungry? Thirsty?"

James nodded without letting go of his clutch around Trevor's back.

"Let me make a call to your mom first, then Gretchen will fix you up with something to eat." He reached for his phone to call Julie. He'd put it back into his shirt pocket when he'd gotten out of the car. James's hand shot out to intercept.

What was that about?

Everything went still, and Trevor honored James's hesitation. He glanced downward and found a boy's version of Julie's huge hazel eyes staring up at him. "Are you my father?"

Trevor took the time to swallow a sudden thickening in his throat. So that was what all this was about. If they'd just made time last weekend…ah, hell, now was no time for guilt.

"I am." He thought of a dozen sentences to add, but something about the moment called for simple and straightforward. He'd let James lead the way on this particular conversation. Not as he and Julie had planned, but nevertheless.

"Why didn't you want me?"

Not wanting to place blame anywhere, Trevor still needed to be honest. Julie would have to explain her side of the story when she felt the time was right. "I didn't know about you until a few weeks ago, after you and your mother moved home, and she came to work for me."

Tears welled in the boy's eyes. "All I ever wanted was a dad."

"And now you've got one. And I'm never letting you go, son. But you've got to understand that you have the greatest mom in the world. She's done her best all these years to love you enough for two people."

"Why didn't things work out with you guys?"

"That's a long story, and your momma deserves to be here when we tell it. Plus I can hear your stomach growling." Trevor moved his hands up from the boy's shoulders to around his neck, put him in a friendly headlock in the crook of one elbow and messed what he could of his short hair with the other hand. "I'm going to tell you a secret, just between you and me. Now that we're all together, I want us to be a family just as much as you always wanted a dad. And you know what that means."

"You're gonna marry Mom?"

"I'm going to do my best to convince her, but, no matter what, you're my son and I'm never letting you out of my life again."

To downplay the moment, as monumental as it was, Trevor eased the boy out of his arms and gently prodded him forward. "Let's get you some food before you pass out on my boots."

"She's pretty stubborn, you know," James said as they walked across the circular driveway toward the house.

"Tell me about it. But, hey, don't let on about my plans to your mom, okay? We're going to have to work this out one wrinkle at a time." He held James with one arm as they walked, and speed-dialed Julie with the other hand, and the moment she answered said, "I've got something you've been looking for."

Julie burst into the kitchen, smiling, crying and with her hair bouncing around her head, almost blocking her vision. Wondering how in God's name she'd made the drive over. She made a beeline for James, the most beautiful sight in the world, who'd stood the instant she'd entered the room.

"Mom, don't get mad."

"I'm way beyond that, James." She took him into her

arms and squeezed him nearly down to the bone. He felt great, even though he smelled like he might have stepped in a pile of horse manure somewhere along the way. "But I do expect answers, like how in the world did you get here?"

"The boy has a clever streak." Monty spoke up. "How much did you pay that teenager in Laramie to drive you almost fifty miles?"

Thankfully, James didn't look proud, though Monty's tone clearly said he admired her son's ingenuity. "Twenty dollars."

"The money I gave you for snacks all week?" Once Trevor had told her that her son was safe twenty minutes ago, her full-out alarm had switched to a different kind of concern and worry, and, of course, anger for his putting everyone, especially her, through this mess today. Was this behavior going to be a pattern? "What about the rest of the way?"

Trevor spoke up. "He rode in the bed of old man Mc-Gilvary's truck, then broke in his new skateboard the rest of the way."

"Until it got too bumpy, then I walked."

She clutched him to her heart again, even as that particular organ seemed to retreat to her toes with fear. His risky plan could have gone wrong in so many directions. New panic over all of the possibilities took hold, and she refused to let herself go down that path. The boy was here, in her arms, safe. Thank you, God. "That was crazy and impulsive, and…"

"And dangerous, I know, Mom, but—"

"No buts, you can't do things like this." She stared her son in the eyes, forcing him to look at her. She saw his own brand of regret mixed with confusion and maybe a little anger.

Trevor's firm hand latched onto her shoulder. "His grandfather did a great job of reading him the riot act. And it seems James had something on his mind that couldn't wait until the weekend."

His *grandfather*? "He knows?"

"Evidently the question was burning a hole in his brain."

And heart? Oh, but she'd handled everything wrong.

"If we'd told him last weekend like we'd planned," Trevor continued, "none of this would have happened."

"Mom, I promise I won't do anything stupid like this again. I was totally scared, too, but I needed to know if Montgomery was my dad, and I wanted to ask him in person."

She hugged him and kissed his stubbly hair, as a wet path trailed down her cheek. She sniffed, loving the stinky smell of her son, as long as he was safe and in her arms.

"Please don't make me go back to the academy. I promise I'll straighten up. Why can't I go to Cattleman Bluff Junior High?"

He couldn't be rewarded for running away, even if his desire to confront his father had been the reason. "Sterlings aren't quitters. You finish off the semester at the academy, prove you can be trusted, that you're back on track, then, after summer, we'll see about the fall semester."

In frustration, James looked at Trevor, presumably for backup. They'd better not have already had this conversation with a different solution, the new dad taking a soft line. With her hackles raised and ready for a fight, she nailed Trevor's unwavering eyes.

Trevor had the good sense to raise his hands and step out of this battle. "I won't interfere with whatever your mom decides. I wouldn't dare," he added, to lighten the quickly intensifying atmosphere.

Surprisingly, James didn't complain, he just nodded sullenly, in defeat. After all, it was his first encounter with both of his parents, and maybe, underneath the disappointment of not getting his way, he actually appreciated having rules he couldn't stray from. Having parents, and a grandfather, who laid them down in a united front. Julie could hope anyway.

Jumping back to even more practical thoughts. "Have you eaten?"

"He had two sandwiches and three glasses of milk!" Gretchen spoke up, from her quiet spot in the shadows pretending to move crumbs around the counter with a sponge so she could stick around for the fireworks.

"Thank you." Julie looked around the room at what could be a bunch of strangers to James, but found three pairs of caring eyes staring at her son. "Then we need to get you showered and take you back to school. Oh, my gosh, we've got to tell them—"

"Already taken care of," Monty said. "I gave Chief Jorgensen a call. He said he'd see to everything else."

"I need to call the school and make sure they haven't expelled him or anything, I guess."

"I doubt they'll expel him, but I'm sure James will have some kind of punishment," Trevor said. "You agreed to take it like a man, right?"

James nodded again, if only halfheartedly. "I should probably leave my skateboard here, so they won't take it away from me."

James's last little attempt to get away with something made the entire group in the Montgomery kitchen crack up.

After the day she'd been through, the laughter over

the audacity of her son was welcomed beyond this frazzled mother's wildest imagination.

Julie and Trevor managed to deliver James back to the academy twenty minutes before lights out, where he quickly learned of his fate. He'd miss out on free time for the next month, and he wouldn't be able to go home the next weekend, instead having been assigned to the groundskeeper as extra help. He didn't complain, maybe because Trevor was there and he didn't want to come off as weak, but Julie was grateful he took his punishment without complaint.

They did however learn that just because he couldn't come home, it didn't mean they couldn't come and have dinner with him on Sunday, and so they made plans to bring him something special.

After a long hug, and many silent prayers of thanks that her son was safe, Julie stepped back and let Trevor have his turn.

Trevor moved in, and when James held out his hand for a shake he sidestepped it in favor of a fatherly hug. "Don't even think about pulling any more lame-brain escapes, okay?" Though he said it sternly, it was clear he'd laid down the law with love.

James must have realized the same thing, because he pulled back from the hug with a tentative smile. "Today's will last for a while, I guess."

"The next time you have a hankering to come home, you call your mother or me and we'll see what we can do. You're too damn young to hitchhike. What were you thinking?" He grabbed James back and pretended to rough him up a little. James ate it up and dished some out, too.

"Okay, you too, quit competing for most immature."

Julie smiled, though sad and feeling a little empty knowing they had to leave her son behind.

As James was escorted off to his room, he looked over his shoulder. "Bye, Mom, I love you."

"I love you, too."

"Uh, do I call you Dad now?"

"I'd be honored if you would."

It was almost midnight when Trevor delivered Julie home. They'd been at it nonstop all day with work, two deliveries, news of James having gone missing, going crazy waiting for word about him, then the surprise beyond all surprises, James finding his way to Trevor's ranch in order to ask if he was his father.

What a day. Yet, spending so much time with Trevor had been her life saver. He'd kept her sane and functioning, and just thinking about how it would have been without his steady presence made her queasy. She reached across the car and took his hand. As always, his response was quick and welcoming.

He glanced at her just before turning into her driveway, that familiar look she'd come to know as desire and something deeper. As emotionally wrung out as she was, his obvious need was contagious.

When he parked, she leaned across, took his face in her hands and kissed him, silently promising they'd be spending more time together tonight. "I don't know what I would have done without your help today."

His hand cupped her ear and eased her back toward his mouth. Tender, warm lips waited to start slow, but soon devour her mouth. The car windows steamed up and the thought of seducing him here versus on her big and comfortable bed helped Julie break away.

"Let's go inside. Will you stay with me tonight?"

He didn't need to answer; the sexy smile lifting the corner of his mouth said it all.

Over the past few weeks they'd explored just about every position and technique for making love, and Trevor proved to have quite a repertoire. She'd become the lucky recipient of his single-minded attention. Surprisingly, he'd brought out a creative side to Julie that she'd never known she had before. To be honest, though being with Trevor was exciting no matter what they did, she preferred good old vanilla, face-to-face sex, watching his eyes and expressions in the most intimate moments.

Right now he sat with his back against the headboard, her on his lap, him straight and tight inside her. His hands held her hips as she moved over him, lifting, lowering, speeding up, slowing down, all while their heated stares fused together. His nostrils flared when she moved a certain way, her breath caught when he bucked from beneath. The scent of sex as intoxicating as the sounds of their bodies slapping together. The only time she wasn't looking at him was when his mouth was locked onto hers, pillaging with his tongue, as she did the same. Frantic and crazy, they tore away at each other as if the cares, tension and worries of the day couldn't be worked out any other way.

They needed each other with a capital N, and the level of stimulation they'd whipped up in record time tonight felt nearly earth-shattering. She grabbed the headboard on either side of his ears to anchor herself as her desire heightened, driving her to bear down on his arousal, then let him work his wonders from beneath as she held perfectly still.

Tongue deep in a kiss, he pulled away from her mouth, delving into the side of her neck with his wet lips, panting as she quickened her movements. "Marry me, Julie." His strained whisper blew over the shell of her ear.

She was over halfway to that wonderful land of sexual free fall when his words, like a taut bungee cord, pulled her back. What had he just said?

He moved her arms from the headboard and pinned them behind her back with a single hand, then lifted her up and flipped her onto the mattress with the other, and came at her with purpose and determination she'd never experienced with him before. He slowed his thrusts just long enough to get the words out. "Marry me."

Stunned to silence, and nearly lost to sex-over-reason, she tightened her thighs around his hips and bucked into him, selfishly going for release to avoid his mind-boggling question.

He obliged her raw need and took her deep, deep inside to the center of her universe where big things were about to happen. His rapid-fire penetration made tingles turn to shimmering eruptions, then delectable spasms before she went helpless to the explosions pounding through her nerve endings. Her guttural moan and inner gripping and throbbing around his rigid lunges soon took him to what she knew was his blackout place. All that seemed left of the world for those few priceless moments together imploded inside as she came again, and she sensed how his climax wiped him out, one synapsis after another, until he was totally spent, just like her.

It took forever to recover, to crawl out from her cave of stimulation and release. But out of that sexual fog she emerged as her head cleared one thought at a time until she remembered. Trevor had just asked her to marry him!

Trevor held Julie by her arms, the fresh-from-sex blush blooming across her chest and cheeks. Her hair was damp and tightly curled around her face. This was how he loved seeing her, having been taken by him, defenseless against him, with Julie having the same effect on him. They needed each other. When he'd been with Kimberley, he'd thought he wanted sophistication and high breeding, but that had clearly backfired. His choosing a simpler life, loyal to his roots, had held little appeal for her.

Julie was different; she'd come home to find what she'd left behind, hoping to make things right for her son. Little did she know it was exactly what she'd needed, too. Now older and wiser, how could Trevor make her see that if she didn't get it?

She'd avoided answering his proposal, and he couldn't blame her, having been completely distracted by sex himself, but still, it burned and felt too reminiscent of when he'd opened up to Kimberley. How it had felt as if she'd ripped his heart out with her refusal.

Would Julie do the same?

A soft hand bracketed his face. "Trevor, you took me by surprise asking me to marry you."

He turned his cheek and kissed the palm of her hand. "I mean it, I want to marry you, be your husband and James's full-time father."

Silence lingered between them; it tore at that last bit of scarred tissue. Her gaze intent, she seemed to study every millimeter of his face. Finally, she opened her mouth. "Sometimes the right thing to do doesn't measure up to being right for each other."

"You don't think we're right for each other? We're perfect for each other, and we have a kid. Don't you see, our getting married will solve all your problems?"

"James is still recovering from Mark leading him on, then ripping hope right out of him. Can you imagine how a boy would feel being told, 'You're in the way, kid. Let's do something about that. I don't want you. I just want your mother'?" She pleaded with her eyes. "I wouldn't dare spring another relationship on him just yet. Not even with his birth father."

He grabbed her shoulder and made sure her gaze turned back to his. "That sounds way too clinical. I'm his father, never knew he was born. That was your decision. Now I'm saying it's time for me to make some decisions about the boy. I want to be a family, and I want you to be my wife."

She closed her eyes and crinkled her brows, shutting him out. "It's not fair to work a girl up and pop that question out of the blue. I need to get things straight in my mind, and being naked with you doesn't help at all."

"Are you asking for some space?"

"I think so. Just a breather, some time out. Please understand, this can't be some pat reaction. You deserve better. James deserves better."

"You deserve love, Julie bean. You deserve to be happy. I can make you happy. Hell, I already have. You can't deny that."

She shook her head. "I'm not. I'm just asking you to give me a chance to work this out my way. When I get married I want it to be for all of the right reasons."

Trevor stood, grabbed his pile of clothes from the chair and headed for the bathroom. Five minutes later when he emerged, dressed and a little clearer headed, he found Julie right where he'd left her, lying on the bed, staring at the ceiling. Though now she was covered by a sheet. She glanced his way.

"I want to know one thing before I leave here tonight." He straightened his shoulders and took the plunge. "Do you love me?"

She stirred, sat up; there was that look of doe in head-lights again. How could he have misread all the signs these past few weeks?

"I, uh, I've never felt this way about anyone but you, Trevor, but I—"

She was taking too long, making terrible excuses; he couldn't stand it. "Here's the deal—I love you," he said, matter-of-fact, then turned to leave the bedroom. He made it all the way out the front door without a peep from the woman he'd just admitted he loved and wanted to marry.

Besides slamming his fist into a wall, what the hell was he supposed to do now?

CHAPTER TEN

JULIE ROLLED ONTO her stomach and cried as hard as she
had the night when she'd first found out she was pregnant, and again when she'd realized she would have to
give up everything in her life back home to move to Los
Angeles. She'd been too eager for her happily-ever-after
with Mark and had gotten a swift kick to the gut as a re-
sult. She couldn't set herself up to go through that again.

Trevor wanted with all his heart to do the right thing,
because that was what he did in life: Go to med school
like his brother, become a family-practice doctor instead
of a specialist in some top-paying field, open a clinic
in his sleepy little hometown instead of a big practice
in an exciting city.

Marry a woman because he'd knocked her up once
upon a time?

After spending all these weeks together, she sensed
theirs was a different relationship, full of heat and crazy
good times on one hand, yet still managing a respectful
professional relationship on the other. With herself as the
exception, she wasn't sure a person, Trevor, could fall
in love that quickly, and above all she worried that he
was once again *only* doing what was right and expected
of him.

Yet hadn't she fallen in love with him at seventeen

based purely on a few summer parties and one night of losing her virginity?

But that had been immature love. She was a grown woman now and needed to act like one. Her heart had been hinting at something different these days. Sometimes more blatant. She was pretty sure it was love, but until she was convinced Trevor wasn't forcing the issue because it was the right thing to do, she'd keep her little secret.

She'd literally bit her tongue to keep from saying, *Yes, I love you, with all my heart.* It would have been true, but it was the last thing he should hear right now. He needed to be sure on his own. She couldn't dare influence him. Not at this most delicate juncture with James.

As hard as it would be, she'd have to ride this one out until she trusted Trevor Montgomery loved her for her, and not because she'd made him a father.

Thursday and Friday had been tough at work, but both Julie and Trevor had managed. Word traveled fast, and Rita and Charlotte knew the score about James, and both seemed particularly interested in the history leading up to it, but Julie was in no mood to fill anyone in. Trevor mostly avoided Julie at work, and it hurt, but she'd asked for it with her stupid insecurity.

On Saturday, Trevor also left Julie alone, and she was glad since she definitely needed a recovery day. Though time and time again she thought about James having to work with the groundskeeper as part of his penance. While she pretended to sort through more of her parents' things, she also thought about Trevor. He'd told her he loved her and wanted to marry her. The idea of spending the rest of her life with such a wonderful man gave her chills. Could he really love her for her?

By early Sunday afternoon, she was dressed and ready for Trevor when he showed up exactly on time for the ride out to the military school. He didn't play fair with his two-day beard growth and perfectly combed hair, wearing a taupe-colored corduroy blazer with a brown grid-checked shirt with jeans, and of course his weekend, broken-in boots. Making the blaring statement, *Yes, I'm for real*. Rancher, doctor, sexy as hell, all around great guy.

"Hey," she said.

He nodded, smiled and immediately dipped his head to kiss her hello. He also managed to kiss the train of thought right out of her brain. Whatever it had been. Oh, right—all around great guy.

"You ready?" he asked.

"Yes." They were halfway out to the car when she remembered she'd made brownies for James, and rushed back into the house to get them.

"I thought he might like a cheeseburger tonight, but guessed we should wait until we got there to pick one up," Trevor said once she was in his car.

That was exactly what she'd been thinking! "Good idea. Now all we need to do is find where his favorite burger chain is in Laramie."

"Already looked it up. It's five minutes away from the school."

The guy was the most intuitive and considerate man she'd ever met. Not to mention he already knew James's favorite hamburger joint.

James was happily surprised to get his burger and fries for dinner, and Julie's homemade brownies brought a wave of nostalgia to his eyes. But he didn't complain about his punishment for running away from school.

"I know I shouldn't brag about getting in trouble, but

a couple of the senior high school kids think I'm cool now. Before they didn't know who I was."

"Don't let that go to your head," Trevor said.

"I won't."

The ease with which Trevor interacted with James amazed Julie. They'd missed twelve years and now seemed to pick up as if they'd always known each other.

On the ride home, Trevor brought up the taboo subject. Again.

"So I've been doing some thinking," he began while heading down Interstate 80. "Since you're all into the practical side of things, I guess it will be up to me to convince you to listen to your heart and what it's telling you, and to tune out your brain. Just tune it out."

"Easier said than done."

"Here's how I see it. I'm the missing piece in your family puzzle. All I'm asking for is a chance to be there for our son." He glanced her way, then added, "And a chance to love you like you deserve." He looked back to the road before adding, "Without reservation."

Oh, what she'd give to let go and love like that. She'd done it once with Trevor when she was really young and it'd changed her life. She'd had to give up her romanticizing and dive into the realities of life and never look back. Now, here he was again, dangling the perfect little family fantasy, and it tore at her better judgment. Being practical and toughened by the hard knocks in life had been her survival. Could he make that dream come true? Should she dare to believe him?

"So I've decided," he continued. "We have to start over."

"What?"

"The only way I'm going to win you over is to do some old-time courting. The way a lady deserves. First we'll date, then we'll see how things go before we jump into marriage. How does that sound?"

"Like the craziest idea I've ever heard." But she loved it. Loved him for thinking it up.

"Well, you better clear your calendar because I've got the whole week planned, and the week after that and if necessary the week after that."

"Three weeks to marriage? I'd call that speed dating."

"Call it whatever you like, but that's what we're going to do." The man looked so utterly pleased with himself, she could hardly stand it.

"And you're just expecting me to go along with this?"

"If you know what's good for you. Besides, I've had expert input."

"Oh, really?"

"James has given me a list of your favorites for starters."

"What? You got James involved?"

"Hell, he's the one who suggested it."

Her son suggested they date for a while? She needed to shake her head in order to think straight for the rest of the ride home.

As if the night hadn't been brimming with surprises already, the biggest came when Trevor walked her to the door, kissed her goodnight, then turned and went straight to his car.

The man was definitely up to something. The thought of being the center of his attention put a grin on her face the size of the crescent moon perched up in that huge Wyoming sky as she stood and watched him drive off.

First thing Monday morning Julie found a bright, perfectly arranged spring bouquet on her desk with an invitation for a special dinner that night at Bartalotti's, the only Italian restaurant in Cattleman Bluff. When

they arrived, she found Trevor had reserved the entire
place just for them with the excuse it was their seven-
week anniversary from when he'd hired her and she'd
told him he was a father.

Once again, when he took her home, he only gave her
a chaste kiss, reminded her about their plans for a quiet
walk after the morning clinic on Tuesday, and took off.
This plan of his, where he intended to spend good old-
fashioned time with her and keep hands off the mer-
chandise, left her confused but completely infatuated
with the big doctor rancher.

Tuesday morning clinic turned out to be a madhouse
with Dustin Duarte showing early signs of appendici-
tis, Janine Littleton arriving with tonsillitis for the third
time in as many months and Brian Whiteside suffering
from a massive allergic reaction to last night's shrimp
tacos. While Trevor ran STAT lab tests on Dustin and
arranged for transportation to Laramie General Hospital, and Charlotte began IV antibiotics on Janine, Julie
injected adrenaline into Brian along with a massive dose
of Benadryl, and stayed with him until the periorbital
swelling began to recede.

By the time one o'clock rolled around, Julie was ready
for a nap, not a walk, but Trevor wouldn't back down.

"It's a beautiful day—the fresh air will do you good.
Besides, I'm taking you to my secret place, the one with
a waterfall."

"How many secret places do you have?" How could
she refuse?

Two hours later, after sharing a bottle of three blended
red wines with crusty bread and Gretchen's homemade
Asiago cheese, which smelled like yogurt and butter,
but tasted surprisingly sweet, she sighed. Didn't most
things taste or seem sweeter with Trevor?

Her head rested on Trevor's lap beside a beautiful and secluded natural pool and waterfall. It was shallow enough to wade in, but they didn't on this April day. They were on a blanket and he tenderly stroked her hair. She thought she might be in heaven, except for the strong stench of steer roaming the family ranch in the distant background wafting over her nostrils thanks to a constant, though gentle, breeze.

"Growing up, I used to come here when I needed to think. This is where I first planned we'd bring James to tell him. It's where I came when they told me Cole had broken his neck and would be in the hospital for a long time." He played with a group of curls along the nape of her neck, tingles fanning out over her shoulders. "I came here when I found out my mom had cancer." His fingers quit fidgeting with her hair. "And I came her the morning after I took a certain girl's virginity. I wanted to kick myself over that."

Julie's hand reached for the fingers now resting on her shoulder, and squeezed. He bent forward and kissed her lightly.

"Was I your only virgin?" His face was upside down over hers, yet she saw his eyebrows lift.

A look passed through his eyes as if he'd never really thought about that aspect before. "I'm pretty damn sure you were." He bent and kissed her again, but only a fleeting kiss. "And you're the only woman I have a son with. That makes you pretty damn special, too, doesn't it?"

She sat up and kissed him again, but on purpose he kept things from heating up.

Wednesday morning Julie found a box of chocolates on her desk with an invitation to share dawn with him on horseback Thursday morning. Presuming she'd say yes, he went ahead and gave her directions for where to meet and even what to wear. When she opened the candy, she was amazed that all of the dark chocolates she loved were there. He'd definitely had inside information from James on choosing every single one of the truffles, nuts and caramels. The thought of Trevor and James whispering over the phone, collaborating on Julie's likes and dislikes, tickled her, and she spent her day wearing a silly grin.

The next morning, still dark before sunrise, when she showed up in broken-in jeans and old hiking boots— because she hadn't been on a horse since she lived in Cattleman Bluff—Trevor looked handsome, as if he'd been up for hours. He introduced her to O'Reilly.

"This is our very own Connemara pony. Dad brought her home from Ireland about five years ago."

The dark brown pony had calico markings on her legs, which made her look very sporting. "She's beautiful, but I haven't been on a horse for—"

"This girl is perfect for you. She's sure-footed and has a calm temperament. Now quit worrying or we'll miss the sunrise." With that, he helped her onto the saddle, gave her a few quick instructions about how to use the reins, which quickly came back to her, then he got on Zebulon and they took off.

The crisp morning breeze chilled her cheeks and hands as O'Reilly followed Trevor and Zebulon's lead, cantering toward the low eastern hills in the distance. The distinct scent of open-range grass brought back memories from when she'd been a kid. Within minutes peach-colored clouds broke open for a bright burst of sunlight. The sight would be embedded into Julie's heart along with a sense of wonder as she realized—and was totally thankful—that these were special gifts Trevor shared with her. When had she felt this alive or important, other than when she made love with him?

He circled around, loping, then rode up beside her and pulled out his cell phone. "I promised James a picture." He took her reins and moved O'Reilly closer. Julie leaned in and, with the breaking dawn behind them, he took a few selfies of them smiling like the sunrise, until he found one he really liked tinted with that special golden glow of early morning. Her heart felt the way the picture looked.

"There," he said, as he pushed send. "That will make Jimmy smile."

"Jimmy? I've never called him that, not even when he was a baby."

"He doesn't seem to mind when I call him that, Julie bean. Here, I'm sending you a copy, too."

She heard Trevor's phone ding. "See, he already responded. He said 'awesome.'" Trevor's full-out grin nudged brighter that golden feeling building inside.

"How often do you talk to him?"

"I call him every night to catch up on things. Sometimes we text during the day. He thought that black widow spider bite we treated yesterday was both gross yet dope. You know that means—"

"I know what dope means." She'd been a mother for twelve years but suddenly Trevor was an expert? Rather than annoying her, it endeared him to her beyond explanation.

It didn't go unnoticed how Trevor's eyes lit up every time he talked about James. It also didn't go unnoticed how the dawn's soft colors made this already-handsome man downright stunning. Which made her miss making love to him all the more. The last thing that hadn't gone unnoticed since he'd started courting her was how he only kissed her hello and goodbye. And, somehow, that was pretty damn sexy, too.

By the time he'd taken her for a quick breakfast and they arrived at work, Julie felt more alive than ever before. And one more feeling nudged its way into her thoughts—love. What wasn't to love about Trevor?

These dates went on for the next two weeks, driving Julie crazy with longing for Mr. Proper Medicine Man, but he seemed hell-bent on not pressuring her about sex. The problem was she was about ready to beg him to strip naked and jump into the sack with her. Pretty please with sugar on top.

The second Friday morning of their two weeks of dating, Julie found a small box on her office desk. Her pulse stumbled over what the meaning might be. Jittery fingers found it hard to untie the bow and open the box, but, determined, she made her way inside to find a beautiful smoky topaz pendant on a delicate gold chain.

He must have been standing right outside, because the instant she gasped over the gift his grinning face popped around the corner of the door. "I chose smoky topaz because it reminds me of your eyes."

She stepped around her desk and approached him, pulled him inside by gathering the stethoscope hanging around his neck and tugging, then closed the door. Up on her toes, she threw her arms around his neck and kissed him the way she'd missed since he'd started courting her.

His hands settled at her back, hip level, as he eased her closer, massaging and kneading her hips. Yeah, just as she thought, he missed making out, too.

"You're driving me crazy," she said, over his lips.

"Crazy with love, I hope." He nipped her pouting lower lip, sending a thrill straight to her navel, and below.

"Definitely crazy with lust." Playing hard to get really was fun. She went off her toes, forearms still rest-ing on his shoulders, as she studied his face. "You're one damn fine-looking cowboy, Dr. Montgomery. Want to see me naked?"

She saw the flash of hunger in his eyes. These two weeks had to have been just as hard for him as they'd been for her. "I think about it every day." His coarse whisper turned her on more than any crazy make-out session. She really *needed* to have sex with him!

"Then why are we doing this?"

"You don't like being courted?"

"I love it, but I liked what we had before, too."

He inhaled slowly, savoring what she figured was a passing image of what they'd shared before. So expres-sive was his face that she could practically see what he was thinking. "I loved what we had before, too, but it didn't get me anywhere."

She made an incredulous face. "It got you everywhere, mister."

He bit back something he started to say, and she re-alized he'd told her he loved her and she hadn't been able to say it to him. But things had changed in the past two weeks. She'd let herself fall harder for the guy she'd fallen hard for years ago. He'd gone out of his way to show her how much he cared. Now it was her turn to show—and tell—him.

"Be at my place at seven on the dot," she said.

A knock on the office door drew them out of their lovers' standoff. "Julie? Your first patient is in Exam Room One," came Lotte's reedy voice.

"I'll be right there," Julie said without tearing her gaze from his.

"Wear that necklace tonight," he said, releasing her from his embrace.

"It might be all I wear," she teased, loving the way his deep, dark eyes instantly went darker.

Julie thought about wrapping her body in kitchen plastic wrap and putting a big red bow on her chest to greet Trevor, but decided against that as it seemed too desperate, not to mention hard to get out of. But if she didn't get through to him tonight about how much she loved being with him, she'd definitely try that next time.

She wore a slinky little black number, cut high enough to show lots of leg, and put on the highest heels she owned, which happened to be red. She'd skipped the bra, wearing only a lacy thong beneath. And of course the topaz pendant slipped perfectly between the tops of her breasts. She'd let her hair go wild, the way it always wanted, and brightened her eyes with mascara, then her lips with red lip gloss. She'd dabbed perfume behind her ears, inside her elbows and along her shoulders, though her finger had traced downward to her cleavage before she'd finished. Not bad for a heavy hint, if she did say so herself.

Now, when the moment was right, she'd tell Trevor that she loved him. And mean it with everything she had.

His knock came at precisely seven, and she flung open the door, anxious to see that blaze in his eyes just for her. He didn't disappoint, with the addition of a slow, sexy-as-hell smile. That smile alone set off a tingle fest.

"Hi." Someone had to say it.

"You look great," he said, stepping inside.

"So is that enough small talk? Can we make love now?"

The corner of his mouth quirked upward. "I'd like to take some time looking at you like that, if you don't mind."

"Feel free to sample the wares." Okay, apparently she *was* going for desperate.

He stepped closer but didn't touch her. "You really want to get together tonight, don't you?"

Feeling stripped naked by his eyes, and maybe a tiny bit embarrassed over being so blatant, she nodded. "Are you going to drop that courting stuff and get down to business?"

One brow made a subtle rise. "On one condition."

"Again with the rules?" She sighed, desperation flooding back in.

"I'll do everything you want me to, and more, then do it all again if you'll answer one question."

She stood quiet, waiting.

Not losing eye contact, he dropped to one knee and took her hand. "Julie Sterling, will you marry me?"

She gulped in a breath, feeling forced to make a quick decision that wasn't just for her, but for her son, too. She'd been prepared to tell Trevor she loved him, but was she ready to marry him? Why was he always one step ahead of her?

Her brief hesitation gave Trevor time to take his cell phone out of his back pocket and speed-dial. "Hey, son, would it be okay with you if I asked your mother to marry me?"

All she heard on the other end of the cell was *"Whoo-hoo!"*

"I take that as a yes," Trevor said, smiling, after the noise quieted down. "Okay, now all I have to do is convince your stubborn mother." He shut off his phone, then stood back up and took her hands in his. "I know I've been hitting pretty heavy on this topic, but I know it's right and the best thing I've ever wanted. But I'm not hearing the same from you."

Her resistance on principle and practicality had forced Trevor to prove how much he loved her. And boy had he ever! As long as she'd had the tiniest doubt, she would have carried a secret around that her man only married her to be a father to their son, and the thought of that stung too much to consider. But they'd had these past two weeks together, and he'd changed everything. A wise man.

"Trevor, if I didn't know positively, beyond a doubt, that I love you, I'd never agree to marry you."

His grip tightened ever so slightly. "Have you figured that out yet?"

Her smile had to give her away. "Yes. I love you. I do." Now was that so hard? "I thought I loved you when I was seventeen, but I was so wrong. Thank you for showing me what love is, for helping me trust again, and for giving me feelings I never dared dream I could have. I love you, Trevor."

He pulled her tight to his chest, the leftover cool night air on his clothes soon disappearing. Julie couldn't believe how happy she felt. How completely sure that she'd found her perfect man—a country doctor with a heart of gold.

Her hands bracketed his jaw as she kissed him. A kiss she'd never forget.

A text ding went off in his pocket. Both knowing it was from James, Trevor answered it. "He wants to know what your answer was."

They grinned at each other, as if they'd been a family for years. "Tell him yes, all caps."

Trevor did as he was told, his grin stretching wider

while he sent it, then shut down his phone. His dark eyes found hers again, a mischievous glint dancing between them. "Well, you kept your end of the bargain, I guess I'd better keep mine, Julie bean."

With that, he bent and picked her up, then carried her toward the bedroom. "Nice shoes," he said on their way.

* * * * *

FATHER FOR HER
NEWBORN BABY

BY
LYNNE MARSHALL

Published in Great Britain 2015
by Mills & Boon, an imprint of Harlequin (UK) Limited,
Eton House, 18-24 Paradise Road, Richmond, Surrey, TW9 1SR

© 2015 Janet Maarschalk

ISBN: 978-0-263-24736-7

Harlequin (UK) Limited's policy is to use papers that are natural,
renewable and recyclable products and made from wood grown in
sustainable forests. The logging and manufacturing processes conform
to the legal environmental regulations of the country of origin.

Printed and bound in Spain
by CPI, Barcelona

To John-Philip and Kaitlyn for helping me see magic
where a gnarly oak tree stood on that ranch.
Your wedding inspired me to write
a gorgeous scene for my characters.

And to granddaughter Thea
for being the inspiration for Flora.

Books by Lynne Marshall

Mills & Boon® Medical Romance™

Temporary Doctor, Surprise Father
The Boss and Nurse Albright
The Heart Doctor and the Baby
The Christmas Baby Bump
Dr Tall, Dark...and Dangerous?
NYC Angels: Making the Surgeon Smile
200 Harley Street: American Surgeon in London

**Visit the author profile page at
millsandboon.co.uk for more titles**

PROLOGUE

LIZZIE SILVA PUMPED the air. "Yes!"

I've got a job. Thank you, world! She glanced at Flora, nestled in her arm having just finished nursing, and then went completely still, afraid the sudden movement might set the baby off again. Maybe it had been the turmoil of her pregnancy, and stress and medical school had certainly taken a toll, but Flora had been born crying and had rarely stopped since. Or maybe it was because Flora sensed Lizzie didn't have a clue about being a mother. Her heart squeezed as it always did when she thought about that. But wouldn't things be better now?

She held her breath and lifted Flora to her shoulder and patted her back. "We're going to have our first adventure together," she cooed as Flora burped. "Good girl." As if the delivery and first three months of her daughter's life hadn't been adventure enough already.

She'd just ended a phone call with her favorite professor from medical school, the man who'd become a surrogate father, probably out of pity, or guilt, but nevertheless. Even now, since she'd broken up with his son, he was looking out for her and his granddaughter.

"We're moving to Wyoming. Can you imagine?" She

smiled and rubbed her cheek against her baby's fuzzy head. So far, so good; Flora was sleeping. At last!

Never in her life had she felt such love. This precious little child would know how to trust because Lizzie promised with all of her heart never to let her down. Ever since Flora had been born, she'd dreamed of getting her out of the city, of giving her a better start than she'd had. Now this job opportunity had come out of nowhere, as if answering her prayer, and deep down she believed better things would follow if she said yes.

She'd walked off her last temporary job at the Boston clinic dealing with drug addicts. Especially when she'd had to counsel the meth head who was pregnant. It'd hit too close to home because of her own mother. Add in her new-parent stress and little sleep and she'd quit that very afternoon.

Flora suffered with colic and kept her up most nights, and Lizzie was always tired, but she'd never leave her daughter. She knew how it felt to be left behind as a baby by her mother, and ten years later by her grandmother, even though the dear woman couldn't control the stroke that had killed her. She knew the constant disappointment as foster home after foster home had let her go. Until she was fifteen and met Janie. Thank God for Janie, yet even she'd let her down. *Why did people choose to keep cancer a secret?* She would have dropped everything to be by her side. But then maybe that was what Janie had been afraid of. The woman had been intent on helping Lizzie get a hand up in life.

If it weren't for Janie Tuttle she'd never be a new graduate doctor, licensed and all. She never would have reached for the stars with a dream of going to college.

She cuddled Flora closer as the baby finally settled

into deep sleep. She'd been at her wit's end all evening, as usual, not knowing what she was doing wrong, or why her baby cried so much. Not to mention worrying about how she'd support the two of them. She'd finally calmed Flora by nursing her again, then the cell phone had buzzed, and, as she'd often found herself doing at any little noise, she'd held her breath waiting for her daughter to start crying again. But this time she hadn't. Then the new temporary job offer had come. Beggars couldn't be choosers. Maybe this was a good omen?

No matter how much of a challenge this little one was, she loved how her child smelled and felt, and how she breathed unevenly. Basically, she loved everything about her, even when she was inconsolable with colic. Could the colic somehow be her fault? Mother's love cut to the center of her most sacred feelings. Poor kid got stuck with her. Tears welled in her eyes. "I'll never let you down, sweetheart. I promise. Never," she whispered, shaking. There was no way she'd ever be able to live up to that promise, since she basically didn't know what she was doing as a mother. Yet she hoped her unstoppable love would get through to her daughter.

Fear shuddered through her for her daughter's sake, as she worried that life might prove her wrong. This time she blamed it on postpartum hormones rather than her mounting insecurity as a parent. She had to face the fact she was a mess, a total wreck.

All the street smarts in the world couldn't make up for not having a clue how to be a mother, and the tough facade clearly didn't work with parenting.

She'd been anything but a skilled mother so far, feeling nothing short of a feeding machine, completely out of her depth. Due to Flora's colic, she functioned on minimal sleep; most days she felt like some kind of half monster, half human thing slogging through the hours. But so far they'd both survived. Somehow.

Becoming a mother had been a shock. Especially without backup. Dave Rivers had been another in a long list of disappointments, turning out to be nothing more than a biological father. And the most recent disappointment, not getting a residency at any of the hospitals where she'd applied, was further proof she was a screwup. Then walking off the only job she could find…

She gingerly laid Flora in her cradle, held her breath again and watched the baby settle into deeper sleep. *Whew.* Lizzie sat on her own bed in the single-room apartment she'd rented all through medical school, trying her best not to make a single sound.

Panic had riddled her when she'd gotten the same rejection five different times. And she hadn't exactly been able to hit the pavement looking for work when she'd been about to pop with a baby on board, so she'd taken whatever she could get—the free clinic. She'd never felt more helpless in her adult life, but she'd gone into labor and become a mother, and now three months later was still trying to get her life back on track.

Lying back on her pillow, she willed the negative thoughts from her mind, choosing to take the opportunity to rest while Flora slept. She had a chance to start afresh, to give her baby an opportunity she'd never had. Dr. Rivers had promised the small medical clinic could accommodate her every need. She needed the job and believed it could be the start of a new life for her and her daughter. She needed that new start. *Please, please, make it so.*

Anxiety grabbed hold again. There was so much to do

before Saturday when she'd board a plane for Wyoming and begin their new start.

Thank you, Dr. Rivers, for believing in me. And for helping these last few months.

She had a job.

Yes!

CHAPTER ONE

It was Cole Montgomery's turn to step up for the family. He'd been absent far too long. While his brother, Trevor, was away he needed to oversee the ranch and help his father, the man he'd avoided most of his adult life. And because Cole was a doctor, he'd promised to keep the Cattleman Bluff Medical Clinic running while Trevor took a well-deserved honeymoon and vacation. At his sides, his fingers twitched. To be honest, he didn't know if he had what it took to take the reins at home, or the patience to deal with his father.

He stood off to the side of the wedding party, feeling more of a bystander than a part of the family. It was his younger brother, Trevor's turn to shine today, being the first of the brothers to marry. Plus, Trevor had a ready-made family with his beautiful new wife, Julie, originally a Cattleman Bluff girl, and the son Trevor never knew about until four months ago, James. At thirteen, the boy looked ecstatic, practically bouncing out of his skin, as he watched his parents finally take their vows.

What must it be like to get married and already have a family to look out for? If anyone could handle it, Trevor could, but the thought of raising kids sent a shudder from the tip of Cole's spine all the way down to his toes. Especially after his recent and total failure with Victoria and her five-year-old son, Eddie. Yeah, he'd pretty much proved his inability to be a boyfriend and potential father with that year-and-a-half dating nightmare.

Trevor and Julie's ceremony was intimate with only a handful of family and friends. They'd opted to have it in the silo portion of the ranch, the circular part smack in the middle of the house Dad had built around it. The silo had been their mother's art studio many years ago. Skylights made for perfect, almost magical lighting showering over his brother and the new bride, and seemed like a posthumous blessing from their mother who'd died several years ago. Cole knew she would have loved every moment of this simple yet ideal ceremony. There'd been a reason she'd chosen this section of the house to paint her pictures.

He took a moment to remember his mother, the peacemaker. She'd had to work extra hard when Cole was a teenager, since he and his father seemed to butt heads on every little detail in life. His dad wanted to train him to take over the ranch when the time came, and all Cole had wanted to do was show off at junior rodeos. After the accident, when his father pushed him to spend weeknights learning the ins and outs of cattle ranching, Cole had signed up for the high-school academic decathlon, which assured he wouldn't have an extra minute to learn anything from his father. And that earned him the nickname of Wonder Boy, said with contempt not pride by his father.

When Cole eventually announced he wanted to be a doctor, not a cowboy, well, Tiberius hadn't been able to hide the disappointment. What father in his right mind got upset when his son wanted to go into medicine?

A "cantankerous old cowboy first, father second" kind.

Cole wished his mother were here so he could hug her

and tell her how much he'd always loved her. But rather than slide into a sentimental slump, he shifted his gaze from the overhead skylights back to the bride.

Julie Sterling, soon-to-be Montgomery, looked stunning in an off-white cocktail-length dress, her unruly brown hair piled high on her head, dotted with baby's breath and tiny yellow daisies, making her big eyes look nothing short of huge. He couldn't help but notice she had great legs, too—Trevor's favorite part of female anatomy. And by the way she looked at his brother, that wide stare was meant only for him. A good thing.

Cole wondered what that might be like—had a woman ever only had eyes for him? It seemed there was always a link to his accomplishments, or a secret wish for what he could offer, and when those things got stripped away, the love light fizzled out. That was how it had worked with Victoria when he'd never gotten around to proposing. He glanced at his lucky-dog brother.

Trev looked nothing short of dignified in his Western tux and new boots, and Cole hadn't exactly held up his end of the bargain if he was supposed to dress in kind. Instead, he'd opted for one of his tailor-made city suits, the type he wore for fund-raisers or exclusive speeches, of which, in his new role as cardiac educator, there were many.

He continued to study his brother, a refined version of himself. Where Cole had inherited his father's rugged, rangy looks, Trevor had the luck of their mother's delicate features blended in with the coarse Montgomery genes. Mom's DNA might have cut a couple inches off Trevor's height, making Cole a truly "big" brother, but the good looks and confidence his little brother possessed had sure worked wonders in life, and especially with the ladies. Always had. Being six years older than

Trevor, Cole had never felt particularly close to the kid, even though his brother had always looked adoringly up to him. Was it any wonder they'd both become doctors? Yeah, Dad sure loved that, too. He ran his hand over his short hair, noting Trevor had let his grow out a bit more, maybe at Julie's request? Who knew the influence a woman could have over a man.

He sure didn't. None of his relationships had ever come close to love or commitment. He blamed it on his job. His single-minded quest to improve cardiology, to take mitral-valve replacements to a new level. His success. His laziness? Or maybe it went all the way back to being fifteen, when Hailey Brimley, the first girl he'd ever loved—and the girl he'd literally broken his neck for—had taken one look at him all banged up with rods sticking out of his skull and walked out of the hospital never to come back. He'd risked everything for young love and she hadn't been able to get past how he'd looked in that damned halo brace. Yeah, there was that link to accomplishment, or lack of, even back then. Whatever the reason, at forty, he was a single guy with zero prospects for true love, and watching his brother get married forced him to think about his own circumstances. Well, guess what, that was how he liked it. Single. Unattached. *Sorry, Victoria, but that's the truth.* Busy with his career. He cleared his throat and straightened the knot of his silk necktie. At least that was his side of the story and he was sticking with it.

His father, Tiberius, stood to the right of Cole as the couple took their vows. With one hand on the carved wooden walking stick—since he'd chucked his clunky quad cane for the ceremony—his father was decked out in his finest Wyoming duds, including his prized Stetson, which he'd removed and held with his free hand for

the duration of the ceremony. Cole noticed something
he hadn't seen in years: a contented smile on his father's
face. He'd personally stopped seeing that look when he'd
shown off for a girl at the high school rodeo and had broken his neck. Twenty-five years ago. Or maybe it was
when he'd flat out told his old man he never wanted to
be a stinkin' cattle rancher. But today was a day of celebration, and Cole didn't want to focus on the past. So
he shifted his gaze once again, and looked to the future.

James, Julie's son, grinned as if he knew the world's
biggest secret and was about to share it. Personally, the
thought of raising a teenager, or any kid, in today's world
made Cole shiver inside, but since the boy's happiness
was palpable and proved to be contagious he joined in
and smiled. Why not? He was at a wedding. His brother's
wedding.

The couple pledged their unending love and kissed,
and soon the crowd of twenty broke out in a cheer. Cole
applauded and gave his nearly forgotten rodeo whistle,
adding to the noise reverberating off the circular silo
walls.

Though it was a special day for Trevor and Julie, Cole
felt somehow uninvolved, holding back to himself. Truth
was he didn't have a clue what to expect filling in at the
Cattleman Bluff Medical Clinic, which, thanks to his
brother's extended honeymoon and family-bonding trip,
would take up almost his entire summer. Cole had taken
a leave of absence to accommodate their trip. As he'd
known in his gut, it was time to step up for the family.

The couple had waited until the school semester
ended for James before they got married, thus the mid-
June wedding. They planned a weeklong honeymoon in
Montreal while James went back to LA with his great-
aunt Janet. The week after that they'd go out to LA to

pick up James and to take in some tourist sights, then they'd all come home and head off on a monthlong road trip around Wyoming, camping, hiking, fishing, horseback riding, anything they felt like doing, but most of all bonding. That was the word Trevor had used over and over while telling Cole his plans. He didn't know the whole story since he and his brother had hardly had a minute together before the wedding, but Trevor and his son sure had a lot of lost time to make up for.

The wedding party had moved on to the second champagne toast, and everyone suddenly looked towards Cole. He hadn't given a single notion to what he should say, so he thought quickly. "I want to wish the bride and groom as much happiness as our own dad and mother had in their marriage. Love doesn't run any deeper than that. Cheers!"

Cole caught a glimpse of his father's tearing eyes as the man raised his glass and toasted new love along with everyone else, while most likely remembering the loss of his own. His dad had fallen apart when Mom died from cancer. His life had literally stopped, and, though he'd tried to pick up the pieces over the past several years, his health had never been the same. That kind of love scared the hell out of Cole. Was that what Trevor was setting himself up for, too? Another good reason for Cole to stick with his current life trajectory.

Bittersweet moments clogged his throat, and he didn't have a clue why that tended to happen much more often when back home. He didn't like it—those deep feelings, the kind that ripped at a person's heart. Maybe that was why he preferred his hundred-mile buffer zone, living out in Laramie half the time and in Baltimore the other, except whenever he was on the road, which seemed to be close to 80 percent of the time lately.

He took another drink of champagne. Staying put for two months in the house he'd grown up in, seeing the continuing disappointment and blame in his father's milky, aging eyes, and sensing the lingering love from his mother would prove to be a challenge. How long before he and his father finally had it out?

The old man's health was failing; he grew weaker by the year yet still insisted on running the ranch. Cole couldn't very well blast him with accusations and force an apology, could he? Damn, he needed more champagne.

When everyone else was joining in with the celebration, laughing, cheering, making a racket, Cole slipped a little farther back from the crowd. Julie prepared to toss the bouquet, and once she turned her back and threw the flowers over her head, the dozen or so ladies in the group started to squeal. The young blonde from the medical clinic, Rita the receptionist, caught it and screamed with delight. Her glittering eyes flitted toward his, and he quickly looked away, deciding now was the perfect time to refill his glass with bubbly.

Briefly, while on his quest for the server, he engaged Jack, the ranch foreman, in conversation. He felt him out as to how the family business was holding up, assuring Jack he'd be as helpful as possible in Trevor's absence. In fact, Cole looked forward to getting on a horse again. The rodeo had been his passion in life throughout his childhood and early teens. He'd made a name for himself on the junior circuit, riding bucking broncos, until...

"Incoming!" he heard Jack say.

Cole looked up in time to reach up and pluck a shiny white lace garter out of the air, rather than let it hit him in the face. *What the—?* He glanced up at his brother's mischievous dark stare, a smile stretched from ear to ear. Was that a challenge?

"You're next, Cole," Trevor said, laughing, knowing full well the absurdity of the remark.

Playing along, only to be polite, Cole mock kissed the garter, then stuck it in his handkerchief pocket. "I'll keep you posted, Trev, but don't hold your breath." He made a shrewd effort to avoid Rita's coy gaze at all costs.

He got his refill of champagne and finished it with three large gulps, enjoying the floating-in-water feeling in his head.

When he was a kid, he used to think the sky in Wyoming was the limit, and anything was possible on any given day. Wasn't that why they'd called him Wonder Boy? These days, not so much. Still smiling, since everyone seemed to continue to stare at him, he hoisted yet another glass in another toast. "Cheers!" he said as expected, waggling his brows, as any lucky guy who'd just caught the garter on a glorious wedding day should. Then he took one more drink of champagne, letting that pleasant buffer of booze make everything fuzzy around the edges, and followed the crowd outside for the reception and lunch.

Tomorrow he'd saddle up and ride the range with Jack. He couldn't remember the last time he'd ridden the entire Circle M Ranch or seen the thousands of head of pure English-bred steer roaming the grasslands, and, being honest, he'd missed it. Of course, he'd need a refresher course on the challenges of raising grass-finished cattle for meat. His father's specialty. Genetics was the key, his old man had always said, and, being a scientist, Cole could easily wrap his brain around that. But all the finer details of animal husbandry he'd leave to Jack.

As for right now, he couldn't very well zone out on the rest of his brother's wedding party, so he stood, straightened his tie and headed toward Trevor's table to tell him not to worry about a thing while he was on his honeymoon. His mother would want it that way.

"Just the man I need to talk to," Trevor said, eyes brightening as Cole approached his table.

"I thought you'd already told me everything I need to know." Cole had a sudden sinking feeling.

"I lined up some extra help for you at the clinic while I'm gone."

Cole wasn't about to complain about that. "Thanks. Someone from Cattleman Bluff?"

"Boston."

"What?"

"It's a complicated story, but, medically speaking, the doctor is qualified. Lawrence Rivers highly recommended her."

Larry Rivers was a respected professor who'd mentored Trevor during medical school, and he'd become a trusted colleague for Cole when he'd made the decision to learn transcatheter heart-valve replacement. "But?" Cole's instincts waved yellow flags, waiting for Trevor to come clean with the rest of the story.

"The problem is, she only applied for internal medicine residencies at the top five most competitive hospitals in the country, so she didn't get a single spot."

"She's fresh out of medical school? And that's supposed to be a help, how?"

"You know Larry wouldn't recommend her if he didn't believe in her."

"Believing in and actually being competent are two different things." Ah, hell, Cole didn't want to get in an argument with his brother at his wedding. Mom wouldn't like that. He'd back off for now.

"She might be a little rough around the edges."

Are you kidding me? "You're joking, right? Is this some sort of weird wedding joke?"

"Larry said she's a tough Boston girl, from the wrong side of the Charles River. She can handle anything."

"So Larry's playing both of us, right?"

Trevor bit his lower lip and grimaced. "She needed a job. I said she could have it. You'll need help at that clinic, trust me."

"And I want all the help I can get, but—"

"Come on, Trevor," Julie said, a huge smile on her face, a warning gaze in her eyes. "It's time to change clothes for the send-off. The limo is going to be here in twenty minutes."

Trevor lifted his brows, cast a quick glance at Cole, then put his arm around his new wife.

"What's this doctor's name?"

"Elisabete Silva."

Great, he'd be working with a wet-behind-the-ears doctor who probably thought she knew it all. Didn't he think the same thing when he'd first graduated from medical school?

Trevor was the most conscientious man Cole knew, and wouldn't set him up for failure. Instead of acting like his father, blowing a gasket before getting the whole story, he'd take his mother's approach. He'd reserve his opinion until he'd met the new doctor at the clinic himself, but he suddenly had a kink in his gut that had nothing to do with the baked chicken served at the wedding-reception dinner.

Trevor started to walk off with Julie, but turned back. "Oh, one more thing. The doctor will be living here at the ranch. Dad said it's okay."

What in the hell was going on?

Trev looked as if he wanted to say something else,

but Julie snagged him firmly by the elbow and led him
off. Cole stood and watched as they headed off to change
clothes while those waving yellow flags in his head
started turning red.

Ten minutes after tossing rice and grinning along with
everyone else, then watching the new couple drive off
in the fully decorated "Just Married" limo, Cole saw a
town car heading up the long road. The Circle M Ranch
wasn't exactly on the main highway—anyone coming
out this way generally had a reason.

He looked on with interest from the yard as the car
came to a stop in front of the house and Jack, his father's
ranch foreman, along with the family cook, Gretchen,
rushed toward it.

"Cole, come and dance with me." Rita, the attractive blonde medical-clinic receptionist, linked her arm
through his, her still-lingering potent perfume overpowering his nostrils. "It's tradition for the bouquet and garter catchers to have a dance together."

First he'd ever heard of that tradition. Cole didn't want
to come off as impolite at his brother's wedding reception—his mother would be disappointed—especially
since he'd be working with Rita all summer, so he let
her lead him to the dance floor, losing sight of the limousine and the house as he did.

CHAPTER TWO

THE LAST OF the wedding guests had finally left. It was getting dark, and Cole had handed the mantle to the lead of the cleanup crew. He'd done his brotherly duty for Trevor's wedding, and looked forward to getting out of his suit and unwinding with a good novel before calling it a night.

He wandered toward the porch and the front door. Gretchen, the family cook, met him with an anxious look.

"Hello, Cole," she said, trying to sound calm but not coming close.

"Hi. What's up?" He remembered the limousine from earlier. "We have company?"

"Uh, yes." She wouldn't look him in the eyes.

"Is something wrong?" He stopped and waited for Gretchen to look up.

"Uh. No. I was just a little surprised, that's all." Still not looking at him, she turned toward the screen door.

"Surprised? About what?"

Tiberius appeared on the other side of the screen. "That she has a baby, that's what."

"Who has a baby?" His feet stuck to the porch floorboards.

"The doctor Trevor hired," his father said with a lopsided grin.

"A baby?" What was going on? The new doctor was here already?

"You know, the little tykes in diapers, a baby." His dad seemed to take great joy in rubbing in the news, though he looked tired beyond his years just then. It'd been a long few days preparing for the wedding; Cole would cut him some slack. "They cry a lot and need undivided attention?"

Cole sped up the last few steps to the front door, pulling out his cell phone on the way, ready to speed-dial his brother. "Trevor didn't mention that." In all honesty, Trevor hadn't had the chance.

"Of course not, because you would have thrown a fit if he did," Dad said, not splitting hairs, holding the door open for Gretchen and him to go inside.

"That's not necessarily true. But it would have been nice to know."

Before he could press dial, a tall and slender, dark-haired woman with vivid green eyes and ivory skin appeared in the entryway. She'd come from the east wing where she must have left her baggage, and had some sort of swaddling sling across her torso with a good-sized bulge buried inside.

"Hello," she said, a natural rasp in her lower-than-usual female voice. "I'm Elisabete, but everybody calls me Lizzie."

Out of the blue, Cole wondered how her laugh would sound. He guessed smoky and...

She reached out a thin hand with long delicate fingers, and, instead of dialing Trevor to curse him out, Cole pocketed the phone, took her hand and shook. Warmth emanated from both her grip and her wide gaze, which was truly stunning, and stole some of his thunder.

"I'm Cole. Nice to meet you. I'm a bit surprised

by your...er...bundle there." He nodded to the lump dangling snuggly from her middle.

She gave a fatigued smile and glanced down beneath fuller-than-usual dark brows at her baby. "My little Flora screamed the entire flight from Boston. I think she's worn herself out. At one point I thought the flight attendant wanted to shove me out the door." She lifted her gaze, tension dwelling in those lovely, though bewildered, eyes even as she tried to make light of her situation. "I'll carry my load at the clinic, Dr. Montgomery. I promise."

Had she read his mind? Only then did he think to let go of the comfort of her hand. Those deeply inquisitive eyes studied him, obviously hunting for a sign of his humanity.

"With an infant that will be a huge challenge. Are you sure you can handle the job?"

"I don't know how much Dr. Rivers told you—"

"Dr. Rivers spoke to my brother, who left for his honeymoon today. I don't have a clue if Trevor knew about the bambino part or not." So much for his humanity.

"I've made some tea—why doesn't everyone sit down and I'll bring it?" Gretchen said, having never been able to handle tension, even though, having worked for years for the Montgomery family, she should have gotten used to it by now.

"Yes, why don't we?" Tiberius said, an amused smirk on his face. He led the way to the living room.

Cole gestured for Lizzie to follow, noting her jeans-clad long legs, narrow hips and flip-flop-covered feet, thinking how impractical the footwear was for a ranch. But there was something else he noticed beyond her travel-weary appearance, and besides the single long, thick braid down her back: it was the confidence with which she walked. The way she held her head high even under his less-than-gracious welcome. This one was a fighter. Maybe she had to be.

"What kind of name is Silva?" Tiberius asked just before he sat in his favorite overstuffed chair.

"It's Portuguese."

Cole wasn't exactly sure what he'd signed on for taking over his brother's practice, but, with the arrival of Lizzie sporting a baby, that task had suddenly gotten a hell of a lot more challenging.

While Gretchen served tea in the living room, Cole asked Lizzie about medical school, but got distracted with the dozens of other questions flying through his head.

"And after spending a month in the emergency department, I knew for a fact I didn't have what it takes to work under that kind of pressure. That place made me wicked crazy," she said without seeming to take a breath. "Internal medicine seemed the right fit for me. It's kind of like taking a good mystery—the patient's symptoms—and step-by-step solving the case by diagnosing and treating them properly. Makes me feel like a medical sleuth, kind of like that TV show, *House*, you know? So I'm really looking forward to working in your clinic, Dr. Montgomery."

Just what he needed, his own *House*. Didn't she understand that guy would have lost his medical license a hundred different times because of his antics? Cole definitely had his work cut out for him training a new, dreamy-eyed doctor.

Plus, she spoke rapid-fire, with a thick Bostonian accent, and to be honest he often had trouble following her. *Depahtmint. Pressha. Lookin' farwid.* But it was kind of amusing at the same time. He suppressed a smile as she talked on and on, probably nervous and wanting to make a good first impression. Meanwhile, he grasped for ways to make this situation work. New doctor. New mother. New clinic. And he'd thought he was out of his depth taking over the clinic before!

For a new mother, she certainly seemed to have a lot of energy, or maybe she was just a hyper type. He hoped she wouldn't talk his ear off all the time because that would get old fast. *Gee, thanks for sticking me with your sight-unseen doctor, Trev, old buddy.*

She continued on with her story, and Cole hoped she'd get around to mentioning the baby, but she conveniently skipped over that part. Instead she talked about experiences in medicine and kept assuring him she'd carry her load at the clinic, then stopped midsentence when her eyes settled on Tiberius, who still had an amused smirk on his face.

"Is that how you always smile?" she asked bluntly.

Granted, it was an odd lopsided smile, but Cole figured it was typical of Dad to be a smart aleck over the mixed-up circumstances Cole had found himself in. Then he looked closer. She was right: something was off.

Lizzie popped up from the chair and walked straight to his father. "Smile again," she said. "Hmm. Give me your hands. Squeeze." She glanced over her shoulder at Cole, her full arched brows raised, then quickly back to Tiberius. "Are you feeling numbness or tingling on either side?" Tiberius looked confused. "Cole, he's noticeably weaker on the right. Is this always the case?"

Cole jumped up and strode toward his father and Lizzie. "No."

"Raise your arms for me, Mr. Montgomery." The right arm went only half as high as the other. "Can you say 'the sky is blue'?"

It came out slurred and jumbled. "Sy…boo."

"I'll call 911." Cole dug for the phone in his pocket and made the call.

"He seemed to walk in here just fine, but then I noticed his droopy smile." Lizzie went down on her knees to look Tiberius in the eyes. "Is your vision blurry?"

He made a tiny shake of his head.

"He needs thrombolytics ASAP. Time is brain," she said, slipping into doctor mode, stating the obvious door-to-IV necessity for early treatment. "We've got a three-hour window."

Cole filled in the emergency operator. "We need a stroke team ready to go," he said when he'd finished. She assured him an ambulance would be on the way with estimated time of arrival twenty minutes. The nearest hospital was in Laramie. He did the math and knew time was of the essence if they wanted the best results with his father's evolving stroke. Panic ripped through him at the thought of losing his dad. He went to him and squeezed his shoulder. "We'll get the help you need, Dad."

Tiberius glanced up, seeming a bit disoriented. Trevor's wedding had taken more of a toll than Cole had realized.

"We should give him an aspirin right now," Lizzie said.

"He's already on daily aspirin."

"Let's give him another. Research shows the benefits outweigh the risk of causing bleeding in the brain."

Cole also knew this was an ongoing debate among clinicians. Some researchers said early aspirin was beneficial, others said it could prove risky. The key was whether a clot or a burst vessel was the cause of his father's stroke, and only a CT scan could prove that. Yet, the overemphasis of TPA, tissue plasminogen activator, as the only treatment could also cause bleeding in the brain. He wasn't about to take up that debate now with Lizzie when his father was in the middle of a stroke.

"Out of…" Tiberius mumbled.

What? "You're out of something?" Cole repeated what he thought his father meant.

"Asp." He looked and sounded like someone who'd just had Novocain injections at the dentist.

His father had a history of TIAs, transient ischemic attacks, and that was caused by blockage. Why hadn't he gotten a new bottle of aspirin immediately? Cole wanted to wring his dad's neck, but quickly remembered there'd been a lot of activity going on over the past week with wedding plans and parties and Cole moving back home. Today's wedding had been an all-day affair. He'd cut his father some slack, but still wondered if this TIA could have been prevented, and whether or not it would turn into a full-blown cerebrovascular accident this time around. The thought sent a shard of fear deep into his chest.

"Let's do it, then," Cole said, jogging to the closest medicine cabinet in the hall bathroom. "There isn't any here," he called out. Frustration blended with panic.

"I've got some in the kitchen," Gretchen said, close on his heels. "You should have told me you were out, Monty," she called over her shoulder.

When they returned, Lizzie had remained with Tiberius, reassuring him and distracting him by showing her newborn to him. She cooed over her baby and smiled up at the man. That lopsided smile returned, and his eyes looked calmer and more focused since gazing at the sleeping child.

"Take this, Dad." Cole gave him the aspirin. "Can you swallow okay?" He tested his dad with a tiny sip from the cup of forgotten tea on the table next to his chair. He seemed to swallow okay, so Cole gave it to him. If this was a true TIA, his symptoms would go away within ten to twenty minutes. If it was a CVA, there was no telling how long or how much worse it could get. By Cole's count it had already been over ten minutes since Lizzie had astutely noticed his father's quirky grin, and as of now the symptoms remained unchanged. A foreboding shadow settled around Cole's vision; worry kicked up the fear he'd tried to suppress. He wasn't ready to lose his dad. Nowhere near.

"I'm calling the Laramie ER, giving them a preliminary report. I already told them to have the stroke team ready to go the second Dad arrives."

"Do you have a blood-pressure monitor in the house?" Lizzie asked as he dialed his cell phone.

It'd been so long since Cole had lived here, he didn't rightly know.

"There's one in Monty's bedroom," Gretchen said, setting off in that direction of the house.

Cole studied his father, then looked at the beautiful baby with a full head of dark hair, just like her mother. The child squirmed and stretched while still deeply asleep, and that simple marvel kept that odd smile on his father's face. Whatever helped or distracted him. The man must be scared as hell of having another stroke. He prayed their actions would be enough for now.

Gretchen produced the portable blood-pressure cuff while Cole gave his report to the ER. He watched as Lizzie carefully placed her baby, who was obviously still exhausted from the big airplane trip, across Tiberius's lap, then she went right to work setting up and checking the numbers. "Well, we can't blame his blood pressure for this CVA." At one hundred and thirty over eighty-five it wasn't greatly elevated.

Cole repeated the BP to the doctor on the phone. He knew that eighty percent of all strokes were ischemic, caused by a blockage of blood flow. The fact that his father had kept his blood pressure under control since his first TIA a couple of years ago, plus his BP wasn't exceptionally high right now, meant the odds of a hemorrhagic stroke were much less. But you never knew, he couldn't be too cautious and the man belonged in the hospital for treatment and best outcome. And just before he finished the call, there was the sweet sound of a distant ambulance siren.

"Our ride's here," he said to the doctor on the other end, then gave his dad a reassuring smile. "ETA an hour and ten." That left a one- to two-hour window to get his father on thrombolytic therapy for best chance of full recovery. He hoped it would be enough.

CHAPTER THREE

WELL AFTER MIDNIGHT, Lizzie struggled with her colicky baby. These fits always seemed to happen at night. The child had been so intent on crying she couldn't calm down enough to nurse. At the end of her tether, Lizzie walked the floor of the cathedral-ceilinged living room, with the spiral staircase winding up to a huge loft library at the back.

She had no business being a mother. Didn't this prove it? She didn't know what she was doing, and poor Flora sensed it. The baby bore the brunt of her overworked and undertrained parent. She wanted to cry right along with her child, but held it in, afraid if she let that gate open she'd never regain control.

She'd put on quite a show that afternoon, walking into a strange house with her baby, acting as if she were the most confident girl in the world. Oh, yeah, move out of state? Take a temporary job? Piece of cake. *How long before Cole Montgomery sees through me?*

Headlights flashed across the arched, church-sized window. Oh, great, just what she needed—now Cole would know what a failure she was as a mother, too. She thought about running off to her room set away from the rest of the house. Maybe he wouldn't hear Flora's wails there. But her curiosity about Tiberius overpowered her desire to run and hide—was saving face really that important?—so she stayed put. Her one hope being Cole wouldn't demand she shut Flora up because if he did, she might have to quit the job before she even started.

She took a deep breath and switched her little one to the other arm and bounced her. Maybe Flora had worn herself out, because she shifted from scream mode to fussy and generally unhappy—an improvement. But could Lizzie blame her for having colic? The poor kid was stuck with her, clueless and unnatural, as a mother.

This move to Wyoming was supposed to be the first step in a better life for both of them, yet Flora's distress seemed to prove otherwise. Why did she have to doubt herself at every turn since becoming a mother? She couldn't very well ask her own mother for help.

A key turned the lock in the front door, and from the darkened room Lizzie saw Cole enter. His head immediately turned to the sounds of the baby's cries.

"Hi," she said, walking toward him, glad she'd thrown a long sweater over her funky flannel pajama pants and overstretched tank top. It was too late to try to do anything with her hair, though.

He nodded, looking tired and grim when he turned on the light. He watched her a few moments as they both adjusted to the sudden brightness.

"How's your dad?" She shifted Flora to her shoulder and rubbed her back as she continued to fuss loudly and squirm in her arms.

"He's stable. The CT scan showed blockage without bleeding, so that's good. They put him on ATP well within the window for best results. Only time will tell."

She thought about the news. It was promising, and that was all they could hope for tonight. "So the CVA hasn't evolved?"

"You still can't understand him when he tries to talk, but the right-sided weakness seems less. At least that's something." Cole threw his keys in a ceramic bowl on the long entry hall table, the sound startling Flora and the fussing turned to crying. "Oh, sorry." He grimaced.

"It's not you. We've been up for a couple hours. I keep hoping she'll wear herself out enough so I can nurse her." God, she wanted to cry, that familiar helpless feeling of not being able to comfort her daughter ripping at her heart.

His brows pulled downward. "You need your sleep just as much as she does." Surprising her, he took off his jacket, laid it over the back of a chair and reached for Flora. "Maybe a change in scenery will help. Give her to me." He took her squirming baby, now looking amazingly tiny in his big hands and arms. "Let's go in the kitchen, and have some herbal tea or something. It'll do us both good."

He led the way—her wriggling, loudly protesting baby leaving him unfazed—and, though feeling embarrassed about her appearance, she followed. Fortunately the kitchen light had a dimmer, so Cole left it at half the usual brightness. That worked for Lizzie. The less he saw of her bed hair and unwashed face, the better.

"I'll put the water on," she said, noticing that Flora still fussed but had quieted down a little. "Where do you keep the tea?" In a kitchen the size of her entire apartment back in Boston, she didn't have a clue where to begin to look.

"The pantry," he whispered, and pointed to the corner, Flora in the crook of his elbow as he unconsciously rocked the fidgety baby. "Second shelf. I like the Sweet Dreams brand, but there's some chamomile, too, somewhere, I think."

It tickled her to think of big ol' Cole Montgomery liking herbal tea and holding babies. Even though he gazed at Flora as if she were an alien from Planet X. After she got the tea she was grateful the cabinets had glass doors, so at least she knew where to find the cups.

Behind her, he chuckled softly. "I think she's hungry—she keeps trying to suckle my neck."

"Oh!" Maybe she should stop everything and nurse that child since that seemed to be her message.

"You have a bottle or something?"

"I'm nursing. Why don't you give her to me?"

He gently handed Flora back to Lizzie, and their gazes caught and held briefly. He seemed to have questions in his, and she didn't want to begin guessing what he wondered. Most likely something along the lines of— *what in the hell are you doing here?*

Good question. Would he believe her answer—*making a better life for my daughter?*

Flora had settled down and showed all the signs of finally being ready to nurse. "If you don't mind watching the kettle, I'll take her back to the living room. I'm already in love with your dad's favorite chair."

He blinked his reassurance. "I'll bring the tea when it's ready."

Five minutes later, with Flora finally nursing contentedly, Lizzie had thrown her sweater over her chest for privacy, and Cole brought two teacups to the living room, lit only by the light of the moon.

"Mind if I join you?" he whispered.

She smiled up at him as he put her cup on the table nearest her free hand. She'd honestly expected him to use a mug, but he sat across from her and sipped his tea as if it was second nature. She couldn't think of a single thing to say to him because her main thought was, *Thank goodness Flora quit crying and is nursing.* Now maybe she could breathe. At least she knew how to do *something* good for her baby. Yet, hadn't Cole calmed the child down? Maybe he had a kid of his own?

"How do you know how to quiet babies so well?"

"I didn't know I did." His surprised-bordering-on-shocked expression said it all. Pure luck, the kind Flora wished she had more of. "I just saw you struggling and you looked like you needed some help." And wasn't that an understatement?

Her first sip of hot tea soothed her strained throat. It never ceased to amaze her how her entire body tensed when Flora was unhappy. She was surprised her milk let down so easily under the circumstances. "I thought maybe you had your own kids or something."

He let go a big puff of air, a sound meant to show the absurdity of the comment. "*No-o-o.* No kids. No wife. Just me and cardiology. See, I understand the physiology of the heart perfectly—the emotional side of things, don't have a clue."

She lightly laughed. "I hear you on that one." Cole had revealed a lot in that last sentence. Maybe they had something in common.

"So is that why you're not married either?"

Sitting in the dark helped shadow her first reaction—pain. A year ago she would have bet her life on her and Dave getting married, but, after his wicked change in character when she'd told him she was pregnant, she was glad she wasn't married to him. In fact, her life, or losing it, might have actually been part of the bet. The guy had gone ballistic with the news. He'd flipped out and grabbed her, shaking her violently, then shoved her against a wall, banging her head several times on the surface. *You think you can trap me with a kid? Think again.* She'd never seen him so crazed; the memory of his wild-eyed stare still sent shivers through her muscles.

She'd never felt more helpless in her life either and vowed that would never happen again. Fortunately, he'd stopped at roughing her up, hadn't hit her or anything, just manhandled her to frighten her for messing with his plans. He'd given her one last shake and left. So much for true love. And so much for never feeling helpless again. It seemed since Flora had been born, helpless had become her middle name.

She reminded herself she'd come to Wyoming to change things. She wasn't helpless. She had a job. "Her dad and I couldn't work things out. He took off. I stayed pregnant."

"How'd you manage to finish med school with a new-born?"

"Called in a lot of favors." It wasn't that she wanted to be abrupt, but, really, they didn't have all night for her to explain that one. Maybe the guy deserved a bit more than her glib answer, though. "When you're raised in foster care you learn to be resourceful. I'd helped a lot of students through the toughest modules, did one-on-one study sessions with a girl who probably would have failed the boards otherwise. You know, that kind of thing. They owed me."

"Wait a second, back up." He leaned forward. "You were raised in foster care?"

"After my grandmother died, yes." So she wasn't exactly being forthcoming. It wasn't that she wanted to be secretive; she was just saving him the sob story. Did Cole really need to hear all of it?

"And what happened to your mother?"

"She went back to being a meth head after I was born."

He shook his head and, since her eyes had adjusted

to the dark, she could make out his sympathetic expression, brows pushed together, lips tight. Yeah, she'd had a hard life, he got it, no need to pound home the point. "And you rose above all of that and made it into medical school. That's amazing."

She pushed her head back onto the soft cushion of the high-backed chair, suddenly needing that extra comfort. Put that way, yeah, maybe she was amazing. "The only thing I had control of in my childhood was my school grades. I guess you could say it paid off. If you don't count the fact that I wasn't chosen for a single residency program I applied for." She didn't want to sound sorry for herself, but the discouraged sigh had already left her lips.

"Didn't anyone counsel you on casting your net wide? From what I was told you only applied to the five most prestigious hospitals in the nation. No offense, but what were you thinking?"

"That I should reach for the stars." She needed to shut him down, be blunt, because she'd gone over her blunder a million times already and it always came back to the same conclusion—there was nothing she could do about that now. And that was why she'd come to Wyoming, to make up for it. To start over. To give her baby a good start in life.

Her little scientific experiment had worked. She'd formed her hypothesis, tested it, and analyzing her data—sitting in silence, the dim light from the hallway making his shadow large and looming, mouth firmly shut—he wouldn't and didn't know what to do with the truth. Yep, she'd been right.

"So how are we going to work this out?" Cole's deep voice cut through her thoughts, his rugged yet handsome face dappled in moonlight and shadows.

"You mean my working for you? Or my living here with a colicky baby?"

He nodded, his laser gaze, noticeable even in the dim light, nearly making her squirm. "Part A."

Under the sweater, she shifted Flora to the other breast and waited until she latched on. "Well, while you were at the hospital I had a long talk with Gretchen. She seems to have an unfulfilled grandmotherly gene. She said she'd be happy to take care of Flora when I work."

"Maybe you should just work part-time at first."

She wanted to yell, *Don't you get it? I'm broke. I need the money!* But she swallowed another sip of tea instead. "But you hired me to work full-time. I want to keep my side of the bargain."

He went quiet again and studied his expensive brand-name shoes. The man oozed wealth. And good looks. "I'm glad to pay you the amount Trevor agreed on, but maybe at first you can come in half days or something."

"You do realize that women only get six weeks' maternity leave in the US and return to work all the time, right? I'm that single mother in med school who never missed an overnight shift, and my only support system was other med students. I graduated the same day as everyone else with my baby swaddled in a sling across my chest. People do what they've got to do, you know? Gretchen said she's happy to help. Let me do what you hired me for, okay?"

Take that!

"That's commendable. I'll give you that." He remained thoughtful, probably analyzing her plea, seeing right through her, figuring out how desperate she was. "I suspect Dad will be in the hospital at least a week, and then be sent to rehab after that. Once he comes home, though, Gretchen will have her hands full caring for him."

"You've got a point, but by then I can find other child-care arrangements." *Keep positive even against the odds. You've got to.*

He thought for a moment or two. "Reasonable enough." *Whew!* He put down his teacup and slapped his big palms on his thighs. "Well, I'll leave you and Flora to your feeding. It's been a long day."

She nodded. "I can hardly keep my eyes open."

Before he left the room, she studied his huge silhouette in the doorway, broad shoulders, long torso, big in every way, a man's man. Fine-looking man. Yet he'd been gentle with Flora. Was it totally wrong to find your new employer sexy? Yet she couldn't deny she did.

"May I ask you a question?" It had been bothering her since she'd noticed the identical scars on his forehead when she'd first met him, and to be honest she needed something to get her mind off how attracted she was to him.

He turned. The epitome of patience...and gentleman cowboy...sexy.

"Did you have a broken neck?"

The hallway light cut across his profile. He scrunched up his face, obviously surprised by her comment. "Another astute observation, Dr. Silva. I take it my halo-brace scars tipped you off?"

She nodded, trying not to look smug, though definitely feeling it.

"When I was fifteen I was riding a bucking bronco, got bucked off and fractured C1-C2. I was fortunate not to have a spinal-cord injury, as you can obviously tell." He held out his arms, palms up, looking over his own body.

"No need for fusion?"

"Three months wearing that brace did the trick. It also changed my life goal of becoming a rodeo star." He smiled and deep vertical grooves cut through his cheeks. Yeah, that was sexy, too.

But his confession made her laugh outright. "A rodeo star?"

"You're looking at Cattleman Bluff's former junior rodeo bucking-bronco champion." He said the mouthful with an amused twinkle in his eyes, as if the title might have carried some clout around here at one time.

But rodeo stars were as foreign as extraterrestrials to a girl from Boston. "I'd say I was impressed, if I had a clue what that meant." If this was her idea of flirting, she wasn't doing a very good job.

His closed-lip smile widened slowly, finally revealing a fine line of teeth, and the effect, combined with the lingering glint in his eyes, sent a shiver through her. *Oh, man, this could be bad. Dr. Montgomery is gorgeous.*

She swallowed. "I'm sure you were a regular star around these parts." She tried out her version of cowboy talk, her accent no doubt falling far short of the mark. *These pahts.* Come to think of it, she could imagine him in dungarees and a torso-hugging cowboy shirt. And what she'd give to see the man wearing a cowboy hat.

"Easy come, easy go," he said.

"Sounds pretty ouchy to me."

"That, too. I guess you can say I'm a doctor today because of that accident."

"Weird how life goes sometimes, isn't it?"

"Yeah." He gave her statement some thought. "Well, I hope you both get a good night's sleep."

"Thank you." She imagined sympathy in his eyes, and, though she didn't want his pity, she appreciated his caring on some level. These days she didn't have anyone in her corner, with the exception of Dr. Rivers, and he was far away.

"I also want you to know that, if it hadn't been for you, my father might have been a hell of a lot worse off. You haven't even begun to work in the clinic, and you've already impressed me."

He'd paid her a compliment, and this from a man who didn't seem to do heartfelt. It made her beam. "Thanks. I hardly know your dad, but I like him. He's got a lot of spunk."

"Yeah. He's probably too stubborn to die, but the thought of dealing with his aphasia, well, let's just say, we'll all be miserable. I'm hoping his symptoms will resolve quickly."

"Me, too."

"Well, like I said, thanks to your fast thinking. Good night." With that he turned and headed in the opposite direction from her bedroom wing. She watched him for a while, thinking that for a big man he moved with grace, and she definitely liked his style.

Flora had fallen asleep. Lizzie rose gently, hoping not to wake her, and started toward her room. It had been a crazy first-day meeting at the Montgomery ranch. How was she supposed to know there was a wedding going on? And a stroke? Sure was one hell of a way to break the ice with the family, though.

Cole seemed more city slicker than rancher, but thanks to his taking the time to talk with her she'd got-

ten a glimpse of his inner cowboy, which had probably shaped the man he'd become. The thing that really
mixed her up, though, was she really, really liked what
she'd seen.

CHAPTER FOUR

COLE WAS TOO keyed-up to sleep. Worries about his father had peaked a few hours back when he'd been assured by the attending physician that Tiberius Montgomery was stable. He'd sat by his father's hospital bedside and watched him sleep for an hour or so after that, then decided, as the doctor had said, that it would be okay to go home. He thought about going to his own apartment in Laramie to sleep and be nearby, but decided to head back out to the ranch because of Elisabete.

The last thing he'd expected was to step in on a tired and frazzled woman walking the floors of the living room doing her best to calm a wailing baby. Her nearly black hair had been set free from the earlier braid, and thick tendrils had covered her shoulders. The contrast with her creamy skin had been unnerving. Then in the kitchen he'd noticed the tiny sexy mole above her upper lip, and had nearly fallen off his chair, which wouldn't have been a good thing considering he'd been holding her baby.

She had the potential to be an incredibly beautiful woman, yet did little to enhance it, and still had managed to make him sit up and take notice. When was the last time that had happened? Maybe that was the special factor about naturally attractive women: sometimes they didn't know it, and that made them all the more appealing. Or maybe it was just her youth.

Not a good thing for their situation, and, he had to be honest, with her fresh out of medical school, he'd be doing a lot of teaching at the clinic.

He sat on his bed, scrubbed a hand over his face, tired to the core, yet restless just the same, and accepted the fact that peace of mind wasn't in his immediate future. He had a father to rehab, a new-to-him medical clinic to run, a diamond-in-the-rough doctor to train, not to mention an innocent baby who deserved a good start in life to look after. And why should he feel even partly responsible for that, too? Because any decent man understood innocence deserved protection.

He shook his head, then lay back on his pillow. And to think all he'd expected to do when he came home was run his brother's medical clinic and keep up with his father's accounting books. Simple, right? He laughed wryly to himself. Since when had life ever played out the way he'd expected?

Good thing he intended to spend the entire day Sunday working the ranch with a couple of Jack's cowhands, then in the afternoon he'd go to the hospital to check in on his father. It would give Lizzie and Gretchen time to bond with the baby, and hard work had always been the best way Cole knew to run away when his personal life got out of control.

Hell, that was how he'd decided to take a fellowship and train for transcatheter heart-valve replacement. He'd chosen to learn the minimally invasive mitral-valve replacement procedure when hardly anyone in the country had heard of it, rather than deal with his mother's death. He hadn't spent more than two days consoling his father after the funeral. He just hadn't been able to take the emotional strain seeing his dad fall apart like that. And leaving early as he'd done, as always, he'd left another burden on Trevor's shoulders.

He rolled over. *Sleep, where are you hiding?*

Lizzie took extra care after nursing Flora Monday morning. She fought back tears when she diapered and dressed the precious baby in one of the few terry-cloth onesies she owned. "Everything's going to be fine today, Flora bear. I promise. Gretchen is a sweet lady who'll take good care of you."

The baby watched Lizzie as she talked, as if trying to understand. Such intelligent blue eyes. She knew her mother's voice, too, and the thought made the brimming tears spill over Lizzie's lids. How was she going to survive today?

I've got to work. "Everything I do is for us." She kissed her daughter's chubby cheek and inhaled her special baby scent, savoring it. Not wanting to let go.

She'd had to leave Flora with so many different people when she'd first been born in order to keep up with medical-school classes and clinics. Then the toughest job in her life: the addiction center. It'd about ripped out her heart to leave her, too, but she'd had to graduate if she wanted to pass the boards and get a job. And she needed an income to pay the rent. At least now, in Wyoming, she'd only have one sweet grandmotherly type watching Flora every day, and she'd see her baby every night and all day on the weekends.

Quality time was what mattered, she repeated over and over to help dry her tears. Squeezing her baby close, she forced a smile, pulled back and put on her brave face, not wanting to leave Flora seeing her cry. "Are you going to be a good girl for Gretchen?"

A gurgle and coo answered her question.

"I love you so much!"

Lizzie kissed Flora goodbye in Gretchen's arms. Cole could have sworn he saw her eyes well up, yet like a trooper she pulled herself together and didn't utter a word about missing her baby on the drive in to work. Though frequent sighs and constantly fidgeting hands in her lap gave her away.

His back was stiff from hard labor yesterday, walking the range, sinking posts, but it was the kind of ache that did a man good. But the pain wasn't distraction enough to keep him from noticing how Lizzie had pulled her hair back in that braid again and wore silver hoop earrings large enough for shooting practice. Even though she'd chosen a long-sleeved white tailored shirt with dark slacks, sending a clear unisex message, he couldn't help but notice what seemed to be all woman beneath the wrapper. Yeah, this couldn't be good.

"How's your dad doing?" She broke into his spiraling sexual thoughts.

"Pretty well. He's recovering his strength quickly, which, as you know, is always a good thing with CVAs. Fingers crossed his speech will turn around, too. Another day or two of observation, and they may even skip sending him to rehab if he continues on this trajectory. The doctor said a home occupational-health worker and speech-recovery therapist may be all he needs."

"That's fantastic. Wow, we dodged the bullet there, didn't we?"

He liked how she'd already thrown herself into the center of his family using *we* as if she were one of them. "Yes, *we* did. Keep sending good thoughts for his speech. You know how recovery can change day to day in the hospital."

"Yes, and I certainly will."

It got quiet then, as if the early morning drive had been their routine for years. She sighed and glanced out the window; he snuck a peak at her intently watching the scenery. He'd forgotten how amazing the Wyoming landscape was, how the sparkling blue sky over this big box-shaped state accentuated the brown and golden shades of strata on the low-lying hills, and made the prairie grass look like one huge shaggy carpet.

"How're we gonna work this today?" she asked, checking back in, one foot suddenly tapping a quick rhythm on the floor of the car. He didn't peg her as someone to get nervous about a new job, though she did seem to run on adrenaline and nerves.

"The patients?"

"Yeah, are you willing to let me work on my own unless I need your help?"

"I'd like to supervise, if you don't mind."

She started to protest.

"At first," he said to appease her, but mostly to shut her up because he didn't feel like debating the topic. He was the senior doctor and she might as well get used to it. "Then we can evaluate the situation and go from there."

"I guess that's reasonable."

"You didn't think I'd just cut you loose, did you?"

She tossed him a teasing smile. "A girl can hope."

"Charlotte, the RN, is going to triage the appointments. Give the more complicated patients to me, and maternal/child to you. Oh, and I'll take all of the cardiology patients. Obviously."

"How sexist is that?"

"It's not sexist if it's practical. I know squat about

maternal child health, and I figure, since you recently had a baby, not to mention the fact that you've just graduated from medical school and most likely studied the topic more recently than I have, you're more suited to the job." *Not to mention that you're a woman. Okay, so it did sound sexist. It was beside the point.*

She shook her head, but moved on, apparently deciding not to argue. Good choice. "I'd like to do as many procedures as possible."

"Fine with me. I'm spoiled by having a team of nurses do my dirty work."

"See, you are sexist and since when do cardiologists ever get dirty?"

"Who's being sexist now? There are plenty of male nurses."

She smiled, clearly liking the verbal sparring. "Point taken. But I don't think of cardiology as a profession that gets dirty."

"You've heard of angioplasty, right?"

"You do those?"

"I do, and I take it a step further, I replace mitral valves, too."

"But that's open-heart surgery."

"Not the way we do it these days. I use the same route as angiograms. TAVR or TAVI—have you heard of that?"

She turned her head toward him, disbelief in her eyes. "You do transcatheter aortic-valve replacements?"

"Also known as trans-catheter aortic-valve implantations. Yes—" he sounded smug and couldn't help it "—that would be me."

"Oh, my gosh." Except it sounded like *ohmahgosh*. "You're, like, a star in medicine!" Except it sounded like *stah*.

"You've heard of me?"

"You're, like, the god of cardiology. I can't believe I didn't add that up." She tapped her hands on her knees. "Wow. I'm working with a genius!"

"I wouldn't go that far."

"Oh, I would. You launched a whole new minimally invasive approach to mitral-valve replacement. No major incisions, the heart doesn't have to be stopped or put on bypass, there's quicker recovery time. We learned all about that in my fourth-year cardiology module. This is freaking amazing."

"Hold on, it's not like I created it. All I did was hear about a great new product, and ask to be trained by the medical-device company. Granted, I was one of the first in the country to do that. Okay, the first." He tried his best not to look too proud. "You know the old saying with medicine: watch-one-do-one-teach-one. Now I travel the country doing in-services training for other doctors. Spreading the word. Kind of like a TAVR evangelist." He enjoyed her gushing, but went the humble route anyway. "I'm just a teacher."

"The procedure sure has changed a lot of lives for the better. It probably doesn't cost nearly as much as the old way of doing things either."

"Well, the surgery isn't for everyone, but, yeah, it has helped a lot of people."

He pulled into the parking lot, which put an end to the conversation. When they got out of the car, he thought he noticed a fresh blush on her face, and she looked at him differently than when they'd left the ranch. Okay, so now he knew she was the kind of woman who was impressed with what a man could do, not only his appearance, which was a definite plus for him. Yet there was that link to a man's abilities again, rather than the person. Yeah, but that was all beside the point, because nothing was going to happen between them.

Why did he need to remind himself?

She walked ahead, as if she couldn't get inside the clinic fast enough. There was a spring in her step, and when she looked over her shoulder at him she displayed a giddy grin. "I can't wait to actually start practicing medicine as a real doctor. Finally!"

Doctah!

Oh, good grief. Why didn't she just click her heels and declare to the world *I heart medicine*? He refrained from rolling his eyes, not wanting to dash her rookie excitement.

"Charlotte, our RN, is going to give us a tour of the clinic before we get started," he said.

"Makes sense. We don't want to spend the day looking for things, right?"

So far he liked her logical way of seeing things.

As they approached the clinic door he reminded himself Elisabete Silva was only twenty-six years old, fourteen years younger than him. A different generation, a millennial. His job was to refine, educate and send her out into the world of medicine as a better all-around doctor.

That was all.

So why did he keep checking out the natural side effects of that bouncy walk of hers? Because he was a man, and, unless he was dead, it was what a man did.

Inside the clinic, after general introductions—Cole had met the head nurse at the wedding on Saturday—Charlotte lifted one silver brow above an obvious appraising stare. "Well, I hope you know how to work hard, because there's no room for slackers in this clinic."

Ah, a tight-ship lady. Hmm, Trev had left off that

part. Was that a subtle threat to Cole, too? "Don't worry, Lotte." He used her preferred name, since Trevor had already filled him in. "We'll all pull our load. I know Trevor is a tough act to follow, but I'm older and wiser." He liked to think he was anyway. He winked.

Lotte softened her stern expression at the mention of Trevor. Or maybe it was the wink. "You'll do fine. All you Montgomery men are overachievers." At least she was free with her compliments. "It's just the new one I'm worried about."

Uh-oh, Lotte played dirty, landing a sucker punch below the belt. Did she not know Lizzie was standing right there? He glanced at Lizzie, expecting to see insult, but she wore an amused smile, keeping her true reaction to herself. Good call. But what he'd give to know what was running through her head.

"If it's all the same, I'll look after Dr. Silva," Cole said. "I'm sure we'll all get along just fine."

By the expressions on both women's faces, he wasn't the least bit sure about his prediction.

"Now, how about that tour of the clinic?" he said.

Midmorning, their routine was sliding into place. Granted, Lotte had only allowed half the usual appointments for the next couple of days, but between Cole and Lizzie they were tearing up the house, if he did say so himself.

He sat in Trevor's office, inputting the necessary computer data on his last patient; Lizzie tapped on the opened door. He glanced up, and the vision of youth and eagerness changed his serious outlook to something more in the carefree department. The woman was contagious.

"I've got a patient who doesn't want to take birth-

control pills. She doesn't want the implant or the shot.
I've talked her into using an IUD."

"Okay?" *And what does this have to do with me?*

"You said I had to run everything by you."

"Oh, right. Yes. So can you do what she wants?"

"I've only inserted a couple of them." She'd lowered
her voice to a whisper.

"Do we even have intrauterine devices in the clinic?"
he whispered back, playing along. Since when had playful been a part of his clinical routine?

"Charlotte says we do, and she's willing to assist me.
That okay with you?"

"It'll have to be, because I don't know the first thing
about placing an IUD birth-control device. Should I have
whispered that?"

That got a broad smile out of her, a reward far greater
than he could have imagined. "Okay, great." She charged
off, like an athlete getting called into the game.

"Let me know how it turns out," he said, but suspected she didn't hear him since she was already back
in the patient-exam room with the door closed.

Twenty minutes later, Lizzie emerged from the room
with a victorious smile on her face. Cole watched in
amusement. Lotte followed behind. "You did fine," the
nurse said, matter-of-fact.

"Thanks!"

Shortly afterward the patient stepped outside the
door, dressed and ready to leave. Lotte started to give
instructions, but Lizzie cut her off, taking full responsibility for her patient. The nurse's disgruntled expression didn't go unnoticed by Cole.

"Remember you may feel mild cramps like you're
getting your period for the next couple of days. That's
normal. But if you have excessive cramping or begin

moderate to heavy bleeding, come back and see me right away."

"I promise." The young woman stepped closer to Lizzie. "Dr. Silva, thank you so much for helping me choose a method of birth control that doesn't involve hormones, shots or pills."

"I'm glad we found something that works for you, Gina."

When the patient exited the hallway, Lizzie scrunched up her face, raised her shoulders, fisted and shook her hands in a super-happy gesture. "She called me 'doctor.'"

Cole shook his head just before he went in to see his next patient, though, for the record, he thought her enthusiasm and excitement over the job were cute, even if they did tick off the RN.

During lunch she locked herself in Julie's office, the one she'd taken over. He stood outside and listened, positive some crying was going on in there. Wow, she hadn't given the hint of being homesick for her baby, yet he couldn't deny the sound of crying. He was about to knock to invite her along to the café in town, thinking it might make her feel better, when Lotte informed him that Lizzie was expressing. Expressing what? Then he heard some weird mechanical noises start up inside.

Feeling the urge to put fingers in his ears, he strode out of the building to buy some lunch, trying his damnedest to put the image of a woman pumping her breasts with a machine out of his head.

"TMI, Charlotte. TMI," he called just before he closed the back clinic door.

Lizzie couldn't believe how great the day in clinic had gone so far. Then it hit her: she hadn't thought about Flora for, what, an hour? Her chest clinched and her eyes immediately stung. More proof she was a terrible mother. Flora's sweet face appeared in her mind's eye and she ached to cuddle her. But she'd just finished a pre-summer-camp physical for a ten-year-old boy, which he'd passed with flying colors, and she was printing out a copy for his mother to turn in to the camp nurse when Cole snagged her in the hallway.

"I've got something for you to hear," he said.

"Okay, just let me give this to my patient's mother and I'll be right there." She'd called Gretchen during lunch, and she'd promised everything was going great with her baby, so she'd focused back on work. But, oh, how she missed Flora whenever she came to mind.

Once she'd finished her appointment she went directly to Examination Room Two, where she'd seen Cole step back inside. Still feeling guilty over letting Flora slip out of her mind from time to time, she forced those thoughts away and knocked before entering. Tomorrow she'd bring a picture of her baby and put it on her desk.

"Mr. Harrison, this is Dr. Silva. I wanted to have her listen to your heart, if you don't mind."

"Not at all, Doc," the skinny older man said. He sat on the examination table topless, having removed the worn and faded clinic exam gown.

"Dr. Silva." She loved hearing him call her that. "I was doing a routine physical and, since it is rare to hear all four heart sounds on auscultation, I thought I'd share it with you. The fact that Mr. Harrison is thin helps a lot. Have a listen."

He'd said the sounds were something to share, but she knew it was a test. He didn't just want to share heart sounds with her, there had to be something more going on, and her hunch was it would be up to her to find the reason.

She pulled her top-of-the-line stethoscope from around her shoulders. It had been a gift from Dr. Rivers when she'd graduated near the top in her class. She put the ear tips in and placed the bell on the man's chest in the first of the five positions for listening to heart sounds. True, most of the time doctors and nurses only heard the *lub-dub* sounds, but, seeing as this was an over-sixty and thin male, all four sounds were in fact fairly loud and clear, a rarity. She listened again, more carefully, then heard the faint click between S1 and S2. A murmur. Mitral-valve regurgitation.

"How long have you had mitral prolapse, Mr. Harrison?" She skimmed her gaze over Cole before giving the patient her undivided attention, and she'd seen it, the pleased glint in his eyes and the slight nod of the head. Yes, she'd heard exactly what he'd pulled her in here for.

"What's that?" the man said.

Cole stepped in. "Normally Mr. Harrison doesn't visit the doctor unless he has to, but since he turned sixty-five his wife insisted he have a physical. He's never been diagnosed with mitral prolapse, and seems to be symptom-free, but we'll do a cardiac workup, get a twelve-lead EKG and send him to a specialist for an echocardiogram, then decide how best to treat him."

She nodded in agreement, then, realizing the test was over and she'd passed, she said goodbye to the patient and Cole and went back to work. She still had three more patients to see before the clinic closed. One would be a pelvic exam and Pap smear, another a follow-up for asthma and the last a surgery follow-up for gallbladder removal—a clinic schedule just like a real doctor.

Lizzie loved doing this job. It was the one thing in her life she was sure of...she'd been meant to be a doctor.

On the way home she talked Cole's ear off, but

couldn't help herself, because she was bursting with excitement and needed to share it with someone. Plus, she was on her way home to see Flora. What more perfect way to end a day than that? When she got this way, all worked up and happy, she talked way too fast and slipped into her strongest Boston accent, and Cole probably couldn't understand half of what she was saying, but she couldn't stop. Unlucky Cole was the guy sharing the car with her, so she talked and talked and talked. Poor man had to listen to her full-speed-ahead monologue almost the entire ride home.

As her day wound down, and her breasts tightened with milk, she could barely wait to see her daughter. Thoughts of helpless and beautiful little Flora washed over her, making her want to instantly hold her. She'd missed her daughter, of course she had, yet the breather, doing something she also loved, had been a welcome relief from nonstop child care. What an awful thought! Her face screwed up in confusion, and she needed to either break down and cry or talk about it. Sobbing in front of Cole after her first day at work was not an option. "Is it wrong that I enjoyed being away from Flora today?" she said, her chin quivering.

"Are you asking me if you should feel guilty?" He took his eyes from the road and glanced at her.

She nodded, without a shred of confidence in what his answer would be.

He hesitated, obviously searching for the best words. "I wouldn't dare judge, but I suspect it's normal for any mother to want a break. Nothing to feel guilty about. It's got to be stressful as hell to be totally responsible for another life."

How could this man who'd never been a father nail her exact feelings? "Yes. Very."

"And your being away for a few hours has probably done both of you some good."

"You think? You know, I never heard from Gretchen this afternoon and I'd asked her to call with any questions, or if Flora got too colicky, so that's a good sign, right?"

It was his turn to nod. "Believe me, if Gretchen needed to contact you, she would have."

Swimming on a stream of insecurity, she couldn't help herself. "So you don't think I'm a horrible mother?"

"Not at all. Plus, I think you are a fine doctor in the making who gives her patients a hundred percent of her attention. Which they deserve."

Insecurities duly banished, she sat straighter, her eyes wide and heart warmed from the compliment. "You think?"

"I know." He smiled and that Wyoming cowboy grin nearly knocked the breath out of her. This man was downright dreamy when he smiled.

"Thank you!"

He looked relieved when they got to the ranch. When Gretchen appeared at the back door with Flora in her arms, a rush of motherly emotions flooded every pore, and all Lizzie wanted to do was rush to her baby and hold her. To kiss her and make sure the little one knew her mother was back, and they'd be together the rest of the night. From the distance of the car, she studied her precious one, the face she swore had changed since just that morning, and beamed with love. Her daughter was the icing on the cake of her first dream day on the job and she started to rush toward her.

But Cole pulled her back by the arm, first.

"I couldn't get a word in edgewise on the drive home, but I just wanted to tell you that I think you were outstanding today. You carried your load and you've got a lot of potential and I'm going to see to it that you turn into that top-notch doctor you obviously want to be."

This was the wildest compliment she'd ever gotten, and being that her confidence had been lagging lately, she was so grateful he'd said it. One moment she couldn't find a placement in a resident's program, and the next she was impressing one of the finest cardiologists in the country. How crazy was that? Enthusiasm riding on adrenaline spilled over and coursed through her veins, it pumped into her head and washed her brain in happy juice, further proving she'd made the right decision to come to Wyoming. She couldn't control herself.

She popped up on her toes and threw her arms around Cole's neck for a tight hug. "Thank you so much." Then without thinking she pulled her face out of the crook of his neck and kissed his cheek, complete with end-of-day stubble. "Thank you, thank you, thank you," she said, staring into a pair of startled light brown eyes.

Afraid to linger too long, getting lost in his sexy gaze, she rushed off toward Gretchen. Riding another flood of thanks, she took her precious baby into her arms, kissed Flora's chubby cheek, cuddled her close and thought this had been one of the best days of her entire life. Thanks to Cole Montgomery and the kind surrogate grandmother. Then, getting walloped with a sudden surge of how much she'd missed her daughter all day, she burst into tears.

CHAPTER FIVE

By Friday, Cole was worried how Lizzie would survive. He'd heard the baby crying in the still house in the middle of the night, most nights. He'd witnessed the dark smudges beneath her eyes worsening each new morning. Because of his ongoing neck issues he preferred to stand at the nurses'-station torso-high counter to do his charting in the clinic, and he'd had to step in more than once to ease the friction developing between Lotte and Lizzie. Both were strong-willed women, and wanting the best for the patient; their outspoken styles often clashed. Tension had built all week and something needed to change.

As they drove to the clinic Friday morning he glanced at Lizzie, who'd closed her eyes for the duration of the ride. Her thick hair pulled back tight into the usual braid, the same silver hoops in her ears, the white tailored shirt and black slacks that had turned out to be her personal uniform—perhaps that was the extent of her wardrobe?—her long, delicate fingers twitching lightly from time to time as she stole a few last moments of rest.

He needed to step up as her employer, to guide her and offer gentle advice on how best to serve her patients along with the medical staff. She was a ball of hyper-insecurity one moment and suffered from overconfidence the next, was edgy yet overly sensitive, and she'd been driving the head nurse crazy. That couldn't continue. He'd let her rest for now, but once they arrived at the clinic he'd invite her into his office for a friendly chat.

She made a quiet snort waking herself, then sat straighter and, with bleary, though still sensational eyes, glanced at Cole. "Sorry."

"For what?"

"I think I snored." She rubbed her makeup-less eyes and stretched minimally under the confines of the seat belt.

He smiled, not wanting to make her self-conscious. So he lied.

"I didn't hear anything."

"Oh, good, then."

But, since he'd lost sleep over it, he did need to broach the subject foremost on his mind. "Listen," he said. "I've been thinking we should start having weekly meetings at the clinic. You know, to talk about our patients and share information. As your senior staff person, I should mentor you and as the newest doctor, you can share your discoveries with me, too. What do you say?"

"I've been running everything by you at work." She looked doubtful, like a person realizing they're being set up.

"Yes, but we rarely have time to discuss anything in depth. If you were a resident you'd have daily rounds with fellow doctors and senior staff, you'd be questioned and tested on all the medical possibilities, given assignments, and questioned again. I owe it to you."

She inhaled slowly. "I don't know how we'd squeeze that in at work, though. There's hardly time to breathe, and when I take lunch I need to express for Flora." Without warning she broke into tears, the mark of a stressed-to-the-limit person.

Cole was at a loss for what to say or do, so he let her cry until she recovered a modicum of composure.

"I'm sorry," she said. "I had no idea how hard both working and taking care of my baby would be. How do mothers do it? I think I'm losing my milk." She bit her lower lip, fighting back emotion.

He didn't have a clue how to comment on that at first other than to say, "I'm sorry," but then decided to go the scientific route. "I'm pretty sure science has proven that machines can duplicate most human functions, but they don't ever come close to replacing the soul of the matter." Idea fresh in his mind, he touched the handless smart-phone connection on the steering wheel, desperately needing female backup. "Call Gretchen," he recited.

Within seconds he heard her voice. "Hello, Cole, is everything okay?"

"Gretchen, can you bring Flora to the clinic around eleven-thirty today?"

"Sure. Is there a problem?"

"No problem. Just make sure she's hungry when you leave." He hung up and looked at a clearly flabbergasted Lizzie. "From now on you can nurse your baby during lunch. I'll have a big healthy meal delivered in every day, and you and Flora can have some bonding time on the job."

"You don't have to…"

"Of course I do. It's my job to keep you from melting down. You're here to help me, not to become my next patient."

"I'm sorry."

"Nonsense, no apologies needed." He needed to hit the right tone with his explanation, not make her feel guilty or coddled. "This is purely selfish on my part, so I'm being practical. You need to be a high-functioning member of my staff. You've been doing a commendable job under the circumstances, but there's always room for improvement, right?"

She dutifully nodded, a side of Lizzie he hadn't seen before. Then it occurred to him that there was more to say; there were more ways he could help her, since they lived under the same roof. "Furthermore, if Flora wakes you more than once a night, I'll expect you to come and get me. Not that I can nurse her or anything, but I can walk a floor just as well as you, I suspect. We can share the insomnia between us, then it won't be so bad. And if that helps my new doctor look more alive and keeps her head about her on the job, then I'm happy to do it."

The grateful expression on her perfectly lovely face was hard to resist, but he kept his eyes on the road after a brief peek. He'd never once offered to help with Eddie, Victoria's five-year-old son. Probably because the kid couldn't stand him, and to be honest the feeling was, well, mutual. Victoria had overindulged him and the boy thought he was the center of the universe. But a three-month-old baby like Flora needed to feel cared for and soothed.

"I can't ask you to lose sleep, too," she said.

"You're not asking me anything. I'm telling you our plan to get both of us through the next few weeks. Men are task oriented, in case you hadn't noticed. That's all."

"You're serious, aren't you?"

"You bet I am. Oh, and while I'm on a roll here, let's make those staff meetings back at the ranch." He'd been going to the hospital to visit his father every night after work, but Gretchen had kept him informed about a few things back home. "You've been having dinner in your room, and that's fine for now, but since my father is doing so well, he might be coming home soon. They've agreed to send daily home-health caregivers for the initial week, Gretchen has agreed to sleep over for the first couple of weeks, and we'll see how it goes from there. But my point is, once he's home, we should all take dinner together. He'd want it that way, and, out of respect for him, it's the least we can do. And that includes you. Then after dinner you and I can retire to the library to discuss medical business."

"What about Flora?"

He'd expected a huge protest, but got a maternal-minded question instead, which proved she was a better mother than she gave herself credit for.

"Bring her with. Or let Gretchen bathe her and put her to bed. You figure that out. Bottom line, we need to get on with the job of making you the best resident material out there so you won't sit out another moment from your medical career."

He figured putting it that way she couldn't possibly argue with him.

"Okay. Thanks. I'm in." Amazingly his plan had worked. "Let's make this a miniresident program. Teach me everything you can. It's the best thing for me and the baby, and hopefully your father will benefit from the family dinners as much as I will. Now I know I made the right decision coming here." She beamed.

Cole smiled at the road, thinking his crazy plan had actually worked. Then a chill slipped down his spine at the implications—Lizzie Silva was about to become a part of what was left of his family. Was he ready for that?

At least it was only for the next few weeks. If growing up and surviving medical school, residency and two fellowships had taught him anything, it was to take each huge project one single step after another, never looking at the big overwhelming picture, but concentrating on every small achievement along the way. The days and weeks would click off quickly over the next few weeks, and soon his job would be over with Lizzie. If he worked it right, she'd find a resident placement. She and Flora would pack up and leave once Trevor and Julie returned home, and his life would finally get back to how it was supposed to be.

Traveling. Teaching. Working hard. Uncomplicated by personal relationships.

Alone.

He pulled into the clinic parking lot wondering what in the hell he'd just accomplished, and, since he hadn't a clue, he screwed up his face in confusion. Why did he suddenly feel he was getting the short end of the stick in this clever plan?

Thirty minutes later, after seeing her first patient of the day, Lizzie appeared at Cole's office door.

"I've got a question." She stood smack in the middle of the frame, neither stepping inside nor remaining in the hallway, her stethoscope draped like a shawl over her shoulders, dark hair pulled into a ponytail and piled high on her head.

"Okay, shoot." He stopped typing his notes on the laptop to give his undivided attention, and it never took much for him to give Lizzie Silva all of his attention. Basically, all she had to do was show up and, *boom*, he was all eyes and ears.

"Mrs. Ruth Overmoe is in my exam room complaining of ongoing bloating and nausea unrelieved with over-the-counter gas and acid medicine for a few weeks now. I have a hunch it's more than that. She mentioned today's weight was a few pounds more than usual and attributed that to the bloating. No dietary changes. No history of heart disease. What do you think about my running a CHF workup on her?"

"Are her ankles swollen?"

"Not much, and she says they've been that way for years. The belly bloating is the new issue."

"Any signs of JVD?"

"Nope, her jugular veins don't look distended."

"What do you propose for the workup?" It was a test, yes, but he needed to make sure she didn't miss any labs or other tests that might be useful to make an initial diagnosis.

"CBC, lytes, UA, BUN, FBS, EKG."

"Don't forget liver-function tests and get a chest X-ray."

"Yes, that's a given. Too soon for natriuretic peptide levels?"

"Let's see what we find first with these studies," he said. As she thought, her lips puckered and smoothed, stealing his undivided attention, nearly making him lose his medical train of thought.

"Got it." She smiled and turned to leave.

"Good find," he said, pleased with her level head and solid medical background. From over her shoulder, as she walked away, she flashed him a wide smile, one that reeked of confidence and pride. "I'll expect a full report on congestive heart-failure symptoms exclusive to women at our first meeting."

"You got it," she said without turning around, un-fazed by his challenge.

Cole wasn't sure how helpful these after-dinner sessions would be for Lizzie, but, as for him, he definitely looked forward to them.

"Here's your girl," Gretchen said, making her daily clinic entrance exactly at 11:30 a.m. in Lizzie's office the following Friday morning.

"Thank you!" Excited to see Flora, Lizzie reached out and took her baby into her arms. In one short week, it had quickly become the highlight of her work day. Whether sensing her mother or smelling milk was nearby, the child opened her eyes, squirmed and soon fussed. "Oh, honey, I miss you so much." She kissed her baby's cheek, which was growing chubbier by the day, and cuddled her close to her body. "Mommy loves you."

Gretchen had been nothing short of a godsend these past couple of weeks. She glanced up at the older woman in deep appreciation. "You know, since you started giving her the evening bath she has really settled down at night. It seems her colic may have passed."

"I have a little trick I remember from when I had my babies. Not that they've given me any grandbabies to try it out on or anything, but that's an issue for another day." Gretchen gave Lizzie her pretend disgusted expression. Having chatted a lot since arriving at Circle M Ranch, Lizzie had learned how much the woman longed for grandchildren, but neither of her daughters were married. "I use an old rubber water bottle filled with warm water and lay it across her tummy after her bath. Then, when I put her down, I give her a pacifier to suck on."

"That's a great idea, and it certainly helps Flora settle

down faster," Lizzie said as she unbuttoned her blouse and opened the nursing-bra flap, then watched with delight as Flora nuzzled close to nurse.

"I think she senses you're settling down, too."

"What do you mean?"

"You've come a long way since arriving at the ranch. You were one edgy and nervous lady at first. Now we've all gotten into a comfortable routine, and Flora must sense it. Babies love routines."

"You may have a point."

"Well, the test will be this Sunday when Tiberius comes home. If anything can disrupt the peace, he will."

"Have you been to see him?" Flora was eagerly nursing, and, though it was always great to have alone time with her, today Lizzie chose to use the time to quiz Gretchen.

"A couple of times. He's doing really well, gets most sentences out the way he wants, but once in a while he can't quite express himself, and it bugs the holy hell out of him." Gretchen's eyes widened. "Oh, pardon me for cussing in front of the baby."

"I don't think she noticed." Lizzie grinned, thinking how terrible she'd been the first few weeks alone with her colicky baby. Not that she'd cussed *at* her precious one, no, but she'd been so exhausted and frazzled that she'd been short with a lot of people, some who had even been trying to help her. And sometimes, feeling under a pressure cooker, she'd revert to cussing a blue streak like when she'd been a rebellious teenager. Realizing those days seemed to be behind her, or maybe it mostly had to do with nursing Flora, but whatever the reason, she completely relaxed and slipped into the moment. Life was good. For now. Two weeks ago it had been like living a nightmare in Boston with zero prospects, staying in that dark and tiny single-room apartment after quitting that horrible job.

Now she had a new job and a great place to live, she enjoyed her work and the one-on-one mentoring time with her boss, and she owed it all to the big handsome Wyoming hunk, Cole.

"I'll leave you two alone now," Gretchen said, tiptoeing toward the door. "Be back at twelve-thirty."

"Thank you," Lizzie said, glancing at her contented baby then making a blanket statement for everything good in her life in the right here and now, kind of like saying grace and meaning it with all of her heart. "I can't thank you enough," she whispered, and closed her eyes.

By the end of Lizzie's second week at Circle M, Cole realized that Lizzie hadn't knocked on his door once in the middle of the night. Could bringing Flora for midday nursing have helped fine-tune the baby's schedule? He shook his head no. He'd taken the time to read up on colic in babies and knew that, though the problem still remained mostly a mystery, the biggest help turned out to be time. Sometime around three or four months, except for extreme cases, the colic issue seemed to cure itself. Whether it was a baby's metabolism finally figuring things out, or all the mother's efforts to avoid spicy foods and caffeine paying off—whatever the reason, or maybe for no reason at all—sometimes the problem simply disappeared.

He put his hands behind his head and turned out the bedside lamp, then closed his eyes. Instead of letting himself fall asleep, he remembered Lizzie's luscious expressions earlier as she'd listened while he went over the day's list of patients and quizzed her on each one. Thinking of her inquisitive green eyes, and how her mouth pouted slightly while she thought, assured he wouldn't find sleep in his near future. Crying baby or no crying baby, Flora wasn't the source of his insomnia. His father's health wasn't either. Or the huge cardiac conference he was missing in NYC this weekend, nor was the running of the Cattleman Bluff Medical Clinic with its outdated computer hardware. No. The source of his insomnia was simple to identify—Lizzie Silva.

CHAPTER SIX

COLE BROUGHT TIBERIUS home Sunday midafternoon, and Lizzie stood in the entryway. She waited for him to come through the door while wearing Flora in a front-facing baby carrier, the child's current favorite place to watch the world. Plus it was an online tip as another way to help decrease colic in babies.

The older man begrudgingly used his quad cane to stabilize himself as he made the trek from the parked car to the porch. His wild mane looked whiter than she'd remembered, but someone, most likely his nurse, had done battle with it and his hair lay somewhat flat against his head. Cole was directly behind him watching his every step. He obviously played down the fact he was within catching distance in case his father lost his footing or anything. Tiberius would throw a fit if he caught on, so he stayed a foot or two back and allowed his father to be independent. Once they crossed the wide porch, Cole shot ahead to open the front door for him.

"I can do it," Tiberius said, grumpily. "I'm not an invalid." Then quietly he muttered, "Yet."

"Just trying to be helpful, Dad." For that comment, Cole received an impatient squint, and Lizzie ached for him. "Gretchen, have you got something for Dad to eat?"

"Blasted hospital food is worse than airplane food."

More grumbling from Mr. Cheerful. Then he noticed Lizzie and Flora, and his irritated expression softened a little. "Well, look who's still here. I thought you'd have high-tailed it back to Boston by now." He walked toward her, and she was about to answer him, but Mr. Montgomery hung a left before she could think of a good comeback—which was unusual for her—heading for his chair in the living room. She suspected he recognized a kindred spirit in her, one blustery phony to another. At least that was how she saw him, all bark yet tenderhearted. With Tiberius clearly in a sassy mood, she followed his lead.

"You can't get rid of me that easily, Mr. Montgomery." Lizzie understood the best way to deal with a grump was to be grumpy right back. "You've inherited us for another four weeks, so just get used to it." She followed him, and beat him to his chair, then puffed the pillow tucked into the corner of the arm rest. He sat, hanging on to his annoyed expression, but he couldn't fool her, because, like a thin veil, right behind the grouchy gaze was a "happy to see you, too" glint.

"Weren't you the one who saved my life?"

She sputtered a laugh. "Hardly. We all did our part, and you turned out to be stubborn enough not to let anything too bad happen anyway."

He sat with a thud. "How do you know me so well?"

"Maybe you're the grandfather I never had." Which set a whole other connotation into place—but the last thing she'd ever think of Cole as was a father, not with the way she'd already developed a crush on him. True, he was fourteen years older than her; she'd done the math. They'd grown up in different generations, he was a Gen X and she was a Gen Y—a millennial. She didn't write letters or listen to voice mail. She didn't know what the world was like before computers took over. Their taste in music had to be light years different. But sometimes she fantasized about him.

Realistically, besides practicing medicine, what did they have in common? Yet, each day she felt more drawn to him because of his calm, his maturity, his knowledge…not to mention his excellent looks and how he was sexy without even realizing it. She especially liked that. She sighed as she repositioned the pillow exactly where Tiberius pointed behind his back, forcing her thoughts back on track.

"No, thanks. I've already got a grandson. James is enough."

"Now you're just hurting my feelings," she said.

"Didn't mean to do that." The sincerity in his eyes nearly bowled her over. "I'm still cranky from being stuck in the hospital for a couple of weeks. Torture. Pure torture."

"Can I get you anything?" she said, a sudden puddle of compassion.

At that moment, Gretchen appeared in the doorway with a tray of food in her hands. Cole rushed to find and open a TV tray to set it on. With three people and a baby circling his favorite chair, Tiberius protested. "Back off, folks, I'm not going to croak today or any day this week. Give me some breathing room, would you?"

Watching to make sure he had use of both hands, without residual weakness on the right, Lizzie stepped back and passed a sheepish glance at Cole. He raised his dark brows in warning, obviously implying, *Be prepared—you ain't seen nothin' yet.* She liked passing secret messages with Cole, especially since it meant she got to look into those handsomely wise eyes.

"I think I'll take Flora for a walk," she said, heeding his warning, deciding to leave Tiberius to Cole and Gretchen. Besides, it was a beautiful warm and sunny afternoon, and if she timed it right she could make it all the way out to the ash and maple-tree grove with the pond before Flora's next nursing was due. She could sit in the shade in privacy and enjoy Wyoming's big sky and abundant nature, and feeding her baby all at once. Which reminded her she was hungry, too. She bent her knees, since bending at the waist was impossible with the baby carrier, and snatched half of Tiberius's roast beef and cheddar cheese sandwich. "Mind if we share?" She passed him a mischievous look, raised her brows, and, when she had his full attention, took a big bite before he could utter a word.

The corner of his wrinkled mouth lifted in a near smile. "Wouldn't want to rob a woman of nourishment. But don't even think about touching that gingerbread cookie."

"Not even half?" she said, her mouth filled with wheat-bread sandwich.

"Don't push it, girlie-girl." He feigned a grouchy glance, and she gave him a genuine smile, because she really liked the old guy, and she suspected he liked her just as much. Then, with the smile lingering on her lips, her gaze settled on Cole, who watched the odd interaction between his father and the newest boarder at the ranch. A tiny hiss and sizzle snaked down her chest as she walked out of the living room and into the great outdoors where the sun warmed all of her, not just the hot, fluttering part planted there by Cole.

Later, after nursing Flora and dozing off to sleep for a few minutes, Lizzie wandered back to the ranch and the stables. She'd already figured out that Flora loved to see the big horses.

"You ever want to take a ride, just let me know." Cole surprised her from behind.

She turned away from petting the big reddish-brown horse. "I've never been on a horse, wouldn't know what to do."

"I'd be happy to teach you. All you have to do is ask." Their gazes met and held firm, and she wondered if he'd just offered something more than horseback-riding lessons. Nah, she'd probably read too much into that supersexy gaze.

"If Gretchen's hands weren't full with your father, I might take you up on it right now."

One brow curved toward the other. "Good point. Any thoughts on how she's going to be able to watch Flora and my dad?"

Lizzie inhaled and let her air out slowly. Fortunately, she'd given this topic lots of thought. "I'm one step ahead of you, Cole. Remember Gina, the woman I helped with birth control?"

He nodded, looking so darn much like a real cowboy she thought she'd traveled back in time.

"Well, she and I have been keeping in touch, and it turns out she has two kids under three. She could use some extra money and when you mentioned your dad was coming home, I asked if she'd consider watching Flora. She'd love to, even said she'd bring her by for midday nursing."

"That's great. I'm glad you're making friends."

She tossed her glance upwards. "Too bad Lotte and I can't be friends, too."

A benevolent smile coursed his mouth. "She's what

we call a crusty old nurse. Got a lot of opinions and isn't afraid to push them on everyone."

"Someone needs to tell her she's a little outdated because she won't listen to me."

Suddenly losing the sexy cowboy gaze and taking on a diplomatic expression, he squared his shoulders. "Well, you do have a way of pushing the limit, in case you're not aware of it."

She shook her head. "Look, I know I'm not exactly an ambassador of goodwill, but I'm the one fresh out of medical school. When did she get her RN license? Thirty years ago?"

Cole walked to the horse Flora was watching while she cooed and squealed, and patted its cheek. The horse blew hot breath through flared nostrils in appreciation and the sound drew another shriek from the baby. "She's a wealth of experience that you could tap into. Being fresh out of school can sometimes be a disadvantage, you know?" he said, admiring the horse rather than look at Lizzie. "You might just learn from her if you give her a chance."

She'd honestly never considered Lotte a wealth of information, but seeing the sincerity in Cole's avoiding eyes, and more so in his demeanor, she realized he'd just used a velvet hammer to call her out. Maybe her head was bigger than her knowledge? "Is this where I'm supposed to eat humble pie?"

Instead of seeming frustrated, he grinned. "I remember being full of myself, too. Just ask my dad—he'll tell you story after story. The thing is, a lot of the old ways still work just fine. You might learn some time-saving tricks if you give Lotte a chance."

"And no one, including you, likes a know-it-all, right?" How had she gotten called to the vice principal's office in a stable? And more important, why did she have the strong desire to change immediately? Couldn't he see her overconfidence was just a ploy to cover her insecurity?

He dipped his head and studied his boots, maybe a little disconcerted by her usual full-speed-ahead approach, then sent her a narrowed gaze. "If you're here in Cattleman Bluff to learn, I'm suggesting you find every opportunity available. Nurses are a great source of practical knowledge and it never hurts to make them allies."

He turned to leave, and partly because what he'd said made perfect sense, plus the fact he looked like a real-life cowboy in those tight jeans and that button-up shirt, except without a hat, she couldn't let him go just yet. "Thanks," she said. "I get it." Really she did. She needed to soften up around Lotte. She waited for him to turn, expecting a surprised expression, but she found so much more. His eyes examined her as if he'd just seen her for the first time. Couldn't the man see how she felt about him? His extra attention sent a shiver up her neck. "Um, Flora's due for a nap—any chance I can take you up on that horseback-riding lesson offer?"

"The old man's taking a nap, too, and Gretchen's watching over him like a mother hen. No reason she can't look in on Flora, too. Let's do it."

Excited over the prospect of taking her first ride, she rushed to Cole, popped up onto her toes and bussed his scratchy cheek, thinking he'd put her in her place without humiliating her and now he was kind enough to take her horseback riding for the first time in her life. This guy was too good to be true. "See you soon." When she pulled her head back, the flash of fire in his dark eyes sent more hiss and sizzle slicing through her, except this time it sank deeper. She couldn't very well stand there locked in his sight, not when Flora's little hands flapped like a hummingbird, so she turned and headed out of the stable. As she strode toward the house, she realized she was out of breath and it had nothing to do with walking or carrying Flora.

Cole refused to be a cliché, damn it—boss falling for his attractive employee. But he stood there, watching her walk away, enjoying every sway of her hips and the bounce of her dark hair, and liking the way it made him feel alive in a way he'd forgotten lately. This was crazy.

And it had to stop.

He started to saddle O'Reilly, the Irish pony from Connemara, dark brown with calico markings on her legs, for himself—his father had brought her over five years ago for the ranch—thinking Trevor's aging buckskin Appaloosa, Zebulon, would be good for Lizzie. He relaxed and enjoyed the process of saddling the horses, not having to think, just mindlessly following the steps. He should let go and see what the afternoon would bring, think of it as nothing more than a relaxing ride with a lovely lady. What harm could that do? Then tomorrow, back at the clinic, he'd go back to business as usual. Because he couldn't let his growing attraction to Lizzie interfere with what was best for her. Best for both of them.

Thirty minutes later, Lizzie showed up in jeans and tennis shoes—better than flip-flops anyway—obviously eager, though nervously chewing her lower lip. That expression alone nearly stopped him dead in his tracks. He really needed to quit focusing on her mouth.

"Ready?" he said, going into forced casual mode. The horses were saddled and waiting.

"As ready as I'll ever be."

He couldn't stand there staring at how cute she

looked, so he moved in, weaving his fingers, making a footrest for her to launch off. "Put your left foot here and swing your right leg over Zebulon's back."

For once, she didn't resist, but followed instruction to the T.

"Now slip your feet into the stirrups, so I can adjust them. You can hold on to the horn for now." He shortened the stirrups to fit the length of her legs. "How's that feel?"

"About right, I guess." She looked all around stiff and anxious, and he tried to remember how he'd felt the first time he'd sat on a horse. But he'd been way too young to remember all the details now. Come to think of it, he kind of had grown up on a horse.

Not wanting to prolong her worries, he handed her the reins. "Hold these gently, no need to pull them. When you want Zebulon to walk, just squeeze your inner thighs right here." He patted the area just behind the horse's girth. "When you want to stop him lean back a touch and pull back on the reins. Not too hard, though—he'll get the message." He stroked Zebulon's neck and kept talking. "Just don't do too many things all at once 'cause that will confuse him and he'll ignore you. Oh, and horses prefer gentle voices."

Her eyes were large, concerned-looking and maybe a little panicked.

"Don't worry," he said. "Zebbie's gonna follow O'Reilly, and we'll take it easy for your first time. Okay?"

She nodded, still looking uncertain, an expression he'd rarely seen on her.

"I'm not gonna let anything happen to you, Lizzie, so relax. Zebulon will pick up on your nervousness and he's known to be stubborn. You don't want to set off his stubborn button."

"Okay." Her nostrils flared slightly when she said it, and Cole understood the city slicker felt completely out of her element, so he grinned warmly to help soothe her.

"You're going to do fine," he said in his gentlest voice, as if he were talking to a spooked horse.

"If you say so." She sounded breathy, and he liked it. A lot. He gave her a quick lesson on how to turn the horse right and left, and let her practice a time or two with him right there in case anything got fouled up.

Once he'd mounted O'Reilly, they set off at a measured pace until he sensed Lizzie was settling in. "See that ridge way out there?"

She followed his direction and narrowed her eyes. "Yes."

"From there you can see the entire ranch. Feel like giving it a try?"

Obviously hiding her nerves, she gave a courageous firm nod, and he admired her for that. But he admired her for a lot of things, and not all of them strictly physical. This woman had a lot to offer, and some guy down the road would be lucky to have her. "Let's go." Not him. "Remember, whenever you want Zebulon to go, squeeze your thighs together. If he doesn't respond right off, squeeze a little tighter."

She suddenly shared a shaky yet beaming smile with him. "No wonder women like to ride horses."

He laughed—now that was the lady he was used to—and led out, wondering how it might feel to have Lizzie Silva squeeze her thighs around his hips. Oh, damn, he wasn't going to be a cliché. *Don't forget.*

The clear sky left the sun alone to bake their backs as they rode at a trot toward the trail to the ridge. "How you doin'?" he called back.

"Surprisingly well. This is fun."

He turned to look at her and was rewarded with her happy expression along with a lightly flushed complexion. Yeah, he didn't know one person worth their salt who didn't enjoy riding horses. With one last glance and smile, he switched back and led the way to the ascending trail.

"What's up with you and your dad?"

Whatever peace and tranquility he'd gathered up so far on this ride vaporized as chaotic memories broke in. "What do you mean?"

"There's some major tension between you two. Am I right?"

He hated when people saw right through him, especially when he'd worked so hard to cover it up. "We have some old business, I guess you could say, like everyone."

"It seems pretty current to me."

Was it her street smarts or her training as a doctor that had her zeroing in on the situation? "Well, if you want to focus on the current issues, he's getting old and neither Trevor nor I want to take over the ranch."

"It's his legacy, right?"

"Yup. Key word being *his*, not mine or Trev's."

"He's worked hard to build it."

"That he has. I think he holds me responsible for Trevor following me into medical school. I was the first-born and it was taken for granted I'd take over someday, maybe build an empire for the Montgomery name—best steer in the country. You know how that goes."

"Not really. Foster care, remember?"

"Oh, right, I'm sorry. So you probably fall on the ungrateful-son side with my dad, then, right?"

"No judgment from me."

He decided to leave it at that, since he hadn't figured out how to bring up the subject with his dad and didn't think a woman who'd never had a dad could be empathetic. Things were complicated. He'd made a great career for himself yet his father still thought of him as a runner. "I've used my career to avoid dealing with him."

"You don't come home much?"

"Not since my mother died."

"I can kinda tell he still loves and misses her. Probably why he likes to play grumps all the time."

"I didn't hold up my end of the bargain. Never did. Tried to impress a girl and fell off a bucking bronco, broke my neck. Then got it in my head I wanted to be a doctor, not a rancher. Then, to make matters worse, Trevor followed my lead. My mom used to keep me and Dad from killing each other when I was a teenager. Theoretically speaking. After my neck, I went the academic route when all Dad wanted was more help with the steer. He wanted to teach me everything he knew, didn't give a crap about my winning the county scholastic decathlon three years running. Mom put her foot down when he refused to pay for college."

"Wait a second. You broke your neck for a girl?" That low and husky laugh tumbled out, and, realizing the absurdity of his story, he laughed with her.

"Yup. 'Cause that's how I roll. At fifteen anyway."

She laughed until Zebulon protested, then covered her mouth and pushed the last of her chuckles back down her throat. What else was there to say after that? He'd been involved with Victoria for almost two years and had never told her about why he'd broken his neck. Now all he did was take a short horseback ride with Lizzie and spill his guts. He squinted toward the sun, inhaled more fresh air, deciding to chalk it up to the great outdoors and the woman with the green eyes that drove him wild.

Twenty minutes later, with only the creaking of their

saddles and the plodding of the horses' hooves, his lungs filled with crisp air and mind with earned solitude, they'd made it to the ridge.

"Let's take a break here." He dismounted, and led O'Reilly to some grass, then started for Zebulon, who'd taken it upon himself to share that patch of prairie grass with O'Reilly and had already moved closer. "Whoa," he said gently, stopping the horse long enough to allow Lizzie to swing over her leg. He grabbed her from behind by the upper hips and helped her down the rest of the way, liking the weight of her in his hands and the heat simmering from her body.

How many times did he have to tell himself reacting to her like that was crazy?

She turned quickly in his arms, cheeks flushed from brisk air, mood clearly exhilarated from the ride. "That was incredible. I loved it."

She'd taken right to riding, and discovering she loved it set off a light, flighty sensation in his chest. "I thought you might."

"Wow!" She'd skipped right past their warm moment that evidently he was the only one feeling, trading him in for the view, but not before he zeroed in on that sexy little mole by her upper lip. "Would you look at that?"

He'd rather look at her, but he followed her invitation toward the cliff. The entire Circle M Ranch sprawled out before them, neatly divided into sections of green and brown grazing land for their steer, separate grazing areas for the horses, perimeter and pasture fencing protecting the cattle from the roads, and irrigated areas where they grew much of their own hay and grains to help feed the steer. Even all the way up here, he could smell the hay. From this angle the view was impressive, even though he'd seen it hundreds of times.

The prairie grass had turned light brown due to summer, covering the rolling hills and flatlands dotted with greener shrubs and trees. Their home was dwarfed by the panoramic view. It was the first time he'd been up here since coming home, and the view, as always, caused a swell of pride in his chest. His father had taken a dream and made it come true. Truth was, Cole wanted to impress her with the Circle M Ranch and all it stood for, to give her a clue how sacred this land was to his father. After their earlier conversation, it was also a lesson for him.

Unless he or Trevor stepped in, their family ranch might be gone in a matter of years. Or the *M* would be torn down and replaced by someone else's initial. He didn't want to dig into those consequences right now, not with Lizzie by his side, but the realization helped him understand better his father's frustration.

"I don't think I've ever breathed fresher air," Lizzie said, breaking into his thoughts. A light breeze had kicked up and loose ends of her hair, though mostly pulled back into a ponytail, flicked and tickled around her face.

"Welcome to our little bit of heaven on earth."

"I can't imagine what it's like to grow up in a place like this."

"I'll be honest, I took it for granted. Now that I live in Baltimore half the time and Laramie the rest, I appreciate the peace and solitude when I visit."

"Which isn't that often, right?"

"Don't ruin my moment." Something about Lizzie made it easy to say exactly what he thought without worrying it would be taken wrong—another exact opposite from Victoria.

"You ever think about moving back?"

He raised his head, taken aback by her comment. Did he? "Let's just say sometimes I wonder what will happen if I don't."

"You think you could live all the way out here and continue to be cutting-edge in cardiology?"

And there was the rub.

"Another good question that I don't have an answer to." She'd managed to make him edgy, even while gazing at the cattle kingdom his father had staked out for himself and his family. He had a lot of thinking to do on the subject, especially now with his father growing more frail by the year, hell, by the month.

He really didn't want to think about that right now, though, not with the tall, intriguing woman standing so near, sharing the view with him. He'd much rather be close enough to smell her shampoo and to see the tiny golden flecks he'd just recently noticed in her soft hazel-green eyes. That tiny mole. Or to think about, for instance, how it would feel to put his hand on her waist.

She must have sensed his thoughts because she turned toward him, pushing hair out of her eyes as she did, smiling and practically willing him to come closer. He took a step or two and she met him halfway. They reached for each other as if they'd planned this lovers' getaway for weeks. What was going on? He didn't care; he pulled her into his arms as she stepped closer and soon his desire to sniff her hair and nuzzle her long neck became reality.

They stayed there, hugging, getting used to the feel of each other, and him liking every little discovery. Like how she fit so well against him; her being tall meant he didn't have to hunch over, which took a lot of discomfort away from his neck. Her head fit neatly beneath his chin, and sharing the view with her made him want to fly. So much of what Lizzie Silva did was disturbing to his equilibrium, yet uplifting, too. He wondered what he did for her, and worried it fell far short of what she managed to bring out in him.

He needed to shut down his brain, to quit overthinking every little thing, because all of these thoughts were stealing from their moments together. Lizzie was normally like a skittish colt, yet right now she snuggled into his chest, relaxed and calm; he couldn't let this slip by. Soon, though, her head moved from under his chin. He looked downward to her questioning gaze, and without a second thought, he answered her by pressing his mouth to hers. Their lips settled together in a warm and exhilarating seal. Hers were soft and smooth, and he swore he caught the scent of vanilla and tasted it from her lip gloss.

Though knowing this was exactly the opposite of what he should be doing if he didn't want to be a cliché, he deepened their kiss. She obliged, opening her lips enough for him to touch the tip of her tongue and then to discover the velvety-smooth inner side of her mouth. He tasted hints of peppermint even as he inhaled that vanilla gloss.

Being a man, he knew exactly two gears, On and Off, and right now On took control. His hands wandered down her surprisingly fragile back and then lower to her hips, enjoying all that he grabbed on to. He was vaguely aware of her arms tightening around his neck when he did. She'd heated up the kiss, canting her head, probing and delving deeper with her tongue, and the entire front of his body tensed in anticipation of what might come next.

With blood rushing through his veins from her being so close, he didn't stand a chance she wouldn't notice his natural reaction. But he didn't care. She'd started it. She was a doctor, knew all about physiology. He just wanted to keep kissing her and feeling her. And she seemed to want the same, kissing harder as her hands kneaded and rubbed his neck and shoulders.

Minutes passed as their kisses danced and whirled into a passionate knot. He tasted and breathed her, and made it very clear that she'd turned him on. The problem was, there was nowhere to go from here. Sure, some heady kisses were great, but, really, he knew this had to end. She'd been brought on board to help at the clinic, and he hoped to help her, too. She wasn't meant to be a playmate.

She was a new mother, for crying out loud—what was he doing working her all up when reality screamed that this wasn't supposed to happen? He *was* a cliché.

Then he felt it. His guy switch turned to Off.

Yeah, they couldn't keep this up. Not now.

Not ever?

His hands lightened their grip on her hips. He removed his lips from hers as he drew back. With regret he looked into her eyes and saw the hesitant disappointment there, and for that he was glad, because he was definitely disappointed, and didn't want to be the only one. At least he hadn't thrown himself at her; every part of this make-out session had been mutual. Beyond a doubt.

But what the hell had they just done except complicate things?

"Must be all that fresh air, huh?" She broke the stretching silence, answering his unvoiced question.

Sure, they could always blame it on the weather.

He glanced sheepishly at her. "Yeah. I hope I—"

"Please don't apologize, because then I'll have to, too, and, to be honest, I really liked kissing you."

Since she put it that way... "Me, too, but we have no business dragging sex in to this situation."

Her eyes shifted downward beneath her full, arched brows. "Then we should probably ride back now."

Damn, he'd hit a nerve or something and now she wanted nothing more to do with him. He didn't want to force the subject of sex or no sex, so he agreed. He ran one feather-light knuckle over her smooth cheek regretfully. "Okay, let's go, then."

Cole barely needed to help Lizzie mount her horse this time around, and before he got on O'Reilly she'd already turned Zebulon around, heading back toward the trail.

He'd let his most honest feelings loose just now, and all it had done was confuse things. That couldn't and wouldn't happen again. Because he was damned if he would be a cliché.

Lizzie rode down the trail in silence. She'd let down her defenses and kissed Cole. What a stupid idea. Cole had reprimanded her about dragging sex in to their situation, and she really should have known better. Men these days got called out for inappropriate behavior with employees and slapped with lawsuits all the time. For all he knew she might have been setting him up. Wasn't that how Dave had felt after going out with her for six months, then finding out she'd gotten pregnant? The last thing she'd needed was a baby while going through medical school—how could Dave possibly think she'd gotten pregnant on purpose? Yet he did. The fact that her schedule had been crazy and she'd messed up on the birth-control pills had never entered his mind. Nope, he'd flipped out and roughed her up to make his point, too.

A powerful man like Cole couldn't be cautious

enough, and she'd just allowed something as simple as a horseback ride on the ranch let her make a bad choice. Of course Dr. Cole Montgomery was off-limits, and the fact she'd thrown her arms around him and kissed him as if they were on a date proved she was suffering from new-mom brain.

Seriously, what had she been thinking?

That he was the sexiest man she'd ever met. That there was something special about him and his family. That she'd give anything in the world to belong to someone like that, to be a part of it and for Flora to have a man in her life like Cole.

When they got back to the stables, she dismounted without his help, didn't want him to have to touch her again since he'd backed off pretty quickly after they'd kissed. Was it something she'd done? When their gazes slipped over each other's, she sent him a secret message—*Don't worry, Doc, it won't ever happen again*—then headed back to the house, pretending she needed to rush back to her baby.

Sunday dinner was mandatory. Dad was home, cranky and restless. Gretchen had cooked his favorite meal of prime Montgomery beef stew with root vegetables even though it was summer, had baked corn bread and made cold cucumber salad. Cole wanted to avoid Lizzie, but wouldn't dare stand up his father for dinner—especially since he'd made such a big deal out of it to Lizzie—and definitely not on his father's first night home.

They gathered at the huge heirloom table, big enough to seat twenty people, seeming sadly lacking as a party of four and a half—that was if Lizzie and Flora showed up. Maybe it was time to start eating in the kitchen. Ah, what was he thinking? That would never fly with his traditionalist father, especially not on Sunday nights.

The moment Lizzie walked in to the room, things brightened. A little buzz zipped through Cole, reminding him of earlier, making him wonder if she'd replayed those moments as many times as he had in the few short hours since they'd shared those kisses. Or had she thought of it at all?

Their eyes met and held briefly, and something told him she'd already taken his words to heart—*we have no business dragging sex in to this situation.* It didn't matter if they liked kissing each other or not, they'd messed with their work dynamics and it would take a while to get over that. At least for him, because, as he'd already established, he *was* a sad cliché.

Yet he still had to sit across from her at the table and couldn't very well avoid looking at her.

She'd pulled her hair back and put it in a loose roll on the top of her head, wore bright pink lip gloss and a dark blue short-sleeved blouse. Her eyes stood out as always, and her gentle smile of greeting made them turn upward at the edges. It suited her.

In such a short time he'd already gotten accustomed to her face, to seeing her every day, which was a very bad thing. He frowned and she must have taken it personally by the flash of confusion in her gaze as she pulled it away and settled on his dad, instead.

"Mr. Montgomery, you're looking dashing tonight," she said, even though his father wore a faded plaid shirt, with an obvious stain on the yellowing crew-necked undershirt.

"Call me Monty, like all of my friends, and cut the crap." He shook out his napkin, signaling it was time to eat.

Lizzie laughed good-naturedly, something else he liked about her, adjusting Flora in the wraparound sling she wore across her torso. "Okay, Monty, I feel honored to be considered a friend."

Monty fretted, as if he'd already regretted opening the door to friendship with her. "Pass the stew, would you?" he barked gruffly.

Cole stood and carried the large ceramic tureen to his father, lifted the lid and let him serve himself even though it took more effort than usual, then walked around the table and held it for Lizzie to dish out hers. Just because he'd kissed her like a randy teenager earlier didn't mean he'd forgotten how to be a gentleman. He figured things were awkward because he was sending mixed-up messages, and she focused on the food rather than look at him. He wanted to kick himself for kissing her—uh, no, honestly, he didn't, but right now he hated the repercussions—because it fouled up their working relationship. She had so much to learn and he wanted to help her.

"Gretchen, this smells fantastic," Lizzie said.

Gretchen dutifully brushed away the compliment. "Oh, I've been making this for the Montgomerys for years."

"Best food I ever had since coming here. You're a great cook."

"Oh, not really." Cole had made it over to Gretchen and let her serve herself. "Thank you, Cole."

"She's right," he said. "I've been away so long I'd almost forgotten." She patted his hand in appreciation once she'd filled her bowl.

Cole sat to the right of his father and served himself. The corn bread got passed around and after his father's terse grace they all dug in.

"I'm not really used to eating family-style." Lizzie wasn't afraid to break the silence, and Cole was glad about that.

"Families don't eat together in Boston?" Monty plunged ahead without a second thought.

"Didn't have a family. I was mostly in foster care." She spread butter on her corn bread. "I never really felt part of those families."

That stopped Monty cold. He quit chewing and stared at Lizzie, obviously trying to decide how to put his other foot in his mouth, too. "Now, that's a cryin' shame." He shoved another bite into his mouth, deep in thought.

"I had my grandmother until I was ten. Loved her to bits. But she died and it wasn't until I was fifteen when I met Janie Tuttle."

Cole didn't want his father to make any more lame comments so he spoke up. "Was she a foster parent, too?"

Lizzie glanced appreciatively at him, knowing she'd already shared a part of her history with him. "Yes. She's the reason I got scholarships to college and she put the notion in my head that I could be a doctor if I wanted to be."

Achy warmth clung to his chest, making him wish everyone could have a solid home as he and his brother had growing up. "She must have been a great lady."

"She was an old spinster school teacher, didn't have a clue how to handle a teenager, but she took a chance on me. I guess I had the good sense—well, after being in a whole lot of not-so-great foster homes—to appreciate her interest in my education. She died my second year in medical school, but at least she knew I'd made it there." She blinked away the moisture that had gathered and made her eyes look large and dewy.

The achy warmth increased and clinched like a vise.

He forced his gaze to his food to give her space to recover, if that was what she wanted to do. Lizzie had lost
everyone who ever cared about her; now all she had was
Flora. The last thing she needed to feel was that she had
been taken advantage of by him. Sometimes life really
didn't seem fair.

"You're an inspiration," Gretchen said. "You've made
yourself a success."

Lizzie laughed lightly. "Hardly. After I'm through
here I don't have a job."

He didn't think for half a second before the words
popped out of his mouth. "I'm going to do something
about that."

Her full, arched brows lifted a good inch. "How are
you going to do that?"

"I'm going to get you an interview with the head of
the internal-medicine resident program of your choice."
He was? "I'm going to coach you and help you present
yourself in the best light and I will guarantee you make
a great impression."

"My choice? You have that much clout?"

Probably not, but he'd work out the details later. "The
key is you can't pick the same hospitals you just tried
to get into. Come up with your secondary list. Give me
five choices, and I'll get you in."

"You'd do that for me?"

He wanted to. "Yes." Maybe partly to get her out of
his life, or partly to impress her? Oh, hell, he wasn't sure
why he wanted to do this, but he did. That was the important thing. He wanted to help Lizzie and Flora. He
liked them, cared about them. In order for them to have
a good life, she needed a resident placement. Hmm, he'd
make some calls this week to see if any spots were left

open in any of the east-coast programs. "Are you willing to consider a list of programs I compile for you, too?"

"How can I say no to that?" She offered a somewhat disbelieving grin, and Cole knew he'd have to prove to her that he was a man of his word. That he could be trusted. And their kissing had nothing to do with this.

He took a bite of beef, wondering one thing. Was he the kind of man who could be trusted?

Soon after Lizzie had finished eating, Flora got squirmy and fussy. "I'm so sorry but I'm going to have to take care of her." She looked earnestly at Gretchen. "I really wanted to help with the dishes, too."

"Don't bat one eyelash over that. Go take care of our sweet baby."

Looking relieved, she glanced over at Tiberius. "It's great having you home again. If there's anything I can do, please let me know."

Cole could tell his father, slowed by the latest TIA, was searching for some witty comeback. "Thank you, I've got all the help I need," he finally said. "Take care of the little one." Or maybe finding out about Lizzie's childhood helped him bite his usual acerbic tongue.

Cole didn't have a clue what age babies sat up, but it seemed that sling thing wouldn't be the best way to hold Flora much longer. All anyone could see was the top of her head at the dining table and that shock of dark fly-away hair. It made him smile. But he kind of liked seeing her face and those inquisitive baby eyes, so awed by everything. So intelligent in a totally innocent way. Since he had some free time that night, he got it into his head to do some extra research. Truth was, Lizzie wasn't the only one to have gotten under his skin.

CHAPTER SEVEN

MONDAY MORNING, Cole and Lizzie agreed to travel to work in separate cars, since she had to deliver Flora to the new child care. He'd gotten the okay and loaned her his father's car, and was grateful not to be stuck in the same car since things had gotten awkward between them the rest of Sunday after their kiss. He lingered on at home and enjoyed an extra cup of coffee while making a quick online order before leaving, then listened to the weekend sports wrap-up on the radio for the ride in to work.

He'd no sooner walked in to the clinic when Lotte rushed him with laser-like tension in her eyes, and with Lizzie right behind her. His first worry was that they'd had another argument and he wasn't sure if he was ready to be diplomatic yet or not. *Work it out yourselves, ladies.*

"Been a horrible accident out at the Waltons' ranch," Lotte said. "One of the cowhands got butted and gored. You'd better get out there."

Cole glanced at Lizzie with alarm. When was the last time he'd worked the ER? "Ever see that in your big-city ER?"

"No, but I certainly saw my share of stab wounds. A deep puncture is a deep puncture, right?"

"You're probably right." Trauma medicine was far from his specialty, but he'd been raised on the ranch, had seen all kinds of injuries related to spooked cattle. He could at least help until the ambulance arrived. If he recalled right, his father had told them the Waltons were raising buffalo now.

"Where's the trauma kit?" she said.

"Good question."

"This way," Lotte said.

They set off for the procedure room where the trauma and delivery bags were kept, right on Lotte's heels.

"Everything you should need is in there."

Lizzie grabbed and opened it, and did a quick inventory.

"I'll call an ambulance and have Rita cancel the morning appointments," Lotte said. "If anyone shows up, if they want to stick around, we can try to squeeze them in the afternoon."

"Sounds good." He gathered extra gloves and gowns, since there might be a lot of blood involved, even though his biggest fear was internal injury from the patient getting rammed by a bison. "Let's go."

"This should be all we'll need until the paramedics get there," Lizzie said, closing the bag and looking calmer than Cole felt.

On the drive over, to keep his mind occupied, he quizzed her on deep-puncture-wound care and signs and symptoms of internal bleeding. As always, she aced it.

Fifteen minutes later while they were still in the car, a young cowboy on horseback led them to the corral where the man was down. They parked and rushed to the scene. Hell, it was Mike Walton; they'd gone to school together. The guy had been working the ranch all his life, which proved you never knew what might set off a steer, or, in this case, a bison.

The cowhand chattered every step of the way, filling them in on the particulars. "We was moving them through the chute, this guy was the last one. Something must have spooked him and set him off."

Cole found Mike in the corner of the corral on his side, moaning.

"The damn thing hooked him with his horn after he rammed him into the post. Just picked him up and threw him back down like he was tumbleweed or somethin'."

Cole knew that big animals found comfort in groups and got nervous when they were alone. Any number of things could have set off that bison. He figured they'd spent their time and manpower energy getting the bison out of the corral after that, and probably hadn't looked after Mike at all. He dropped to his knees.

"Mike, you with me?"

Mike moaned and opened his eyes. "Hurts like hell. He gored my ass." He lifted his head a little while he talked, which was a good sign his upper spine was okay.

One thing Cole understood for sure was if a person had to get gored, the buttocks were by far the best place. Lots of padding and minimal nerves ran through the area, unless he'd been gored deep enough to hit the obturator nerve—then there could be a lot of damage. "Can you move your leg or foot?"

Mike tested out moving his foot. It worked well enough, another good sign.

"This is Dr. Silva. She's going to help me."

Lizzie nodded hello, then didn't waste a second. She grabbed large bandage scissors from the ER kit to cut off the jeans. "We need to get a better look, okay?" she asked, but only after she'd sheered through most of one pants leg.

Mike gave a tense nod with thick dust in his hair and mud smudges all over his face. His cowboy hat lay trampled a couple feet away. "Pardon my derriere, ma'am."

"Not a problem."

"So the bison butted you with his head before he gored you?" Cole asked, engaging him in conversation just to keep Mike focused, and so he'd feel like he was doing something.

Mike gingerly moved his hand over his abdomen. "Knocked me against the post and I fell on my face. Couldn't breathe. Then he gored my ass."

Lizzie stopped cutting long enough to see where Mike gestured. "You in pain in the stomach area?"

Mike nodded again. "A little, but my butt hurts like hell."

Cole knew cowboys often had high pain thresholds. There was no telling what a little meant. Also, the fact he could talk in sentences was a good sign that one of his ribs hadn't punctured his lungs. "I'm going to get rid of your shirt so we can see anything obvious, okay?"

Another stoic nod.

He popped the buttons on his shirt and opened the front; the guy was already bruising. "Check this out," Cole said to Lizzie.

She gently pressed around the area. "The good news is the area doesn't feel hard or stiff." Though Mike definitely flinched when she touched him. "I'm going to take your blood pressure. See where we stand." She motioned for Cole to pick up where she'd left off with cutting off the jeans and took over the examination.

While he did battle on sturdy denim with the bandage scissors, going up the back of Mike's leg, she checked his vital signs. Fortunately the BP was in normal range, maybe a little high from the pain, and his pulse wasn't quick or thready according to Lizzie. Mike might have been tossed around by a bison, but maybe he'd survived without rupturing his spleen or a kidney.

Cole finished cutting off the jeans and they saw the baseball-sized puncture wound on Mike's right buttock. Blood trickled out from the angrily torn edges of flesh.

"We'll have to leave the deep cleaning and debridement for the hospital, but we can at least go ahead and clean and bandage the wound for now," she said and went right to work. "The hospital can do computerized tomography to look for any intra-abdominal or retroperitoneal hemorrhage or organ damage."

Cole understood the ER would need to assess damage to his pelvis and hip, and his respect for Dr. Silva was growing leaps and bounds.

"You'll need surgery to debride the wound."

"How long will I be off work?"

Cole knew Mike had a ranch to run, but the healing would take as long as the puncture needed to fill in with new granulation tissue. The process of secondary intention worked from the inside out.

"That's hard to say," Lizzie spoke up. "Let's just concentrate on getting you to the hospital for now and see what happens after that, okay?"

Once discharged, they'd see him in the clinic for follow-up care. Eventually, knowing Mike, he'd be the guy at the bar with a great ass-injury story, and if anyone doubted, all he'd have to do was drop his trousers. The odd thought put a smile on Cole's face, but mostly what made him smile was the expert way Lizzie handled the situation, making him feel like nothing more than a supervisor. She had everything it took to be a fantastic doctor. All she needed was a little more polishing and general experience.

Soon the ambulance pulled into the long drive and Mike got transferred onto a gurney, and while Lizzie gave her report to the paramedic, Cole called ahead to the hospital and gave a thorough rundown of the event to the emergency-intake doctor. While he did, it occurred to him what a great team they'd made, he and Lizzie. By ten o'clock they headed back to the clinic, and, since Lizzie had taken over at the scene, he felt compelled to do a little teaching.

"Steer, cows and bison have eyes on the sides of their heads so they can see almost three hundred degrees. They can graze and watch for predators at the same time," he said.

"No, *suh*!"

"Pardon?" Must be one of those Boston idioms?

"Really? That's so cool. If we had three-hundred-degree vision, we wouldn't have any blind spots when we drove." She showed some interest, and, as usual, added her unique take on the subject.

Being in that corral had brought back a truckload of memories, and since he'd felt fairly useless back at the scene, he went on. Granted, the information would only be of use if Lizzie planned to live in Wyoming or some other ranching state. Which of course she didn't, but nevertheless...

"They have something called a flight zone that handlers need to respect. In a corral situation the handlers are already deep in the bison's flight zone, so the animals are in a moderate state of fear. All it takes is sudden movement or a loud noise, just about anything can cause the bison to go into a high state of fear, and that's when they start crashing fences or goring other animals, or in this case the handler. Mike was lucky today. It could have been a lot worse."

"And this from the man who wants nothing to do with his father's ranch." Lizzie's deadpan analysis hit the bull's eye. Cole turned his head enough to meet her smart-aleck eyes, planning to deliver an irritated stare, but the instant their eyes met they both broke into laughter. She'd called him out. What else could he do?

Maybe it was a way to de-escalate the tension from the medical emergency they'd just worked on together, or maybe she shot from the hip about ranching and he got the message, but, whatever the reason, they spent the rest of the ride into the clinic making immature comments about the cowhand who'd been gored in the backside by a bison. Childish, yes. Shamelessly enjoyable? Yes again.

Had he ever laughed until his sides hurt with Victoria?

"So a bison handler walks into a bar..." Yeah, she cracked herself up as she proceeded to tell a horrible rendition of a classic joke. He laughed along, but he also got a kick out of how "bar" sounded like *bah* and "handler" like *handlaw* when she said it, and that made him enjoy the joke even more.

Cole never acted this way with his medical peers, even if sometimes he wanted to. Nope, he always kept it professional. But then this was Lizzie, and they'd just discovered they could let their hair down together.

Which set off a whole other fantasy.

To help get his mind off his growing desire for Lizzie, he jumped right into bragging incessantly to Lotte and Rita the instant they got back to the clinic. "You should have seen her..."

Tuesday morning Cole sent out texts to several medical-community friends he knew on the east coast, fishing for information on their internal-medicine resident programs. Then he got right to work at the clinic while he waited for information to roll in. Lizzie stopped by and handed him a list of her second-string hospitals, as she'd promised. She'd definitely made her sights more realistic this time around, but he didn't have a contact at a single one of those hospitals.

Midmorning, while completing a surgery referral for cholelithiasis in a forty-five-year-old woman, he got a call.

"Cole, it's Larry."

Lawrence Rivers didn't call unless there was a good reason. Wasn't that how Trevor had wound up with Elisabete Silva? "Hi, what's up?"

"What are you doing weekend after next?"

"I'll be right here in Cattleman Bluff until my brother gets back, why?"

"I saw your text about resident spots and I thought I'd save you some time."

"How're you going to do that?"

"One of the internal-medicine first-year residents may be dropping out of our program for an assortment of personal reasons."

"Are you serious?"

"Yeah, but no one knows about it yet, and it's not a sure deal. Here's the thing, weekend after next is the annual JHH charity event, right? They're having a formal affair at Hotel Monaco in Baltimore, and most of the east-coast hospital administrators will be there, including the resident admin from Boston University Hospital. Even if Lizzie can't get in at our program in Boston, she can meet and make a good impression on a boatload of other administrators. It'd be a good time to try out your

Professor Henry Higgins and Eliza Doolittle routine, don't you think?"

Cole sat in order to take in everything his friend told him. Was that what he'd become where Lizzie was concerned—even bigger than a cliché, a George Bernard Shaw character?

Pygmalion aside, Cole promised Lawrence that Elisabete was hirable, beyond hirable, then he told him all about the recent goring incident. He owed her a hand up, not only for her, but for Flora's future. He could introduce her to a number of important people there and if she made a good impression at the charity event she was bound to find a resident program sooner rather than later. She had a baby to support, she needed a job when Trevor and Julie got home, which was only a few weeks away.

"Send the invitation. We'll be there."

After Cole hung up a long list of worries queued up in his mind. Would Lizzie even agree to going? Would she be prepared for the upscale event? She certainly didn't have the wardrobe for a charity ball at a grand hotel; he'd have to buy her a dress. And not let on what his intentions were, because she'd have a fit if she knew it was a setup. His outlook grew grim, but he was determined to make this opportunity work for her.

If he was successful she'd meet and impress the perfect hospital administrator who'd find a place for her either in the current resident program, or maybe give her some sort of hospital staff position while she waited for next year's list of openings.

All Cole could do was put her in the right place at the right time. The rest would be completely up to Lizzie to make the magic happen. Which was why he'd have to step up their nightly medical conversations, and, while she wasn't looking, sneak in a few tidbits about proper charity-ball etiquette.

He rubbed his palms together, then quickly got lost in another thought—if he was successful, he might never see her again. Some of the excitement dissipated.

Wednesday, Cole beat Lizzie home from work and found the large package he'd ordered the other morning waiting for him. He tore open the cardboard box to get to the baby jumper seat inside. A bright and friendly-looking, freestanding baby jumper required assembly, so he got right to work in order to surprise Lizzie, and most especially Flora, when they got home.

The rotating, comfortable-looking seat would let Flora's legs dangle and her toes touch the ground, which would help develop large motor skills when she pushed off and jumped. Plus, it would be a safe place to keep her while Lizzie needed both of her hands. Like, for instance—and the true reason he'd gotten it—while they sat at the dinner table. Flora could dangle, jump and play with the colorful creatures and attached toys to her heart's content.

Once he'd finished the setup, Cole smiled, taking great joy in getting something special for Flora. The more time he spent around her, the cuter she got, and sometimes, when the timing didn't work out right and he didn't see her, he missed her.

Had he once missed Victoria's son, Eddie? Nope.

Midgrin, Lizzie breezed into the kitchen with Flora in her car carrier seat, and Cole stood proudly beside the jumper toy waiting for them to reach the dining room. Flora was making some loud baby sounds, not fussing, just exploring her voice, and once Lizzie pushed through the door she stopped on a dime.

"What's this?"

"Flora's new jumping toy."

"You got this?" He nodded. "Did you know that Gina has one of these at her house and she says Flora loves it?" He shook his head. "Oh, my Gawd, Flora, lookie!" It might as well have been Christmas.

Lizzie set the car carrier on the dining table and Cole did the honors of taking Flora out, enjoying the sturdy feel of her growing body. "Look at this, Flora. What do you think?" Her little legs started kicking before he could even set her in the seat. She squealed the minute her bottom hit the vinyl. Cole flipped on the switch and loud jungle-animal sounds started along with silly music. The baby loved it and kicked her legs, setting off more bouncing.

A tight squeeze on his arm drew his attention away from Flora to Lizzie. She looked sincerely up at him. "This is so sweet of you. Thank you."

"My pleasure." And it was, since he enjoyed watching Flora almost as much as Lizzie.

The love he saw in Lizzie's eyes for her daughter seemed to reach inside his chest and grab his heart. What must that kind of love feel like? One thing he knew for sure, the simple gift had brought a roomful of joy into the house, and he wouldn't trade having the two of them here for anything.

And yet, his most important task at this point in time was to find Lizzie a job and send her away. His wide grin suddenly felt all wrong.

That night after dinner and after Flora had been nursed and put to bed, Lizzie headed to meet Cole in the library loft above the living room. She loved these meetings with him, not only for the wealth of medical knowledge he shared, but also for the one-on-one time alone with Cole. Since he'd kissed her cowboy-style on the open range under that never-ending Wyoming sky, though, he'd pulled back. Way back. Most days he seemed more like the guy she'd originally met when she'd first arrived. Distant and standoffish. Except they'd shared a good belly laugh the other day on the drive back from the Waltons'. And this afternoon he'd surprised the heck out of her with that impulsive gift for Flora. She shook her head, missing the man who'd helped with Flora and who'd diplomatically shown her the error of her pig-headed ways with the clinic personnel when she'd first arrived in Cattleman Bluff. She'd caught a glimpse of who he could be today and wanted more. But all the years in foster care had trained her never to get her hopes up. People never wanted her for long, so they just kept passing her around.

Lizzie didn't have enough time to sort out her confused thoughts. Once she hit the top of the spiral steps to the library, he was already waiting at the table they shared nightly, a hot mug of something steaming to his right. Probably Sweet Dreams herbal tea. A barely there smile didn't come close to his eyes, but he stood and, like a trained gentleman, waited for her dutifully.

"What's on the agenda tonight?" she said, trying to ignore the lackluster greeting, walking heavy-footed toward her chair.

He sat back down and weaved his fingers together, resting his hands on the table between them. "I was wondering if you'd consider taking a trip with me to Baltimore?"

He'd blindsided her with a crazy question and she nearly fell off her chair before she'd completely sat down. "What's in Baltimore?" Was this a test?

"What will be in Baltimore? Nearly every single university-hospital resident-program administrator this side of the Mississippi."

She didn't bother to scoot back into the chair, but stayed balancing on the front edge. "I'm listening."

"Weekend after next the prestigious Johns Hopkins Hospital is hosting their annual charity event, and we've been invited."

"That's where you work, right?"

He nodded.

"Why invite me?"

"Were you not listening? You'll be introduced to the people who can get you into their resident programs. Make the right impression, it can open doors for you."

Nerves twined together making an uncomfortable ball in her stomach. She didn't dare get her hopes up since she'd learned the hard way by failing to get placed this year. Plus she wasn't exactly known for her charm. "I can't do that. I'll blow it for sure."

For the first time since that afternoon with Flora jumping in her chair, she saw an honest reaction from him. He torqued his face in disbelief. "That's not the Lizzie I know. When you put your mind to it, you can do anything."

Did he know her that well?

Feeling like a little girl, she held her breath and glanced upward, her heart jumping its beat. Uncensored honesty kicked in and she let him see the unconfident shadow that followed her everywhere, the part of her she'd locked away all her life in order to get through the tough stuff. Her usual fake facade of confidence and tough Boston girl had been her survival, but right now... He'd pushed her just past her comfort zone, enough to see her true reaction, and she couldn't let him see any more.

Was a measly old charity ball really going to be her undoing?

He must have read her panic and appeared at her side while barely seeming to move. His large hand squeezed her shoulder. "What's up?"

"I don't know how to act around rich people. I won't belong there. I'll stand out like a copper penny with a bunch of silver dollars."

Cole squeezed her shoulder tighter and dropped to her eye level. "Honey, you're the silver dollar. We just need to let them discover that."

Well, that did it. First he bought her baby a wonderful gift, now he paid her the sweetest compliment she'd ever heard. She flung her arms around his neck and hugged him tight to hide the unwelcomed tears springing up and dripping over her lids. His arms wrapped around her back, one warm hand massaging up and down. She thought she could stay like this for eternity and never get tired of Cole holding her—and how she'd missed him since their kiss—but she needed to pull herself together. There were at least a hundred questions she had right that instant, and she figured she'd think of a thousand more as the night went on. He'd just proved he had confidence in her; the least she could do was not let him down. "How do we pull this off? And, yes, I did say 'we' because there's no way I can do this without you."

He pulled back and passed her the sincerest and handsomest gaze she'd ever seen. It made her instantly want to drop to her knee and ask him to marry her. God, she was easy. And starved for love!

"I'll be by your side every step of the way." He kissed her forehead—more like a friend than a man she had the hots for, but right now was no time to protest—broke away from their hug and sat over by his steaming mug of herbal tea again. Back to business. "I'll teach you everything you need to know to knock the argyle socks off those nerdy admins. We'll buy you a dress they won't be able to take their eyes off of, and basically all you'll have to do is smile."

She wiped at the dregs of her tears. "That sounds a little smarmy. And really sexist."

"I'm just saying." His brows pushed down, clueing her in he was only trying to be helpful and had exaggerated maybe "a ttch"—wasn't that the word he liked to use? But his dark eyes let out that little twinkle she sometimes saw when she amused him. "You do have a beautiful smile, you know."

He thought she had a beautiful smile? Her head spun at the news. She blurted the first coherent words that came to mind. "I can't let you buy me a dress."

"You're sure as hell not wearing those unisex slacks and button-up blouses of yours."

"Good point." She shook her head again; there really was no way she could go to this event without his help because she needed every penny she made at the clinic. "I'll pay you back."

"Whatever. Here's the thing—we need to go shopping in town this weekend. Rita told me about a flashy new boutique that's recently opened, and it just so happens I treated the owner for a gallbladder attack today and she gave me a discount card. Small world, eh?"

So that was what he was shooting the breeze with the clinic receptionist over today. Lizzie had to admit it had burned a little to see him spread that Wyoming gentleman charm around, especially with the sexy blonde. Her sensibilities wouldn't let up. "I'm already feeling like a kept woman. Your brother gave me a job, a place to live, and now you're buying me clothes."

"Don't look at it that way—be practical. We hired you with room and board as part of the package. Look, this is necessary in order to make the best impression. You'll thank me for it one day."

"Only after I pay you back." Wait, wait, wait! "No. See. I can't go. What about Flora? Who'll take care of her while I'm at this party?"

"First off, it's not a party, it's a fund-raising event." He licked his lips before following up on his next thought. "I was thinking we'd leave Saturday morning and return Sunday morning. One night. I'm pretty sure Gretchen could take care of Flora for one night."

"Leave my baby? Are you trying to kill me? I'd be so miserable without her, there'd be no way I could be the silver dollar you insist I can be."

Silvah dawla.

"*Are.* You are. Get it?" He leveled his gaze and stared hard at her, and he wasn't going to let up until she agreed. "You'll be you on your best behavior."

"I won't be able to concentrate on anything but Flora. I'll be crying the whole time, ruining the new dress. How can I be charming without my baby?"

"How do you get through work every day?"

"By knowing I get to come home and see her."

"And you will see her. It's just twenty-four hours I'm asking for."

She'd been storing up extra breast milk for the sitter, and Gretchen had proved to be amazing with her baby—would it really be impossible to leave Flora for one day? Especially since this event in Baltimore could change their future for the better? It wouldn't be wise to miss this opportunity. She had to think for two now.

She curled in her lower lip, trying her best to be a team player. And since when had they become a team? "Why go to all this trouble for me?"

"Because I want the best for you, Lizzie. This one night can open doors for you and your daughter's future. Sacrifice one night for your entire future."

He'd punched a heart-shaped hole in her chest with those words. The man was for real. She'd taken a last-ditch job in Wyoming out of desperation, but it turned out she'd come to the best place she'd ever been and face-to-face with the noblest man she'd ever met. She cleared her throat. "Well, what if we don't find a dress in town?"

He laughed at her weakest line of protest yet. "Then we'll go online and use overnight shipping."

She wanted to hate him for being persistent, but loved him for putting up with her. For not giving up. No man had ever done that before, and that tiny swell of love cut loose. It must have shown in her eyes. "You think you have all the answers, don't you?"

His tolerant gaze shifted to the look she remembered after they'd made out by the horses. "In this instance, I know I do." That sizzling dark stare set off a reaction distinctly below her waist.

She was a fool for confident men; the fact her breasts tightened and peaked beneath her T-shirt proved it. She and Cole were having one of those moments that seemed to happen more frequently before that first kiss—the kind where sparks flew both ways—and without saying a word each let the other know something amazing could happen if they let it. But with this new turn of events, most specifically the charity ball, Lizzie needed to keep her head about her. She couldn't let herself get swept away in the big cowboy's supersexy eyes. She hated to do it, but if he wanted to train her up and send her away, she'd have to break this spell because they had plans to make, and work to do.

"I believe you," she whispered, sitting back in her chair, letting their moment trickle away. "So let's get started."

A cloud of disappointment scudded across his gaze but he synced in with her, sat and acted as if nothing short of a hot and sweaty promise had just passed between them. He took a drink from his mug and opened the four-inch-thick Johns Hopkins *Internal Medicine Board Review* book; next to that was an equally thick *Pathologic Basis of Disease* tome. "Okay, then."

Back to business as usual.

Saturday Cole insisted they duck out from the ranch around lunchtime for the boutique on Main Street and Lizzie arranged for Gretchen to watch Flora. They'd timed it to work around her nap. He'd quizzed her over her size and what her best colors were all morning, and had called ahead so some dresses were pulled and ready to try on. Evidently he had limited time because he was bringing his father's bookkeeping up to date, a major job he'd moaned about on the drive over. Of course she loved his sharing his concerns with her, so she kept her mouth shut and let him vent.

Lizzie'd had minimal time on her own since arriving in Cattleman Bluff and, though she'd been meaning to check out the shops, she'd yet to make it into this part of town. She gazed in amazement as they walked under an arch made entirely from elk antlers stretched across a street that could double as an old Western movie set, raised timber boardwalks and all.

"It's the largest in the state," Cole said nonchalantly, knowing exactly what she reacted to. "Jackson Hole has a pretty good one, but nothing like this." He glanced upwards, and she studied the arch closer up.

Was this something to be proud of? "Interesting," was all she could think to say.

The boutique was tiny with only two dresses on display in the window, and both looked far too Western and lacy for a girl from Boston, but she'd keep an open mind since Cole had gone to such an effort.

The owner, Carol, waited excitedly inside. "Hi! Come in. Those are the dresses I thought you might like." She pointed to a rack with four dresses hanging on it right next to a fitting room.

Expecting to see gowns more suited for matronly types, Lizzie was surprised to find a colorful assortment of flirty full-length gowns. She checked the size and worried that since the baby she wouldn't be able to pull off looking sexy. She could always use control underwear for her leftover baby bump, though.

Without looking at Cole, because she was suddenly hit with a pang of embarrassment having to model gowns for essentially her boss, the sexy guy she had a crush on, she grabbed the black one and another red dress and scooted inside the tiny cubicle. She slipped out of her clothes as quickly as possible and first tried on the black one.

"No way!" she said from inside the fitting room. "This one is cut to my waist. I'm not wearing it."

"Okay. I won't argue, but feel free to show me if you want." She heard the teasing, and maybe a twinge of hopefulness in his playful response. Turning sideways, realizing her post-baby figure was definitely curvier, she toyed with the idea of modeling for him. *Yeah. No.* Her new-mother breasts poured out, giving her a cleavage she'd never had before. *He's not seeing me in this.* Then she wiggled out of it and moved to the red one.

"What's this red one called?"

"That's a mermaid dress. You like it?"

The red velvet and lace dress looked more suited for winter than a summer event, but she did like the neckline and the capped sleeves. "I like the cut on it, but I'd like something a little more summery."

"Oh, then, try this one on."

It must have been hanging on the rack, too, because Carol pushed a few hangers across the bar and managed to find something in record time. She handed it over the top of the fitting-room door before Lizzie could get out of the red one.

In pale icy blue, the beaded bodice was offset by laced cap sleeves with sequined stripes and had a sweeping, gauzy skirt flared by wispy godets. A triangle cutout on the back made for fun peekaboo sexy appeal without showing too much skin. She liked it. Really liked it, and hoped it looked as good on as it did on the hanger.

It had lined and lightly padded cups in the front, so she wouldn't need a bra, but her breasts spilled over the classic cut. The fitting bodice actually did all the girding she needed in her waist, and the flow of the skirt made her feel feminine and even a little playful. The question was, what would Cole think of it?

She zipped as far as she could, then needed Carol's help with the hook-and-eye parts.

The woman gasped when she came into the compact room. "You look gorgeous. Oh, honey, this is definitely your color." Carol filled Lizzie to the brim with compliments as she hooked the dress. Then she stepped back, honest to goodness envy in her eyes. "This one's made for you."

Lizzie liked the dress, for sure, but was it really perfect for her? How could she know? She'd never worn an evening gown in her life. Dared she show Cole? He'd see her soon enough, but, hey, the man was paying for this dress, so he deserved to put in his two cents, right? Maybe he'd hate it.

She inhaled and stepped out of the fitting room, and the first chance she got to catch Cole's reaction she glanced at his face. The best she could describe his expression was astonished. Astonished? Really, he was that stunned by her putting on a fancy dress?

She'd let her hair out of the confining rubber band and it hung loose around her cap sleeve–covered shoulders, and she stood on her toes, since the dress required heels she didn't have, which made her feel a little off balance. Or maybe it was Cole's continuing awestruck stare.

"This dress was made for Lizzie, don't you think?" Carol said, gesturing with both hands toward her.

Cole was evidently dumbstruck, only nodding his agreement. Had she ever affected a man like this in her life? As though he were seeing her for the first time, an array of expressions crossed his face in the span of one moment. Amazement, surprise, reverence, desire. Yes, he'd been unable to hide that part, desire, and seeing his reaction made Lizzie feel beautiful from the tip of her head all the way down to her unpainted toenails. A cascade of chills covered her skin; she needed to look away, and so she spun around and pretended to be distracted by the dress, not his reaction to it.

"Is this the one?" she asked over her shoulder, insisting on sounding blasé.

"Definitely," he said, and when she chanced one last glance at him his stare seemed to say, *You're the one*. It shocked and frightened her, making her breath quiver, and she headed for the fitting room hoping he didn't notice.

Maybe she'd imagined his reaction. Or hoped for it. No. She couldn't get her hopes up about Cole Montgomery. The thought of them as a couple was absurd, and...

"Okay, boss. Thanks. I like it too." She did everything in her power to play down the depth of emotions rolling through her. For that one instant, all she wanted in the world was to be *the one* for him. And wasn't that the biggest fool's dream she'd ever invented? Because in her world people always let her down and she couldn't trust them. Especially men.

A little voice in her head countered that Cole had kept his word about everything since she'd met him, even about not kissing her again.

"You'll need shoes." Carol broke into her thoughts.

"Oh, right. My flip-flops won't exactly do this justice, even though they have rhinestones." Self-deprecating humor seemed the only route to take right now, because otherwise she'd have to admit that something substantial had happened between them. She wasn't anywhere near ready to deal with that. Or the significance.

"Try these on." Carol was the fastest shop attendant she'd ever encountered. Usually she'd have to hunt them out in the stores where she shopped, then beg for assistance.

Four-inch strappy silver heels got slid under the changing-room door, ensuring Lizzie would have to get a pedicure to go to this event. And what about her hair? Oh, my, her head was spinning with how disruptive this plan of Cole's had become.

"Get whatever you need," he said.

"What about a necklace?" Carol was quick to add.

"I'll take care of that," Cole said. "Thanks."

His comment started a whole new wave of chills circling Lizzie's body, but the feeling quickly waned. Was
Cole doing this because he cared or because he wanted
to get rid of her?

CHAPTER EIGHT

ALL THE MAGIC and fairy dust disappeared the moment they got back in the car. Cole seemed suspiciously quiet, as if he'd pulled himself together, or had given himself a stern talking-to, and the ride home felt nothing short of awkward. All of Lizzie's quick *what if?* thoughts and fanciful dreams of being his lady dissolved into the thick, odd atmosphere inside the car.

Once safely back at the homestead, all business again, Cole dropped Lizzie off at the front of the house and he took off for the ranch office in the stables. It was as though their moment had never happened, as if what he'd done for her was routine and his desirous gaze had only been in her imagination, and now it was time for him to get on with the show. Bookkeeping called.

"Thanks again!" she said for about the fifteenth time since leaving the boutique as he walked away. Crushed, she stood holding the dress in a travel bag, compliments of the store. So this was how Cinderella felt after the ball.

"You're welcome. You'll knock 'em dead next weekend." He kept walking, didn't even glance back.

She'd never forget that look today when he had seen her in that dress. Never. It had made her shiver from her very center, down her spine and to the tips of her toes.

What would it be like? She sighed and walked toward the house.

The thought of going to this huge event and having to be on top form scared her to death, and there was only one person in the world who could calm her down right now. Flora. With a smile, thinking how much progress Flora had made since coming here, Lizzie entered the house. She'd barely got inside when she found Gretchen laughing and singing along with the repetitious songs coming from the new baby jungle Jumperoo, and Flora squealing with joy, bouncing to her little heart's content.

Lizzie owed Cole so much, the least she could do was knock 'em dead next weekend. For him. Then get out of his life as soon as possible. It seemed he'd want it that way.

On Monday all the exam rooms were filled with patients by the time Lizzie got to work. She'd spent a little extra time talking with Gina, whom she'd come to really like, and wound up being a little late. Cole was already seeing his patients, and she was thankful to dive right into work. Lotte handed her the schedule and made a disapproving expression as she filled Lizzie in on her first patient.

"This one's trouble," she said. "Typical spoiled teenager who keeps coming up with reasons to miss school. Last month it was nausea and vomiting. Before that insomnia. Maybe if she spent less time online she'd get enough sleep. Today, she's got a headache. Good luck." She huffed and walked away, and when Lizzie caught a glimpse of Cole leaving one exam room and entering another she rolled her eyes rather than say what was really on her mind.

Having the prediagnosis of faking it drummed into

her head by the overbearing nurse, Lizzie did what Cole had suggested in order to keep peace at the clinic and bit back her first thoughts. But she was bound and determined not to step into that room with a preconceived opinion of what was wrong with her fourteen-year-old patient.

When she did enter the examination room, what she found was a withdrawn and anemic-looking young teen named Valerie with mousy brown hair and intensely sad gray eyes. It was a look that didn't seem easily faked, and, being only twenty-six, Lizzie still prided herself in seeing through teenage drama. Valerie's mother looked as tense as the daughter, and nearly at her wit's end. Both mother and daughter were nail biters, and both were underweight—not that that had anything to do with diagnosing a headache, it was just an observation, and family dynamics often played into teenage headaches. The first thing Lizzie did was dim the light in case Valerie had photophobia.

"I just don't know what it's going to be next," the mother said, not waiting for a proper introduction or trying to hide her exasperation.

"I'm Dr. Silva." Lizzie kept to her usual routine, offering her hand to the patient to shake, and then her mother. "I've read through your history, Valerie, and I see you've had some problems with stomachaches in the past couple of months?"

"That was from taking too many over-the-counter headache pills." The mother insisted on doing all of the talking.

"How long have the headaches been going on?"

Valerie actually opened her mouth to reply, but her mother beat her to it. "A couple of months."

"Any correlation with the menstrual cycle?"

Mom looked to Valerie, who shook her head, and it seemed even that small move aggravated the pain.

"How long do the headaches typically last?"

"A few hours." Valerie's high-pitched, tinny voice sounded younger than she looked. "Sometimes a whole day. Once two days. I woke up with this one today and I think it started last night."

Lizzie understood that migraines presented differently in adolescents than adults and didn't usually last as long. So far she hadn't ruled out migraine.

"Show me where it hurts." Valerie touched both of her temples. Again, Lizzie understood that migraines in adolescents could be bilateral instead of unilateral as for most adults. "Can you describe the pain?" The teenager gave her a blank look, so she decided to prompt her. "Does it throb or pulsate?"

"Throbs." Valerie sounded on the verge of tears. "Anything I do makes it feel worse."

"Have you vomited today?"

"No, but I can't eat. Just the thought makes me want to barf. Why does this happen to me?"

"I can imagine that these headaches would be frustrating, Valerie. Is it okay if I ask you a few more questions before I examine you?"

The reluctant patient nodded.

After completing a thorough history to establish any symptoms that might precede the headaches like auras, and to help rule out depression and anxiety, since they often coexisted with migraine headaches in adolescents, Lizzie discovered Valerie had pretty classic symptoms. Difficulty thinking, light-headedness, and general fatigue along with the nausea and vomiting and photophobia. Valerie said it even hurt to listen to music when she had the headaches—phonophobia.

With the physical examination Lizzie discovered Valerie also had neck tension and pain, but the rest of the examination, including basic eye exam and neurological testing, proved normal. She still had a hunch her young patient might also be dealing with depression.

Lizzie's biggest job today would be to make sure these were primary headaches, not secondary to another condition such as a tumor, concussion or sinus disease, or several other potentially life-threatening conditions.

"I'm going to recommend something called a CT scan for now, and once we have that information we can move forward with treatment."

"Does she have a brain tumor?" Panic sliced through the mother's voice.

"I don't believe so, but we need to perform standard protocol testing first. I think your daughter has classic early-onset migraine headaches, and we can treat that." She glanced at Valerie, who showed the first sign of hope today. "First we have to make sure what's going on, okay?"

The mother agreed and Lizzie wrote the referral for a stat CT scan at the radiology center the next town over, a forty-minute drive, but well worth it for the concerned mother and daughter. This would buy her time to discuss the medical treatment for adolescent migraine sufferers with Cole tonight in their routine after-dinner meeting.

Now that Lizzie had a car to drop off and pick up Flora from child care at Gina's every day, she arrived home just in time to nurse her baby and change clothes for dinner. When she showed up at the dining table only Gretchen and Monty were there.

"Cole said not to wait, he had an errand to run," Gretchen said as she passed a plate of pasta toward Lizzie.

"Oh, but he said he'd expect to see you at eight in the library like always."

Her initial disappointment lessened. "Okay. Thanks." Lizzie put Flora in her bouncing chair, making sure the sound was off out of respect for Monty. She suspected the elephant and monkey sounds got on his nerves after a while. Flora didn't seem to notice and immediately started jumping and playing with the attached plastic spinning ball filled with colorful beads.

She helped Monty dish out a few extra meatballs, while wondering where Cole had gone and what he might be doing. She didn't have the right to any part of him beyond the clinic and what time they shared in his home, but after last Saturday, when he'd bought her the dress with his seal of approval, she'd felt differently about him. Like she might be falling in love. Couldn't help it. As usual she'd overreacted to his consideration. Was she that starved for attention?

Monty was his usual cantankerous self, complaining about the home-health aide the hospital sent out each day. "Why'd they give me a guy? I can handle letting a woman bathe and dress me. Hell, I don't even need the help with Gretchen around, and this guy has hands like bears."

"My condolences to his wife," Lizzie tossed in drily, hoping to knock Monty off balance and maybe get him to change the topic.

"I doubt he has one," he grumbled under his breath before shoving in half a meatball. All complaining aside, she was happy to hear him talk so much. Each day his words and strength got better. Such a positive sign.

"Will you let me bathe Flora tonight?" Gretchen made a concerted effort to change the topic, too. "Now that she's in child care, I miss her so much." She glanced at the baby and made a silly grandmotherly face.

"You don't have to do that." Lizzie missed Flora after her days at work, too.

"I want to. I can get her all ready for you, then you can read her a story and put her to bed. How's that?"

Lizzie had been making a concerted effort to get Flora in a routine now that she was just about four months old. Bath, nursing, reading a book were all part of her nighttime routine.

"Since you put it that way, I'll take you up on it, but you have to let me do the dishes." Lizzie gazed kindly at the silver-haired woman who had stepped in as the matriarch of this ranch, and thought how much she'd miss her when the summer and this job at the clinic ended. She inwardly shook her head, scolding herself for getting involved with everyone and everything in Cattleman Bluff. Especially Cole.

He'd insisted his plan to take her to the charity event was to make sure she had a solid future, but deep inside she wondered if it was just to get rid of her. The sooner, the better.

That thought melted away some of her happy feelings for Gretchen and grouchy Monty as she removed the dishes from the table and walked into the kitchen just in time to see Cole come in. Then a whole new wave of mixed-up feelings took over.

"Hi," he said, looking steadily at her, his demeanor calm.

"Hi." Her heart got flighty but she recovered quickly enough. "You need some dinner?"

"I grabbed a bite at the diner in town."

Why did he need to do that? Had he been as shaken by their moments in the dress boutique the other day as she'd been? He'd been nowhere to find on Sunday, and had seemed to only slip in and out of his office like a ghost all day today.

He kept walking. "I'll see you at eight."

She dipped her hands in warm dishwater and stared at the window, hoping to follow his reflection on the glass, but it was summer and still too light out. Instead she turned and watched his broad back as he continued on into the house, those big shoulders she'd come to rely on, then she tried to read the closed-down vibes lingering in his wake.

Fortunately she had a lot to do between now and eight, so she couldn't stand around smelling the lemon dish soap wondering what was up with Cole, even though she doubted she'd be able to get him out of her mind no matter what.

Eight o'clock, Lizzie came prepared for their meeting with a specific goal in mind—how best to treat her new patient. Plus she brought her own mug of tea tonight.

As always, Cole had beat her there and sat reading a medical journal while waiting, the light bulbs casting a yellow tint, making his skin almost golden. He glanced up and smiled, and she thought how much she loved the grooves along his cheeks whenever he did.

"I caught you being good today," he said.

What part of the day was he referring to? The clinic? The kitchen earlier? "Why does that make me think of grammar school?"

He went thoughtful, his glance downward. "Maybe because my mother used to say that to me."

"When you were ten?" She was touched by the memory of his mother, but didn't have a clue what was going on so she took the smart-aleck route.

"Probably." His smile settled into more of a pensive expression. "But I was talking about your holding your tongue with Lotte at the clinic this morning, and again later in the day when she insisted her way of teaching asthmatics how to use inhalers wasn't out of date."

Now she laughed. "Ah, so you could tell I had to zip my lips both times, but mostly for her being so judgmental about my patient." She put down her mug and stood beside her usual chair.

"Your body language is pretty easy to read." He shifted forward in his chair, put his forearms on the table. "Yes, that's exactly what I'm talking about, and I thought you wanted to deck her." His brows tented and his gaze drifted toward hers. "I especially liked how you explained to her, after the appointment, how sometimes teenagers really are sick. I think she got your point without your blowing up or her feeling reprimanded. Anyway, nice job. Shows me you can learn and change."

Now his smile came back full force and she decided not to keep being a wiseacre. "If you don't mind, I'd really like to discuss Valerie's case with you. Especially the treatment."

"Of course. We can learn together because teenage migraines are definitely out of my wheelhouse."

Instead of sitting across from Cole, as she always did, she put her books next to her mug and pulled the chair next to his. "We can read together," she said, enjoying the scent of his masculine soap. She could sit and stare into his mesmerizing eyes all night, but that wouldn't help her form an assessment and plan for her newest patient. Sitting beside him would actually help her focus…once she got used to how good he smelled. As if that would ever happen.

She opened the textbook on adolescent health and

read about the similarities and differences between adult and adolescent migraines.

"I've sent her for a CT scan, which I'll bet my next paycheck will be negative. But I get the feeling she has some emotional issues going on, too. I think she might be depressed, as well. Can we refer to mental-health clinics?"

"You can. Might be a good idea. But it would be up to her mother to get her there and whether or not to pay for the extra psychiatric care. And the best place would be Cheyenne."

"I know some people have a stigma about that, but I want to make sure Valerie knows that teenage depression is more common than she thinks. I don't want her to feel like she's a freak or anything."

"Do you think she might open up one-on-one with you? Maybe you could feel out her situation more that way before you refer her to psych."

"Good point. To her credit, Lotte did fill me in on a few things. Evidently Valerie's mom and dad got divorced last year and there were some nasty accusations being flung around by the Mrs."

"So it was a lousy divorce."

"Aren't they all?"

"Wouldn't know, haven't been married. My parents adored each other."

Is that why you've never married? Afraid you can't duplicate what your parents had?

He opened his laptop and, rather than discuss marriage anymore, they went to several pharmaceutical websites and studied up on medical treatment for teenagers.

"Jeez," Lizzie said. "So many of these migraine drugs aren't approved for adolescents. Our choices are minimal."

"Well, you don't want to go too crazy with meds right

off. Looks like treatment should be multimodal with nonpharmacological interventions and modifications in daily living first."

"Agreed. I need to get her on board about noticing triggers and keeping track of what to avoid. That's another reason I'd like some one-on-one teaching time with her."

"If you can address her stressors and any potential mood disorders, that'd be a big help, too."

"We can start her out on nonsteroidal anti-inflammatories and acetaminophen, see how that goes, but the key is to catch the headache early. I'll have to really drive that point home to Valerie and her mother."

"Maybe hold off on triptans for now. See how early treatment works, first?"

"Yeah, that makes sense," she said. "Especially since there's only one or two of those serotonin-binding drugs FDA-approved for teens, plus she'd have to be able to inject it at school if needed and that'd be a whole other learning curve."

"Let's wait for the CT results and go from there. I think you've got your plan mapped out well enough for now."

"Thanks, I feel better discussing it with you."

Once the business-as-usual portion of their meeting was wrapping up, Lizzie recognized tension rolling back into her. If she'd known how life-altering the simple act of trying on a dress could be on their relationship, she'd never have agreed to do it.

Cole kept looking sideways at her as if there was something he wanted to bring up, and suddenly she needed to move her chair back to the other side of the table. How could one man wreak such havoc with her mind?

He reached into his shirt pocket and pulled out a small

black velvet pouch cinched together by a ribbon. "I got to thinking about the charity ball and your dress, and, like Carol said, you need a necklace and earrings to go with it, so I went by the town jeweler's after work and found this." He reached for her hand, since her mind was too boggled by his statement to think about physically responding, then he dropped the velvet pouch into her palm. "If you don't like them, take them back and get something else."

"I...I can't accept jewelry from you."

"Well, you can't very well wear that dress without a necklace and earrings either."

"Why'd you do this?"

"How much explaining do you want? Because I haven't got all night. Now open it and try them on." His attempt to imitate Tiberius Montgomery fell far short, but it did get across the fact she needed to check out the gift. Or was it a gift? Might he expect something in return?

Nah, they'd been through that already and he'd proved to be the perfect gentleman. Something else that was aggravatingly appealing about him.

She loosened the black satin ribbon and shook out a huge aquamarine teardrop on a braided silver chain, with matching drop earrings, and forgot how to breathe. "This is gorgeous. It's perfect for that dress. But I can't accept this gift."

"Seriously?"

"This seems so personal and we hardly know each other...um, that way."

"Then let's be practical. I'm dragging you to a function that requires a certain level of sophistication. It's my responsibility to make sure you fit in. Trust me, this necklace won't compare to the jewelry you'll see there, but it will definitely look good on you. I want you to have it and feel confident."

She dared to look into his eyes and realized something serious was whirling around behind those dark lashes. This meant something more than going to an upscale job-placement fair, and she wasn't ready to figure out exactly what that was. Because then she'd have to fully examine all the confusing feelings she'd been carrying around about Dr. Montgomery, and it might set her up to get hurt. "Can I just borrow them for the night?"

He laughed and patiently glanced around the room before answering. "The Cattleman Bluff jewelry store isn't in the business of loaning necklaces. I bought it for you. Keep it. Hawk it. Return it. Your call. But wear it this Saturday night."

"Now I've ticked you off, and I've taken ungraciousness to a new low. Please forgive me, Cole, I'm just not accustomed to a man giving me a dress and a gorgeous necklace. And earrings. Oh, and shoes. No one has ever done that before and it's just, well, I don't know how to describe it." She'd melted down to the babbling stage trying to explain how big a deal this was, and he'd obviously had it with her.

He stood, leaned over the table and took her by the shoulders. The last time a man had been upset with her and had taken her by the shoulders she'd been shaken up pretty good. She tensed. Cole immediately saw the fearful reaction in her eyes and let up, moving one hand from her shoulder to her jaw, gently cupping it. He bent and moved in and, as delicately as a butterfly, kissed her.

"Do me a favor," he whispered next to her ear. She felt the shell of his ear lightly on her cheek. His woodsy aftershave still noticeable on his throat. "Humor me and keep the necklace and earrings. I want to enjoy seeing you in them, and I want to know you might remember me whenever you wear them."

She switched from hard-headed to a puddle of emotion; her hands flew to his cheeks. She kissed him more purposefully than he'd kissed her, and she enjoyed every warm and moist moment. She'd missed his lips. They took their time with the gratitude kiss, but she had no intention of taking it to a different level. Not now anyway. "Thank you. I'll always treasure this necklace and the earrings because you gave them to me."

Wisdom must have kept him from kissing her again, even though she hoped he would. But, perhaps more intimate than any kiss could be, they continued to stare deep into each other's eyes for several more heartbeats. Her gaze flitted around his face, settling on his strong chin and back to those rich brown eyes, searching for some clue for what was happening between them, until it was time to tuck this moment away with all the others and say good-night.

Friday afternoon, Lizzie's last two patients cancelled and she got back to the ranch early. Cole hadn't been so lucky and was still at work. Once again, she was glad for the independence of using Tiberius's car. She'd finished nursing Flora, who'd fallen asleep, and she wandered into the living room.

Monty sat in his chair thumbing through a magazine. The moment she entered he looked up. "Hey, girlie-girl, feel like taking a ride with me?"

"You mean like run an errand?" He'd probably been waiting for her to bring the car home.

"No. Like sit on a horse and saddle. I've missed my horses. Plus the visiting occupational-therapy nurse gave me the okay to ride again today."

"That's great and I'd love to." There was still plenty of light left, being mid-July. "In fact I've wanted to ride again since Cole took me. Let's do it!" Lizzie let Gretchen know what they planned, and, other than looking a little surprised, she switched on the baby monitor on the kitchen windowsill in order to keep tabs on Flora while she slept.

Monty's gait was strong and balanced now, even though he still relied a little on his hand-carved walking stick. The intricately designed wooden cane went well with his dungarees and cowboy hat, too. "I figured you might want to go, already had Jack saddle up Zebulon and O'Reilly for us. We won't do anything strenuous, just enjoy the evening air."

"Sounds great to me, and dibs on Zebulon." Though she expected the ride would conjure up all kinds of heady memories from the afternoon with Cole on the ridge trail.

A half hour later, when she'd been right about her hunch, they'd ridden to a huge corral where the new mothers and calves were kept separated from the grazing steer. Lizzie was proud of the fact she'd remembered everything Cole had taught her about riding, and was handling Zebulon as if she knew what she was doing. For a city girl, she thought she could get used to riding horses.

Monty sat watching the calves nurse for a while, smiling. "I never get tired of my ranch. I especially love the spring when the calves drop, and the summer watching them grow. Makes me know the Circle M will continue on."

Lizzie kept her wondering thoughts, about who would carry on after Monty got too old, to herself.

He made a clicking noise with his mouth and the horses immediately knew it was time to move on. She tightened the inside of her thighs and Zebulon quickened the pace and caught up with Monty and O'Reilly. They continued on, side by side for a while longer, in silence.

"When I was in the hospital in Cheyenne, I was treated like a specimen." Evidently Monty had gotten tired of the quiet. "All these young doctors trotted in every morning and they talked about me and my condition, like I wasn't there."

"I'm sorry."

"That's not my point. I didn't mind that. What I'd forgotten was that the University of Wyoming Hospital is a teaching hospital. They've got a three-year family-medicine program that is supposed to be one of the best in the country. Doctors there learn how to do everything, even surgery, just like Trevor does. That's where he did his residency. I know it's not a fancy job like Cole's but it's just as important. I also know you're a city girl, but I was thinking Wyoming could use more good doctors like you. And that way Flora could grow up in the wide open instead of cooped up in some city apartment surrounded by cement."

No wonder the speech therapist had released him last week; he'd just said more words in one go than he'd said the whole rest of the time she'd been at Circle M. Plus he seemed to read her thoughts about Flora growing up in wide-open spaces.

"Why, Tiberius Montgomery, are you trying to influence my decision?"

"I'm trying to talk some sense into you. Couldn't get through to Cole, but maybe you being a mother and all, well, maybe you'll think about it."

"Cole's gone to great lengths to open some doors for me, but please understand I am honored that you care.

And, more importantly, that you think I'm a good doctor."

Maybe she'd gotten too syrupy for Monty or something, but he made that clicking sound again, and both horses picked up speed trotting back toward the ranch and the stables. End of conversation.

Besides thoroughly enjoying the evening ride, regardless of his flighty attitude, Lizzie was flabbergasted that Tiberius Montgomery had given her career any thought. As they dismounted and the stable guy walked off with the horses, an odd niggling, way in the back of her mind, made her promise not to disregard Monty's heartfelt and practical suggestion. Maybe he was on to something.

Walking back to the house she let down her guard and imagined a life with Cole, living in Wyoming, raising Flora together. Her head swirled at the possibility of being his woman. Loving him. Watching him flourish as his fatherly skills grew. Then she stumbled on a rock and nearly fell to her knees. As usual, whenever she got her hopes up about something, the universe had a way of knocking her off balance.

It had been a senseless fantasy anyway. Cole couldn't love her, he was too busy with his career to settle down, and he'd never move home again.

Saturday morning Lizzie was having a fit in her bedroom. "How can I leave my baby?" Those large, pleading eyes nearly broke down Cole's resolve, but there was too much at stake for her to back out now.

Nearly out of patience, Cole paced. If Lizzie couldn't get it through her head that this small sacrifice of twenty-four hours would be worth her entire future, there was nothing more he could do.

He reached for Flora, removing her from Lizzie's

clutches. "Finish packing. I'll take her for a walk." With-out giving her a chance to respond, he left with a beam-ing baby, because Flora always brightened up when Cole held her, and headed for the door. Flora really liked Cole, and Lizzie could tell by his demeanor whenever he held her that the feeling was mutual.

"I'll be back in twenty minutes to get your bags, and we're leaving. Understand?" He gave Lizzie a stern stare, made sure she knew he wasn't horsing around, then, looking at little Flora's happy blue eyes watching his every move, he made a silly face and snorted like a pig as they left. It worked; the baby smiled and squealed, her arms around his neck. "Want to see the horsies?" he asked in a voice a full octave higher than usual. Flora sucked her fist and pumped her feet in answer. "Okay, then. Let's go."

A half-hour later both Lizzie's and his overnight bags were in the trunk of Cole's car and they set off for the airport in Cheyenne, barely speaking a word. He could read her, though, and she was one big ball of fear, sepa-ration anxiety and maybe a touch of excitement. He had to admit he was nervous, too. Part of what he was doing felt wrong, as if he'd found and trained a prized mare and turned her into a show horse. Yeah, that definitely didn't feel right, but wasn't it for the greater good? Her greater good?

The thought of not seeing Lizzie every day hit hard. Regardless of whether she got a residency after tonight or not, by summer's end they'd both go their separate ways. He sighed and stepped harder on the gas pedal, nearly hitting eighty on the speedometer.

Lizzie spent the entire drive thinking of things to make calls to Gretchen for, to remind her about caring for Flora. She reached for her phone once again as they parked at the airport, and Cole leaned across the car to stop her. "I think you've covered everything Gretchen needs to know." He forced Lizzie to look at him for the first time that morning. She connected with his eyes, apprehension coloring her expression. "Flora's in good hands. You know it. Now relax and think about rewriting your future tonight."

All she could muster was a nod along with a quivery breath, but at least some of the anxiety fizzled from her gaze.

Forty-five minutes later they boarded their plane and settled in for the three-and-a-half-hour flight. Cole planned to quiz Lizzie part of the time, but as soon as he began she tossed him a glance that begged to be left alone.

Truth was, if she didn't have her routine down by now, cramming for the test would be of little help, so he let her be with her thoughts. Closing his eyes, he faced a fact he wasn't prepared for. What happened after tonight? Or after Trevor and Julie came back to the clinic? Had he done such a great job of shaping up Lizzie that he'd lose her?

The lose part had never been meant to be a part of the equation. This exercise had been a test of his teaching skills. Could he take a young doctor with potential who'd been rejected by all the most prestigious hospitals in the country and turn her into the doctor everyone wanted? His success was supposed to be a feather on his cowboy hat, not an aching, gaping hole in his gut. After spending nearly every day and evening with Lizzie for the past month, he'd grown accustomed to being around her. He looked forward to seeing her serious yet hopeful face each morning and to watching her concentrate each evening in the library as she puckered and smoothed those delicious lips while she read and thought.

What would a day be like without looking into those extraordinary green eyes?

He couldn't go there. Not now. Because right now he needed to work on his act: the guy who was indifferent to her leaving. The guy who only wanted her placed in a resident program so he could get back to business as usual. Busy days in the cardiac clinic at Johns Hopkins, envelope-pushing cardiac procedures, nonstop travel around the country, hell, around the world. Why not? Once she was gone he'd have his old life back.

But since meeting Lizzie, Cole wondered what kind of life that would be.

CHAPTER NINE

LIZZIE HAD AGREED to be ready by 6:00 p.m. and, because her entire future seemed to depend on this blasted event, she didn't want to mess up. Cole had put so much time and effort into making her hirable—even down to scheduling an in-suite mani-pedi at the hotel—she couldn't let him down now.

She'd never been in such a beautiful hotel in her life and she felt like a princess in the huge marble bathtub, the bubbling bath gel smelling of lavender and vanilla, and her toes barely able to reach the end of the tub. She wanted to stay here all afternoon, but knew she couldn't. Wow. Was this how Cole was used to living?

He'd thought nothing of tossing down his credit card to pay for both hotel rooms at the ornate and luxurious Monaco hotel. Until that moment, she hadn't been sure—and sure as hell hadn't been about to ask but had hoped anyway—if they'd be roommates or not.

She'd thought she'd walked into a royal palace when they'd first entered the classic beaux arts building with its sparkling marble floors, crystal chandeliers, grand winding marble staircase and Tiffany stained glass windows. Every bit of history had been preserved yet the lobby was modern and inviting and beyond everything else, due to armloads of flowers in several huge vases, colorful. A girl from Southie, Boston, she'd never had a fantasy come close to the reality of this hotel. Dreams like those were for people who lived in the Back Bay, the upper class of Boston.

Lizzie lay back in the tub and dunked her hair and face under water, suspending herself in time and space. Cole came to mind, as he often did, now. His handsome, all-guy face. His sturdy hands, and how they felt on her shoulders. His lips, soft as a butterfly one moment and demanding the next. The way he heated her up from the inside out with one smoldering glance.

She sat up, the water running down her hair and over her face. The little fantasy from yesterday returned. What would it be like to be his wife, loving him, sleeping with him every night, waking with a smile on her face every day? What if she seduced Cole tonight, to force him to see how good they could be together, to prove she had as much to offer as he did? She'd surprise him with her love, drive him crazy with total passion for him. But she'd know when to leave him alone, too. Yes, they'd be so in touch they'd know without saying what each other wanted. She'd be that kind of wife for him. She dreamed. Plus, they'd be a force to be reckoned with as lovers, and parents. The two of them raising Flora to be... Flora!

Then it hit her: she hadn't thought about Flora in... how long? More proof she was a selfish and terrible mother. She stood up, water falling away, panic replacing the calm she'd just enjoyed. She climbed out of the tub and draped herself in the extra thick and soft bath towel, searching for her cell phone.

Gretchen hadn't called, true, but Cole had probably put the fear of God in her about only calling for an emergency. She speed-dialed and waited.

"Everything's just fine, Elisabete." Gretchen had never called her Lizzie like Monty and Cole. The relaxed sound of the woman's voice poured over Lizzie, automatically helping her calm down. "She's taking her afternoon nap." Baltimore was two hours ahead of Cattleman Bluff; of course it would be nap time for Flora.

"So everything's okay, then?"

"She's as good as gold."

"You're not just saying that, are you?"

"I've never been good at lying, Elisabete. Please trust me with your precious baby. I'm giving her all of my attention. Even Tiberius is helping."

The reassuring words and the sudden sense of family back home put a smile on Lizzie's face. Her little fantasy about Cole returned. She glanced at the crystal clock on the ornate mantle above her hotel-room fireplace. She needed to speed up if she planned to be dressed and made-up by six. And what was she going to do with her hair?

"I'll never be able to repay you. Thank you so much," she said.

"Darlin', you've brought new life back into this family. We love Flora. Now, go and knock 'em dead." Wasn't it interesting how Gretchen naturally considered herself a part of the extended Montgomery family? If Gretchen could, why couldn't Lizzie?

Lizzie hung up, grinning and planning to do just that. But in all honesty, there was only one person she really wanted to knock dead in the figurative sense tonight, and that was Cole Montgomery. She was on to his dirty little plan to get rid of her, but she had a surprise in store for him. Tonight, she'd make him an offer he couldn't possibly refuse…unless ice water ran through his veins. And she'd kissed him enough to know that wasn't the case. Tonight she'd make him want her, no matter what it took.

Decked out in his tux and black dress cowboy boots, Cole knocked on Lizzie's hotel room door at one minute to six, then waited. He'd already made a few calls to various hotel rooms, setting up plans to meet with several residency administrators during the gala cocktails in the Paris foyer. They'd have to wait to see who they'd be sitting with for dinner in the ballroom. Fingers crossed they'd be near the recruiters from Massachusetts General Hospital in Boston and New York Presbyterian Cornell campus since he hadn't been able to contact them so far this afternoon.

The door opened and a vision straight from heaven stood before him. She seemed a little taken aback by seeing him, too. Maybe it was the boots and the Western-styled tux he'd taken out of storage before the trip.

Lizzie's dark hair had been piled in high ringlets on top of her head. Her full brows highlighted those amazing eyes that she'd colored and lined with make-up. Wow. Her skin looked creamy and he fisted his hands inside his pockets to dampen the urge to touch her all over. The ice-blue evening dress fit like a glove, and the choker-style necklace looked perfect on her long neck, the aquamarine stone dangling just below the delicate notch of her throat. If he concentrated, and he definitely was, he could see the faint beating of her pulse there.

She stood watching him taking her all in, waiting with an eager, open gaze. *Well?* He could practically hear her thought.

It required great discipline to speak. "Are you ready?" He couldn't very well let on how overwhelmed and turned on he was by her beauty. Or how his skin practically vibrated with desire. How easily he'd slipped into the most basic of all reactions of a man to a woman. It wasn't the purpose of this night. No, her wow factor was meant for the old tired-eyed doctors recruiting for next year's internal-medicine programs on the East Coast.

But he couldn't ignore the immediate disappointed expression she bore from his silence either and he had to let her know how great she looked. Where had his manners gone? "You look fantastic. I've said it before—that dress was made for you."

She let out her breath. "Whew. Thanks. I don't recognize myself. And by the way, you look sexy as hell."

He stood a little taller, liking that she thought he was sexy looking, and he could think of a million more things to say about how great she looked, too, but this wasn't a date or a mutual-admiration-society meeting. It was business. He couldn't think of tonight in any other way. Tonight was all about the business of getting Lizzie a job. "Got all the names memorized?" Back on track, even though her appearance distracted the hell out of him.

"Yes," she said, turning to pick up her clutch bag, immediately clicking into the purpose of the night. Except he noticed the fine, sequined lace covering the backs of her shoulders and the triangle-shaped cutout area revealing her skin at the center of her back. *What would it be like to touch Lizzie all over?*

She glanced up, a message in her gaze: *touch me, I won't break.* He swallowed and pushed down the desire.

"All you have to do," she said, turning back and straightening to her full height, "is mention the hospital program they're from and I'll remember the name." She glanced at him, narrowed her eyes and nodded. "I'm ready for this, but wish me luck anyway."

She sounded breathy and he lost his train of thought for a moment, thinking of how that breathiness might feel blowing gently across his chest, then on reflex he cupped her upper arm and kissed her cheek. "You're beautiful." He'd meant to wish her luck, but it'd come out wrong.

There was a question in her eyes when he pulled back and he mentally scrambled to cover as he canted his head. "Good luck."

She tucked her lips inward and nodded, seeming suddenly nervous, or disappointed. "I had something else in mind."

"For?" Her dazzling appearance had made him suddenly stupid.

"For wishing me luck." She moved toward him, wrapped her arms around his neck and kissed him hard, her lips already parted.

He sank right into the kiss, could have chucked the whole night for the chance to stay here and seduce her. But that wasn't the kind of man he wanted to be for her. He wanted to help restore her faith in men, not add more evidence to her case against them. He broke off the kiss, but not before her smoldering gaze begged him to take her.

He knew in that moment he wanted her more than any other woman on the planet.

Just not right this instant. They had work to do, a battle to win, a job to conquer. They needed a victory before they celebrated.

He took his pocket kerchief and wiped away the lipstick he instinctively knew she'd left behind on his mouth. Doing his best to recover his breathing and tame the sex-starved beast she'd nearly unleashed with her kiss, he glanced in the mirror in the hotel sitting room, inhaled slowly and let it out.

"You're going to do great," he said, knowing she'd knock dead every doctor she met with her great looks, then impress them with her intelligence and hopefully she'd throw in a little charm. She had it all, he knew beyond a doubt. He had to keep his head clear, for tonight was her night. All she had to do was showcase the polished version of herself.

"Thank you," she said, standing beside him, gazing into the mirror, reapplying lipstick and fixing a few stray curls in her hair, trying her best not to sound disappointed by his not throwing her on the bed and making love to her.

Or was that his thought and disappointment?

He had to focus on the task at hand. Tonight Elisabete Silva was bound to land a job.

"Ready?" He offered his arm.

"As ready as I'll ever be," she said, taking it.

On the elevator ride down to the Paris ballroom he savored the fresh, modern and flirty scent of her perfume, and the way her deep red fingernails matched her toenails. Every part of her had been perfectly put together—even the wisps of hair from the updo falling on her neck seemed flawlessly placed. He was thankful she hadn't lacquered down her hair with spray. He thought all of this while staring straight ahead, watching her reflection in the polished brass elevator door, hoping she didn't notice.

The elevator dinged and the doors parted. A wave of loud chatter hit them as they exited. He glanced at her reassuringly. "Showtime," he said with a confident smile and nod as they stepped onto loud patterned gold-and-maroon carpet and into the ballroom foyer with violet blue walls and ceiling-to-floor magenta velvet curtains.

Cocktails were served in the foyer and they'd taken exactly three steps before a black-vested waiter offered drinks. Lizzie looked to Cole, thinking briefly before accepting a glass of some kind of fun-looking pale cranberry-colored drink.

"What's this?" she asked.

"That's a cosmopolitan, ma'am," the server said, clearly enamored by her beauty. "Vodka, triple sec, cranberry juice and lime."

"Thanks." She took the drink and moved her head close to Cole so no one else would hear. "I'm not nursing tonight and don't plan to keep whatever I express, so why not, right?"

He grinned over the insider information. "Why not?" He took a glass of red wine, and soon his eyes scanned the gathered group for familiar faces. "Ah, George Eckhart, from the Philadelphia program. Follow me." Why waste time?

On task, she took a quick sip of her cocktail and matched him step for step around one group of people then another to reach his mark.

"George! Good to see you."

Dr. Eckhart's eyes reflected respect when he greeted Cole, then they lit up with new interest when Cole introduced him to Elisabete Silva, MD. After that, as hoped and planned for, every doctor he introduced her to reacted nearly identically, and Lizzie became a force to be reckoned with over cocktails.

By 7:00 p.m. someone used a mallet on a brass gong to announce that dinner was served and to direct people to the Paris ballroom. The epic room was set with round dining tables covered in silver cloth, sparkling crystal goblets and the best hotel china and silver, and with vases of white hydrangeas at the center. Cole had checked the seating chart and was happy to see the head of the MGH resident program in Boston would be at their table.

Taking Lizzie's hand, and thoroughly enjoying the feel of her cool fingers wrapping around his, he led her to table number thirty, midway into the ballroom. Dr. Linda Poles might not respond to Lizzie's beauty, but she was sure to appreciate her intelligence and Boston wit. Cole traded a name plate to make sure Lizzie was next to the doctor and watched as the friendly-faced, middle-aged woman in a standard black evening dress approached.

He'd been right, Lizzie and Linda hit it off immediately, talking about their favorite city, Boston, and the rest of the night played out like a well-rehearsed dream.

By 10:00 p.m. the event was winding down, having raised more money for their cause than on any previous year.

Cole made sure Lizzie bid good-night to Dr. Poles, and also to the doctor from the New York internal-medicine program, Joseph Steinberg, who'd been sitting at a nearby table, and whom Cole had made sure Lizzie had spent time chatting with between the main course and dessert with coffee. Both doctors seemed genuinely taken with Lizzie, as had all the other doctors he'd handpicked to introduce her to tonight. She couldn't have made a better impression.

"Ready to go?" he asked.

"I'd like to finish my drink first." She'd found a favorite in the cosmopolitan and this was her second… or third? But he couldn't fault her since he'd put on so much pressure about tonight. Cosmos or not, she'd performed perfectly.

He took the opportunity to say good-night to a couple more people, glad-handing as he'd never done before, on Lizzie's behalf. After tonight she was bound to get placed in any number of internal-medicine resident programs. She probably wouldn't even have to wait until next year—that was if she was willing to step in late. He stood chatting, hands in pockets, with the wife of another doctor, biding his time until Lizzie was ready to leave, when an arm snaked around his elbow and tugged him near.

Lizzie. "I'm ready." She smiled, that beautiful beam he'd admired all evening, looking no less for the wear over the past few hours.

They squeezed into an elevator with a dozen other people and disappeared into the corner letting everyone else talk and laugh.

"I'll see you to your floor," he made a point to say, since he had in fact gotten their rooms on different floors so as not to encourage rumors.

"Thanks," she said, fiddling with one of her earrings.

On the fifth floor they both got off, she stepping out of the elevator first. She didn't wait for him, but kept up a quick strut all the way down the hallway. For the first time that night he noticed she maybe wasn't enjoying herself as much as he'd imagined.

"You okay?" he asked before she reached her door.

"As a matter of fact, no."

"Something I do?" This came out of nowhere.

He got the long drawn-out stare, communicating he'd probably just asked the dumbest question of the night, and when she'd made sure she'd gotten her point across she answered. "I'm on to you, Dr. Montgomery." Then she shoved her key card into the slot and pushed her door open.

He stopped right where he was, trying to figure out what was going on. A couple he'd seen at the gala came down the hall, acknowledging him with nods before heading on to their room, but not before he noticed the woman's raised brows. He didn't want to give the wrong impression about him and Lizzie, so he stayed where he was. Just before Lizzie's hotel door banged closed, she caught it with her foot in those strappy silver heels.

"You coming in?"

He couldn't very well leave it at that, with her angry, not after all the hoop jumping he'd made her do tonight, so he followed her inside.

Lizzie had felt like a prized pet all night the way Cole had showed her off. She'd gone along with it only because he'd pounded it into her head that this was all about her future. But it didn't feel right.

"What do you mean you're on to me?" Cole asked, from her hotel doorway, one brow raised, an amused glint in his eye.

"You wanted to look good." She folded her arms. "I made you look good tonight."

He narrowed that gaze, tenting his brows, and walked into her sitting room. "What are you talking about?"

"You've made me your pet project, and tonight was the science fair." She made a huge circle with her arms. "I took first prize. You get the blue ribbon."

"Look, Lizzie, that wasn't the case at all. Tonight was all about your making a memorable first impression on the people who will take hundreds of faceless applications and decide who gets into their prized programs and who doesn't. It's a scientific fact that it's harder to

reject a person with a face and a personality than a piece
of paper with a passport-sized photo on it."

"That's not my point. I felt fake. Like I had to be
someone I'm not."

He shook his head and stepped closer to where she'd
dug in her heels. "You are Elisabete Silva, in a prettier-
than-usual dress, that's all. Oh, and with a great hairdo,
too. Meant to tell you that earlier. Not that I don't like
the braid and unisex clothes the rest of the time." He
worked at a charming smile, but somehow knew how
fragile she felt and toned it down.

He looked sincere in wanting to make her feel better,
though, and that was what mattered. But she needed to
get the next part off her chest. "It's all because you want
to get rid of me. Don't lie."

His enticing expression changed to far more serious.
"We both knew our time together was temporary. I don't
belong at the ranch and you certainly don't belong in that
clinic in Cattleman Bluff."

"Who says you don't belong? It's your home."

"Not really. Not anymore." His answer bothered her;
didn't he see everything he had in Wyoming? But right
now, she needed to stay on point.

"Well, I like it there. I feel connected with the people
at the clinic."

"And that's a gift you'll be able to carry with you into
your residency wherever you go. When Trevor and Julie
come back, they'll take over again. We were only there
for the summer. After tonight, your fall and New Year
should be set. No, *will be set*. You'll have your choice of
programs to accept." He took another step toward her.
Why did she feel fragile and invaded, the complete opposite of how she'd felt before they'd left earlier? "We
accomplished something special tonight, Lizzie." The

tone of his voice modulated to kinder. Gentler. "Flora will thank you one day."

"What about us?" She refused to feel fragile, hated it, made up for it by being brazen. Her fantasy, no matter how silly, deserved a shot. Then she moved closer so she could get a better look at his eyes, since he'd suddenly become evasive with eye contact.

As she expected, he looked perplexed, as if she'd blindsided him. "A few kisses and a lot of desire doesn't add up to much, does it?"

His words stung, but she warded them off with resolve. She put her hand on his arm, needing to make contact with him. Needing to force him to feel something for her, even if it was only sex. "It could have added up to a lot more, but I get the feeling I'm not good enough for you."

"That's crazy." He nailed her with his disagreeing stare.

"No, it isn't. Your whole goal was to change me. To make me hirable. I mean, I know I came from a completely different background than you. Maybe I seem tough and maybe too aggressive but that's how I survived. I needed to be that way to get by. You've kept me at a distance from the beginning. Like I make you uncomfortable or something. Except for when you needed to teach me stuff. Then I became a project."

"I couldn't take advantage of you. Not that I didn't want you. It wouldn't be right."

"Do you think I'd let you take advantage of me? Come on, whatever you're referring to is mutual. Tonight, though, I think you took advantage of my looking great in this dress." She gave a wry laugh.

"Not so. We seized the moment for you and Flora. You needed tonight. Not me."

"So you could be done with me. Right?" She waited for him to look back into her eyes. "Well, your job is over. Now what?"

He went silent for a beat, cleared his throat. "Now we go back home and finish minding the clinic for another couple of weeks. Then I go back to Baltimore and you'll hopefully have a spot waiting for you in a resident program."

She sighed over his being obtuse, guessing she'd have to spell it out for him. "What about earlier? What about right now?" Her fingers walked up his arm and across his shoulder. "In this hotel room?" She lightly tugged his earlobe.

"That wouldn't be wise."

"Are you always this shut off?"

"I'm your boss. You've had a couple of drinks and you're not using good judgment right now."

"And if I came on to you, you'd be taking advantage of me?"

"Something like that."

"Baloney. I know what I'm doing. I look hot in this dress. Tell me you don't think so." She'd made him look more uncomfortable than she'd ever seen him—and she'd put him in his share of tough positions since she'd moved in to his home and worked with him at the clinic. Her heart pounded with worries he'd shut her down and leave, but she pressed on, needing proof he did or didn't want her as much as she wanted him. "We're in a hotel room and no one will know but us."

"You're playing with fire here. One of us has to be levelheaded—"

"Why?" She'd taken her stand and nothing would turn her back now. She unbuttoned his jacket and slipped her hands inside, exploring his shirt-covered chest and broad back, loving his lingering classic cologne, letting his gorgeous build and rugged face rule her thinking. "I like the fire I see in your eyes." She reached for his jaw, his nostrils gently flared as some of his resistance eased. He did have feelings for her, just as she did for him, and now was the time to let them all out. "I've missed kissing you." Being in heels, she didn't have to lift her chin much to make contact with his lips.

Melding their mouths, tilting her head for better access, she welcomed him full on. His hands shot to her and pulled her tight and close as his tongue delved deep. She moaned with approval. They fought through their kisses without a hint of tenderness. His was a battle of resistance, and hers a fight for what she wanted. Needed. Him. Right now!

Off came his jacket and shirt, and her dress was nearly torn away when he reached the stubborn hook and eye, but he fought them and won. They wound up rolling onto the sitting-room couch, desperate to be naked and making love together. She didn't want him to be gentle, and he couldn't be if he tried. They'd suppressed too much for too long and now was their moment to set everything free.

His hand cupped and pushed up her breast as he kissed her neck and shoulder raggedly. He got rid of his boxers, and she took the moment to look at his imposing figure. Long-waisted, broad shoulders, built for hard work, yet with muscles subdued by his medical career. His strong legs and fully aroused state were a sight she never wanted to forget, but right this moment she needed to touch him.

He moaned when she did, and she eased him back onto the couch as she straddled him, her fingers stroking the smooth skin of his long ridge. His large palms cupped her bottom, massaging the hunger for him, and she dipped her head to his face. They kissed more out of desperation than desire. They'd quickly reached the point where they needed to connect, for him to be inside her, for them to be close and tight and rocking their way to release.

"I'm still nursing and haven't gotten my period yet—" she had to be practical for this one second "—but it's your call. Now's the time."

"I need my wallet," he said, on the exact same wavelength.

Ah, so the traveling cardiologist knew about being prepared. It surprised her, even made her a little jealous, but she took that energy and helped him find and place the condom in record time, rather than let it hold her back.

She stayed on top and controlled his entering her. Things were definitely different since giving birth, but he felt great and she hoped he enjoyed it as much as she did. Glancing at his tense yet euphoric expression, she immediately quit worrying about how she might feel to him. He loved it. She drove him crazy.

He watched her body as she moved on him, worshiping her with his gaze. His hands gripped and guided her hips just so, his head lifting, mouth nipping at her breasts. Now and then his lids dipped closed with pleasure, but he didn't stop looking at her otherwise. She fed his lust, and she loved how that made her feel. Powerful. Wanted. Soon, he needed to go deeper and, with her legs wrapped around his waist and her arms around his neck, he lifted and repositioned her beneath him on the cushions.

He thrust into her fast and frantic and she lost her grasp on sustaining the pleasure, zipping right along to nearly there and, oops, over the edge. Wow. He groaned all the while her waves of orgasm shot through her spine and down to her toes, and she could feel how her reactions made him harder, brought him closer to release. Soon, with a few long, slow thrusts, he moaned when the moment hit and he hardened even more just before throbbing deep inside.

The whirlwind minutes of having sex with him were worth every risk as her body took over and, having already been shown the way, she came again with a vengeance around him, lengthening his free fall. They rocked together long afterwards, liking the feel of being joined, not wanting it to end. She loved having her breasts crammed against his chest, and the vision from this angle of his straining shoulder muscles while maneuvering the narrow couch. Damn, he felt fantastic and she wished their being together could be more than just now. But knowing Cole as she did, that would never be the case. She'd forced this. He never would have initiated it, being too much of a gentleman. Like always, she'd plowed ahead in her bullheaded fashion and insisted on having her way. With him.

He might be wiser than her, but she glanced up at his face and, from his *What just hit me?* expression, she was convinced he was just as glad she'd forced this completely physical conversation. In fact, it had been long overdue.

After Cole and Lizzie moved to the bed, pulled back the covers and got comfortable snuggling together, he couldn't deny the energy and heat this woman brought him. And when in the last ten years had he performed like that? The thought helped him pinpoint what had been missing with his long string of girlfriends ending with Victoria last year—passion.

From the very first day, Lizzie had managed to pull out of him the strongest reactions, no matter what the circumstances, be it annoyance, anger, joy, surprise…lust. Oh, yes—lust. And now, realizing there was no place for this relationship to go since she'd be leaving, sadness. He pulled her closer and kissed her forehead; she sighed contentedly, completely relaxed in his arms. All natural beauty, not polished and practiced, just her, the way he liked her. Loved her? The fire that had burned in his belly for her minutes before got replaced with a dull ache of loss.

He inhaled the flowery scent of Lizzie's hair, which had fallen over her shoulders when they'd made love— if he could call it that. What they'd just done had nothing to do with love. It had been totally raw. Focused. Feral. Amazing.

His throat went dry as he prepared to say the toughest thing on his mind, because he knew it was the best thing for her. He pushed aside his selfish desires, for her future. "This can't happen again."

Her head shot up. She stared at him. "Why not? I'm in Wyoming for a few more weeks."

"It's unethical. You're my colleague, not a playmate."

Her brows crinkled in a quizzical way. "And if I like being your playmate?"

"That's beside the point. I'm always on the road. We'll be living in different states. The most we could ask for was the occasional hookup. Is that what you really want?"

"Isn't that how you usually do it? Keep a safe distance from people. Stay too busy to commit to anything or anyone outside of work?"

His hand clutched her shoulder tighter. How had she nailed him so easily? He kept that distance because he'd disappointed everyone who'd ever cared for him, including his mother. He'd never been able to be what those close to him wanted, to be there when they needed him most, and there was no way he could survive loving with every fiber and losing, as his father had. Women walked away from him as soon as they realized his profession was his first love. Eventually, Lizzie would too, and that wasn't what was best for her or Flora. He forced himself to lighten his grasp. "I have a demanding job. I've managed to make a name for myself, and traveling is the key to keeping my status."

"So you let status rule your days?"

"Like I said, I didn't set out with that in mind." She'd cut to the dirty truth: he'd settled for status over feelings. Over really living. "Things just fell into place." Or had he made sure to hold on to his wonder-boy status at all costs, because that was the only way he knew how to be?

"And now those things keep you away from your family, your father, and heaven help any woman who wanders into your life."

On defense, he fought to sound casual. "You bug the hell out of me, you know that?" He shared an annoyed though nonthreatening smile. "And you're far too accurate in your assumptions. Look, this is me. It's the way I live."

"Who says I want anything from you? In case you haven't noticed, I'm a new mother and I'm searching for a job and my plate is pretty full. Truth is, I don't have room for you."

She'd taken his hint and run with it, immediately relieving him of any guilt or responsibility. How did she have such a knack for reading people? Maybe getting tossed from one foster home to another growing up taught a young girl to read people and to never get her hopes up for anything permanent. Back came the guilt in a rush. Didn't Lizzie deserve more out of life?

No. He really needed to stay out of her life so she'd have a shot at a real relationship with someone who cherished her and Flora. That person wouldn't be him. Life didn't work that way for him.

"I'm not good enough for you, am I?"

He couldn't hide his shock since that thought had never entered his mind, and yet it was the first conclusion she'd jumped to. "Good enough? It has nothing to do with that."

She laughed. "Am I about to hear the 'it's not you, it's me' speech?"

He could see right through her tough and cynical mask, but wasn't it better to let her down now than later when it would really hurt? As he thought of Flora's future and how she deserved a father who loved her his heart sank. That baby had already managed to steal his heart, but that wasn't the point; they both deserved a better future than he could give them. He might be able to offer wealth and protection, but they deserved to be loved, a feeling he'd lost the day he broke his neck. When he'd risked it all for love, he'd nearly killed himself. "Thought I'd already given it."

Her wry laugh offered relief from the tense moment and begged for him to join in.

"So," he said. "After tonight—" he said, hurting in a place he'd long forgotten.

But he'd only gotten half of his thoughts out before she rolled on and straddled him. "Who says tonight is over?"

She ducked her head and nailed him with an open-mouthed kiss, and there was no argument from him.

She'd made a great point about their night together. He'd
been honest with her and she still wanted to make love.
He wasn't about to talk her out of right now. His hand
cupped the back of her head and he kissed her as if there
were no tomorrow.

This kind of escape he could handle, as long as feelings didn't enter in.

But wasn't it already too late?

They'd barely woken in time to shower and make their
flight home, Sunday. An uneasy tension wove between
them on the airplane, nearly erasing the amazing night
they'd spent in each other's arms.

Lizzie watched out the window as they flew over
Wyoming, her heart swelling at the beauty. Such wide-
open spaces. A little piece of heaven she wanted for her
and her daughter. As they landed she thought about her
odds at getting placed in one of the programs from the
administrators she'd met the night before.

Cole had set her up for more possibilities than she
could ever dream up herself, yet she couldn't quite get
Monty's comments from their last horseback ride out of
her mind. What kind of future did she want for Flora?
Her little fantasy about Cole would never play out. It had
been foolish of her to even dream it up, because it already hurt like hell and there was nothing she could do
to move Cole out of his lifelong rut. Now all she wanted
was to get home to hold her baby again.

She glanced at Cole, diligently reading a cardiac-
medicine journal, wishing things could be different between them but knowing better. She was a big girl, after
all. Besides, his noticeable indifference this morning
proved he hadn't been lying last night. There wasn't
room for her, and especially for Flora, in his life. The

man was honest on all levels, even the tough-as-nails topics. At least she could always count on him for that.

Maybe she could still make an impact on one aspect of his life, though. Because she cared, she opened a topic he'd pushed aside years ago. "So you'll only be in Cattleman Bluff a couple more weeks. Are you planning to set things straight with your father?"

Cole lifted his head slowly, removing his stare from the journal and placing it on her. "Has he talked to you?"

"I didn't need it spelled out. All I had to do was observe."

"Hmm." He started to go back to reading and she wasn't about to let him get off with a single-syllable response.

"And Monty and I talk all the time—" his head lifted, though he didn't look at her "—but not about the trouble between you two. Nope. Like I said, I figured that out myself." She waited a moment to make sure Cole was still listening. "He isn't getting any younger, you know."

Cole inhaled, immediately seeming uncomfortable about the conversation. "And he'll settle for nothing less than having both of his sons completely change their lives in order to accommodate his dream. *His* dream. Do you understand how unreasonable that is?"

She glanced down at the hands in her lap, not wanting to step on anything Cole needed to say, but thinking at least he had a family. Didn't he understand how precious that was?

"Trevor never got out of town. He could have had a far more lucrative and respected career but he stayed in Wyoming after medical school and took his residency in family practice. He got strapped with the clinic in Cattleman Bluff, and has never left since."

"But he was with your mother the last days of her

life, and he wouldn't have met Julie again if things had worked out your way."

He went immediately thoughtful on the first part of her response, quickly passed over it to her second thought. "True, but who knows what opportunities he's missed because of sticking around?"

"Is life only about opportunities or missed opportunities to you?" He went silent, so she prodded more. "What's wrong with family medicine?"

"Nothing, if that's what a person wants. But I always got the feeling Trevor wanted more. And having my brother around still hasn't made Dad happy."

"I think it's because neither of you have taken an interest in the ranching business. Your father really has made a name for himself. I think he's worried all will be lost when he dies."

"Jack is perfectly fine at handling the everyday issues, but Dad really does need to find a partner to handle the business end of it. Raising prime beef doesn't mean squat unless you have places to sell it."

"Circle M steer may not keep their reputation if an outsider steps in."

"What are you getting at?"

"Don't you have any interest in your family business? It's given you all the *opportunities* you've had in your life, to use your favorite word. Isn't it time to give a little back? Like you said, your brother has stuck around and is keeping a promise to the community with the clinic. You seem very business savvy in the medical field because of TAVR. You've marketed it all across the nation. Like you said, you're always on the road."

"And that makes me a meat magnate, how?"

"Same skills. Connections. Just different product."

He tossed his gaze upward with an unbelieving expression. Maybe she'd knocked him sideways and he was ready to pull the oxygen down and take a breath or two, or maybe it was just good old impatience. She understood she had a way of drawing that out of people.

The plane finally taxied to a stop and they jumped up to grab their carry-on bags, putting an abrupt end to the uncomfortable conversation. All she could hope was to plant a seed in Cole's thoughts about his future. To somehow make a difference in his life, even if she wouldn't be in it. Because wasn't that what you did when you cared about someone?

Cole hoped neither Gretchen nor Dad would pick up on the change in his and Lizzie's dynamics when they arrived home and came through the kitchen. Though it would take nothing short of award-winning acting to avoid it. After greeting Monty and Gretchen, Lizzie rushed to gather Flora from Gretchen's arms and, after kissing the baby hello, took off for privacy to nurse her. He was surprised by his own surge of happiness at seeing that bright and sweet baby face, wished he'd had a chance to kiss her, too. Instead, he got down a glass and filled it with water, then drank. Tiberius hung back in the kitchen along with Gretchen, waiting for a report, no doubt.

"She did great," he said after he'd emptied the glass. "Those hospital administrators were eating from her hand. It'll only be a matter of time before the offers come in."

For some odd reason, both his father and Gretchen looked disappointed. Didn't they want the best for her as he did? He gave them a couple of seconds to say something, anything, but neither did.

"Well, I'm exhausted, so I'll see you at dinner." Cole

had a long to-do list. He needed to make arrangements for several upcoming trips, one in particular including an in-service for doctors at the University of California at San Francisco. He'd be demonstrating TAVR, then assisting with the head of cardiac care; next he'd talk him through another procedure and finally be an observer, but ready to step in with any glitches. Once he certified that doctor, if the hospital brought this life- and cost-saving procedure into their facility, it would be a huge West Coast win for his premier cardiac procedure. The medical-device company he worked for part-time would send a substantial bonus check. Maybe he'd skip family dinner tonight.

Though as he headed for his room he couldn't keep Lizzie's intruding conversation on the plane out of his mind. As with hers, his time on the ranch was coming to an end, and he really should hash things out with his father once and for all. There was so much more to discuss than who was taking over the ranch so the man could retire, but he really didn't have the energy to tackle that today, thanks in no small part to her. God, he ached for her already.

He halfheartedly cursed Lizzie for bringing up the tough topic, while loving that she'd cared enough, knowing he couldn't very well sidestep that conversation much longer.

CHAPTER TEN

IT ONLY TOOK until Wednesday for the first residency offer to come through for Lizzie. She whooped and hung up the clinic office phone, then raced to Cole's door.

"Linda Poles just called to say she has an opening for me!" There was no way she could keep the excitement out of her voice.

"Great!" Cole's response didn't sound convincing. "And since she's a woman, you can't claim I pimped you out." His sardonic smile made no attempt to involve his eyes.

"This is true." She wasn't going to let him drag down her moment of victory. Besides, this was a typical good news/bad news deal. "There's only one drawback."

Now she had his full attention. He rose from his chair, circled around the desk and stood a couple of feet before her, waiting for her to fill him in.

"I need to start next week."

The perplexed and downright sad look on his face, a complete contrast to moments before, nearly made her stomach zip-line to her toes, until he quickly covered it up. Saying it out loud drove the point home, though. She'd be leaving. Very soon.

"I…uh…um…" she stammered, trying to work out how to best phrase her words. "I tried to talk her into letting me finish my time here, but she reminded me the program began July the first and that I've already missed weeks. She said I need to get back to Boston and jump right in. I've got a lot of catching up to do."

"And, of course, you're thrilled to get back on old turf and start the program." He'd schooled his expression, and gave nothing away from his reaction. His true thoughts and feelings would never see the light of day around Lizzie. Showing enthusiasm as only Cole could, he flashed that charming smile.

She needed to let him know how she felt, though, which was near panic. "I'm scared witless. I've got to find a place to live, make child-care arrangements. Let my patients here know."

"Lotte can take care of that part." Picking up on how frantic she was, Cole dropped the facade and stepped closer, drew her near, took her into his arms and closed the office door. "You know I'll help any way I can."

"Thank you." She stood there in his arms, savoring the feel of him, touched all the way to her marrow by how she'd missed him since Saturday night. How could she just walk away from everything she'd only just found here? As he'd opened the door for her dreams, even if they were last month's dreams, he'd soundly closed it to anything between them. She had to remember that.

Since coming to Cattleman Bluff and meeting Cole, her goals had subtly shifted, but she couldn't very well say thanks but no thanks to Boston. *I'd like to stick around in Wyoming now, if you don't mind.* She couldn't refuse, after all of his work on her behalf. This was her one big chance to prove herself in a resident program. To eventually find a solid job in a good hospital. To make the best home she could for Flora.

"The MGH program probably has suggestions for

housing," he said, "and I'll pay you for the full six weeks
you were hired for."

"I can't let you do that."

His grip grew tighter. "You don't have a choice in the
matter. I'm in charge of who I pay."

And that, unfortunately, summed up the position she
was in with Cole, once again. She'd moved to Wyoming
without a choice and now she'd leave the same way.

"Your next patient is in the room." Lotte tapped on
the door, figuring out where Lizzie was.

"I'll be right there," she said, wanting to kiss Cole, but
sensing he couldn't handle that any more than she could.
"Thanks again," she said, stepping out of his arms,
willing herself to be ready for the rest of the afternoon
appointments. Because she had to be.

Cole bit back every natural reaction he'd had to the news
of Lizzie leaving, and rendered an award-winning performance, if he did say so himself. And wasn't he getting damn good at that? As the afternoon went on, with
spot conversations here and there while passing in the
hallway, or entering or exiting patient rooms, he'd informed her he could pull some strings to find an afford-
able apartment in a decent part of town. Later, he'd told
a bold lie and said he could even find the best child-care
facility available for little Flora. He'd set up something
with Dr. Poles and the residency program. Lizzie didn't
need to know.

*Keep telling yourself it's what's best for Lizzie. And
Flora.* The thought of not seeing those two bright and
shiny faces every day pinched in his gut. Even now he
longed to take Lizzie in his arms and show her how
much he felt for her. He'd let himself grow too accustomed to both of them. And exhibiting the biggest fail-

ure of wisdom in his life, he'd spent the most amazing night making love to Lizzie. How right they'd been for each other. He could definitely grow accustomed to that.

She'd forced him to feel again; he owed her more than he could ever repay. And since he'd already been monumentally unethical, he'd pay for Flora's child care and lie that it was free to the residents. He'd call Linda as soon as he finished his next appointment to set things up.

Oh, and there was one more call he'd make before he left work today. Larry Rivers. He had some questions to ask.

A bitter taste settled in the back of his mouth.

"I got Elisabete placed," Cole said, leaning back in his swivel chair, facing away from the door, feet propped on the desk corner. "She's in *this* year, not *next*."

Larry praised him, but the accolades only made his stomach churn.

"One thing's been bugging me," Cole said. "Why have you been so invested in Lizzie?"

Silence. "My son fathered Flora. Elisabete could have had him arrested for what he did to her."

Cole closed his eyes and pinched the bridge of his nose. "I see. So this was nothing more than repaying a debt."

He listened briefly while Larry summed up his troubled son, then quickly changed the topic back to Cole working wonders, though Cole's gut churned over Lizzie's ongoing hard-luck story. All the more reason to rejoice in having helped her move on. So why did he feel so bad?

"Yes, yes. I know, Larry." He worked hard to hide his true feelings. "They don't call me the Wonder Boy for nothing. Is there anything I can't do? Sure. Listen,

Larry, next time I'm in Boston you can buy me dinner." Cole glanced up in time to see Lizzie standing in his doorway, having obviously not already left work as he'd assumed, and hearing his every word. The hurt and betrayal covering her face nearly knocked him out of his chair. She took off.

"Listen, I've got to go." Cole hung up the phone, but Lizzie had already made it to the door. He chased her out of the building, not knowing what in the hell to say, but having to say something. She'd practically made it to her car when he caught up.

The hurt he'd glimpsed inside had turned to anger. "Dr. Rivers was behind this?"

"He wants to help you just like I do." He didn't dare step too close.

"You sounded like you'd worked a miracle or something."

He studied his boots, speechless, deciding to be honest, because Lizzie deserved it. "He's been invested in what's best for you. I needed something to take my mind off your leaving. He offered me dinner, that's all."

That stopped her briefly, but the indignation quickly returned. "I hope you choke on that dinner." She swung the car door open and got inside.

He stepped out of the way when she started the engine and backed out of her parking space. There was no stopping her, and he had nothing left to say. He'd just blown every bit of trust he'd earned from her.

There was no hiding the tension between Cole and Lizzie back at the ranch that night. She insisted on eating in her room, and he copped out to feeling relieved he wouldn't have to face her again. Dad and Gretchen looked at him over dinner as if he were the grim reaper. He hardly touched his meal.

"If you'll excuse me, I've got some matters to take care of in my room." He pushed out his chair, preparing to get up.

"What's going on?" Monty didn't hesitate to ask.

Might as well come clean, though he'd been waiting for her to break the news. "Lizzie got a resident spot in Boston. She'll be leaving this weekend, I suppose."

"And you're going to let that girl walk away?"

In what way did his father mean? Evidently he hadn't done a very good job of hiding his feelings for her. "It's out of my control," he said as he tossed his napkin on the table, trying his best to act nonchalant. He left the dining room, but not before he heard his father's final words on the matter.

"Like hell it is."

He hadn't been able to talk to Dr. Poles during clinic hours, but had arranged to call her that night. After bargaining with the Massachusetts General Hospital doctor over how best to provide for Lizzie without her knowing, he put his full attention to making arrangements for his upcoming trip to San Francisco. Anything to keep the sorry circumstances and the pain out of his mind. He booked a first-class flight and made reservations at a five-star hotel. It was after eleven when he heard Flora crying. He stopped briefly from updating his mobile-phone calendar to listen. The baby didn't stop crying, and it was reminiscent of when she'd first arrived.

Had colic come back with a vengeance? Was Flora picking up on Lizzie's tension?

He stood in his room listening, waiting, wondering what to do.

After five minutes the wails escalated. The poor baby sounded in pain. Gretchen had gone home for the night. Someone needed to help Lizzie. He opened his bedroom door and shot down the hall, and found Lizzie in the living room pacing the floor. Flora was safely secured, arms and legs dangling from the snuggly baby carrier wrapped around Lizzie.

Stress diffused from every inch of Lizzie's body. Her brows pressed down, near panic shown from her eyes. "She's got a fever, but I don't know what's wrong with her. She never got fevers with colic."

"Did you look in her ears?"

"They seemed okay."

"You want me to double-check?"

"She's starting to calm down. I don't want to upset her again."

"What's her temperature?"

"One hundred and two."

"Did you give her acetaminophen?"

"A half-hour ago. It hasn't made any difference yet."

He wanted to go over to her, put his arms around both of them, to magically make things better, or at least help calm things down, but knew he'd only upset Lizzie more if he got close. So he stayed where he'd planted himself, and worried. "Anything going around at her child care?" He kept his voice level, unimposing.

"Gina didn't say anything."

"No cold or rashes?"

She just shook her head, exhausted and pushed to her limit.

"Let me take Flora for a while. Your back is probably tired."

Lizzie looked torn, but her weariness won out. "Okay." He undid the fastener of the baby backpack and slid it from her shoulders once she knew he had hold of everything. "Let me help you," she said as she adjusted the straps to meet his bigger size, and he cupped little Flora's bottom even though she was safely snug inside.

Without thinking, he bent and kissed her head, the fine black hair tickling his nose. He'd missed holding her, smelling her, wanting nothing more than to protect her from whatever it was that hurt. "It's okay, sweetheart. We'll figure something out here."

Once Lizzie knew everything was under control, she sat in Monty's chair, hanging her head in her hands. "I'm no good at this. She gets sick and I quit thinking like a doctor, go right into panicked, helpless-parent mode."

Having never had a fatherly bone in his body, he'd learned a few things over the past few weeks. He knew babies liked to be walked around and lightly bounced or rocked. He also understood how precious a small child was, which nearly blew his mind, but mostly scared the daylights out of him. "It's hard to be clinical when your heart is invested so much. Family members change things, so don't be hard on yourself."

"How am I going to handle being a single mother in that program?"

Why was she doubting herself now? She'd always given the impression of pushing full speed ahead at all costs. That she could handle anything in her way. Why was she suddenly questioning herself? Maybe because she'd grown since coming here, just as he had. Maybe he'd helped her see the importance of making the right choices. What she needed right now wasn't a philosophical discussion on the matter. She needed support. "Same as you've handled it here. With backup. I've heard they've got child care for the hospital employees, even a sick bay for the little ones."

"I won't be able to af—"

"It's offered for residents. The single mothers anyway." So he lied just a little—hadn't he already blown her trust? In Lizzie's case, it *was* being offered. She didn't need to know he was paying for it.

"Do you think she could have a bladder infection?"

She'd started grasping at straws, but if it was her way of coping he didn't want to get in the way. "That's a possibility."

"Can we take her to the clinic and do a urine test?"

He stopped walking and rocking. "We'd have to catheterize her to get the specimen. You just said you get crazy when it's your flesh and blood, and I sure as hell haven't catheterized a baby since medical school. Are you sure you want to put her through that?"

Her face dropped with the prospect of having to wait until the morning with a sick baby, to find out what might be going on. Worry converged with fear and Cole suspected Lizzie might be on the verge of tears.

He snapped his fingers. "Hey, let me call Lotte. She's a whiz at pediatric procedures."

"It's eleven-thirty. We can't ask her to come in."

"Sure we can. We just can't demand she come in." He took out his cell phone and dialed her number. "Knowing her, she'll do it, though."

Twenty minutes later, Cole turned off the alarm system at the clinic and let them all in. Lotte hadn't hesitated an instant to offer to meet Lizzie and Cole to test Flora's urine. He'd had a hunch it would work that way. As Lizzie removed Flora from the baby carrier, Lotte gathered her supplies and Cole stepped out of the room rather than watch. No way.

Within two minutes, and with minimal crying from

the wee one, Lotte handed him a jar of urine out the door. "Go test that," she said.

He dutifully took the specimen to the clinic minilab and dipped the test strip in it. Sure enough it was positive for nitrites, a byproduct of bacteria. "It's positive," he called out, then smiled when he heard Lizzie consult Lotte for what liquid-suspension antibiotics they had on hand. Practical as always, the nurse recommended a cephalosporin, right down to the amount per kilogram of Flora's weight and the number of ccs needed per dose.

Lizzie gave Flora the first dose before they left, and as Cole and she were packed up and ready to leave, Lotte sent them off with one more tidbit.

"Now, don't freak out when her poop looks maroon. It's just a side effect of the drug."

They both laughed with relief.

"Thank you," Lizzie said, her confidence in mothering secured once again since her hunch had been right. She glanced at Cole and smiled for the first time since that afternoon before overhearing his phone call. "I know you said I needed to tap into the older nurses as great sources of practical information. Now I'm a believer. My God, she was a genius at catheterizing my baby. No way could I have done that."

Not wanting to push their delicate circumstances, Cole simply nodded. He knew in his gut, as far as the two of them were concerned, he'd already stomped on any trust she'd developed in him, and that was something he couldn't change. For now he'd settle for relief that little Flora was going to be all right as soon as the medicine kicked in.

Saturday had come sooner than Lizzie could imagine. She sat on the corner of her bed, nearly all packed, trying to ward off her emotions, praying she could keep control until she left. But she couldn't help but go over the past twenty-four hours' events. Yesterday, she'd been overwhelmed by the number of former patients who'd stopped in at the clinic to send their regards and give thanks. Even Valerie's mother had made a special point to thank her for diagnosing and treating her daughter's migraines with a sock-it-to-me cake. To the best of Lizzie's understanding, everything but the kitchen sink was part of the recipe.

She'd come back to the ranch with her arms full of cooked and baked items, deciding to share them with the ranch hands rather than let them go to waste. Everyone's kindness had nearly brought tears to her eyes at the clinic, but she'd fended them off...until it had been time to say goodbye to Lotte and Rita and the rest of the help at the clinic. The rush of tears had surprised her as she'd hugged each person goodbye. It hadn't taken long at all to get attached to them, almost as if she belonged there.

Lotte had grabbed her and held tight. "You've got what it takes, Dr. Silva. We could use more doctors like you around here."

Coming from the crusty older nurse, it had meant the world and gave her confidence she could handle the residency in Boston, too.

When she'd picked up Flora from daycare, a second stream of tears had sprung, forcing her to realize how much she trusted and liked Gina, who'd started out as a patient and had quickly become a friend.

She'd miss Cattleman Bluff more than she could imagine.

Lizzie smoothed her hand over the comforter on the bed. She couldn't allow herself to think about Cole. This interim assignment was over, she'd gotten more out of it than she could ever have hoped for or dreamed of and now it was time to leave. Heck, packing and leaving had been her specialty growing up. Plus she'd always been good at hiding her emotions when it came time to leave. She could do this. Hell, she had to!

Now, of course, it took longer with packing for two, plus adding all the times she'd had to stop to dry her eyes. Thankfully Gretchen took Flora for her while she finished.

She came to the gorgeous blue dress in her closet and her thoughts shifted. She'd thought Cole was a man with great potential, but had changed her mind now. Sure, he was a brilliant doctor, but he fell far short of the mark as a son, and pity any poor unsuspecting woman who dared to fall for him. Like her. His disconnect with his feelings was beyond repair and there was nothing she or anyone else could do to fix it. Nope. She'd learned that lesson early on with her mother's drug addictions. That task would have to be his and his alone.

Forgetting about herself for a moment, she switched her thoughts to Tiberius and Cole, and she said a little prayer they'd work something out soon, before it was too late.

She glanced at her watch. Five more minutes and the packing was done. She dreaded having to face Tiberius and Gretchen for the last time, not to mention Cole. Oh, God, she couldn't go there. Not just yet. The dull ache she'd been carting around all morning in her chest suddenly pushed up a notch. She used her palm to massage the area between her breasts. Prickles started behind her lids. Again. Leaving a place where she'd grown to feel completely welcomed would be the hardest thing she'd ever had to do. After saying goodbye to Cole.

Leaving the man she'd accidentally fallen in love with

would take every ounce of courage she possessed. Did she have enough? To save face she'd do everything in her power not to let on about her truest feelings. No matter how hard or seemingly impossible. She patted her cheeks and took a deep breath. *Keep It together, you have to.* Then rolled her baggage into the living room.

Cole was quick to relieve her of that duty. "I'll put these in the car," he said, not making eye contact, and for that she was grateful.

Gretchen had already started crying, even while holding Flora on her hip. "This place is going to feel so empty without the two of you, Elisabete." She reached for Lizzie's head and pulled her down to her level, then kissed her cheek. "I'll miss you. Please come back to see us."

Lizzie had to be honest. "I'll see how that goes. I can't promise anything right now." Tears streamed down her cheeks and she wiped them away with both hands. "I'll miss you, too. But I'll keep in touch online and I promise to send pictures and videos of Flora, okay?"

Gretchen hugged Flora close, snuggling her neck and kissing her chubby cheek. "I'm going to miss you so much, sweet potato. Don't forget your old granny Gretchen."

The two women circled Flora for a group hug and cried until they both felt embarrassed, then laughed uneasily and wiped at their wet faces. What else could they do? She had to leave.

"Are you about done?" Tiberius waited impatiently for his turn. "Come over and say goodbye to me, girlie-girl. We haven't got all day."

Lizzie turned and wandered into Monty's surprisingly open arms, unable to turn off the faucet. He hugged her as if he was a bit out of practice. When his mouth was close to her ear he said in a low voice, "Don't forget our little talk."

"I won't. I promise. How can I thank you for everything?"

"By being happy. Make that little one a happy home, okay?"

She hugged him like a sloppy drunk, *I love you, man*, not caring what he thought. "Yes, sir."

Tiberius's eyes watered when she pulled back her head, and she read every bit of sincerity in his wish for her just by looking into his craggy old face. So this was how it felt to be loved. Wow.

"I hate to break things up—" Cole's cautious voice cut through their moment "—but you've got a plane to catch."

She couldn't deny the truth. Maybe they'd have some time to talk things through on the drive to the airport, because it would be completely awkward otherwise. She hoped they would anyway.

He took Flora from Gretchen's hip and led the way out the front door...to a limousine?

"I've already put her car seat in place in the back."

Was the man serious? He wasn't even going to drive her to the airport?

Lizzie wanted to kick her own butt for being so stupid and hopeful. She'd actually thought she'd gotten through to him on some level, but his calling a car service to drive her off his property, the same way she'd arrived, proved that the only thing inside his chest was a cement block.

Well, two could play this ridiculous game. Egged on by anger, she shored up every last nerve and willed herself not to react. "Okay. Thanks." She refused to look at him as she got into the back of the town car. Only after she sat did she glance his way.

To his credit, he did look sad...*ish*. The one last thing she'd have to do was chuck every single good feeling she'd let sneak through her usual barriers for Cole and keep this goodbye strictly business.

"Thank you for giving me a job when I needed it the most." *Even if it was only because you had to.* "I'll never forget it." *Or you.* "Or Wyoming."

"You're welcome." His voice gritty, his hand grazed her fingers as he closed the car door, then, rather than move it away, as she expected, he covered her hand briefly with his, his warmth quickly spreading up her arm and fanning out across her shoulders. "I know I've been an ass, but I *will* miss you."

"Ready to go, sir?" The driver was behind the wheel checking his watch.

"Yes, yes."

"Okay, then." She didn't have a clue what to say next. *I forgive you? I love you?*

"Oh, there'll be another chauffeur in Boston. He'll have a sign with your name at the baggage-claim area. He'll take you to your resident quarters." He stepped back to let the limo pull out.

"Okay. Thank you for everything." *I'll never forget you!*

"Just be you and knock that hospital on its ear."

She couldn't help but smile at the implications of that comment. "And take care of your father," she called out the window as the car drove off, but not before she glimpsed a look of devastation on his face. He did care.

Cole stood watching the limousine drive off with the woman who'd changed his world as the corners of his life turned in on themselves, making him feel empty and dead. If he'd been hit by a car it wouldn't have hurt more than he did right now. But he had to let her go. It was for the best. For Flora's future.

Lizzie deserved better than him. He wouldn't stand in the way of that. Maybe, with this coveted residency in internal medicine, she'd finally put her life on track and become the huge success she'd worked diligently for all these years.

Maybe, with time, the crater in his chest would heal without her.

Tiberius and Gretchen instinctively knew better than to go near him just then. They'd waved goodbye to Lizzie from the porch as she'd driven off. Now they'd disappeared inside.

Cole stepped slowly into the ranch house, then found himself walking toward Lizzie and Flora's room. He could still feel her here, but knew this too would fade with time. He curled in his lips and pressed hard, damned if he was going to let himself react to the roiling deep in his chest. He hated that she could make him remember how impossibly hard it was to lose someone you...loved.

He inhaled, hoping for one last whiff of her before she vanished forever, then glanced toward the opened closet. Empty except for one item.

She'd left behind the blue evening gown. So she wouldn't have to remember their one night together?

Or to make sure he'd never forget?

CHAPTER ELEVEN

Two weeks later. San Francisco.

COLE MADE A SMALL incision near the premedicated hand-picked patient's groin to gain access to the femoral artery. The surgical nurse handed him the special sterile catheter. Cole took the stainless-steel stent with its attached trileaflet equine pericardial valve with fabric cuff and threaded it through the vein, using fluoroscopy to follow the venous path on the X-ray screen. It was a long and tedious process traveling from the groin to the heart, and it required meticulous technique and total concentration.

Several minutes later, once he reached the diseased valve in the patient's heart, Cole advanced the sheath from the femoral artery, steering around the aortic arch and through the stenotic valve. He made it look easy, but this was his specialty and he'd trained for years, perfecting the technique long before becoming a TAVI evangelist.

As instructed, the surgical team used rapid cardiac pacing to reduce cardiac output while he introduced and inflated the balloon that delivered the special prosthetic valve. He carefully positioned the new prosthetic valve adjacent to the calcified natural aortic valve and secured it in place. Then waited for the new valve to take over.

Angiography and echocardiography were performed to assess the patency of the coronary artery and the new valve competency. All checked out as per his plan, and he began to remove the catheter. Once completely out of the patient, he surgically repaired the access site in the groin. When he was done, the surgical RN placed a pressure dressing over the incision and a five-pound sandbag over that to prevent bleeding or hematoma formation.

As the team finished the procedure, Cole discussed the success with the head cardiologist.

He'd just saved a man from open-heart surgery and the hospital thousands and thousands of dollars with a minimally invasive procedure that required a short recovery and little time in the hospital. It was a win-win situation and the way of the future and, most important, he believed in it.

He stepped out of the surgical suite and changed clothes. Later he'd meet with the team to discuss the procedure and to offer time-saving techniques, as well as a critique on their performance.

He'd spend the next few days here teaching the procedure to the few qualified cardiology staff members. Once he was positive they could perform the percutaneous aortic valve implantation on their own, he would certify them and his job would be done.

The first doctor on the list was a female cardiologist who reminded him of Lizzie. He'd thought of her every single day since she'd left the ranch. He'd started to call her several different times, but left well enough alone. She probably hated him, and, after the way he'd detached himself from their relationship, he couldn't blame her. She'd never understand it was for the best.

Her best. Which reminded him: he'd gotten a disturbing message from his bank, saying that his automatic payment to Massachusetts General Hospital for Flora's child care had been returned. He needed to find out why.

First he called his bank to clarify the message, then he called Linda Poles at MGH for an explanation.

"She left," was Linda's exasperated response.

"What? What happened?"

"She changed her focus and took a residency at another hospital."

"Where?"

"Wyoming. Cheyenne."

Cole needed to sit down. He'd bent over backwards to accommodate her and she'd turned her back on the prestigious placement for...

He scratched his head; the only resident program he knew about at Wyoming University Hospital was for family practice, not internal medicine. His brother, Trevor, did his residency there, They were always searching for more residents.

What in the hell was going on? With trepidation, he called Lizzie, amazed by how moved he was just hearing her voice on the mobile answering system. He'd missed that fun accent. Her. God, he'd missed her, cursed himself every single day for letting her go. But he'd kept telling himself it was for the best. For her and Flora's future.

Maybe if he kept repeating it, he'd eventually believe it.

"Hi, Lizzie, this is Cole. Just got some surprising news and wanted to verify it with you. Call me when you can."

A few days later, it was almost time to board the plane back to Baltimore. Lizzie had never returned his call and it was driving him crazy. Was this her thumbing her nose at him or had she strategically put herself in Cheyenne to be closer to him? Laramie was only forty-two miles away. He'd spent enough time kicking himself for doing the wrong thing, and now, as illogical as it seemed, he needed to set some things straight. To finally do the right thing.

He stepped up to the gate counter to make an inquiry with the booking clerk.

Lizzie promised this move would be the last. Thank heavens she didn't own any worldly goods beyond all of Flora's things. Wyoming University Hospital agreed to let her rent a furnished room in the dorms for the married students. The apartment was tiny with one bedroom and a galley kitchen, but by her standards it was perfect, and she could walk to work every day. Also, the university had a child-development center that accepted Flora into their care program at a steep discount. If these weren't all signs she'd made the right decision, she didn't know what other proof she needed. She was back in Wyoming, and this would be home to her and Flora for the next three years, and after that? Well, she couldn't even predict day-to-day events, so that would be anyone's guess.

She hadn't returned Cole's call, couldn't, because she'd almost gone weak in the knees just hearing his voice. Obviously he'd found out about her abrupt change in plans. Well, it was her decision and she'd do what she felt best for her and her daughter.

She'd taken Tiberius's words to heart about his state needing more doctors. She'd had a long conversation with Trevor Montgomery over the phone about the pros and cons of switching from internal medicine to family practice, and he'd given a great endorsement for this program.

The oddest thing had happened when she'd flown back to Boston after spending her summer in Cattleman Bluff: she'd felt completely out of place. She'd been born and raised there, yet a little over a month in Wyoming had opened her eyes to a different kind of life. A life with big skies and clean air, miles and miles of wide-open land, ranches and horseback riding, where life slowed down and the people were down-to-earth. She felt cramped back home, but here a girl could stretch out and breathe. She liked it here.

Check that. She loved it here. She hummed contentedly while putting away the last of Flora's clothes as her baby napped.

There was a tap at the door, and, eager not to disturb Flora, she rushed over to open it. Her stomach dropped to her knees when she saw Cole on the other side. He'd cut his hair recently and looked tan. He wore a brown Western-style suit with an expensive-looking white polo shirt. From the tips of his boots to the top of his head, he looked all man, and his brown, cutting eyes nearly sliced through her. Yeah, he was angry.

"Don't get mad," were her first words, even knowing it was way too late for that. "I listened to my heart and this is where I needed to be."

He shook his head and stepped through her door. She got the message he wasn't the least bit glad to see her, but if that was the case, why did he come here?

She'd totally messed up his efforts at finding her a residency, she'd essentially spit in his eye, rather than show gratitude, yet not for one second did she fear that he might manhandle her. He wasn't anything like her ex.

"Does this have something to do with my father?"

"If you had any kind of relationship with your father, you wouldn't need me to answer that."

He cocked his head, narrowing one eye. "Are you saying he did have something to do with your decision?"

"Contrary to your assuming you can call all the shots, I make all my own decisions. Your father just pointed me in a different direction."

"Are you aware Laramie is only forty-two miles away?"

"I thought you spent most of your time in Baltimore, and, besides, your living one town over shouldn't be a problem since you're always traveling. No worries about running into each other." She raised her hand in an oath. "I promise to stay out of your way."

He stepped closer and she couldn't budge. Nor could she breathe. All she could concentrate on was the face she'd missed so deeply; she had dreams about it every night.

"Forgive me for being cold to you," he said. "I never expected to—" He stopped.

"To what? Try to control my life? Use me to prove your Wonder Boy status?" Yes, she was still angry.

Not listening to her jeers, he studied and reached for her hair, lifted and dropped it back onto her shoulder, as if reacquainting himself with it. That simple act sent an avalanche of chills down her body. She prayed he wouldn't notice.

"To fall in love with you," he said, low and grainy, as if coming to this conclusion had worn him to the bone. "I never expected to love you."

She let the magic words settle in the air. She breathed them inward, savoring the feel of them, trying them on for size, deciding they fit perfectly with her feelings for him. But he didn't deserve to get off that easily. He'd thrown her life into chaos, then let her go without lifting a finger.

He'd broken her heart! "You wanted to get rid of

me—you forced me to leave. Didn't even have the decency to drive me to the airport. How can I believe you?"

With nothing less than an agonized gaze, he dropped to one knee, reaching into his pocket and pulling out a ring. "This was my mother's engagement ring, and her mother's before that. I'd like you to wear it, to be my wife. Will you marry me?"

Wait, wait, wait. None of this made sense. He loved her and wanted to marry her? She must be hallucinating. "You kicked me out of your bed and sent me out of state. Why the change?"

There was that agonized expression again. "I'd gotten too used to being around you. I still needed to hear your voice…see your face…hear Flora coo." He started to stand up, but she pushed on his shoulder to keep him on that knee. So distracted by his confession, he didn't notice and stayed where she'd put him. "I want you with me. I have to be with you."

She wanted to stay angry at him, wanted him to hurt as much as she had when he'd let her leave. But he'd just as much as told her he'd been miserable without her, had missed her enough to come after her, knowing how angry she was, and ask her to marry him. He loved her.

Realizing she wasn't jumping right in with a yes, he added more. "I just cancelled my flight from California to Baltimore, to fly to Cheyenne, then drove out to the ranch to get this ring to ask you to marry me. What more proof do you need? Can you at least give me an answer?"

Okay, she wasn't imagining this. Cole was reverting back to his usual demanding self. But not before he'd begged her forgiveness and admitted how he felt. Thank God!

Seeing the big man on his knee, risking his pride by asking her to marry him completely out of the blue, and knowing without a doubt he meant it, undid her. She dropped to her wobbling knees before him and cupped the hand that offered the beautiful, delicate antique ring. "You can't keep messing with my life, Cole Montgomery."

"I promise to stop if you say yes."

She laughed through her tears. "Like hell you will."

His slow smile broadened, forming those natural brackets on either side of his cheeks. She loved that grin.

"Yes, I'll marry you." He freed his hand from hers, reaching for her shoulders so he could tug her closer and share a kiss that felt as if he'd been saving up since the day she'd left Cattleman Bluff.

She wrapped her arms around his neck and gave him a kiss he'd never forget either because that was what a girl did when she loved a man with all her heart.

Moments later, she tore away from his mouth. "But first you've got to promise to have that talk with your father."

"Now who's messing with whose life?"

"You needed a kick in the ass on behalf of Monty."

"Before I hold you to marrying me, maybe you should know that I'm giving up the TAVR teaching. Already talked to Trevor about joining his practice. I won't have nearly the prestige I do now."

"Wow. You really have changed! That's the best news *evah*!"

"So you love me, then?"

"You know I do."

She dove for him and knocked him backwards, then picked up the kiss where they'd just left off. After wrestling to get her hand, Cole slid the ring onto her finger, and it fit surprisingly well, as if it had been made for Lizzie. "I love you," he said, again.

"I love you, too." Thrilled to the core, she stopped and admired the platinum, gold and diamond ring with those dewy eyes. He looked on with pride, love surging through his veins, just as Flora woke up from her nap with a shriek.

Cole's brows shot up. "Mind if I get her up?"

"Be my guest." She rolled off him.

"You think she'll remember me?" He squeezed her arm affectionately as he got up.

"It's only been three weeks," she said as he helped her stand.

He walked lightly into the bedroom, Lizzie following behind, and he spoke softly. "Hey, little Flora bear, it's Cole."

The baby squealed with delight when she saw him, and relief circled his body. "Hey, she's sitting up—when did that happen?"

"Last week. Look a little closer."

He did, and with the baby smiling he saw her first tooth. "Look at that—you're growing up!"

Lizzie came up beside him, stretching her arm around his back. "Since we'll be getting married, maybe from now on you should call yourself Daddy?"

Cole lifted Flora, kissed her chubby cheek, then turned his megawatt smile toward Lizzie. "I like the sound of that."

The next night Cole sat down with his father in the living room at the ranch. Lizzie had blackmailed him into doing it by refusing to sleep with him until he did. But as she said, there was no time like the present, and he really couldn't argue with that advice. This conversation was way overdue.

"Can I get you some tea or something?" Cole said, hoping to steal more time to gather his thoughts.

Tiberius scrunched up his face. "You got something you want to talk about or not?"

So that was how it was going to be, but, honestly, did Cole actually think things might be different? He sat and leveled his gaze on his father, trying not to notice the butterflies in his belly. "As a matter of fact, I've got a lot of things to talk about. First off, I've asked Lizzie to marry me and you're the first to know."

The shocked double take almost made Cole laugh. "Well, that's the first display of good sense I've seen from you in years." His old man smiled and shook Cole's hand, after delivering the backhanded compliment. "Congratulations."

"Thanks. I'm glad you approve. And I think you already know you played a role in it."

"I didn't want that filly to get away. She's a real catch. And you're way past your time to get married."

Rather than take offense, Cole focused on what really mattered most. "She reminds you of Mom, doesn't she?"

Tiberius nodded thoughtfully. "She'll be good for you."

"Agreed." They sat in silence, enjoying the rare truce.

His father cleared his throat. "You know, neither of us ever wanted to admit it, but we're a lot alike."

Cole shook his head. "Don't I know that. Mom had her hands full trying to keep peace in the house."

"That's 'cause you were always trying to prove how tough you were."

"And you never did that, right?"

Tiberius nodded mildly, a small smile creasing his lips spawning an expression packed with memories. "I'd come off the rodeo circuit and survived, assumed you would, too. Didn't your momma call you Wonder Boy?"

"Maybe it went to my head a little." The toughest memory of his life flashed before him. "I sure as hell never expected to break my neck."

"Yeah, you went and let that horse almost throw you into a funeral parlor, and—"

Cole knee-jerked the challenge; he leaned forward to make his point. "I didn't let it happen, it just happened." Yeah, his voice might have sounded gruffer than he'd meant.

"You made a poor choice that day, riding bareback for that *girl*."

"I was fifteen." *I had just made love for the first time in my life the night before with the girl of my dreams.* Yet he couldn't deny the truth. "And you never did anything stupid when you were young, right?"

"Like I said, we're a lot alike. That's why I've always been so hard on you. That's why I expected you'd take over the ranch one day. I couldn't believe how you dumped anything to do with horses, rodeo and ranching after you broke your neck."

Cole wanted to scrub his face in frustration, but he sat still, willing himself to stay calm and talk this out with his father, not to let this conversation turn into a yelling fest like all the others. "I found a different calling, Dad." He changed the tone of his voice. "I honestly believe I was meant to be a doctor."

"And you had to drag your brother along, too."

"That was his choice."

Cole could see the fight slip out of his father. "And now I'm getting too old to run this ranch and I don't have anyone to step in, to keep it running, just a couple of fancy doctors for sons."

Cole couldn't let the slight slide by. "You know, I do save lives. How come I've never gotten the feeling that you respect what I do?"

"Of course I respect what you do. I'm proud of you, always have been, but that doesn't fix my ranching problem, does it?"

Cole rested his elbows on his thighs, waiting to make eye contact with his dad. Wasn't this the perfect example for how he'd learned to be selfish? "Not everyone is meant to be a rancher, Dad, not even the sons of the best rancher in these parts."

"You'd think that at least one of you would have taken an interest." Tiberius leaned his head against the cushiony chair, squeezing his eyes closed like a little frustrated kid.

"You've got the best man for the job right under your nose and you can't even see it."

"Trevor?" One eye popped open. "Hell, he's too busy with the clinic and my grandson and that new wife of his."

"Jack, Dad. Your foreman knows this ranch inside out. He's been working here for, what, twenty years?"

Now both eyes were open and ready for a fight. "Of course he knows the ranch but he doesn't have an ounce of business savvy."

"Trevor's good with bookkeeping."

"I'm talking about connections. Finding new venues to sell our steer for meat. Without buyers, we're nothing. We won't have a future. Do you know how many people are vegetarians these days?"

Cole chuckled. It had never occurred to him exactly how many hats his father had worn running Circle M all these years. It wasn't just about tending steer and selling them for the best price—he had set up the buyers and accounted for all the business investments along the way, too. Not to mention raising his boys and taking care of his wife. Hell, the man had probably only taken three vacations in his entire adult life. His health was waning and he couldn't keep up anymore. Cole weaved his fingers together and thought that was the sad and undeniable truth. He finally understood it was time to pitch in and help, just as Trevor already had.

"I've got connections all over the country. You tell me what you need, and I'll do my best to open some doors for our steer. We can make this a family business, but with the help of Jack. Isn't it about time you made him a Circle M partner?"

He could see the surprise and glimmer of hope in his father's milky eyes at the prospect of making Circle M Ranch a group business. A small corporation. Maybe it wouldn't be a traditional family business, as he'd always hoped for, but wasn't that the way of the world now?

"I'll think about it." Tiberius crinkled his brow, already considering the change.

Cole reached across and squeezed his father's forearm. "Dad, one more thing." How should he put this? Probably best to keep it simple, and straight. "I haven't told you nearly enough. Hell, probably never." He waited for his father's gaze to rise so he could look him in the eyes. "I admire you. You made something out of your life. You started out with nothing. Not many people can claim that. In case you're still wondering, I do respect you."

He'd hit home on that one. His father's eyes got watery, his lower lip quivery as the compliment sank in. "And I've always been proud of you, Cole. Sorry I wasn't so good at showing it."

"Like I said, or was it you who said it?" A wry smile

twisted Cole's lips. "We're a lot more alike than we'd ever like to admit."

In the next second Cole felt a cool hand on top of his, and something about his father's bony grip warmed a huge and growing area smack in the middle of his chest.

EPILOGUE

Two months later. A cool and crisp Saturday afternoon in autumn...

FOR THE SECOND TIME in four months Cole wore a suit and waited for a wedding to start. But this was a brand-new Western-styled tuxedo, not that other city-style deal with the bad memories. The small group of guests gathered near the mossy pond beside the cluster of Glory Red maple trees on the Circle M Ranch.

Tiberius had promised a big surprise and instructed Cole to quit looking at his watch and enjoy the day. He stood beneath the portable seven-foot pergola draped with sparkly white chiffon and bright-colored Gerbera daisies, breathing in the chilled air and letting it calm him. Was he really getting married one month before his forty-first birthday, to a woman only halfway through her twenties?

He grinned to himself. You bet he was, and she was the most beautiful woman in the world, as a matter of fact. The best choice he could ever make.

He glanced at his soon-to-be daughter, dressed like a little white fairy in the arms of his new sister-in-law, Julie, then noticed the tiny silver slippers Flora wore and grinned even more. He'd never totally understood the word *cute* until he'd met that baby.

Trevor waited at the back of the rows of chairs instead of standing by his side as his best man. Cole figured there must be a reason and stood where he'd been placed like a good unquestioning boy. A first!

Tiberius had agreed to walk Lizzie down the aisle— if you could call a path covered in windblown autumn leaves an aisle. The guests sat on white vinyl foldable chairs that Trevor's son, James, had spent all morning setting up. The rows were crooked, seeming more diagonal than straight, but what did Cole expect from a thirteen-year-old? And they served their purpose. He wasn't about to complain.

Soft Celtic string music started playing through speakers and all eyes traveled toward the grove of trees on the opposite side of the pond. Cole's pulse jumped as he watched and waited for his bride.

Slowly emerging from the ash and maples came one, then two young women dressed in cocktail-length dresses, red like the leaves on the maple trees. Lizzie had chosen her two newest friends to be her bridesmaids. Both had started out as acquaintances at the clinic but one had become Flora's caregiver, Gina, and the other was Rita the receptionist. This time around, instead of catching the bouquet, Rita got to carry one.

Next Zebulon walked between the trees and, just as Cole wondered what in the world the horse was doing there, the most beautiful sight Cole had ever seen appeared. Lizzie sat sidesaddle, straight and confident, her flowing white dress blanketing the horse's entire back, loins-to-tail and all the way down his belly. The ball-gown cut of her dress made a wide V across her shoulders and dipped to the top of her breasts. A thick, sparkly pearl belt cinched in her waist. She didn't wear a veil, just a feathery flower on the side of her head, and Cole was happy to see she'd left her hair down, with tiny braids weaving an intricate pattern around her head. Breathtaking. Especially knowing that beneath that dress she wore the garter he'd caught at his brother's wedding. His heart had never felt as full as now, with this vision of his soon-to-be wife.

So that was what all those Saturday-afternoon horseback rides with his father were about. Lizzie had embraced Wyoming life with a vengeance since they'd gotten engaged and she'd committed to becoming a family-practice doctor like his brother. The old ranch hadn't felt this much like home since his mother had died. He glanced upward—*I hope you're watching*—then to the front row.

In honor of Lizzie's grandmother and her favorite foster mother, Janie Tuttle, two chairs had been left empty on the bride's side. A third reserved chair had been placed on the groom's side for his mom.

With Zebulon pacing the bridesmaids, and the violin music swelling, Lizzie held the reins comfortably and single-handedly, wearing elbow-length fingerless white lace gloves. With the other hand, she held a fire-burst-colored bouquet.

She circled the mossy pond under the bright blue sky, with occasional puffy white clouds floating overhead, trees in a range of fall colors surrounding her and the hauntingly romantic music drifting on the wind. A perfect moment. The love of his life was coming to him, to take her vows to love and honor, as he would her. He'd cherish her no matter what lay ahead, never more determined to put another person's needs and desires before his own.

It occurred to Cole that his father and brother both understood, and he'd never felt closer to them than right now.

His brother met Lizzie at the back of the chairs as the bridesmaids paced the makeshift outdoor aisle toward the arbor, where Cole waited. He couldn't take his eyes off her, afraid if he looked away this moment might disappear. Trevor lifted Lizzie from the horse, then let Gretchen adjust the train of the dress before she made her final walk down the aisle on the arm of her new father-in-law, the obviously proud Tiberius Montgomery…to him.

Lizzie's amazing green stare connected with his and melded, sending waves of love to ripple over him, her angelic smile stealing his breath. His father handed her over to him and stepped back as the pastor began the ceremony, but Cole couldn't quit looking at her.

Holding her cool, mildly trembling hand, he thought how fragile his bride was beneath her confident exterior. He promised to protect and treasure her, and as the rest of the vows became a blur he saw only Lizzie, until the pastor prompted him to say the best and most important words of his life.

"I do."

* * * * *